The Girl from Snowy River

The Girl from Snowy River

Jackie French

Angus&Robertson
An imprint of HarperCollins*Publishers*

Angus&Robertson
An imprint of HarperCollins*Publishers*, Australia

First published in Australia in 2012
by HarperCollinsPublishers Australia Pty Limited
ABN 36 009 913 517
harpercollins.com.au

HarperCollins*Publishers*
Level 13, 201 Elizabeth Street, Sydney NSW 2000, Australia
31 View Road, Glenfield, Auckland 0627, New Zealand
A 53, Sector 57, Noida, UP, India
77–85 Fulham Palace Road, London W6 8JB, United Kingdom
2 Bloor Street East, 20th floor, Toronto, Ontario M4W 1A8, Canada
10 East 53rd Street, New York NY 10022, USA

National Library of Australia Cataloguing-in-Publication data:

French, Jackie.
The girl from Snowy River / Jackie French.
ISBN: 978 0 7322 9310 9 (pbk.)
French, Jackie. Matilda saga ; 2.
For ages 10+
Country life—New South Wales—Snowy Mountains Region—Juvenile fiction.
Orphans—New South Wales—Snowy Mountains Region—Juvenile fiction.
Australia—Social conditions—1918–1922—Juvenile fiction.
A823.3

Cover design by Jane Waterhouse, HarperCollins Design Studio
Cover images: Girl © Jutta Klee/ableimages/Corbis; Mount Hotham by Peter Walton Photography/Getty Images; all other images by shutterstock.com
Typeset in Sabon 10/15pt by Kirby Jones
Printed and bound in Australia by Griffin Press
The papers used by HarperCollins in the manufacture of this book are a natural, recyclable product made from wood grown in sustainable plantation forests. The fibre source and manufacturing processes meet recognised international environmental standards, and carry certification.

5 4 13 14 15

To Nina, Fabia and Evangeline, who keep the spirit of the girls from Snowy River; to Angela, with love and gratitude always for helping create the horses in this book and so much more; but most of all to Robyn, who rides the mountains with love and understanding, and who fights to keep her valley safe.

Chapter 1

22 November 1919

Dear Diary,
Today I met a ghost …

He came out of the fog unexpectedly. Though how else *do* you appear in fog? One moment the two flat slabs of the Rock loomed dark in front of her, the mist sifting about them thick as flour, then suddenly there was a stranger — a young man in a bathchair — wheeling across the stone and gazing out over the valley.

Empress snorted and tried to back away, her hooves cutting deep into the mud of the track. Flinty patted her neck, trying to assess the stranger. He didn't look like a swaggie, not with that too-pale skin. And how could a swaggie travel in a bathchair? No, Empress was just nervous. Horses hated passing the Rock.

'There's ghosts up on that Rock,' old Dusty Jim muttered, especially between fencing jobs when he'd been at the bottle harder than usual. But Dusty Jim saw fairies and once an elephant that turned out to be another of the mountain's boulders. There was no such thing as ghosts. Except, she thought involuntarily, in my brother's eyes.

But even if you didn't believe in ghosts, the Rock felt different from the mountain slopes around it. Long ago, perhaps, mountain giants had played catch with a massive boulder, and had dropped it here at the edge of the mountain, from such a height that it split in two. Now the two flat halves perched like a verandah above the valley.

Most days the fog drifted down from the gullies higher up, like icing sugar sprinkled on a sponge cake. Other times a saucer of mist, looking as solid as white sauce on a dish of cauliflower, sat on the Rock between Rock Farm and the valley below. The air around the Rock was always cold, as though the sunlight slid away down the slopes on either side.

Suddenly Flinty was glad of the solid farmhouse up the track behind her. Rock Farm might have got its name from the Rock, and even been made of mountain stone, but the house that Dad had built looked like it had drunk in years of warmth and happiness.

Empress quivered again. Flinty stroked her neck. 'Good morning!' she called to the stranger.

The man glanced at her from his bathchair, surprised, as though he hadn't heard the hoofbeats approaching. Young, twenty-one perhaps — Andy's age; four years older than her — dressed in a blue shirt and thick blue trousers that ended in emptiness below his knees. His mouth looked carved in a straight line, too hard to smile.

'Is it?' His voice wasn't bitter, exactly. It sounded blank, like Andy's at the train station when he'd finally come back from the Great War, when they'd had to tell him Dad had died of the influenza while he was half a world away on the ship coming home. Andy had sounded like that the day he'd left them to go droving too, his eyes shadowed as though they still saw the mud of France and not the twisted shapes of snow gums.

Now here was another man maimed by the war. Flinty tried not to stare at the place where the empty trousers dangled over the chair. She forced her voice to sound cheerful. 'Well, it's not raining. Or snowing. Or blowing a gale. Are you visiting nearby?'

She wondered who could have wheeled a crippled man onto the Rock. The Mullinses' farm was an hour's ride downhill, and this man looked too well dressed — and sober — to be staying with old Dusty Jim. Captain McAlpine had chosen his house site for its snow gums and their irregular trunks weathered cream and green and orange, for the high peaks that glinted in the summer rain, or gleamed blue-white in winter: not for close neighbours, or even good soil.

But men back from the war did odd things. A crippled ex-soldier would find peace on the Rock, if he didn't count the trickle of gum leaves in the breeze, the faint *hoosh* of the creek below, the background song of magpies and a few cicadas.

The stranger didn't answer her. Instead he swung the wheels of his chair so all she could see were his back and the chair's. It was made of silver metal, not clunky looking like the wooden ones she'd seen in the newspapers.

Another ex-soldier who refused to talk. Being crippled didn't excuse his rudeness. Suddenly she wanted to yell, 'Speak to me!' It was as though war was a secret girls weren't allowed to share.

The men who'd marched away weren't the only ones who'd suffered. She'd lost a brother at Bullecourt, Mum to heartbreak, Dad to the influenza brought back by the soldiers. Her older brother was off with cattle, fleeing his memories. The boy she loved had come back a man she hardly knew.

I may not have lost my legs, she thought, but I've lost those I love forever. The war had savaged Mum, and Mrs Mack, and every woman in the valley. The war was over but the pain was still there, for her and the families left behind, not just for the men who had been maimed.

We're all bits that the war didn't take, Flinty thought, gazing at the stranger's back. But those left behind had a right to know more about the beast who'd chewed their lives and spat the remnants out.

Well, maybe, just maybe, she'd get one soldier to talk today. She turned her back on the stranger and his bathchair, and walked Empress through the edges of the fog till the track ahead was clear, then cantered down through the puddles to the valley.

Chapter 2

12 January 1916

Dear Diary,

Sandy kissed me! Proper kisses, on the lips. Three times, and the last two times in front of everyone.

The last two days have been … I'm not sure what they have been. Strange. Wonderful, except I'm crying as I write this now. I don't know what I feel. My brain is overfull, like Mum's mixing bowl when she makes the Christmas puddings.

Two days shouldn't have so much in them. I feel like I've turned a corner and suddenly everything has changed.

We all got up even before the kookaburras yesterday morning to go down to meet the enlistment march from Delegate. It said in last week's newspaper they were coming to Rocky Valley. Dad reckoned it was about a three-hour march to get here from their last camp, but we didn't know what time they'd set out, so we all wanted to have everything ready early.

I wore my Sunday dress, the one with the blue flounces, even though it meant I had to sit in the cart instead of riding

Empress. Joey and Kirsty kept singing, 'Oh, we don't want to lose you, But we think you ought to go.' *Mr Ross made us all come down to the school to practise.*

Mum didn't sing. She was quiet the whole way down. Dad kept giving her little hugs when he thought we weren't looking. I think they were remembering how Andy enlisted at the start of the war. Joey and Kirsty are too young to read the pages in the newspaper about all the men who have been killed or wounded. But that's why this enlistment march is so important. We can't beat the Huns without more men to fight, and not enough are enlisting now, and that makes it more dangerous for the men already over there, like our Andy, and Rick and Toby Mack, and the other valley boys.

I couldn't sing either, looking at Mum's face, and neither did Jeff. He looked funny, sort of determined and scared. I thought maybe he was embarrassed because he was only fifteen, too young to enlist.

We were the last in the valley to get there, but we had the furthest to come. There was bunting all across the schoolhouse. I helped Mum carry in the plates of food — she'd made her coconut cake, and I'd made egg and ham pie. There was enough food on the trestle tables to feed the whole army. We didn't know how many men were coming. Fourteen men enlisted when the march began at Delegate, but there'd be the recruiting sergeant and other army people, as well as the men who had enlisted on their way here. I hoped there were a hundred men, but I don't suppose there are a hundred men between here and Delegate.

And then we waited. I talked to Amy for a while. Her dress wasn't as pretty as mine. She said she was going to try to get one of the soldiers to write to her 'as the boys here are all useless', which just means they know she's got a tongue as mean as a red-bellied black snake. She'd set her cap at Andy for a while, but I know he doesn't write to her. Anyhow, she is only thirteen, same as me, so Andy is miles too old for her, and miles too good too.

So I went to talk to Jeff and Sandy instead. They were whispering together but stopped when I came up, which hurt a bit, because they are my best friends in the world, and I didn't think we had any secrets.

Then suddenly there was this weird wailing sound, like the bunyip is supposed to make, but it was music too. Dad yelled out, 'Bagpipes!' and grinned — I suppose Dad remembered bagpipes from when he was in the Indian Army. All of us from school lined up, ready to sing.

The piper came first, a red glint among the she-oak trees. The music wailed but challenged you too, like it was telling the enemy, 'We're here, and we can beat you.' The piper wore a skirt and long white socks, which should have looked funny but looked fierce instead.

The men marched behind him, and a boy with a drum. We all waited as they marched up the track. I counted twenty volunteers and three soldiers in uniform. Then Dad yelled out, 'Three cheers for our brave young men!' And everyone called out hip hip hurray. Mr Ross lifted his arms and we began to sing.

'Oh, we don't want to lose you,
But we think you ought to go,
For your King and your country
Both need you so.

We shall want you and miss you,
But with all our might and main,
We will cheer you, thank you, kiss you,
When you come back again.'

Everyone cheered, and then Snowy White, who'd been sent home from the army when he was shot in the knee at Gallipoli, yelled out, 'Well, the kissing can start now then, ladies. I'm ready!' And we all laughed.

Mr Ross made a speech. He quoted Lord Nelson — he always quotes him at school — about how 'England expects that every man will do his duty'. Then Reverend Postlewhistle, who comes up from Gibber's Creek to give the services every month, said that no man of honour could see women and children maimed and slaughtered, and how the Huns don't spare women and spear children on their bayonets. He said, 'Go, for the glory of God and for your country.'

The recruiting sergeant sat at Mr Ross's desk so that any of the valley men could enlist. I felt bad because there were hardly any men here left to join the army, only Horace Brown who turned eighteen a week ago. All the others are too old, like Dad and Mr Mack, or married and can't be spared, like Johnno Mack, now his brothers have gone.

Mum, Mrs Mack and Mutti Green gave the marchers a cup of tea and a scone to last them till dinner. The schoolyard smelled of grilled mutton chops and smoke. I watched the bagpiper stride back and forth by the sliprails, then Sandy came up and said, 'I've joined up. And Jeff.'

I looked at him with my mouth open. A fly could have buzzed in and out and I'd never have noticed. 'But you're only fifteen.'

'Mum signed the papers. And your mum too, for Jeff. And I'm tall for my age,' said Sandy. Then he added, 'I thought you'd be proud. It's for Andy and Rick and all the others. We can't let them down.'

'I am proud,' I said. I was too. I started to cry, and Sandy said, 'Flinty.' He grabbed my hand and led me down to the creek behind the schoolhouse.

I thought he just wanted to get me away before Amy or someone saw me crying. But he put his hands on my shoulders and then his face came closer to mine and somehow I knew what to do, or almost. I don't think Sandy has kissed anyone either, not properly. Our noses got in the way at first, and then we didn't want to stop, or let each other go. I wanted to feel him warm against me forever. He tasted so good, like apple teacake. I know that sounds silly, but it's true.

Then someone clanged the bell to say it was dinnertime. We broke apart and Sandy said, 'You'll write to me?' and I knew he meant write to him because I was his girl, not just a friend.

I said, 'You'll take care?' and I meant, 'Don't get killed, please come back safe, I couldn't bear it if you didn't come home.'

And then we went, holding hands, and everyone saw and smiled, and Amy smirked at me, but I only cared about Sandy. We ate chops, and cheese and tomato pie, and apple cake. He kissed me good night, just quickly on the lips, in front of everyone, when we went back up the mountain that night — Jeff had to pack, of course.

I could still feel Sandy's lips on mine, all the way in the cart back home. I can still feel them now.

I didn't sleep that night. I don't think Jeff did either, or Mum or Dad. I could hear them talking in the kitchen. I think Dad was telling Jeff things a soldier needs to know, and Mum — I think Mum was just looking at him, making every second with him count.

I kept thinking: Sandy, Sandy, Sandy. It's funny. I've known Sandy all my life. All us kids played together — when there's only eleven of you at school it doesn't matter how old you are, or if you're a boy or a girl, and anyway, there were only two of us girls at school, me and Amy. There are always more boys than girls born in the valley, even with sheep and horses. It's a good thing roosters taste good.

I remember when I was six years old, and Sandy was eight, and he tackled me when we were playing football so I fell down and split my lip. Sandy saw me dripping blood and stopped to say, 'I'm sorry,' and then I grabbed the ball and scored a try. Another boy would have been mad, but Sandy laughed, and always chose me for his team after that.

I can't really remember when we stopped touching, not even sitting wedged side by side in the cart to school. I was ten, I think, and he was twelve. It was almost like we knew there was something special going to happen for us, and we had to stop touching till it happened.

We went down in the cart before dawn. I had my blue dress on again — I'd sponged off the gravy stain. Jeff sat between Mum and Dad on the front seat, not in the back of the cart with me and Joey and Kirsty.

The marchers had slept in the schoolhouse. Mrs Mack and the other women were serving them scrambled eggs and making toast on a campfire with about a hundred pots of jam. Sandy was sitting with them but he came over to the cart and helped me down, just like I was a lady, not waiting for me to jump down myself. I don't think I let go of his hand till the drum began to beat again. The piper puffed into his bagpipes and started to play.

Sandy said, 'I've got to go.'

I said, 'I know.'

He kissed me again, on the lips, in front of everyone, then ran to where the men were lining up. Jeff hugged each one of us, but Mum longest. He said, 'I'll be right, Mum. You're not to worry,' then he went and stood beside Sandy.

Sandy didn't look at me then, or Mrs Mack, just straight in front, like all the other men, with Jeff beside him. They didn't look young. They looked like men, like soldiers. I knew exactly what I was feeling then: proud. It hurt, but I was proud of that too. Like Dad says, it's supposed to hurt when you make a sacrifice for your country. That is what sacrifice means.

The sergeant called, 'Attention! Quick march!'

They began to march. Sandy did look back then, and so did Jeff.

I waved, and cried and smiled at the same time, like Mum and Mrs Mack, so Sandy and Jeff remember us smiling not sobbing as they left. The bagpipes wailed again, and the drum beat. I wanted to run after them, like the little kids did, but I wanted to be a young woman too. If Sandy is a man now then I have to be a woman, not a little girl. I stood there and listened till I couldn't even hear the echoes. But maybe the bagpiper stopped playing once they were out of sight.

And then I helped wash up and we got into the cart and came home.

Mum looked too tired to put on dinner. I said I'd make shepherd's pie with the leftover mutton in the cool safe.

I'd just put it in the oven for the potato to brown when I heard this wailing, like the bagpipes. For a second I thought they had all come back, that the war was suddenly over. Then I saw Mum, sitting down on the Rock, her face in her hands. Suddenly I realised Jeff was gone too — I mean really realised it — and I'd hardly even paid attention, didn't even know if he looked scared or excited, I'd just watched Sandy all the time.

I ran down to the Rock. Mum saw me and stopped sobbing. Her face was swollen and wet. I hugged her and we just sat on the Rock together, because there wasn't anything to say.

The wind muttered down the valley. It almost sounded like Jeff's voice. I remembered that time my loose tooth came out, and I was wailing that now the tooth fairy wouldn't come, and he grinned and got me a sheep's tooth and said, 'There. Now the fairy will have to give you twice as much.'

I suppose you're always closest to the brother who's just older than you. Me and Jeff, and Sandy. We all sort of fitted together. Now there was just me left, on the Rock, with Mum.

At last we walked back to the house. I served out the shepherd's pie and Mum pretended to eat.

The marchers will have camped again for the night now. They are going to stop in every town, all the way to the training camp in Goulburn. I hope there are hundreds and thousands of volunteers marching then.

And because this is my diary and no one will read it ever except me I can say here 'I love Sandy Mack'. I wish I had said the words to him. I will say them when I have an address so can send him a letter, and socks, and a cake. Mrs Mack will send him those but I want him to have them from me too, because I am his girl now, forever and ever.

Here is another confession too. I feel jealous. Just a bit. They are off to fight the Huns and I have to stay here, and go to school. It's always been the three of us, collecting wood or swimming in the creek or riding down to the Snowy to go fishing. Now it's just Sandy and Jeff, and me back here.

I love you, Sandy Mack. I always will.

'Now you sit down and tuck in, Flinty love,' said Mrs Mack comfortably, wiping her buttery hands on her sacking apron and shoving an extra chair in next to hers at the kitchen table. 'There's two apple teacakes just out of the oven.'

Flinty forced herself not to look at Sandy, down at the other end of the table. Mrs Mack had seated her next to where Sandy usually sat, but when he'd seen her he'd sat down near Mr Mack instead.

It hurt. Seeing Sandy always hurt now.

Why had he changed? He'd written 'All my love, Sandy' in his letters, right up to when he had been wounded, that terrible time when Jeff had been killed, and Mum had her heart attack. They hadn't even known Sandy had been wounded for weeks — there'd been a mix-up with his name — and by then he was recovering, safe back in England.

She'd sent Sandy a pair of bedsocks she'd knitted, and a stomach warmer, and a ginger fruitcake because he loved ginger. But he didn't write any more letters after that, or not to her, just notes to Mrs Mack, not even saying 'thank Flinty for the cake', and a letter to Mum saying he was sorry about Jeff, how he was a good mate, and had died quickly, with no pain.

She'd tried to tell herself it would be different when he got home. She'd even gone down to Gibber's Creek with the Macks to meet his train, in her blue dress with a bunch of everlastings, all of them wearing masks because of the influenza epidemic.

And there was Sandy, looking taller and thinner and sort of bent, from his wound in the war she supposed, but still totally and always the Sandy who she loved.

Their eyes met for half a second, then he looked away.

He hadn't met her eyes since.

He'd hugged his family. Not her. She'd thrown the flowers away in the station rubbish bin, and hoped he hadn't noticed.

That had been eight months ago now. And it still felt like a knife slice every time she saw him, even here, in the warm comfort of the Macks' kitchen.

Mrs Mack plonked the cakes next to the loaf of bread sliced into doorstops, the piled, steaming pikelets, the dish of butter freshly churned that morning, the five pots of jam (strawberry, plum, apricot, blackberry and crab apple), the apple chutney, the hunk of Mutti Green's cheese and the sliced cold mutton — the dishes the Mack family regarded as a normal afternoon tea.

Nine pairs of eager hands reached for bread or passed the butter. The Macks' kitchen table always had as much food as you could cram onto it, and as many Mack sons and grandsons who could be crammed about it too.

There were no empty places at the Macks' table, not like there were at Rock Farm, despite the loss of the Macks' daughter Valma early this year in the influenza, and their Rick at Passchendaele. Today the table was crowded with five Mack sons and one grandson — even married Johnno Mack ate lunch and afternoon tea at his mum's, going back home for tea with his wife and younger children — as well as Mr Mack with his straggly grey whiskers, skinny as a rake despite his wife's good feeding.

Dear Mrs Mack, thought Flinty, with her bottom as big as a sofa and ankles bulging over her laced shoes. She fought down the guilt about Joey and Kirsty at home up on the mountain, with only two-day-old bread and golden syrup for afternoon tea. She hadn't had time to make fresh bread today, not and come down here. The jam she'd made last summer (a lonely task without Mum to sing with and share stories while they chopped and stirred) had been eaten, and there was no money to buy sugar to make more, or fruit on the trees yet, for that matter. If only you could make jam from rock and rabbit skins ...

'Eat up, Flinty love,' said Mrs Mack encouragingly. 'You're thin as a match with the wood shaved off. Isn't she, Sandy?'

Sandy didn't look up from his strawberry-jam-laden pikelet. 'She looks all right,' he said.

He still looked like the Sandy who'd ridden after brumbies with her and Dad and her brothers, the Sandy who'd helped her with her mathematics, the Sandy who'd kissed her; although he still had that strange crouching twist to his shoulders, from the wound he'd never speak about.

But he was still freckled; his hair was still the same colour as his name; he was still all knees and elbows. He was still her Sandy.

Except he wasn't.

She took a pikelet from the dish Toby passed her, trying not to look at the two missing fingers of Toby's left hand. He'd lost those at Passchendaele too. A sudden memory slapped her: Toby and Andy grinning as they posed for a photo when they enlisted together the week war was declared.

This is still the world of war, she thought, even here, despite the generous plenty of the Macks' kitchen and the full table. But outside there were wombat holes in fences left unrepaired while so many men were at the war, the plagues of rabbit, with none to shoot or trap them, and no horses since the army took them all.

It was as though the families in the valley struggled to be free, to make their lives again. But the war wouldn't be left behind.

'How are you and the youngsters doing up top there?' asked Mrs Mack, a bit too casually, pouring her husband a cup of tea strong enough to melt the teaspoon. Mrs Mack may have lost her second son to the war, and cared for her crippled daughter till she'd died in the influenza epidemic that had taken Captain McAlpine, but she still had a heart big enough to care for the whole valley.

'We do all right,' said Flinty.

'Heard your Andy's gone to Queensland droving for Miss Matilda,' said Mr Mack, around a mouthful of bread and mutton. Mr Mack was as strong as the draught horses that pulled his plough, but too old to have gone to war. 'Drinkwater's goin' in for sheep again now there's no need for cans of bully beef, I hear. Well, she'll get a better price for them cattle up in Queensland.'

'What's your Andy doing, going so far away again?' demanded Mrs Mack. 'Seems like he'd have wanted to be at home after all those years away. It's the lad's duty to look after his brother and sisters.'

'We manage,' said Flinty.

'That's as may be. But when the young 'uns go back to school after the summer holidays you'll be all alone up there. And Joey's what? Twelve? Not old enough to be the man of the house.'

'Joey and Kirsty aren't going back to school.'

Dad's pension from the Indian Army had stopped with his death. Selling rabbit skins was the only way they had to get money just now and she couldn't do the chores by herself as well as keep up Joey's traps. Kirsty was too young to ride down the mountain and back every day by herself.

Nor were there horses to sell any more. Rock Farm's horses had been sold to the army in the first year of the war. Now the proud animals lay dead in Palestine maybe, or drudged in the Indian Army. Only roos and rabbits roamed the mountaintop paddocks now.

Flinty bit her lip to try to stop the sudden tears. Tears always seemed to be lurking these days. The horses had trotted off so bravely, Prince Henry and Good Queen Bess and all the others, bred with such dedication ever since Dad had been invalided out of the Indian Army with fever, thirty years back. The mountains had given Captain McAlpine life again, he'd said, and given him a family and his horses too.

Till early this year, and the influenza.

She looked up to find Sandy passing her the apple teacake. 'Better get in quick or it'll be gone,' he muttered.

She took a slice and sniffed instead of blowing her nose, hoping no one would notice her wet face. There was tenpence halfpenny in the jam jar under her kitchen floorboards. Dad's funeral had been paid for, and the doctor's bill ... but the rates ...

Flinty tried to shut her mind to the rates bill, sitting accusingly under the clock on the mantelpiece. It was only three pounds two shillings, but three pounds two shillings was as far away as the moon.

She just had to keep going as best she could. In a few months Andy would be in Brisbane, the Drinkwater cattle sold and sheep filling Miss Matilda's paddocks again, paddocks half empty since the men went to war. Andy could telegraph them a money order from his first wages. And maybe Joey's rabbit skins would bring in a pound or even two as well. How long could rates go unpaid before the government took away your farm?

'More mutton, Flinty love?'

'I beg your pardon? Oh, I'm sorry, Mrs Mack.' Flinty was suddenly aware that Mr Mack and the boys were getting up for a last few hours' work before sundown. 'No, thank you. I wondered,' she took a breath, 'I wondered if I could speak to Toby. Privately,' she added.

'Toby?' Mrs Mack gave Sandy a quick glance. Sandy stared at his jam-laden pikelet, expressionless.

Toby pushed back his chair from the table. 'No time to sit round yakking. Need to fence the river paddock. Spring flood ripped out the floodgate ...'

Mr Mack looked at Flinty, then at his Toby. Mr Mack knows what I want to ask, she thought.

'Nothing that can't wait till tomorrow, lad,' said Mr Mack gently. 'You have a talk with the girl.'

'But Dad ...'

Mr Mack laid a cracked and calloused hand on his son's arm. 'She's owed that,' he said quietly.

Toby stared at his father. He was as tall as Sandy, broader across the shoulders, his nose still crooked from where Bluey White had broken it when they were eight years old. 'What would you know ...?' he began. He stopped at a cry, almost a sob, from his mother. Mrs Mack's hands were suddenly busy with the teapot, her face resolutely intent on refilling it with hot water.

Toby stood up. 'All right then,' he muttered. 'Out on the verandah?'

Flinty nodded. She glanced again at Sandy. For once he was actually looking at her, his expression impossible to read. Well, Sandy wouldn't talk to her. Toby was her last chance. She followed Toby along the passage, smelling of Sunlight soap from Mrs Mack's spring-cleaning, then outside. She settled onto one of the shaggy armchairs and looked out across the valley, the silver thread of the creek that led down to the broad flats of the Snowy River, the mountains purple against the sky's blue.

You could see the other valley houses from here, the Mullinses' cottage with its shingle roof, the one-room schoolhouse, with the schoolmaster's house beside it, the hint of heat rather than smoke from the Greens' chimney. The Greens had been the Grünbergs till the war, but no one in the valley remarked on their sudden change of name when Germany became the enemy. Beyond them were the Browns and then the Whites.

Dad said that Mr White had been 'Bruiser Snodgrass' and wanted for cattle theft in two states before he'd changed his name and come to the valley. The White boys still stole any calf that wasn't branded and assumed that any land not fenced belonged to them and their cattle, which included the thousands of square miles across the Snowy. You didn't want to cross any White boy after a night on the booze — or even before it.

But Ginger White was buried in France with Jeff and Rick now, and when old Ma White heard Dad was sick the other White boys had ridden up and chopped enough wood to see them through a month. The Colours of the Valley, Dad had called them all, when the Grünbergs changed their name to Green.

One of the sheep dogs gave a sharp bark. It jumped up onto the verandah and onto Toby's lap. He patted it absently. Flinty kept her eyes from the scar where his fingers had been lost.

'What do you want?' Toby asked shortly.

She took a deep breath. 'I want to know about the war.'

Toby glanced up at her defensively. 'Sandy wrote to your mum all he knew about Jeff's death. It was quick, like Sandy said. Jeff didn't feel a thing.'

Her brother's name still had the power to hurt. 'I know. That's what his captain said in his letter too. That it was quick. That Jeff felt no pain.' She clasped her hands together, digging the fingernails into her wrist. 'Toby, that's what the letter your mum got said about Rick too. And what they said about Ginger White. That it was sudden; that they didn't feel a thing.'

'What of it?'

'The letters can't all be true,' she said softly.

He stared at her. 'What do you know of it?'

'Nothing. That's why I'm asking. Sandy won't talk to me. Not about anything. Andy wouldn't tell me anything either. So I'm asking you.'

'There's nothing you need to know.' He looked down at the dog, automatically caressing its fur. 'Jeff was Sandy's best mate. He was my mate too. You think I don't miss him as well? And Rick? What difference does it make now how Jeff died? He's dead, Flinty. Gone. Like Rick and all the others. And we have to go on living.'

She had to force her voice to stay steady. 'I didn't come here to talk about Jeff. I need to know about Andy.' And Sandy, she thought. But if Sandy won't even talk to me maybe I don't have the right to know.

Toby looked up at that. 'What do you mean? Andy didn't get more than a scratch the whole four years. We called him Butter Boy, because he seemed to slide through any trouble. What do you need to know about Andy?'

'I need to know what's sent him away from his sisters and brother, why he's run all the way to Queensland when we need him here. Why did he scream with nightmares every night? I found him crying out by the well once —'

'And you want to know why the poor bloke's gone droving?' For the first time Toby's voice rose. 'Just listen to yourself, Felicity McAlpine. Maybe your brother's gone because you've driven him away. Telling you would make him live it all again. It's bad enough that we had to see it, day after day, year after year, without bringing it home for all you too. You and your questions —'

'You leave her alone.' Sandy stood in the doorway, in that strange new crouch, his lips a hard straight line. Toby stopped as though an axe had chopped off his speech.

Flinty stared at Sandy, then at Toby, his face suddenly expressionless. 'Got to help with the fencing,' he muttered. He flung himself off the verandah and headed round the house.

Sandy still stood there, not quite looking at her, but not looking away either. Flinty waited, forcing back tears again, hoping he'd join her on the verandah. But he didn't.

'Do you think I drove Andy away?' she asked at last.

'Yes. No. I don't know,' said Sandy. He seemed to consciously force his body straight. 'Flinty, just leave it, all right? There's some things women don't need to know. Just give Andy time. Give him a bit of quiet.'

'I see,' she said dully.

'No, you don't. I'm sorry. Toby shouldn't have said those things. Shouldn't have said anything. I better go help with the fencing. Dad'll put his back out with the crowbar if I don't stop him. You doing all right for firewood?'

'Yes. We spent all last week hauling branches home.'

'You need some good logs to keep burning all night. I'll bring the axe up next week.'

'I don't need more wood!' she cried. 'Why won't anyone talk about the war?'

'Because you're better off out of it,' said Sandy flatly. His boots sounded hollow as he tramped across the verandah and then off towards the paddock.

Flinty watched him go, the tears cold on her cheeks. Sandy, who'd dammed the creek with her every summer to make a swimming hole, till the next spring's floods hurled their mud and branches down and away. Sandy, who'd punched Tiger White's nose when he tried to kiss her behind the school water tank. Sandy, who had written from Sydney, from Egypt, from England, from France: *All my love, Sandy.*

If only he really *was* different, she thought. But this man was still the boy; more than he had been, but never less.

'Sandy didn't mean it, lovey ...'

Flinty turned as Mrs Mack came out the door.

'Yes, he did.'

'Well, maybe he did at that. But when you get to my age you realise there's no point trying to make a man talk when he don't want to. He'll get round to it in his own good time.' She hesitated. 'Got some things for you to take home. Forequarter of mutton, some of my jam. Your ma always said I made the best apple jelly in the valley. There's a knack to it, I admit. You sure you're all right up there? What the captain was thinking of building so far up the mountain I'll never know.'

'Dad liked the view,' said Flinty.

'Well, he got a view all right,' said Mrs Mack, looking at her own comfortable farmyard, the tamed paddocks of young corn and potatoes, the dusty hens clucking in the yard. 'You're sitting in the clouds half the time. And that big Rock. Spooky, I call it. I've heard stories ...' She stopped, as though realising that ghost stories weren't going to reassure a young girl who'd lost her brother and her parents, who had an even younger brother and sister to look after in an isolated house. 'It don't seem right, three children on their own,' she said instead.

'I'm seventeen,' said Flinty.

'Yes. Well.' Mrs Mack's pursed lips said more than her words about what she thought of seventeen-year-old girls keeping house.

'And Andy will be back by the end of summer.' Please let him come home, thought Flinty desperately.

Mrs Mack patted her hand. 'You let us know whatever you need. Your ma and the captain were our friends. You just remember you've got neighbours all down the valley who'll help. All you have to do is ask.'

She reached out and hugged her. For a moment Flinty was folded in the scent of floury arms and new butter and wood smoke.

'I'll remember,' she said.

Chapter 3

22 November 1919

Dear Diary,

It all seemed magic on Armistice Day. As though we could step into peace the next day. But it took months and months for all the boys to come back.

Could Sandy have met another girl, a nurse in England, maybe? I asked Jones the postman last week if the Macks had got any letters. I pretended Joey was still collecting stamps. It wasn't a lie — he kept every stamp we got, from Andy and Jeff and a few of their mates who didn't have anyone else to send them socks and cakes, and wrote back to thank me and Mum and Kirsty. But Jones said the Macks don't get any letters at all, just the weekly paper and the rates bill. 'Waste of me time coming up here,' said Jones. 'Now everything is back to normal all I bring anyone is bills and no one thanks me for them.'

'You bring the wool cheques,' I said. That made him smile. Mum would have given him tea and cake, but I hadn't made any cake, and I was too embarrassed to give him bread and

syrup, so I just offered him a cup of tea. We're almost out of tea, so I was glad when he said no.

Now everything is back to normal, he said. Except it isn't. No Mum and Dad and Jeff, Andy gone and Sandy like a stranger. Maybe that's why I can think that what happened on the Rock today is even possible. The impossible has happened over and over the last few years.

Maybe even ghosts are possible too.

The sun hovered between the mountains as Empress cantered back up the mountain track to Rock Farm, like a lamp in the window beckoning the way home. The last of winter's distant snow blazed like fire in the sunset.

Dad had called this the shadow time. The sun sucks colour from the world, he'd said. He'd taught her to see the softer colours of the dusk, the green and orange bark, the purple shadows. At times like this Flinty felt her edges vanish, leaving her part of the mountains, like the wallaby pulling wonga vine down from a thorn bush, or the sleepy possum peering from a tree.

She'd stayed with Mrs Mack too long, comforted by the scents of cake and roasting mutton. It would be dark by the time she got home, if she kept to the track. Empress could find her way in darkness — Flinty reckoned Empress could find her way even if rain fell as mud — but Kirsty and Joey would be worried if Flinty wasn't home by dark.

She tugged at the reins. The track twisted back and forth across the mountain; if she cut straight uphill she'd be home before dark. A horse could stumble and break its leg on rough ground. But Dad had put Flinty in the saddle when she was two years old. Empress could sense a wombat hole at twenty paces. She never stumbled no matter how steep the slope, or caught her hoof in a tussock that a bettong had twisted into a nest.

Flinty let Empress have her head. The horse picked her way up through the tussocks, over the little round billy buttons, the tiny white heath flowers and the bigger yellow everlastings. Dad had kept only two horses when the others had gone as army horses: Lord George for himself and Empress.

Now Andy was riding Lord George, up by the Queensland border. Did he still have nightmares, crying out in his swag under the trees as he had in the narrow bed at home? Did anyone make him a cup of cocoa to drink when he woke, sweaty and shaking?

Not that he'd ever told her what haunted the empire of sleep. He'd just sat there, sipping his cocoa, holding it with both hands till the shaking stopped.

Was Toby right? Had her questions driven Andy away? Maybe he didn't want anyone to bring him cocoa, to watch him force his hands to slowly still.

What had taken Jeff and eaten Andy's laughter too? Hearts can break, Mum whispered, when she read the telegram that said that Jeff had died. And Mum's had broken, even if hers hadn't stopped beating till a month later.

Sometimes it was like the war still growled around the windows in the darkness, lurking, snickering, waiting to snatch even the men like Andy who'd seemed to come home safe, and drag them back, at least in dreams.

What was war really like? What vast crack had buried Jeff down in the mud, had sent Andy off with cattle? What had changed her best friend so much he could hardly look at her now?

Empress broke through the hop bushes back onto the road again. Flinty glimpsed the house in the last of the light, tucked among its apple and plum trees, above the mist. Rock Farm was bigger than any of the houses in the valley, its walls of stone, its roof of she-oak shingles, as lichen covered as the tree trunks now.

The mist still covered the Rock. The man in the bathchair was a dim shape just visible through the white.

The soldier.

She urged Empress to a canter again. The horse responded instantly, hesitating only slightly this time as they reached the mist's edge, her hooves clacking on the stone of the Rock.

The mist stopped at the edge of the Rock. The valley stretched below her, trees and tiny patches of paddock, the houses hidden among the green. Here and there Rocky Creek glinted red and silver in the last of the sunbeams, on its way to join the great spring rush of the Snowy River further down the mountain. Between the ridges one last mountain top of snow glowed pink as the sun descended.

The young man must have heard her, but he didn't turn even when she dismounted. Empress backed off a little, showing the whites of her eyes. Flinty stroked her nose till she quietened, trying to control her anger. How dare he not even look at her? The Rock was her home, not his. How dare he not even speak?

And then he did. 'What do you want?' He still stared out across the valley.

It was as though her anger fizzed up like a shaken bottle of lemonade. 'I want to know what it was like.'

'What do you mean?' The man wheeled the bathchair around so it faced her. Its wheels were made of shiny metal edged with black rubber. She had never seen a metal wheel before.

'The war!' she cried. The sound echoed across the valley: *War ... war ... ar ... ar ...*

He stared at her, almost wary, his mouth still that hard harsh line. His hair was black above his white face and shadowed eyes — none of the families in the valley had black hair. It made him look even more a stranger. But his shoulders were square, like the men she knew, even if they looked too thin. His hands and arms were muscular, she supposed from wheeling his chair. 'You want me to talk about the war?'

'Yes!'

'Why?'

'Why do you think? Because it killed my brother. Because ...' She buried her face in Empress's warm neck so he wouldn't see her cry.

'I'm sorry. I didn't know about your brother. I only got here yesterday.' He didn't sound sorry. There wasn't any emotion in his voice at all. But at least he was looking at her. 'I'm staying at the old farmhouse.'

He must be at Dusty Jim's hut after all, thought Flinty. Maybe he was even Dusty's nephew or great-nephew, though bush rats looked more like Dusty Jim than this young man.

She should be sorry for him, his legs shot away, a stranger. But he was using all he had suffered — all that all the returned men had suffered — as a wall around himself. Didn't any of them realise how much she had to cope with too, just like Mrs Mack, like Mum?

'Please! Just tell me what the war was like.'

He stared at her. She could see pain. Guilt did stab her now. She hadn't wanted to add more suffering. But still she met his eyes, daring him to speak.

'You really want to hear about the war?' He sounded faintly incredulous.

'Yes!'

'No one wants to know,' he said flatly.

'I do.'

'You want to know what it's like to lose your legs? Well, I can't tell you. One moment I was running, the next I was in a hospital bed. No pain. It hurts now more than it did then. Or maybe it hurt so much then that I just don't remember the pain ...'

She tried to keep her voice steady. 'I'm sorry about your legs. But I didn't mean that. I want to know what it was like to be *in* a war. The newspapers just told us where the fighting was, and who had died or been hurt. I need to know what it was like *being there*. Please.'

'You want a tour of war? All right then.' Suddenly there was so much emotion on his face that it felt like he'd slapped her. 'You think war is battlefields, but it's not. No country starts out as a battlefield. It's farms and houses and women and kids, but any one of them can kill you, even a boy peering from behind a door. Every time you see a face you have to think, is this someone I need to kill or someone I must protect? You never know. Never.' His breath ran out and he stopped, then managed, 'You want more?'

She nodded.

'The smells. That's what you can't forget. Every smell is foreign, every smell is etched on your brain. Rice paddies, jungle, even the markets, not a single smell of home. Nothing.'

She hadn't known there were rice paddies in France or Flanders. Dad had had the paper delivered with the mail, once a week, so he could put little flags on the big map in the kitchen to show the battlefields and Mum would know who had lost someone and when to bake a cake for the memorial. But the newspapers just gave names and places, not what the land was like.

The soldier was looking out across the valley again now. 'There's noise. But the silences are worse, because then you're waiting for the shelling and the screams. And even when you think you've won, you've lost.'

For the first time he looked down at the dangling blue trousers where his feet should have been. 'We won the Battle of Long Tan. We won! A hundred and eight of us Aussies facing thousands of the enemy. We should have been heroes. You know what happened back in Sydney, the day I left hospital like this?' He touched his chair. 'A girl spat at me. A protestor.'

Flinty stared at him. She had heard that some people had been against the fighting. Pacifists, they were called. She had never heard of any woman spitting at a soldier.

'I can still hear her,' he said. She could hear the anger now, pushing its way through his control. '"Ho Chi Minh!" she shouted. "Dare to struggle, dare to win." Like the enemy was the only brave one, not us. We Aussies secured the whole Long Tan area. But it hasn't made any difference. Nothing we did then, not my legs, not the blokes who died. Not the blokes still dying over there —'

'What blokes? Who's dying?' Flinty stepped back towards Empress. She'd heard some of the men had come home touched in the head. Or maybe he'd been drinking Dusty Jim's moonshine. 'The war's over,' she said cautiously, in case he really was drunk, or mad. 'It stopped at the Armistice. Everyone's come home.'

The young man looked back at her. 'What armistice? Are you crazy? Just turn on the news at night if you really want to know what's happening in Vietnam. Not that they'll tell you the whole truth. Either way, stop bothering me about it.' He turned the wheeled bathchair again, as though to go.

'Vietnam? I ... I didn't know there was a place called Vietnam in France, or Flanders. Is it in Palestine?'

The mist grew colder. Empress gave an uneasy whicker and tried to back away. Flinty pulled the reins, patting the horse's neck automatically, staring at the man.

The soldier gazed at her, then at the horse. He gave a sound that might have been a laugh. 'I thought it was just a story. I didn't believe it. Don't believe it! I'm imagining all this. Too many painkillers for too long —'

'Don't believe what?' she asked, desperate to understand.

'You're a ghost.'

Chapter 4

This morning I didn't believe in ghosts, especially not ones from the future. I'm still not sure that it really happened. But I saw it! It was as real as my hand. And I'm not mad. Neither is he, though he is unhappy.

Is he really a ghost? I keep going over and over it in my mind. If only there was someone I could talk to about it, but the only people I could talk to about things like this were Jeff and Sandy. I don't want to scare Kirsty or Joey by talking about ghosts, and Mrs Mack would worry it's all been too much for me, that I'm seeing things like Dusty Jim does when he's on a bender, or that poor soldier down in Gibber's Creek who ran away screaming during the fireworks, yelling that the guns were firing.

The man on the Rock this morning was real all right. I was upset about Sandy and Jeff and, well, everything, but not upset enough to imagine a ghost.

He didn't seem like the sort of man who'd play tricks either. I think he believed everything he said. But if what he said was true then he's seen enough to imagine things, like ghosts from the past.

Except his ghost is me. And I am real.

So that leaves only two solutions: he's staying with someone around here, and is having hallucinations, thinking he is from the future — someone who carefully wiped away all the wheel tracks from the bathchair, to make me think his story is true.

Or there are ghosts on the Rock, just like people said.

'I'm not a ghost.' She spoke automatically.

His face looked even whiter, like a bleached sheet; the shadows under his eyes had deepened. He shook his head, drops of mist wet on his hair, peered out at her. 'The people I'm staying with warned me I might meet a ghost down here. I thought it was a joke. Like drop bears.'

'Drop bears?'

'Killer koalas that jump down onto your head from the trees. We used to trick the Yanks about them.'

'How can there be killer koalas?' She still kept carefully away from him.

'How can there be ghosts? Except you're here, just like they said. And so am I.'

'That doesn't make me a ghost.' She tried to smile at him as she pinched her arm. 'See? I'm solid.'

His hands still clenched the arms of his bathchair. 'And you're fifty years in the past. Just like they said.'

Someone was tricking him. Dusty, with his drunken stories. The White boys, maybe. But surely even they wouldn't trick a returned soldier. And none of them could have convinced this man he was from another time.

'It's a trick,' he said, almost as if he'd been reading her mind. 'You're pretending to be from the past.' Suddenly he stopped, staring at the track behind her. 'It's not a trick.' His voice had lost all emotion, but his eyes looked wary. 'There's the proof.'

'Proof I'm a ghost? What is it?'

'Look at the road. It rained a couple of hours ago,' he said flatly. 'But there aren't any hoof prints.'

She looked back. Empress's hoof prints were plain in the mud. 'Yes, there are. Look.'

'I *am* looking. The only prints are my wheel tracks.'

There was silence while she tried to see whether he was lying or mad. Was he dangerous? He couldn't get up the steps to Kirsty or Joey in that chair, and she'd be on Empress's back before he got within six feet of her.

'Maybe you really are a ghost.' He stared at her, then suddenly he laughed. 'You're supposed to be scared of ghosts, but who can be scared of a girl and a horse? You're Flinty McAlpine, aren't you? The girl from Snowy River. They showed me a photo of you, a few years older than you are now, just last night. You're a ghost, from fifty years ago.'

'I'm not dead,' she said quietly. 'You have to be dead to be a ghost. I had apple teacake for afternoon tea. You can't eat apple teacake if you're dead.'

'What year did you eat the cake? What year is it for you, I mean?'

'1919, of course.'

'I'm in 1969,' he said flatly. She looked at the track again. There were Empress's hoof prints. But there were no wheel tracks from his chair. How could you wheel a bathchair up to the Rock and leave no prints? Unless he *was* a ghost.

Her head reeled. 1969? He *couldn't* be real! She tried to stay calm and look at him properly.

His clothes. The too-long hair. Most of all the bathchair — that strange slim bathchair with its shiny wheels. Suddenly she believed that the man in front of her might indeed be from the future.

You were supposed to scream when you saw a ghost, weren't you? But she didn't want to scream. In a funny way this ghost seemed more real than Toby and Andy and even Sandy. At least this ghost talked to a girl, instead of hugging close a coat of silence. 'If one of us is a ghost, it's you, not me.' She tried to keep her voice steady.

'Me?' He looked out through the mist at the track again, so obviously seeing what she could not. Hoof prints in my time, she thought, wheel tracks in his. 'I thought I might die a dozen times back in Vietnam. I'm pretty sure I'm not dead now. I'd have noticed dying. I spent nearly three years in hospital trying not to do it,' he added dryly. 'Trust me. You notice when you nearly die too. Besides, I know your name.'

She stared at him. The shut-off look he had worn before had vanished. He's starting to enjoy this, she thought. Then: three years in hospital! Three years wondering if the war would take you after all. Whatever was happening here had brought him back from his war. Ghosts held no terror for her — not after the loss of so many she loved. And apparently the idea of ghosts didn't scare him either. But which time was the real one? 1919 or 1969? Could she really be a phantom, haunting the place she loved? No! She'd just had afternoon tea at the Macks'. A ghost wouldn't remember that — would they?

'Ask anyone around here if I'm real. They all know me.'

'Well, yes. But you were a girl fifty years ago. Not in 1969.'

'Who do you know around here?' Suddenly his words from a few minutes ago came back to her. 'Who told you that you'd find ghosts on the Rock?'

He looked at her steadily. 'Not ghosts. A ghost. The ghost of Flinty McAlpine, the girl from Snowy River.'

'I'm not a ghost!' Her words echoed back from the valley: *Ghost, ghost, ghost ...*

She thrust out her hand. 'See? Pinch me. I'm real.'

Instead he put his fingers lightly on her wrist for a second, then drew them back. His skin felt warm, despite the chill of the mist.

'See?' she demanded. 'I'm solid. Who told you I'd be a ghost?'

'Someone I'm staying with. In 1969.'

'Who?'

He looked at her strangely. 'The family of a boy I went to school with. His grandmother asked if I'd like to get away from Sydney after I got out of hospital. I ... I'd had enough of Mum fussing, of nurses and antiseptic. I wanted to smell gum trees again. I wanted some place new.' He gave a wry smile. 'Looks like I found that all right.'

The sun had slipped behind the ranges now. The shadows were gathering into dark. Flinty glanced up at the house, a vague shape through the Rock's mist. Suddenly Joey yelled, 'Flinty! Flinty, where are you?'

She was shocked how much relief she felt at the real world — her own world — reasserting itself. Had she began to doubt her own sanity — even her own reality? 'I'm down at the Rock!' she yelled. 'I'll be there soon.'

'Kirsty hurt her knee!'

'What? I'll be right there ... See?' she demanded of the soldier. 'You heard that! They're real! I'm real!'

'I didn't hear anything,' he said softly. 'Just the wind. And you.'

Impossible. But she believed him. Somehow she knew he was real, knew she wasn't dreaming, knew that somehow his world was the future. Could both of them be real? Could she be here, in 1919, somehow meeting a man from 1969? Neither of them ghosts. Both — somehow — real? But she couldn't stay here and try to sort this out. She had to do her duty. 'I ... I have to go. Kirsty needs me.'

'Then off you go, Flinty McAlpine.'

Mounting Empress was one of the hardest things she had ever done. Would she see the soldier again? All at once she realised that if he really was from the future he could tell her so many things. Would Andy come back to Rock Farm? Would they get the rates paid? Maybe even if she and Sandy ...?

After all the changes that had shuddered through the past few years it would be good to glimpse the future. Just to know there *was* a future ...

'Flinty!'

Empress shivered, as though longing to be gone. She broke into a trot.

Flinty looked back. He was still there, growing fainter in the dark and the mist. 'What's your name?' she called.

'Nicholas.'

'Will you be here tomorrow?'

'I don't know,' he called back. 'Maybe ghosts can't choose when they'll appear. But I'll be here on this Rock. Will you?'

'Flinty! Hurry!' Joey's voice sounded increasingly desperate.

'Coming!' she yelled, then added, 'Yes,' to the ghost on the Rock.

But this time when she looked back the mist was empty.

Chapter 5

He just vanished. Men in bathchairs can't just disappear. There's nowhere to go, except over the cliff.

All my life I've heard stories about the Rock. All right, most of them from Dusty Jim when he's been at the bottle. But what if he really has seen strange things there? People from another time?

What is time anyway? The day Mum died went on forever, holding her hand while Dad rode for the doctor, knowing she was dead but still hoping, somehow, that she wasn't, watching her skin change from pink to wax.

Maybe time flows like the air on a mountain. The wind will freeze your nose and toes, then suddenly you'll find a pocket of warmth. Maybe time flows too, and there's a pocket of it that slips and slides around the Rock.

There is something special about the Rock. Mum and Dad felt it too. I'd see them sitting down there together, watching the sunset through the mist. Maybe …

No, I'm being stupid. Someone is playing a joke. Amy,

maybe. They carried the chair down so there'd be no tracks. He pretended to have no legs.

But you can't pretend that. I saw his empty trousers! Saw his face too. He has a kind face, not a cruel one. And even Amy wouldn't joke about a wounded soldier.

One minute I think I've got it all worked out, then the next I change my mind.

I want him to be real so badly. Not mad, not lying. Not a ghost either, because ghosts are dead. I want him to be the person who he says he is, the soldier from 1969. How is it that someone who says he is from 1969 looks at me like I am really here, while Sandy can't?

If he's real — if he's ever there again — then I can talk to him. Someone just to talk to, at last.

'Flinty!' Joey's voice came from the kitchen.

She slid off Empress. The pony gave an abrupt snort as though to say, 'Get in there. Don't worry about me.'

'How badly is she hurt?' Suddenly Flinty had a vision of Kirsty with her leg so badly injured she would lose it too. She should never have left them alone so long ...

The lamp shone on the kitchen table. The fire was alight too, as well as the wood stove — thank goodness, she thought with a small part of her mind. Joey must have chopped the wood as she'd asked. 'Where is she? Oh ...'

It was a sigh of relief. Kirsty sat on the floor looking up at her, patting at the tears running down her face with a lace-edged handkerchief. There was a trickle of blood on her leg. A very small trickle from a cut on her knee.

'I tripped over the step!' wailed Kirsty.

'Oh, for Pete's sake.' It had been Dad's favourite oath. Ladies never swore, but sometimes ...

Flinty grabbed the hanky to press it against the bleeding knee. Kirsty snatched it back. 'No! It'll get all stained! I've already got blood on my best petticoat!'

Flinty gazed at the tear-streaked face. Kirsty hadn't cried when Dad died nor at his funeral, just stood there with a face of ice. When the brown snake came in the kitchen door last autumn her little sister had hit it with a shovel and cut its head off before she yelled for Flinty and her brother. But get a drop of blood or mud or gravy on her pinafore and she howled like a banshee.

'Get the bandage basket,' Flinty said tiredly to Joey. Her brain felt like cotton wool. Today had been too much: the stranger, seeing Sandy. She needed quiet to sort each piece out. But there was no quiet, not just now. 'Joey, wait. I'll get the basket. You see to Empress. Take the lantern. There's a sack from Mrs Mack to bring in too.'

Joey nodded, and was gone. She hoped suddenly that he didn't go seeing ghosts down on the Rock.

She fetched the basket from the linen cupboard in the hall. She wished they didn't need to keep the lamp lit — lamp oil was expensive — but kitchen stoves didn't give light to see by, not like an open fire. Mum had made slush lamps with a wick floating in mutton fat, but they had no sheep left now. Joey trapped enough rabbits to keep them fed, but there wasn't much fat on a bunny.

'It's going to sting,' she said, holding up the iodine.

Kirsty wrinkled her nose. 'You won't spill any on my pinafore?'

The pinafore was almost worn through from so much washing, but Kirsty had embroidered little flowers all along the edge, long nights spent peering at the cloth by lamplight. She had embroidered her petticoats too and crocheted lace along the edges of the hanky that she still held away from the blood.

'No. See? Just a dab and then I'll bandage it up like this.' She tied the clean rag around the skinned knee. 'There you are. All vanished.'

Like the man — Nicholas — down on the Rock. She looked at Kirsty, examining her bandage, heard Joey's voice talking to Empress out in the yard. Should she tell them she'd seen a ghost out there? A ghost who thought *she* was a ghost, a ghost who said he was from 1969 …

They might believe her. Might have nightmares too, dreaming of ghoulies lurking in the darkness. But also …

The ghost was hers. Mine and no one else's, she thought suddenly. She had nothing else that was really hers. Her dresses were Mum's, cut down to size, to be handed on to Kirsty when she'd outgrown them. The shirt and trousers she'd worn today had been Dad's, would be Joey's when he grew to fit them. Her days were looking after her brother and her sister, scrubbing, cooking, bandaging knees. Even Rock Farm belonged to Andy now, as the eldest son.

Nicholas was hers. Her ghost. Her story.

Maybe she'd tell Joey and Kirsty about him, one day, as a bedtime story, but changed so it *was* just a story, not maybe true.

Maybe … possibly … impossibly … true.

Had he even really been there? Or had she dozed while Empress plodded up the road? No. She'd seen him twice. She might have dreamed Nicholas once, but not two times.

What was life like in the future? In the past fifty years they'd had the Great War and the Boer Wars, as well as the battles on the North-West Frontier in India, where Dad had served. Queen Victoria had died and bicycles had been invented ... oh, and motorcars and wireless sets, though she hadn't seen either yet. Would as much happen in the next fifty years?

I'm thinking like he really is from 1969, she thought.

'Kirsty? There haven't been any strangers about, have there?'

Kirsty shook her head. She glanced at the dark out the back door warily. 'You didn't see a swaggie, did you?'

'No, of course not,' Flinty reassured her. 'How about wheel marks?' she added casually.

'Only from the Mullinses' dray last week,' said Kirsty practically. 'But the rain washed them away.' She scrambled to her feet as Joey lugged in Mrs Mack's sack.

Tomorrow, Flinty thought. I'll see Nicholas again tomorrow. Meanwhile there was dinner to make. Joey and Kirsty peered into the sack as Flinty hauled a forequarter of mutton, wrapped in more old sacking, already cut into chops and a big leg roast.

Chops for dinner, she thought with relief. It only took ten minutes to fry chops. You had to boil bunny for an hour, then spend another picking out the bones. Boiled potatoes from the garden would be quick too, with boiled carrots and spinach if Kirsty had remembered to pick them.

'Apple jelly!' yelled Kirsty.

'Fruitcake!' breathed Joey. He picked it up like it was the crown jewels. 'Why don't you make fruitcake any more, Flinty?'

Because we can't afford dried fruit, she thought, but didn't say it. Because my life is full of looking after you, and worrying about the rates and Sandy — and now a ghost. 'I haven't time.'

Joey was still examining the cake. 'How come the fruit doesn't sink to the bottom? Or float up to the top?'

'Because it doesn't.' She knew better than to try to answer Joey's 'why' questions, though Dad had been able to. 'Why is so much of the map pink?' Joey would ask, and Dad would explain it was the British Empire, so big the sun never set on it ...

'Look!' Kirsty gave an excited dance. She was wearing her red shoes, even though they were two sizes too small now. She held up the contents of an old pillowslip.

Three jumpers. One blue, one brown, one smaller and pink. New jumpers — or newly knitted anyway, from wool rewound from ones worn out at the elbows but otherwise still good. A jumper made to fit Flinty, and ones for Joey and Kirsty too.

Flinty felt the lump grow in her throat. Every woman in the mountains had knitted the war away, clicking her needles even as she walked out to do the milking. But it must have taken Mrs Mack weeks to make these.

'Pink,' said Kirsty softly. 'Can I wear it to church? Please?'

It would be too hot. But maybe they'd have a cold snap. And even if it stayed warm Mum herself couldn't have stopped Kirsty wearing a new pink jumper regardless of the temperature.

'Yes,' said Flinty. 'Come on. Give me a hand to get dinner on.'

Life was real again.

Chapter 6

Fried chops and gravy for dinner, with Mrs Mack's fruitcake for afters. Funny, I meet a ghost, then end the day frying chops. But oh, they were good. I am so sick of rabbit. They have built up to a plague since the boys went to war, but rabbit skins still fetch a good price, though not as much as they did when they were needed for army hats. How do you turn a shaggy rabbit skin into a smooth hat anyway? If I asked Joey he might know — or drive me barmy asking me how he could find out.

They ate by lamplight, plates piled high with wonderfully greasy fried chops, boiled baby carrots, last autumn's potatoes and spinach from last summer's plants bolting to seed in the vegetable garden. The fire glowed behind them, the room filled with the sweet scent of gum-branch smoke that Flinty had known all her life.

'Elbows off the table,' she said automatically to Joey, just as Mum had said a million times. 'Thanks for the wood,' she added.

'Wasn't me,' said Joey, around a lot of chop. She almost told him not to speak with his mouth full too. But one nag was enough each meal. 'The Mullins boys rode by and cut up the dead tree in the top paddock for us.'

'I hope you thanked them properly.' If the Mullins had seen a stranger the news would be all over the valley by tomorrow, she thought. And how could a stranger get up here without the gossips noticing?

'Course I did. They brought an apple pie too,' he added.

'Where is it?' There'd been no pie in the food safe.

'Me and Kirsty ate it. We knew you'd be having a grand afternoon tea down at the Macks',' he said defensively.

'With jam and everything,' said Kirsty.

'Fair enough. I did too.'

'What sort of jam?' asked Kirsty, making a small mountain of her potatoes and trying to balance the smallest on top.

'Don't play with your food.' Two nags then.

'I wouldn't if anyone could see me,' said Kirsty reproachfully.

'I can see you.'

'Family doesn't count. Was there strawberry jam?'

'And plum and blackberry and apricot and crab-apple jelly.'

'Apricot ...' said Kirsty wistfully. Mum had planted an apricot tree next to the north-facing wall. It survived the winters — just — but the late frosts always froze the blossom. Trust your father, Mum had said each year, to choose his land for the view and not the weather. And every time Dad had laughed and said, 'But the view's worth it, isn't it, old girl? I've got five mountains to look at, and five children too, each strong as any mountain ...'

Flinty swallowed a lump in her throat, as well as a mouthful of potato.

'Flinty?' Joey's voice was too casual.

'What? You haven't been using Dad's shotgun again, have you?'

'Of course not! Not till Andy sends his wages and we can get more shot. I just wondered,' he carefully looked at his plate, not her, 'if I could borrow Empress on Thursday.'

Flinty looked at him, his hair the colour of winter tussocks, bleached by the sun, his eyes like the sky. The three of them had ridden Empress down to school for more than a year, and old Big Bob before that. Empress might be her horse, trained by her under Dad's watchful eye, but she belonged to all of them too.

'What for?'

'To go down to Mullinses'. Do a bit of work.'

She sighed. 'Joey McAlpine, you never could tell a lie. What do you want Empress for, really?'

He looked up at her from under his eyelashes. 'Billy Mullins says Sandy Mack is going to a brumby muster, down in the hills north of Drinkwater.'

Sandy hadn't told her that either. She swallowed her bitterness. 'You want to go on a muster? Not till you're sixteen, like Dad said.' She looked at Joey suspiciously. 'It's a day's ride down to Drinkwater. How long did you plan to be gone?'

'I'd have left you a note,' he said defensively.

'Well, there's no need for a note because you're not going. We need you here,' she added softly, so as not to say, 'You're too young. You might get hurt, or injure Empress.' He might only be twelve, but Joey had a man's pride.

'You don't understand,' he said earnestly. 'This is a special round-up. Back in '15 Miss Matilda bought this stallion, Repentance. Its sire was Lamentation, out of old Regret ...'

'It's that poem, isn't it?' she said tiredly. 'The one Dad used to read to us?'

Joey gave a cautious grin. '*But the man from Snowy River let the pony have his head, And he swung his stockwhip round and gave a cheer ...*'

'*And he raced him down the mountain like a torrent down its bed,*' chanted Kirsty. '*While the others stood and watched in very fear.*'

Flinty didn't know whether to laugh or sob. 'You think you can be the man from Snowy River all over again? The poem's just a story. It's not real.' You're the girl from Snowy River, the ghost had said. But she couldn't think about the ghost now.

'I know you can't chase a mob of brumbies like that and bring them back alone. This is a proper muster. They've got a canyon marked out already to drive the brumbies into.'

'I don't care. You're still too young.'

'Flinty, listen! Miss Matilda's offered a thousand pounds if Repentance is caught. He's worth even more. That's a hundred pounds, if it's divided between ten of us. It could pay the rates!'

A hundred pounds!

The world lurched. A hundred pounds would pay the rates over and over. Buy flour and sugar so they wouldn't have to scratch every dinner from the vegetable garden and the rabbit traps. Joey and Kirsty could go back to school. There'd be other brumbies worth selling or training up too. The stallion could have covered a good few mares in four years. They mightn't be as good as Repentance — most of those brumby mares weren't up to much — but some would be half thoroughbred, at least.

Good breeding stock would replace the horses gone to war. Rock Farm could breed and train horses again. Andy might come home if he had horses to break in ...

'Please, Flinty,' said Joey.

He was right. The muster could solve all their problems. But she couldn't let Joey do it. She knew her brother all too well. If there was hard riding he wouldn't hold back. He was a good rider, but not that good. Not nearly as good as you are, said a whisper in her mind.

'No,' she said. It broke her heart to say it. 'I'm sorry, Joey. The risk is too great. To you, to Empress.'

'But I've mustered brumbies with Dad, just like you —'

'No! That was just round here, and anyway, Dad did most of the mustering.'

'You're not my boss,' he said sullenly. 'You're just my sister. Andy's our guardian now.'

And Andy isn't here, she thought, not with his brother and sisters, not with the farm he'd inherited. 'Empress is my horse —'

'Pony.'

She sighed. Small horse, big pony, what did it matter? Except to Joey's pride, maybe. 'Pony,' she agreed. 'Joey, it was a wonderful idea. I'm grateful, truly. But we need you too much.' We need Empress too, she thought. And I've lost two brothers. I can't lose a third.

She got them into bed at last. Joey had the boys' bedroom to himself now Andy was gone with cattle. She could have moved into Mum and Dad's room, but that seemed wrong somehow, and anyway, there was something comforting about Kirsty's soft snuffling in the night.

Flinty would have liked to read: something where the hero clasped the heroine in his arms, like *Persuasion*, which was one of her favourite books, or the wonderful *Jane Eyre*. Dad had ordered new books every month, to read out on the verandah. Mum and Flinty took it in turn to read to each other in the kitchen, while the other shelled peas or did the ironing. Things ended just as they should in books. But it had been weeks since she'd even opened one. There was no time, except at the end of the day. Lamp oil for reading in bed was a luxury.

Flinty stared at the stars out the window instead. Impossible to sleep. There was too much to think about.

A ghost on the Rock.

A ride that might make a hundred pounds, or even more, and bring her brother back.

A man from the future called Nicholas.

What was it like for him, legless, in the future? Was he lying in bed thinking about her too? How did a legless man even get into bed?

Maybe he had a nurse ... or a wife. No, she thought. He had seemed the loneliest man in the world, hiding from his family, cast away by those of his own age for what he'd done, and because of what he'd lost.

And he'd liked her. He'd been rude at first, but then he'd really talked to her. He'd called her 'the girl from Snowy River'. She'd been too overwhelmed by his very existence to think about it then, but now the words came whispering back.

The girl from Snowy River. But it was 'The *Man* from Snowy River'. That was the poem people knew. She reckoned they'd still recite that poem fifty years in the future too, like the song about Miss Matilda's father that everyone still sang.

It was 'The Man from Snowy River' ... unless a girl someday did a ride like that too. An extraordinary ride, like the one in the poem, down steep slopes and up the crags, chasing brumbies through the scrub, so that people still spoke of it fifty years later.

Joey couldn't do it. He was a good rider. But she was, well, much more than good. And Empress could outrun on rough ground any horse Flinty had met.

She'd told Joey the truth. They couldn't risk losing him, or injuring Empress. But if there *was* a ghost from the future who knew about a 'girl from Snowy River', he might know if she made the ride safely, if her horse had made it back too.

Hadn't he said he'd seen a photo of her when she was 'a few years older than you are now'?

A hundred pounds. Horses in the paddock. Andy back home again. And a ghost who would know if it could be done, because if it had been done it would be history, unchangeable, the past.

Suddenly she knew she longed for him to be real almost as much as she had longed for Sandy to be safe.

She slept at last, the starlight on her face. She slept restlessly, dreaming of ghosts. The stars were fading when she opened her eyes again.

She glanced across the room. It was still too dark to make out more than a bump under the quilt, but she could hear Kirsty's sleepy snuffling. She slipped out of bed and into one of Mum's cut-down dresses — no riding today and a dress was quieter to put on than Dad's trousers, shirt and belt.

She picked up her shoes and tiptoed out, through the kitchen onto the back verandah, with its neatly stacked firewood. She automatically carried in a couple of pieces and shoved them on the coals in the wood stove and in the fireplace, then slid outside again, the boots on her feet.

It was lighter out here, the sun shoving light into the world from down under the mountains where it had sunk last night. She could just make out the dark of the ridges against the greyer sky. Empress whinnied from the back paddock. Flinty shook her head at her and ran down the road.

Chapter 7

23 November 1919

Dear Diary,

Collected ten eggs today — the hens are laying again. Swept the kitchen chimney — the last thing we need is a chimney fire now — Joey poking the brush down from the roof while Kirsty and I pulled below, then scrubbed the floor to clean up the mess. Baked more bread, made pancakes for lunch, stuffed a shoulder of mutton for dinner, put on a big pot of rabbit and potato stew, enough for three days at least, and darned three socks in the firelight after dinner.

And talked to the ghost. To Nicholas.

Because he isn't a ghost.

He's real.

The mist drifted down the gullies again, wisping through the soft dawn light, more mist than yesterday, resting in a puddle around the Rock. But it was thin enough to see that there was no one there.

Disappointment slapped her. But Nicholas hadn't said when he'd be on the Rock. If he really was somehow in 1969 maybe he couldn't appear to her again even if he was sitting on the Rock in his own time now. Maybe their times had just slipped together once, and never would again.

If Nicholas never came back she'd never know if it had all been real or not.

She turned to go back to the house, then stopped. She hadn't seen him yesterday until she and Empress had been actually in the mist.

Suddenly the whiteness seemed alien, not the fog she'd known all her life. She took a breath, then stepped into it, feeling something more than the early morning chill. 'Hello?' she whispered.

All at once the fog around her thinned. He was there, sitting in the damp white air in his bathchair, holding something square and yellow on his lap, but this time he was staring towards the house, not over the valley. Her heart thumped like a cartwheel rolling over a stone, a rush of emotions too mixed up to sort out: relief, wonder, anticipation, all with a breath of fear that impossible things were still happening to her, Flinty McAlpine, even if life was going back to normal for her neighbours ... He turned and looked at her. She saw a brief flash of pleasure on his face before a bright light shone from the yellow thing, blinding her. She put her hand up to shield her eyes from the glare.

'Sorry.' The light vanished.

'What's that?' she whispered.

'A torch. It was still dark when I set out.' He looked glad to see her; as excited as she was.

She looked down at his torch. It was even stranger than his bathchair, his hair. His clothes looked odd today too. She felt a giggle bubble up through the fear and strangeness.

'What is it?'

'Your shirt has flowers on it!' But at least it was normal strangeness, something that a man from the future might have, a new invention like the wireless players Joey talked about, not something weird from the world of ghosts.

'It's psychedelic, not floral. I'm not a hippy.' He looked at her, assessing. 'You don't know either of those words, do you?'

Psychedelic? Hippy? Nonsense. She shook her head.

'Then you really are in the past. I couldn't sleep last night. Thought the people up here were playing a trick on me. Or maybe I was seeing things.'

'Me too,' she whispered.

'Got up an hour ago, decided I'd wait here all day, just to see if you came back.' He looked at her steadily. 'One second there was no one there. Then suddenly you were here. No tricks. No delusions.'

'It was like that for me too. I could see the Rock as I walked down from the house. It was empty till I stepped into the mist.' She tried a smile. It worked. 'Maybe we're both ghosts.'

'Or both real.'

They stared at each other. I should be frightened, thought Flinty. Instead it felt like she'd tried to stuff her excitement into a bag, and now it was seeping out.

She stood there, the too-long dress clinging damply to her ankles, not knowing what to ask first. She had to ask about the brumby muster, but there was so much else she wanted to know too. About him, where he came from, who his family was. The whole incredible thought of fifty years to come ...

'What's it like, in the future? You said there's war again. But they say now there won't be — that ours was the war to end all wars.' It had been a crumb of comfort to think Jeff had died so there'd be no more war again.

'Well, they're wrong.' Some of the harshness was back in his voice.

I'm glad Mum never knew, she thought. 'When will the next war be?'

He inhaled, then looked at her consideringly. 'I don't know how much to tell you. I've been thinking about it, you see. Just in case you really were real. You might ask me what happens in your life, maybe your brothers' lives, your children's lives.'

'Then I'm going to have children!'

He laughed, a real laugh but with regret too. 'See how easy it is, Flinty McAlpine? I decided not to tell you anything that matters, and now I've told you that.'

'Why can't you tell me?'

'In case I change the past.'

'But if the past has already happened in your time then it can't be changed.'

'Or maybe I'll go out of this mist to find it's a different world because I've changed it.'

'Is yours a good world?' Maybe knowing another war might happen would stop it, she thought. But one girl on a mountain couldn't stop a war, especially if she told people that a ghost told her it was coming.

'It's better than in your time,' he said frankly. 'Except in places where there's war, but that's not in Australia. There aren't even many Australians involved in Vietnam, not compared to the hundreds of thousands in your World War I.'

She blinked, the implications sinking in. 'World War I? That was our war? So there's another really big war? Not just like the Boer Wars in South Africa?'

'I'm going to shut up about the future,' he said. He grinned suddenly, cockily, so she had a glimpse of what he must have been like before he lost his legs, before he got the war shadows like Andy and Toby and Sandy. 'I'm not even going to tell you that men walked on the moon.'

She glanced up automatically, even though the moon was long set. 'I don't believe you.'

'But it's true. When you're sixty-six — if you're ever sixty-six: I'm not saying you're going to be — you can bet a hundred dollars that man will have walked on the moon by the end of 1969. And that won't change the past,' he added.

'All right. I will.'

He nodded, still smiling. His face looked so different with a smile. Suddenly she thought: fifty years. I might still be alive in 1969. 'Have you met me?' she asked sharply.

'No more answers.'

'I can't be a ghost in your time if I'm still alive!'

He hesitated. 'You're still alive. I don't think either of us are ghosts like that.'

She sat down on the Rock. It was cold under her thin dress, but her body felt too heavy for her legs. Somehow talking about her own death had been more real than anything that had gone before. 'Is Sandy still alive?' she whispered. 'And Kirsty and —'

'Flinty, hush. Please. I don't know what's happening here.' He hesitated. 'The people I'm staying with told me I might see a ghost down here — the ghost of Flinty McAlpine. That's how I knew your name yesterday.'

'They *sent* you to see me?'

'I don't know! I thought they were joking. Maybe they were joking. But now ...'

'Maybe they weren't.'

'And maybe I can cause a lot of problems if I say too much. I need to talk to them again. Need to think this through.'

'Who are they?' she demanded.

He just shook his head.

She tried to take it all in, the reality of it, the feeling that somewhere just out of sight there were people from another time, talking about her, knowing what had happened in her life.

And he wasn't going to tell her anything more. Not today, at least. But she couldn't wait even another day or two to know if she should go on the muster — if she had done it, in the past.

I have to get him talking, she thought. If he talks about other things he might make a mistake, like he did talking about my children. 'Please. I need to know one more thing.'

'Only one thing?' He was almost teasing.

'Lots of things.' All at once she knew what would get him talking. And it wouldn't really be a trick, because it was what she wanted to know — needed to know — almost as badly as about the muster. She took a breath. 'If you won't tell me about my future tell me about the past.'

'I don't understand.'

'When I was at school Mr Ross taught us history. About the battles of Agincourt and Waterloo and the messenger who fell dead at Wellington's feet. So do you know what the war was like — my brothers' war? The one you call World War I?'

'A bit,' he admitted slowly.

'I don't,' she said flatly. 'I know the dates, the names of battles from the newspaper. That's all. No one says anything. No one will tell me.'

'In my time no one asks. The war in Vietnam ... most of Australia thinks we shouldn't be there. We didn't come home as heroes, like your brother. Half the girls I know pity me. The other half think I'm a moral coward for going at all.'

'But it's brave to go and fight.'

'Maybe,' he said. 'Sometimes it's easier just to go when you're told.'

'But you *were* brave.'

He was silent for a few moments. 'You know, I think I was,' he said. 'For some reason I never really thought about it before.' He gave her a cautious smile, the teasing over. 'Maybe that's why I'm on this Rock, Flinty McAlpine: to hear a girl say that I was brave. Yeah, we learned about Gallipoli in World War I, how we were heroes then. But I bet no one ever teaches kids in school about the Battle of Long Tan. There were a lot of blokes braver than me there. Still are, fighting over there.'

'So your war wasn't like Andy's war?'

He seemed to think about it. 'I don't know,' he said at last. 'Maybe all wars are much the same once you're inside them. I'm not the one to ask.'

A cuckoo began its soft descant below them. The east glowed grey above the ridges. It would turn red soon. Joey and Kirsty would be up, looking for her.

If they came down here, would they find Nicholas too? Somehow she didn't think so. But she didn't want them to either. Life was confusing enough for two orphans without throwing in a ghost. 'Please. Tell me what you do know about World War I.' It seemed strange giving it a new name.

'It was bad,' he said slowly. 'We didn't learn a lot more than that. Rats as big as corgi dogs in the trenches, that kind of thing. Mostly it was just so big, went on for so long. The poor ba— blokes never got a decent break, just English commanders ordering them out of the trenches into enemy fire to try to take a few yards of ground. Tens of thousands killed in a day. They had new weapons — machine guns and tanks and planes — but the commanders were still trying to fight the old way. I suppose it's pretty crook if being in a muddy trench with rats and the dead around you is the good bit, better than being ordered over the top to fight.' He paused, then said, 'I'm sorry. I know less than I thought. All I can say is that it was bad. Very bad and very long.'

Maybe that's all I need to know, she thought. It was long and it was bad. Now they were home. Perhaps Toby was right, and she should let it go. And maybe, just maybe, if there were long enough good times they might feel better.

A kookaburra yelled. Another echoed it, and another. The sky was pink and yellow above the black line of the ridges now, the cap of snow turning gold. There was no more time to hope he'd accidentally answer her now. She said quickly, 'One more question. Please, just one. An important one.'

'Maybe.' His voice was cautious.

'You called me the girl from Snowy River. Why? Did I ... do I do a ride like in the poem?'

He was silent.

He's not going to answer, she thought.

All at once the realisation shook her. He *had* answered. And she hadn't realised, and nor had he.

He'd talked about when she was sixty-six. He wouldn't do that if she wasn't to be that old. He'd talked about her children!

She was 'the girl from Snowy River'. She'd get her ride.

If she was going to live to be an old woman then it was safe to go on the muster. She tried to keep the knowledge from her face. She didn't want him to worry about what he'd accidentally told her. And it couldn't change the past, because he'd already known that she had done it.

'It's all right,' she said abruptly. 'You don't have to answer.'

She saw the relief in his face, and was glad of it — glad he had stopped worrying she'd demand too many answers, like she had with Andy. Glad that he was a man with a conscience, who cared about whether he should answer questions or not.

Glad to have a friend, she thought. She hadn't realised how friendless her life had become. She had people who cared about her — people who would help her — but no friend her own age. She'd never got on with Amy, even when they were at school. Jeff and Sandy had been her friends, her life. Now Jeff was gone, and Sandy was a stranger.

But it was more than that. She liked this man. Everyone in the valley had known her as a little girl, still saw her as a child in some ways. Even Sandy seemed to have grown up so much more than her during his years on battlefields.

He probably had. But Nicholas spoke to her like an equal, not like a girl to be patted on the head, and told to leave the affairs of war to men.

Could a ghost from the future be a friend?

'What day is it in your time?' she asked suddenly. 'You can tell me that, can't you?'

He looked startled. 'Wednesday.'

'It's Wednesday here too. I'm sorry — I have to go, or my brother and sister will miss me. But could you meet me here in ten days' time? Please?'

She held her breath. Please let him say yes, she thought.

'Ten days?'

'You're not leaving the mountain yet, are you?' Please don't let him have to go, she thought, not when I've only just met him.

To her relief he shook his head. 'No.' He gave a small smile. 'Not when I've just met a ghost. Can't we meet tomorrow?'

She let out the breath at the eagerness in his voice. 'I'm going to be busy.' Busy on the round-up, busy going to Gibber's Creek to pay the rates if she got that hundred pounds. She didn't know how long either of those might take, and she might have to wait till Mr Mack or one of the other neighbours was free to take them to town in their cart. 'I'll be here in ten days' time.'

'Too busy to meet someone from fifty years in the future?'

'Yes. I'm sorry,' she added. 'I'd come if I could.'

'All right.' He gave a lopsided grin. 'I'm probably crazy, dreaming I've met Flinty McAlpine on a mountainside ... Maybe everyone is crazy up in these mountains. Maybe the air up here makes you absurd, the scent of flowers and rock and snow. And I've never spoken like that to anyone in my life before. You're my only friend here, you know that? And you're fifty years away.'

She felt the warmth of the word 'friend' trickle through her. 'People in the valley are nice.' She hesitated. Were they nice in another fifty years?

But he said, 'Yes. They're nice. But I don't know them yet.'

'Don't you have other friends? Where's your family?'

'In Sydney. Dad used to be a country doctor. I miss the mountains — that's one of the reasons I came up here. And to escape their fussing. Friends ...' He shrugged. 'Everyone I used to know sees what I haven't got.' He gestured at his legs.

'Not who I am now. Except you. It's not fair, you know. You've got an apparition who knows what's going to happen in your future. Maybe if I sit here long enough someone will appear who can answer some questions for me.'

'What questions do you want to ask?' She knew the answer before he spoke.

'Will I ever walk again? Ride a horse? They talk about prosthetics. False legs,' he added. 'Not wooden legs in my time. They say the ankle even bends. But it'll take a long time to get used to them. Some people never do. I ... I haven't been able to face starting.' He patted his bathchair. 'Took me long enough to work out how to get around on this. Even having a ... going to the toilet took me almost a week to work out.'

'I think you'll walk again,' she said quietly.

'And how do you know that?'

'Because you're here, up in the mountains. A man who won't ever walk again doesn't go to mountains. He stays on flat land, where he won't be tempted to climb up into the trees, up to the snow line. Every time you see an eagle you'll think, I can't fly, but maybe I can walk. And that's how it begins.'

Had she said too much? The silence grew. No, not silence, birds yelling all around them, the mutter of the creek below. 'I can see why they talk of you,' he said at last. 'You're something special.'

'So are you. You said you were brave at Long Tan. I don't think you're any less brave now.'

'Well, thank you, Flinty McAlpine,' he said softly. 'Maybe you have answered my question at that. How about another? Will I fall in love? Will the girl I love manage to see me, and not a cripple?'

'I know it's yes to the second if it's yes to the first.'

'How can you be so sure?'

'Because *I've* never thought of you as a cripple at all.' She knew he could hear the truth in her voice. 'I've thought of you as a ghost, as a stranger. And as a bit odd,' she added honestly. 'Your shirt, your hair, the way you talk sometimes. But not a cripple.'

'Flinty! Where are you?'

'I heard that this time! Like it was coming through a long bubble. It *is* a sound from your time, isn't it? Is it your brother?'

'Joey,' she said.

'He has a voice like a crow ...'

'Only when he yells. Coming!' she yelled up to Joey. 'Put the kettle on! See you next week,' she said hurriedly to Nicholas, in case Joey decided to come and see what she was up to.

He nodded. Once again she had to force herself to hurry away from him, to do her duty instead of stay. She could feel him watching her as she ran out of the fog, knew that the second he vanished, she vanished for him.

She slowed down to a walk.

He was real. He was back in his future too. But it was as though he'd dragged a new future back for her to ride on, one where she could muster brumbies and earn a hundred pounds.

The girl from Snowy River.

She tried to think of all the things to do today. Make a big stew that would last Joey and Kirsty till Mr Mack could collect them in the cart so they could stay with the Macks. She'd have to leave Mr Mack a note, because he'd argue against her going too if he knew. Cook dampers — she'd need to take food with her. Pack up her saddlebags without the others noticing.

Convince Sandy to take her with him. Work out how to get a mob of brumby hunters to accept a girl.

But she was the girl from Snowy River. She'd work out a way to ride. Somewhere, down the tunnel of the future, she already had.

Chapter 8

24 November 1919

Dear Diary,

I knew Sandy would help me. He mightn't love me any more, or even want to be my friend. But I've known Sandy Mack all my life. Sandy is as immoveable as the Rock sometimes. But he'll never say no if you need him. No matter how much the war had changed him, Sandy is solid forever.

She found him in the paddock behind the Macks' farmhouse, saddling Bessie by lamplight. The dawn was a whisper on the horizon. She had expected he would start early — it was a full day's ride down to Drinkwater, and he'd want Bessie to rest before the muster.

'Flinty! What are you doing here?' Sandy stared at her. Her breasts were bound under Dad's biggest shirt and jacket, the baggy trousers held up by Dad's belt to disguise her shape, a big knitted cap over her plaits and a big hat crammed on top of that; Empress was loaded with her swag and saddlebags. Sandy seemed to force himself to stand straighter, out of that slight crouch.

She flushed, aware of what she must look like, wishing that she could at least have worn clothes that fitted her. 'Going to the muster with you.'

Sandy's eyes examined her again, the swag, the shine on Empress's coat from a recent brushing. 'No.'

'Because it's dangerous? I'm a better rider than you, Sandy Mack. And you know it.'

'Because they won't accept a girl. I didn't organise the muster, Flinty. It's up to Drinkwater's manager to say who goes. I was only invited because I was in France with his son.'

'They'll think I'm a boy dressed like this.' She hoped.

'You move like a girl.'

'No one can see how I move in this jacket. Not till we're on the muster anyhow.'

He turned his back on her and began to tighten Bessie's girth. 'No.'

'Sandy, please! We need the money! There's rates and ... and all sorts of things.'

His hands stopped moving, but he still didn't look back at her. 'I'll give you half my share.'

'I don't want charity! I can do this, Sandy. You know I can.'

'It's not charity. Jeff was my mate.'

And what am I? she thought. A ghost from your past? I'm more real to Nicholas than to you. 'If you won't take me I'll come anyway. Follow you down to Drinkwater. You can tell them I'm a girl then, if you want to. If that's what you'd do to the sister of your best mate.'

She'd meant to hurt him. She'd succeeded. She hadn't known it would hurt her too to see the pain as his shoulders hunched again, defeated. 'I can't stop you, can I?'

'No,' she said, more gently. 'Sandy, I'm sorry. I know it's going to be embarrassing when they find out I'm a girl. But maybe it won't matter once I've proved I can do it.'

He turned so she could see his face again. 'That's not what I care about. What if anything happens to you?' For a moment she felt warm to think he still cared enough to worry about her, until he added, 'Who'd look after Kirsty and Joey?'

'Nothing will happen. I'm sure of it.'

'You can't be sure.'

'Sandy.' Her voice was as flat as his had been. 'I'm coming with you.'

He stared at her for a second more, then finished saddling Bessie.

The dawn air stung her cheeks. It was strangely companionable, riding with Sandy through the trees. He hadn't spoken to her since they'd left the Macks', but they'd ridden like this so many times before. She could almost hear Jeff's horse behind theirs, imagine that any moment she'd hear him say, 'Last one around the next bend is a rotten egg,' his laughter floating back as he kneed his horse and flashed past.

For a moment Jeff's presence was so real she turned to look at him. But there were only trees, the bark curling, only tussocks, only the glint of rock. No brown-eyed brother.

The sobs took over her body: unexpected, as they always were. She'd be forking hay and suddenly think of Dad, worry about Kirsty catching the polio, and wish Mum was there. And Jeff.

She forced herself to be quiet, even as the tears fell, thinking of Jeff. There'd been an article in the Sydney paper, a month back, about a soldier who was supposed to have died but who'd lost his memory and, having been in a French hospital all along, had come back to his family. There'd been the sudden flowering spring of hope — she supposed everyone who had lost a brother, son or lover had felt the same hope when they'd read that. But Sandy had been with Jeff when he died.

Jeff was gone. Two horses through the trees, not three. And she only had Sandy today, and him unwilling. If only ...

'Flinty?'

Sandy had drawn Bessie close to Empress. For a second she thought she saw the old look there: not just concern, but the sort of love that meant you shared each other's pain.

The look vanished. He was the new Sandy again, watchful, his face carefully blank. 'Are you all right?'

'Yes. The wind stung my eyes, that's all.'

There was no wind, but he seemed to accept her words. He reached down and undid a saddlebag, then steered Bessie closer so he could pass her a sandwich. 'Mutton and chutney,' he said.

'I brought my own.' Bread and treacle. Her mouth watered at the thought of Mrs Mack's chutney.

'Mum made enough for an army. There're date scones too. They'll turn into rocks if we don't eat them fresh.'

She took the sandwich; ate a scone too, rich with butter and strawberry jam. She licked her fingers, glanced at him, then said carefully, 'How's the lambing going?' It was the most neutral topic she could think of.

'All right.'

'Any foxes down your way?'

He shrugged.

'Heard the dingoes call last night. Joey said at least if they are up our way they're not at your lambs.'

No answer. He didn't even look at her. Each offering had seemed to make him sit stiffer in the saddle.

He didn't want to talk. Either he was still angry that she had manipulated him into helping her pretence, or he was showing her that there was no point trying to re-establish what there'd been between them before.

She pulled Empress back slightly and let Bessie go first between the trees.

Chapter 9

Dear Diary,

When I cry about Jeff these days I feel more the loss of what could have been, than of the brother I grew up with. For years after the war — even before that, while he was still alive in France — I waited for his voice everywhere, from the boys' bedroom in the morning, from the paddocks in the afternoon, waiting for him to open the kitchen door and throw his hat onto the hat stand — he could land it on the hook by the time he was ten; none of the rest of us could manage it — and yell, 'What's for dinner, Mum?' lifting up the lids and sniffing. Mum said he just inhaled leftovers, the year before he enlisted. Jeff just had to pass through the kitchen and somehow the leftover leg of lamb was just a bone, and the cake tin was empty, and all the crusts had vanished from the bread. Jeff loved crusts. I always gave him mine, and he gave me the centre of his sandwiches.

I still miss him, the boy I knew then. But he'd have vanished, even if he had come home, just like the girl I was has long gone too.

No, what I miss now is what we might have become. I would have smiled and cried at his wedding (to anyone except Amy — I'd had to grit my teeth every time Jeff even danced with her).

He'd have been uncle to my children, and I'd have been aunt to his. Christmases of families together — Jeff gave the worst and best presents ever, like that year he made each of us a penny whistle, and Mum had to hide them in the biscuit tin just to shut the racket up.

Silly, I suppose, to grieve over what might have been. Jeff might have decided to be a butcher and move to Brisbane, and I'd never have seen him again except maybe once or twice for a visit. But he'd never have been a butcher, or moved to Brisbane either, and even if he had it wouldn't have mattered. He'd have been happy, because Jeff was the sort who always was happy, if he could have been; I'd have known that, and been happy for him too.

Undated, probably late 1920s

She woke to the scent of grilling chops, and bread fried in mutton dripping. It took a moment to realise where she was — in the men's quarters at Drinkwater Station, four beds to a room, the others empty now. She'd slept in, tired from almost no sleep the night before, having to pack and saddle Empress after Joey and Kirsty were asleep, and ride down the mountain to find Sandy before he left.

She sat up and rubbed her eyes. They'd arrived late last night and been handed plates of bubble and squeak — dinner's roast mutton, baked potatoes, pumpkin and cabbage all fried together, then cold jam roly-poly, eaten in the strange too-bright 'electric' light, the generator muttering in the shed behind. She had been relieved that the men in the room slept in most of their clothes too, only taking off their boots. Best of all, there was a row of dunnies out the back, for privacy.

She felt to make sure that her beanie still covered her plaits, bent to lace her boots, then stepped outside.

There was movement at the station now. Last night's quiet was over.

All the tried and noted riders from the stations near and far had gathered at the stockyard, between the river and the big main house, shrouded in its dapple of English trees. The word had got around.

It was an extraordinary sight to a girl whose life had been the mountains and the valley, with a few short visits to Gibber's Creek.

The station stretched around her: paddocks of neatly strained fences; stockyards and sheep runs; some kind of green-leafed crop, strangely bright and uniform, between here and the wide glint of the river; well-built smaller houses, each with their own garden, probably for the farm workers; more than a dozen big sheds apart from the one where she'd slept the night before — haysheds, shearing sheds, what looked like a farm shop; and more she couldn't identify.

It was more like a town than a farm.

And people. There seemed to be dozens of them: young men with bright scarves, old men with stubble. There were horses tethered to the railings and horses already saddled. She panicked for a second. A thousand pounds wasn't going to go far divided between all these riders. Then she realised that one knot of men and horses was slightly apart from the others, Sandy among them, with Bessie and Empress already saddled.

Sandy had said you had to be invited to this muster. The others must be there just to see them off — or hoping for a last-minute invitation.

Like her.

But at least Sandy had saddled Empress. Which meant he must have already told the manager he'd brought a friend — unless Sandy expected her to be sent off so firmly she'd want to get on Empress and ride away, fast.

She visited the dunny hurriedly, washed her face and hands in the horse trough, grabbed two chops congealing in grease and a hunk of fresh bread still hot from the morning's baking, then stepped back into the bustle of the courtyard, tearing at the bread and meat with deliberately bad manners, lengthening her stride, her hat well down over her face.

There was a woman among the men by the stockyards now, next to a man in a tweed jacket and flannel trousers, obviously not intending to ride today. He seemed to be the only person here who didn't look excited. He almost looked amused. Beside him a small boy in boots and moleskin trousers stood his ground among the adults and horse legs that towered above him.

Flinty stared at the woman curiously. It was hard to tell her age. Her face was half hidden by a big sunhat tied with chiffon under her chin. Flinty had imagined the owner of Drinkwater would wear moleskin trousers, but she wore a dress — the prettiest dress Flinty had ever seen, and out here in the dust of the horse yards too. It was made of what looked like green silk, belted low on her hips, just like the new fashions in the newspapers.

Kirsty would love that dress, thought Flinty. She'd love the purple lace-up shoes too, practical but somehow also elegant. The woman turned to speak to the man at her side, and Flinty saw what the loose silk dress hadn't quite disguised.

Miss Matilda was pregnant.

So this was the famous daughter of the swaggie, the hero of Australia's most loved song, the girl who'd turned a barren holding into an empire and then given half of it away to her native manager and his sons and cousins. Even at first glance Flinty could see why she was 'Miss Matilda' still, not 'Mrs Thomas Thompson'. Flinty knew of no other property with a native manager. But 'Miss Matilda' did things her own way. This woman needed a name of her own.

And even half an empire was still the biggest property around. The man beside her must be her husband, the inventor of one of the radios they'd used in the trenches, and other things Joey had rabbited on about when she had been half listening, just thinking that inventions and factories had made him rich, one fortune married to another, and that Miss Matilda and Thomas Thompson must be quite a couple.

They were.

Even as Flinty watched Miss Matilda laughed, patting the bulge at her middle. 'I wish I was going with you. But I won't be riding anywhere till this one's dropped ...' She glanced at the boy beside her. 'And I know I said that, but if you say "dropped" about a woman who's expecting, you'll get a paddling.'

The boy grinned, showing a gap where his baby teeth had fallen out. 'Yes, Mum. Just as we don't use words like b—'

'Biscuit,' said Mr Thompson firmly. He gave his wife a look, half amusement, half concern, and total love, so open and even intimate that Flinty felt a pang, and looked at Sandy, who was staring at the ground. 'All this fuss about a horse,' he added. 'At least motorcars don't gallop off by themselves into the bush.'

Miss Matilda laughed again. 'Horses breed other horses. You show me a car that can do that, and I'll go into the car breeding business with you.' She looked at the riders again. 'I wouldn't be riding with you anyway, not in the country you're going to. I don't pretend to have your skill and experience. But my heart will be riding with you today. My great-grandfather had a hankering to win the Melbourne Cup, and the old Regret line is the best chance I know of getting it.' She grinned. 'And when we do I'll invite every one of you who helped bring in Repentance.'

'A share of a thousand pound will do me and the boys nicely, thanks all the same, Miss Matilda. I ain't got a hankering to go to Melbourne town.' The speaker was an old man with skin like cracked leather, a crinkle of white beard, and eyes as green as the Drinkwater garden's English trees. His 'boys' were natives, one with white hair and a wrinkled beardless face under his battered hat, the other a few years older than Andy, with paler skin and a sharper nose — perhaps a half-caste.

'Well, the rest of us'll be there, and with bells on, Mr Clancy.' This man had the dark skin of a native too. Was he Pete Sampson, wondered Flinty, the man Sandy had known in France? Apart from the man who must be Mr Sampson, the manager, the other three riders were white men, all in their thirties or forties, their stockhorses strong shouldered and a good hand higher than Empress, at least.

Flinty made her way through the watchers. She took Empress's bridle from Sandy, trying to look as if there was no question she had a right to be there.

Sandy nodded towards her. 'This is Flinty McAlpine. The neighbour I told you about.' Flinty was glad he used her nickname. It looked like Sandy was doing his best for her, but not lying either.

'Good rider?' Miss Matilda's sharp eyes assessed the figure in front of her.

'Better than me,' said Sandy.

Miss Matilda nodded. 'Pleased to meet you, Flinty McAlpine. Any relation to Andy McAlpine?'

'Brother.' Flinty let out a breath of relief. So far so good. She tried to make her voice as deep — and the words as ambiguous — as she could.

Miss Matilda stepped back and looked at Flinty thoughtfully. But all she said was, 'You lost another brother at Bullecourt, didn't you? And your father earlier this year?'

Flinty nodded.

'I'm sorry.' The words held genuine sympathy. 'There's always a job at Drinkwater for any man who's served his country, and for his relatives too.'

Suddenly Flinty saw Drinkwater's neat paddocks in a different light. There must be many men as rootless as Andy, or just plain jobless now the war was over. Matilda and Thomas Thompson had the money to employ as many men as they wanted — or who needed a job. Drinkwater had benefited from it. But Flinty suspected that the man and woman in front of her would employ any deserving man in need, even if they only had a halfpenny in their pockets.

'Time to go.' The words were said by a dark-faced, dark-eyed man, beard as white as snow against his black skin. Mr Sampson, Drinkwater's manager, thought Flinty. She had never seen an Aboriginal manager before, only stockmen.

Mr Sampson stared at the slender rider in the tattered hat, the shabby jacket not disguising her lack of bulk. 'You're a bit young for this game, lad.' Around them the other riders checked saddle girths. Horses whinnied and snuffled the air.

'Seventeen,' said Sandy. Again, the word was true — she couldn't imagine Sandy lying. But she guessed Mr Sampson heard the reluctance in his voice.

Mr Sampson looked at Flinty's smooth cheeks, her hands — too small for a seventeen-year-old boy's. He shook his head. 'Doesn't look seventeen. It's hard riding where we're going.'

'They breed us tough round Snowy River,' said Sandy.

Mr Sampson looked at Miss Matilda.

'Up to you,' said Miss Matilda.

Mr Sampson shook his head again. 'Can't risk it. Not with a young 'un I ain't worked with before.' He mounted his horse swiftly, as though that was the end of the discussion.

Flinty felt like the earth had slipped away from her. She stared at the ground, willing herself not to cry, here in front of everyone. All her hopes, all her planning, dashed in half a minute. Sandy had done his best for her. But her face was too young looking for a seventeen-year-old boy's. Her slenderness was strength in a girl, but if she'd met a boy with her build she too would have doubted his power to stay the day. Nor could she try to persuade Mr Sampson to change his mind — she couldn't tell them she'd been riding after brumbies with Dad and Sandy and Jeff and Andy since she was ten years old. They'd know she was a girl before she'd said a dozen words.

And why should they risk taking her? There would be a dozen men here today happy to take her place, if they'd wanted more riders. She suddenly realised that taking another rider would mean a smaller reward for each of the others, a one-tenth share instead of one-ninth. She calculated swiftly. Eleven pounds less for each of them. Not a fortune, compared to a hundred pounds, but enough to make a difference to most of the riders here.

She looked up to find Miss Matilda watching her. 'How about two guineas for two weeks' work here, helping when they bring the brumbies back?' She nodded at the riders. 'You can even have your own room with this lot gone.'

Two guineas was good money, more than a young man could expect for farm work. This was charity — and kindness.

But not enough. She couldn't keep up the deception for two weeks either. And she'd left a note for Joey and Kirsty, saying she'd be back in a week, that she'd left another note in the Macks' letterbox asking that they be collected in the cart and kept at the bigger farm till her return. They'd worry if she was gone too long. She had a sudden vision of Nicholas waiting for her in the mist too.

He'd called her the girl from Snowy River. It looked as though he'd been wrong. There had to be some way to get the money they needed. But just now she wanted to get away from this place of humiliation as quickly as she could.

She shook her head at Miss Matilda's offer and managed a smile of sorts at Sandy to thank him for trying. Sandy looked relieved, and excited too. Sandy always looked happiest in the saddle. She hadn't seen him look as ... *Sandy-like* ... since he left for the war. 'See you in the valley,' he said, then hesitated. 'I'm sorry, Flinty.'

She shrugged, not trusting her voice to sound boyish enough with everyone still listening.

She turned and tied Empress up at the stockyard again, then ducked back to the dunnies so that the brumby hunters could leave while she was gone. The brumbies had been last seen at Jackson's Flat, halfway back towards the valley. The last thing she wanted was to have to ride with the hunters through her own country, discarded.

The watchers had melted back to their own jobs or farms when she got back. Miss Matilda and her family had vanished too. Flinty could see the horsemen in the distance, the horses' hooves kicking up sand as they headed up into the ranges, Mr Sampson on his big gelding, Sandy looking young beside the others.

She mounted Empress slowly. She'd be back at the Macks' by nightfall. She signalled to Empress to walk, following the same path as the riders. It was strange to see the horizon meet the sky so far away. She hadn't been down here on the plains for months, not since she'd come with the Macks to meet Sandy's train. It had been years since she'd been to Jackson's Flat too. The last time had been with Jeff, just before the war. Sandy had been at the dentist's in Gibber's Creek, so it had been just the two of them.

Valley legend said there was a cave near Jackson's Flat in which a bushranger had buried stolen treasure way back in the gold rushes. They'd never found the cave — Flinty doubted there was any cave to find, for it wasn't limestone country — but they had found a ridge that was easy riding down to the plains. The bushranger had probably used the route to leave the police bewildered.

I'll use the short cut today, she thought. Empress could scramble up that ridge as easily as she'd walk up the track. She'd be past Jackson's Flat long before the brumby hunters arrived, and not have to ride with the humiliation of the hoof prints and droppings in front of her, reminding her how she'd failed.

She'd be there before the brumby hunters ...

Flinty grinned, and urged Empress to a canter. Too young for mustering in rough country? She'd show them! She'd be at Jackson's Flat waiting for them, Empress not even winded.

How could they not accept her then? She'd show the men of the plains how a girl from Snowy River could ride!

It was mid-morning when she got to Jackson's Flat, pushing through the last of the hop bushes. The scrub was thicker this year. There'd been fewer cattle to trample it since the men had left for war, so many stock turned into cans of bully beef to feed the armies.

She dismounted and gazed around.

Hoof prints! The unmistakeable scent of horse.

The brumby hunters had been here already! How had they got here before her? She looked at the hoof prints again ...

Small prints — foal sized — among the large ones. Suddenly she felt like throwing her hat up into the air. Brumbies! They were still near — no more than a short ride away, for the scent of horse was fresh, the pile of droppings shiny. The wild horses would have found a place to wait out the heat of the day, down in the gully probably, before heading off to the creek to drink and graze at dusk.

She hauled off her saddlebags — no point Empress carrying unnecessary weight on the chase — and lugged them over next to a tree leaning like an old man bent from a hundred years of wind. She drank from her water bag, then poured a little water into her hands for Empress. Not too much, not before the big ride ahead, but enough. Empress's warm whiskery lips were comforting on her skin.

'We'll show them, won't we, girl?'

Empress nickered, as though she'd understood, then dropped her head; her big teeth tore at the tussocks as Flinty sat with her back against a snow-gum trunk. The shadows shortened as the sun drew higher towards midday. A lizard darted onto a rock, grabbed a tiny insect, then retreated.

This was her world. The eagle, soaring on the hot air rising from below, the creak of the branches, the hard ground with its gleams of quartz, the pale everlastings, the little white flowers Mum had called baby faces, the bush cherries Dad had shown her and Jeff how to find and eat ...

She heard the brumby hunters long before she saw them: the *clomp* of hooves, the mutter of the men. She stayed where she was, letting them see her — see a boy, relaxed and confident, waiting for them under a tree, his pony cropping the tussocks. Someone who knew this land so well 'he' could get here long before the older, more experienced riders.

Mr Clancy saw her first. He grinned, and she knew he'd read her message. 'Well,' he said.

'Flinty!' said Sandy. He sounded half exasperated, half proud; he was almost laughing and still wholly *there* in a way she hadn't seen him since the war. 'I might've known. Told you Flinty was good,' he added to Mr Sampson.

'Took a short cut,' said Flinty casually, trying to make her voice as gruff as possible. There was no way she could avoid speaking now. The other riders stared at her. Mr Clancy and his 'boys' laughed. A couple of the men scowled, shown up by a youngster.

The older of Mr Clancy's 'boys' said something to Mr Clancy, gesturing at Flinty, his black face wrinkled like a windfall apple.

At last Mr Clancy nodded to Mr Sampson. 'Let the lad come.'

Chapter 10

3 March 1917

Dear Diary,

It's been different with Andy and Jeff gone. Dad's started treating me like a son, a bit, not just a girl. He let me break and train Empress all by myself, and when he went riding up the mountain after the Macks' sheep last month I went with him. I don't think he ever talks to Andy and Jeff like he talks to me though. Or do men talk to other blokes about watching the shadows turn purple in autumn, or how they wait every year for the swallows to fly back? Dad arrived with the swallows his first year here.

I'm pretty sure he tells them things he wouldn't tell me, of course, especially Andy, being the oldest. But sometimes these days Dad forgets that I'm just a girl.

She'd imagined that she'd have the triumph of telling the riders that the brumbies were just down the ridge, as well as beating them up to Jackson's Flat. But the men had recognised the prints and scent of horses too.

'How far off, do you think?' asked Mr Sampson, as Mr Clancy sniffed the wind from the gullies. The old drover glanced at his oldest boy. The boy shrugged. Mr Clancy nodded as though the shrug meant something. 'Over the next ridge from this, I'd say. The gullies all lead down to the creek below the Flat,' he added.

Mr Sampson sucked his teeth thoughtfully. 'That's where we'll drive them then. Down whichever gully we can. Need a pen across at the creek where the gullies meet.' He pointed at Flinty, then Sandy, then Mr Clancy's oldest boy. 'You head down there, and get the pen set up. You know the sort of thing. Ropes between the trees, white rag tied to them — a galloping horse will see it as a barrier. Brush piled up on the rope too, if you've time.' He turned to stare across the ridges again, evaluating the country.

No! thought Flinty. She hadn't come all this way just to put up brush fences! She glanced at Sandy. He shrugged at her. Suddenly she realised that this was exactly what he'd expected. Sandy had been asked on this muster because Pete Sampson knew he was hard working and reliable. Sandy hadn't even ridden much since he'd left for war. So this is why he didn't argue more, she thought. He'd expected that their job would be stringing rope, then patrolling the pen to make sure the brumbies didn't break past.

Well, she hadn't spent her childhood behind a horse and plough at the Macks'. She'd come here to ride!

She nodded at Sandy as though to say she agreed. She saw him relax and turn Bessie to troop back down the hill to find the point where the creeks ran together, while Mr Sampson, Mr Clancy and the stockmen vanished down the hillside. She let them get half a minute ahead, then turned Empress to follow them.

'Flinty!' yelled Sandy.

She ignored him. She heard the clatter of hooves on rock as he urged his horse next to Empress. 'Flinty, don't be an idiot. You'll get your share of the reward anyway. That's what you want, isn't it?'

'Yes. No!' She didn't know what she wanted. She'd come today for the money, that magic hundred pounds. But there was another important idea driving her too.

Ever since Dad died, she'd been left out of the world of men. Andy had inherited the farm, just because he was a boy; and as if that wasn't enough it was Andy who was free to go to Queensland droving, while she stayed behind scrubbing floors and making rabbit stew ...

But Nicholas had said she was the girl from Snowy River. Today she'd show them how a girl could ride.

Sandy stared at her with almost desperation. 'Flinty, for Pete's sake, you can't follow them. It's dangerous!'

'I've been riding these hills since I was two years old. You'd better go get that yard ready.' Flinty squeezed her knees into Empress's sides. She could feel Empress's exuberance match hers as they left him sitting there.

She saw the other riders again within a minute. Their horses ambled down the slope, picking their way through the hop bushes, following the brumby tracks.

Mr Clancy noticed her first. He drew his horse close to Mr Sampson and said something. Mr Sampson looked back at her too.

She waited for someone to yell at her to go back. Perhaps, if they had insisted, she might have. But instead the men seemed to ignore her, lounging back relaxed in their big saddles, letting their horses choose their own paths and pace, skirting wombat holes and lichened rocks.

They're waiting for me to give up when the riding gets tough, thought Flinty. But I can ride this country! This land is mine, and Empress's.

She patted the pony's neck. Empress gave a short snort, as though she understood. She kept well behind the group as the riders crossed a gully and climbed the ridge beyond. There was still no sign of the brumbies yet, beyond the hoof prints and droppings.

Once up on the narrow ridge she urged Empress faster. If she were too far behind she wouldn't be able to catch up when they found the brumbies. The pony surged forwards.

Mr Clancy held up a hand. It wasn't much of a signal — he might have been brushing away a fly. The other riders all reined in. All at once Flinty realised these men had worked together so often that they could read each other's movements. It wasn't just horsemanship they'd be relying on today, but experience, working with each other.

For the first time doubt flickered. She could ride and scan terrain as well as any man, but she had never worked with this team.

It was too late to head back now. She urged Empress along the ridge top, with its thin trees and sparse tussocks, towards the group of riders. Then she saw why Mr Clancy had halted.

The brumbies grazed below them on a small flat by a thin creek, all rocks and scrubby she-oaks, about a dozen of them gathered around one big white stallion, his muscles rippling under what was left of his winter coat.

It had to be Repentance. The rest were mares and young horses, all of them shades of brown except for a dappled mare, and a young horse, a colt by the look of him, just beginning to turn the grey that would one day be white. Two of the brumbies were lying down, but even as she watched the dappled mare gave a sharp whinny. Instantly the others scrambled to their feet. The brumbies gazed up at the riders on the ridge, then at their stallion.

The stallion stared at the hunters for a second. He reared in challenge. His hooves struck the ground. Then he was racing. Sparks seemed to fly between his hooves and the rocks below as he led his mob up between the trees towards the far ridge.

Mr Sampson raised his whip in the air and gave a bellow. The riders spread out, galloping down the ridge, their horses leaping, sidestepping, almost sliding at times. Flinty urged Empress to follow them.

It was harder than she'd thought, galloping down a slope she'd never ridden before. Wombat holes lurked behind boulders and the hop scrub hid them all. She could feel Empress tense and focused below her, her own eyes searching for any clue that might show danger in their path.

A stumble here could kill her; it could kill Empress or at best lame her so badly she might have to be put down. But it was almost like she and her pony shared one mind, four eyes. Sometimes Empress would see the danger and step around or leap across; at other times Flinty guided her.

The men were still in front of her, still spread out across the hill. Dust spurted out from under their hooves. The brumbies flowed like water down the hill, keeping close together, then across this gully's pools between tumbled boulders. They picked up the pace as they surged again up the next ridge.

The mountains' still silence was broken by flying dust and hooves striking the ground, the urgent breathing of the horses, the yells of men and cracking whips. The brumby stallion had vanished over the ridge above them, and the young grey horse too; the mares and a few foals were not far behind.

Empress's breath began to blow hard as they pounded up the mountain after them. Now Flinty understood the stallion's cunning. His brumby mob was fresh. The hunters' horses had not only travelled miles today, but carried riders too. They couldn't catch the brumbies in a chase uphill.

The brumby hunters' only chance to get the whole mob was to outwit them, to catch them before they could climb the next hill, to head them off so they fled down the gully to be caught where the crevasses joined and the trap had been set, further down.

She could hear the other horses labouring, their sides heaving. Empress was faring better — she'd had a longer rest at Jackson's Flat, and carried a slender girl, not a large man. But one more ridge might exhaust them all. We have to head the brumbies off in the next gully, she thought.

Mr Clancy reached the summit first, with his boys and Mr Sampson just behind. They paused as the other riders joined them, reining in their horses, looking down. Why had they stopped? The brumbies would get away!

She surged past them, hearing the *clang* as Empress's hooves dislodged a rock. She just had time to notice the shock on the men's faces, then she and Empress were beyond, heading down the hill.

For a few seconds all she felt was triumph, then the wild horses spread out below her. All at once she realised her mistake. The men had stopped for a reason — to work out exactly where each needed to ride to keep the mob together.

One rider couldn't turn a brumby mob. Even as she thought it the brumbies began to separate. Once they straggled across the slope the men behind had little chance of getting them all together again.

Had she ruined the muster for everyone?

Again, it was too late to stop now. The brumby mob had seen her, were already heading in different directions. All she could do was go on, hope that by some miracle she could turn the whole mob to her will. But how?

The dappled mare, she thought desperately. The mare was slower than the stallion, or maybe keeping to the rear to watch out for the others. She had been the lookout. Would the other horses follow her? Flinty raised her stockwhip high and gave a yell.

The dappled mare turned as Empress and Flinty surged towards her, instinctively seeking the easiest way down the gully — exactly as Flinty had hoped — towards the trap. The other mares halted for a moment, their eyes rolling, then they followed the dappled mare down the gully. The young grey colt followed them.

But not the stallion. The grandson of old Regret galloped a short way up the next ridge. He bellowed out a call that was both challenge and warning.

Flinty felt despair bite. It was the stallion that Miss Matilda wanted, the horse that was worth a thousand pounds.

She'd spoiled it all! No one would ever catch Repentance once he'd galloped up the hill.

All she could do now was head after the mares, keep them moving towards the trap, stop any of them breaking away uphill. Unless ...

She glanced up at the stallion again. He'd halted, his eyes looking wildly from the hunters to his herd below. Flinty remembered Dad saying, 'A good stallion looks out for his mares.'

Repentance thought his mares were safe now, heading fast downhill. He couldn't know that a trap awaited them. He planned to sniff them out again tonight, tomorrow, or in a few days' time.

She needed to convince the big horse his mares were in danger. Now!

Even as she thought it she nudged Empress with her heels again, to keep her moving down the gully. She reached for her other whip, the big one Dad had plaited for her sixteenth birthday. She swung it up around her head and yelled, just like Dad had done.

'*Hoooo-eeee!*' The whip cracked above her, like an axe striking a billet of hard dry wood. A white cockatoo screamed an alarm call as his flock hurled themselves towards the sky.

The dappled mare swung her head to glance back, showing the whites of her eyes. Another mare whinnied in terror. Flinty cracked her whip again. One of the mares stumbled in fright, then righted herself. They were running faster now, truly frightened for the first time since they'd seen the hunters, heads tossing, eyes rolling, as they stumbled down the gully.

Dimly she was aware of Mr Sampson and the others making their way behind her down the mountainside. But they'd never catch Repentance now. She galloped after the mares, keeping well away from the stallion, leaving him free to follow the herd if he chose. The great horse hadn't moved, still staring from his mares to the hunters. And now she didn't dare look back at him. The hidden ground was full of wombat holes, and any slip was death. Empress's neck was white with foam, her breath heaving.

Suddenly she heard hoofbeats behind her. Has Mr Sampson caught up already? she wondered, just as a white shape flashed on her right. Repentance!

She edged Empress further up the slope, leaving the stallion a clear path so he could pass her, think he'd beaten her. She watched, almost too exhausted for triumph, as Repentance rejoined his mares, the one great thundering bunch of them, imagining they were escaping as she galloped more slowly after them, letting them tire themselves like a torrent down the creek bed in their rush to be free.

But the men still had to get the brumbies into the trap. All at once she was aware of other riders on both sides of her, a line of them, in case some of the horses tried to make a break back up either slope.

But they didn't. Down and down the brumbies galloped, fleeing the sound of men, of whips. The muster pounded after them, whips cracking, yells echoing from the cliffs, a mob of grey currawongs rising too, shrieking at the noise.

And Flinty was with them now. She'd never ridden so hard, so far. Nothing in all her rides with Dad had been like this. She felt Empress's ribcage swell and fall and knew she would have to stop soon. She peered desperately ahead, hoping for the flash of white rags among the trees.

Where was the trap? Were they even driving them down the right gully? Had she got it so wrong that the brumbies were heading the wrong way? But this gully *had* to lead to the trap in the canyon: she knew this country like she knew her own feet. One more bend and they'd be there ...

And there it was. Not much of a barrier — rope stretched between the trees, hung with white bits of cloth, branches tucked in and out. Repentance alone could have broken through it.

But he didn't know it. The stallion halted, confused, at what looked like a solid barrier. His mares stumbled around him, baffled, blowing and beaten, as the men closed in.

Flinty was aware of Empress's shuddering frame. The sweat ran down her own sides and pooled under her; somewhere she had lost her hat and her knitted cap — her plaits were flying free.

'Got them,' said Mr Sampson calmly, his white beard not even blown by the wind.

Chapter 11

26 November 1919

Dear Diary,

Some things you know happen only once in your life. Your first kiss, the first time you stand on a mountain you have climbed all by yourself, the first time you know that you and your horse are working as one.

Even when I was riding after the brumbies, even when I had no idea what would happen later, I knew I'd never chase brumbies like that again. This wasn't just the first, but the only.

No one said anything about her being a girl. No one congratulated her on her ride either. I was, thought Flinty as she rubbed Empress down roughly with some dried grass, both very good and very stupid. Her ride was one only a horse and rider who knew the land and each other could have made. It could also have lost them all the prize.

Now Sandy and the men from Drinkwater worked at making the barrier more solid, keeping an eye on the brumby mob, huddled together and bewildered, while Mr Clancy's boys made a fire and boiled the billy.

Flinty let her mare catch her breath, then led her to a pool above the brumby enclosure to drink a little, before guiding her back towards the campfire, where she could graze. Empress didn't need to be hobbled to stay close. Flinty busied herself collecting dead wood, dragging the branches over to the fire where the billy tea already boiled and, by the smell of it, a damper was cooking in the ashes.

Suddenly she was starving.

The older of Mr Clancy's boys grinned, a white smile in the dark face under the big hat. A slender hand grasped a green branch and hauled the damper out of the coals, broke it open into two white floury halves, and handed her one of them with another grin. The native's big grey shirt finally showed the shape inside it.

'Oh,' said Flinty.

The 'boy' nodded, amused. The other boy — who was really a man in his twenties, with dark skin paler than his mother's — reached into the saddlebags and brought out a jar of pale green bush honey. Flinty poured a bit onto the damper. She bit down into the heat and sweetness, then gulped at the tea, strong as boiled wattle bark, sweet with honey.

'Any left for me?' Mr Clancy crouched beside them. 'I see you've met the missus,' he added to Flinty.

'I ... I don't understand.'

'White man, black wife.' Mrs Clancy shrugged. Her voice was sweet, with a slight accent. 'People shake their heads. But when they see a native in trousers, all they see is just another stockman. We went to Queensland droving, when we first met.

Didn't come back till folks had forgotten the white man, black wife. People see what they want.'

'But the men today ...' Flinty gestured at the Drinkwater stockmen, at Mr Sampson.

Mrs Clancy laughed, as if that was all the answer needed. She poured a mug of tea from the billy for her husband.

And maybe she's right, thought Flinty. If you didn't talk about something you didn't have to defend it. It just ... *was* ... like the mountains, like the snow. The Clancys' marriage was a partnership so solid it didn't need a house and wedding ring to make it real. Mrs Clancy's disguise meant the white man could pretend — even to themselves perhaps — that the person they rode with and respected was a 'boy', not a wife. At another time, or another place in town, or even their homes — they might think differently. Not here.

And somehow she couldn't see Mr Clancy, or his wife or son, ever wanting to settle down in a town — where people might talk or, worse, refuse to talk to them, to throw stones or horse pats at their windows. Flinty would go back to her house when this was over, and live under a roof, even if it was surrounded by mountains.

The Clancys' roof was the sky.

Had Mrs Clancy guessed Flinty was a girl, back there at Jackson's Flat? Was that why she asked her husband to let her ride with them? Mrs Clancy must know better than anyone — except maybe her husband — that a woman could ride as well, and as long, as any man. Perhaps she had seen the need to do just that in Flinty's face as well.

It didn't matter. Nothing mattered now except the good damper in her hand, the knowledge that — somehow — she hadn't messed this up.

Meanwhile the other riders were gathering at the fire, with only Sandy and Pete Sampson still on horseback in case the brumbies broke out of the makeshift yard. But the captives were still quiet, their heads down. Even Repentance looked subdued, as though he knew what was coming now and didn't find the memory of the Drinkwater paddocks too bad. Some of the mares were even drinking, or pulling at the grass. The grey colt looked up at Flinty, meeting her eyes for a second before turning away to the others.

A grand horse, thought Flinty. One day that colt would be as white as his father and as strong, or even stronger. The stallion was magnificent. But the young horse had gone almost as fast today, despite his youth. Even now he held his head up as though to say, 'I stay here because I choose to be with the others. But if I wished I could leave you all behind.'

'Good pony you have there,' said Mr Clancy, leaning back against a tree and nodding at Empress, her head down among the tussocks. He took a sip of his sweet tea, his expression strangely grim. 'Favouring her right hind leg. You noticed?'

'No!' Flinty leaped up and ran across to Empress. The pony stepped towards her, limping slightly, as Mr Clancy had said. Flinty ran her hand down her leg and lifted the hoof, trying to find the trouble.

'Strained a muscle, I'd say.' Mr Clancy had come up behind her, his mug still in his hand.

'How bad?' asked Flinty anxiously.

He shrugged. 'Give her a week or two, and she might get over it. Might always limp too.'

Dad had shown her how to put hot fomentations on a horse's leg, warm cloths or hot bran poultices, or even a hot cow-manure plaster. She had no bran or cow manure, but she could warm her spare shirt in hot water and stay up all night, like Dad had sometimes done with an injured horse, reapplying the hot cloths ...

Mr Clancy must have guessed some of this from her expression. His face lost its grimness. He looked at her over his mug. 'That was a wild ride you gave her.'

'But we got them,' said Flinty defensively.

'Reckon that's the last wild ride your pony will ever manage.' He nodded to himself. 'Saw a ride like that, must have been forty years ago now. Bloke wrote a poem about it.'

'"The Man from Snowy River",' said Flinty.

Mr Clancy nodded again. He ran his hands down Empress's leg. The mare let him, shivering slightly.

'Could be worse.' Mr Clancy straightened. 'Reckon she'll get over it if you let her go easy for a while, as long as she's never ridden that hard again. Poets, well, they like things exciting. You know what really happened on that ride?'

'The man from Snowy River brought all the brumbies back by himself.'

'Well, he did that. He did something else as well. That boy rode his horse to death. Oh, he headed off the brumbies all right. The colt from old Regret went back where he belonged. But I saw the mount break his heart trying to do what his rider wanted. He just went down, the young man tumbling after him. The boy was all right. A few bumps and bruises. But his horse ...' The old man shrugged. 'About the size of your mare here. Touch of Timor pony, three parts thoroughbred, maybe. Lying there among the hop, his sides white with foam, still as the rocks. Grown men cried,' said Mr Clancy. 'It's a sight you don't see often, something like that.'

'What ... what happened to the rider?'

'He sat there, the pony's head in his lap, while we rounded up the brumbies. Was still there the next morning too. I gave him one of my spares to ride. Had to leave the pony where he was. Can't bury a horse,' said Mr Clancy, all emotion gone from his voice. Like Andy's, thought Flinty, when he spoke about the war. Some things were beyond feeling.

'You think I could have killed Empress?'

'Or lamed her. But you were lucky,' said Mr Clancy. 'And you've earned a hundred pounds.' He gave Empress a final pat and sloped back towards the campfire.

Chapter 12

I kept waking up that night, wondering why I was in a blanket on hard ground and not a feather bed, hearing the sugar gliders in the gum blossom above me, the horses whinnying, the possums growling and the dingoes howling — we'd taken over their rocks and creek. Every time I woke I'd think, Did I really do that? and then remember, I really did.

'A hundred pounds each and the brumby of your choice,' Mr Sampson said the next morning to the riders around the campfire, their legs still stretched out towards the last of the heat. The fire was old coals now, ready to be raked out of existence when they broke camp.

Flinty was comfortably full of damper and honey, as well as the mutton chops that Mrs Clancy had somehow conjured out of her saddlebags, enough for all of them. There'd also been three wild ducks over the fire for dinner, though Flinty had no idea how Mrs Clancy had caught them, and some sweet fibrous roots baked in wet leaves that she and the Clancys ate but the stockmen ignored.

Flinty looked automatically over at the brumbies, still subdued in their pen. They know they are prisoners, she thought. Only the white stallion and the grey colt gazed at the humans eye to eye.

She would love to choose that colt. She could almost feel herself riding him, breaking him. She could see Andy working him too. He'd be a joy to train, a horse with pride like that.

A horse needs to feel good about himself, Dad always said. Look at the way he carries his head, his tail. A sulky horse will try to slide you off under the next branch, or turn stubborn and head for home. But a horse who knows he's as good as you — a horse like that will be with you all the way.

The colt turned, as though he knew she was looking at him. She scrambled to her feet, while the men sipped the last of their tea and Mrs Clancy gathered her billy and saddlebags, and walked over to the horse yard. The brumbies edged away from her. She slowed down so she didn't spook them. The last thing she needed was to make them break through the barrier now.

'Hello, boy,' she said. The colt flicked his ears at her. Without thinking she held out a bit of damper. Silly — she knew that as soon as she did it. A wild horse wouldn't even know that she was holding out food.

He lifted his head, his nostrils twitching. It seemed he liked the smell of damper.

'It's good,' she said softly. 'The best damper ever made. Don't you want to try it, boy?' Words didn't matter, Dad said. But the horse needs to get used to your voice. A horse heard what you meant to say, reading your face and your movements as well as your tone. What you said had no meaning, but what you meant did.

'Come on. You're a good boy, aren't you? A wonderful boy.' She held her hand still.

Suddenly, magically, the colt took a step towards her. Flinty stayed motionless, holding out the damper.

Repentance whinnied a warning and pawed the ground, but the grey colt ignored him. He took another step, and then another.

She heard hooves behind her. Empress's grassy breath whiffled over her shoulder. Flinty was glad that the small horse wasn't limping this morning, merely favouring her hind leg when she stood. Empress reached her head down and nibbled the bit of damper.

Flinty laughed. She broke the damper in two and fed half to Empress, still keeping one eye on the colt. 'See? Empress knows she can trust me.' Or she can trust me now, she thought guiltily, remembering Mr Clancy's reproach the night before. She'd dreamed of the dead horse last night, the boy holding his head through the dark. When she'd woken the dingoes had been howling. The poor dead horse would have fed them, and the crows and eagles and goannas too. Better than being buried in the ground.

Now two horses watched her: Empress, butting her shirt in case there was more damper, or lumps of sugar; and the colt, stepping nearer still.

The grey was now so close she could touch him, but she had to let him take the final step.

And then he did. His warm lips swept her palm for the damper; he ate it while she touched him lightly on the chin, keeping her body motionless, only her hand moving.

'Your name's Snow King,' she whispered. 'One day you'll be as white as snow. One day you'll be a king.'

All at once the colt jerked away. He tossed his head and cantered over to the others.

'Well,' said Mr Clancy behind her. Mr Clancy could put a lot of meaning into a single word. This one sounded approving. More than that: amazed.

'He's beautiful, isn't he?' she said, still gazing at the colt.

'He is that.'

'Have you chosen him for yourself? Or does Mr Sampson want him?' Because of course they would get first choice, as senior riders.

'Sampson's not taking a horse — he's in partnership with Miss Matilda in this. I was going to take the colt. But the wife says I should give him up to you.' He chewed a bit of grass thoughtfully. 'Usually right about things, the wife.'

'Why? The colt's the most valuable horse here,' she added frankly.

'And he came up to you. That means something. But a colt like that needs training. Oh, I could break him in fast. Sell him fast too. He'll be a racer, like his dad. But the wife says he deserves better than that. Says he deserves to be broken in slowly, kindly. Think you can do that?'

Hope rose in her, incredulous. Did he really mean it? 'Yes. My brother can train him too,' she said quickly, in case Mr Clancy thought that a girl wouldn't be good enough. 'Andy'll be back by the end of summer. Dad taught us well.'

'Did your dad teach you not to take your horse at full gallop down a strange hill?'

'Yes,' said Flinty honestly.

'Well. Long as you remember it. Long as you never do that to another horse again.' He bent and plucked another stem of grass, bit off its soft end, then stuck the harder bit in his mouth, slowly chewing the rest. They watched the colt together. At last he said, 'Give me ten pounds for him.'

'He's worth much more than that.'

'I know it. But me and the lad and the wife have made three hundred pounds the last two days, and part of that's due to you. Oh, you could have ruined it all, all right. We could have lost the whole bunch of them. But we didn't. You brought them home, and that's what matters. Our lad can buy his own place now, up the river past Drinkwater, next to his cousins' place. Wouldn't do for me, but that's what he wants. So I say, ten pounds.' He held out a hand of grime and leather.

Flinty put hers in his. 'Deal.'

Chapter 13

Mrs Clancy's recipe for damper:

Put some ash in the bottom of a mug and cover it with water to let it settle. Then mix the water from the top with the flour and more water till it sticks into a ball. Roll the ball in wet green grass or a tussock, then shovel out the coals of your fire, put it in the hole and rake the coals back over it. Wait till the shadows move one and a half fists when your arm is held out right in front of you, then retrieve it. (You can leave it longer but the crust will be tougher.) Mrs Clancy says you roll it in green grass before putting it into the coals so you can eat the crust — it isn't hard and ashy.

The men moved the stallion and the rest of the brumbies in a mob down to Drinkwater the next day, leaving her and Sandy and their horses and the colt. Sandy had accepted an extra five pounds instead of a brumby to be broken in.

The mob moved quietly up the ridge towards the track, still cowed by the crack of the whips, the stockmen riding slowly around them to keep them together. Even Repentance seemed to have accepted that his time in the mountains was over. Perhaps, thought Flinty, he remembered that no dingoes would threaten his foals in the Drinkwater paddocks, that there'd always be good feed in the trough when it was dry or cold. Only Snow King showed distress, anguished at being left alone, running along the edge of the pen, whinnying and rolling his eyes.

The Clancys were the last to leave.

'You all right here?' asked Mrs Clancy, as Flinty helped her pack her swag. She nodded at Sandy.

Flinty glanced over at Sandy. He was reinforcing a smaller yard for Snow King with wattle saplings. He moved awkwardly today, even more hunched over. She wondered if his wound hurt him. Dad had always said his scars ached after a long day, or a night in his swag on the hard ground. 'Sandy was my brother's best friend.'

Mrs Clancy nodded, accepting it.

'Might call in one day, see what you've made of the colt,' said Mr Clancy.

'You'll be welcome,' said Flinty, meaning it. She wasn't sure Mum would have invited a native woman to her dining-room table, and Dad had talked of 'half-castes' a bit like he'd talked about dingoes after the lambs. But once you got over the shock of the colour of her skin Mrs Clancy was just like Mrs Mack, only better in the saddle and at conjuring up food on the road.

'Yes. Well,' said Mr Clancy. 'It was a grand ride you did, girl. Just don't do another, eh?' He raised his hand in farewell and squeezed his horse up. It cantered easily up the mountainside after the brumby mob, his wife's and son's horses on either side.

The gully was empty. Emptier than when they'd arrived, as the horses had eaten most of the grass, and half emptied the waterholes along the creek too. The bush smelled of horse and wood smoke. Empress grazed a little way off, still favouring her hind leg. Flinty added more wood to the fire, then went to join Sandy at Snow King's yard.

It still seemed impossible that the colt was really hers. One day he'd accept her as his leader, just as he'd obeyed his father. A girl, able to command so much strength and beauty.

Sandy leaned against the fence, watching the colt. The young horse still paced around, his sides sweaty as he whinnied at the departing mob. He'll try to break through the yard at any sudden noise, thought Flinty. Hurt himself, perhaps, against the rails. What must it be like for him to be so suddenly alone, after a life surrounded by his clan? Even worse than your brothers going off to war, your mum and dad dying. At least she still had Joey and Kirsty, and Andy when he came back, and a home she loved.

The colt had lost everything. All he had was her.

'He's beautiful,' said Sandy. 'I'm glad he's yours,' he added.

She smiled at him, grateful. Sandy had not said a word about her almost ruining the round-up, or being embarrassed when they'd discovered she was a girl. He didn't say, 'Be careful how you handle him,' either. Sandy knew who she was and accepted it. Like the Clancys accepted each other, in a way, she thought.

'Are you all right?' she asked.

His face closed up again. 'Why shouldn't I be?' He looked at the frantic colt, not at Flinty, unconsciously straightening his body.

'I just thought maybe ...' She stopped and said instead, 'What are you going to do with your hundred and five pounds?'

'Put it in the bank.'

'What then?'

He shrugged. 'Get a place of my own one day. I've applied for one of the new Soldier Settler blocks. Batlow, maybe, or down the Murrumbidgee. But I'll need money to set it up properly. Some of the blokes taking them up haven't tuppence in their pockets.'

Batlow. The Murrumbidgee. Her heart lurched a little at the thought of the valley with no Sandy in it. Even when he'd been away at the war she'd known somehow that he'd be back. But of course he'd want a place of his own. There wasn't much flat land in the valley, and that was all farmed already. The Mullinses and the Colours all had sons who'd take over their family farms in turn, just like Johnno would take over the Macks'.

She forced herself to smile. 'Sheep farm?'

He gave an almost grin. 'Not in that country. Orchard, more like. And horses too. Saved most of my pay in the army. I'm not far off what I need now.'

'Andy told me he spent all his pay. Said he didn't see any point saving when tomorrow his body might be feeding the soil of some French farm.'

Sandy plucked a head of grass and began to chew it, his eyes still on the horse. 'I reckon saving my pay was a sort of promise I'd get home. All of us dreamed of different things, I suppose.'

'What things did you think about?'

A pause. 'Mum's pikelets mostly.' He pushed himself off the fence, stretching till he stood upright. 'And strawberry jam.

Not plum. They used to give it to us in France, before they sent us over the top. I'll never eat plum jam again.'

Flinty felt a stab of disappointment. What had she expected — that he'd say he'd dreamed of her? And now he'd finally talked about the war, but only to complain about the jam.

She looked at him, standing there, watching the colt, not her. 'You'd better be heading back if you're going to be home by dark.'

He turned, surprised. 'I can't leave you by yourself.'

'What could happen to me?'

He shrugged. 'Swaggies, maybe.' There were some strange types around these days, not just the old-time swaggies who'd been decades on the road, cadging meat and flour and a night in the shed in return for chopping wood. The old-style swaggies were a bit gone in the head sometimes, muttering to themselves, which was why Mum had had a strict rule that none be allowed in the house.

There were new swaggies now, men who couldn't settle after the war, maybe had come home to find parents or wife or job gone, and no home to settle into.

'Swaggies stick to the roads, where there're farms they can beg a bit of food. And Kirsty and Joey will be worried,' she added. 'You can let them know I'm safe. It's going to take me longer than I thought to get home, with Snow King. I need to get him used to me before I can get a halter on him and teach him to lead. I don't think I should ride Empress back either, not yet awhile. I'll have to walk and lead them both.'

Sandy considered. 'All right. I'll come back here tomorrow,' he said at last. 'You can ride back on Mum's Sally. I'll bring Toby or Sam to give us a hand leading the colt too.'

She nodded, grateful, but suddenly wishing she hadn't asked him to go home. One more night wouldn't matter much to Joey and Kirsty. Had Sandy thought she didn't trust him alone with her, as Mrs Clancy had hinted? Maybe if it was just them and the horses in the darkness, with the stars and the calls of the dingoes, he might talk to her again, joke with her like he'd done before he and Jeff marched off to Goulburn, to Sydney, to the war. Maybe he might even want to kiss her ...

Get over it, Flinty, she told herself. When Sandy had kissed her last time she'd been in her blue dress, her hair down with a ribbon in it, not in dusty trousers and a shirt, smelling of perspiration and horse and smoke. If he hadn't wanted to kiss her on the railway platform he certainly wouldn't want to kiss her now.

She wondered what French women were like. He must have met nurses too, English, or even Australian and American. Clean, with soft hands, women who wore lace dresses when they weren't on duty. The nurses in the war posters all looked so fresh and beautiful. She bet they even had lace on their petticoats.

He must have met someone else, even if he wasn't getting letters from her. That was why he was saving so hard for a farm. A farmer needed a wife, and sons to inherit what he'd built.

Suddenly she wondered what Sandy would say if she told him she'd met a soldier from another war, a ghost from the future. Sandy was maybe the one person who'd believe her. She wondered if Nicholas would seem more real, or less, if someone else knew her secret. She was about to speak, just as Sandy turned. 'I'll get more firewood for tonight. You'll need to build the fire up to keep the dingoes away.'

He loped off into the trees.

He'd probably have laughed. No, Sandy wouldn't laugh at her. He'd have worried that she was going batty, up on the mountain. Or demanded he meet this stranger who claimed he was from the future. She had a sudden vision of Mr Mack and all his sons descending on the Rock, interrogating Nicholas. No, she couldn't do that to Nicholas. Besides, Nicholas was hers. She didn't want to share him. She turned back to the colt, fished some damper out of her pocket and leaned on the stockyard rail, the damper in her hand, and waited.

A creaky-door sound echoed in the branches above her, and then another. A mob of black cockatoos passing through. Snow King's ears flickered as the big birds landed, one after another, in the trees around, and then began to rip off the bark to get to the grubs below. Had they been waiting till the men and horses left? She supposed so. Far off she could hear Sandy whistle as he collected firewood.

Snow King was calmer now, or perhaps just anxious for company, even that of a human. She watched as he stepped closer to her.

'Hello,' she said softly. 'You're mine now. Did you know that? And I'm yours, because you are the most beautiful horse I've ever seen. I'm going to break you in, then Andy will train you. You'll like Andy. He's got gentle hands, like Dad's. He'll train you to be a racehorse. You'll like that too — everyone cheering you and the other horses far behind as you beat them all.'

Snow King whinnied, softly, not the desperate cry of before. She nodded, understanding as clearly as if he had used words. 'Don't you worry. When the races are over you'll come back up the mountains, to your home paddocks again. When you get old that's where you'll live forever, with your mares and your foals.'

The colt took one more step towards her. She could feel his warm breath before he took the damper. Once again it seemed a miracle, a gift from the mountains as well as the horse in front of her. She stroked his neck, and this time he allowed it.

'Are you lonely now the others have gone, boy?' she whispered. 'I know all about lonely. But you'll have Empress with you. You'll like Empress. You've got me too. I promise you won't be lonely again.'

Chapter 14

27 November 1919

Dear Diary,

It was as though when the brumbies finally vanished over the hill Snow King decided I was his mob leader. I've never felt that with a horse before — Empress knew all about humans before I began to train her. But I am the first human Snow King has ever known. All that beauty and power — and yet he lets me lead him, tell him what to do. I'll never ever forget that moment, the rich smell of him. Even the clouds seemed to dance in the sky.

She placed a halter on Snow King that afternoon, slipping it over his nose and up behind his ears, the lead rope attached. He resisted only briefly, tossing his head and then considering her, before allowing her to put it in place. He was surprisingly easy to teach to lead too.

'Maybe Empress has convinced him to trust me,' she told Sandy when he arrived with Toby and the extra horse the next day. Empress had been grazing next to the colt's pen all night. Flinty had heard them whinnying to each other as she sat by the fire, glad of its light as the dingoes howled in the hills.

'Nah. Reckon he loves you,' said Sandy shortly, as Toby took their horses down to the creek.

Can a horse love? thought Flinty, and then, Of course they can.

It took them till late afternoon to lead the horses back, going slowly for Empress's sake, eating the mutton and chutney sandwiches, the pikelets and fruitcake Mrs Mack had packed for them, with jars of cold sweet tea.

For a while they walked along the river flats beside the Snowy, the sand freshly swept clear by spring's thaw, dappled with wombat and roo prints, and the longer trails left by horses and their riders. The debris was piled high and dry up in the trees.

Flinty wished she could carry some back — driftwood was the best tinder of all. Rock Farm was too high on the mountain for their trees along the creek to collect much, even after the spring thaws.

Toby talked of the lambing, which floodgates had been destroyed in the rush of the spring melt. He seemed to have forgiven her. She was glad. There was no awkward silence now, as they rode along the sand. But she still wished that she was alone with Sandy.

At last they reached Rocky Creek. They followed it, ambling up into the valley along the shade-dappled creek flats rather than heading over to the road. The hills on either side closer now, the mountains high and clear in the distance, a plume of blue smoke coming from the Whites' place, the sound of wood chopping from the Browns', a cow calling her calf from the Greens'. Only the smoke and fences showed that the valley was inhabited by humans, until they came in sight of the Macks' farm, sitting in its tiny garden of roses and camellias between the paddocks of corn and potatoes.

'Flinty!' Kirsty ran down the road, her plaits flying. Flinty put her hand up quickly, gesturing for her to stop and wait. She didn't want Snow King to pull back and reef the rope from her hand this close to the end of the journey.

Kirsty stopped, jigging from one leg to the other as the horses and people came abreast of her. Then she could hold back the torrent of words no longer. 'You've been so long! I've got eleven new freckles and lost a tooth and Mrs Mack made me a new dress out of your old green one. It's got lace around the collar from one of her shawls. Real lace! And —'

Flinty dismounted and hugged her. It felt like Kirsty had grown, even in the few days she'd been away. 'I'm sorry,' she said.

'Mr Mack brought us down here. We had plum pie last night! Did you know Mrs Mack has a sapphire ring? It doesn't fit her finger any more. She says she's keeping it for the next girl who marries one of her boys. Joey's out with Mr Mack and the boys,' she added, 'dagging the sheep. He says he wants to be a shearer now.'

The month before he'd wanted to be an engine driver. Flinty suspected that Dad and Mum had hoped for something different for their youngest son, but a shearer might be the best he could do now. Though could Joey ever be satisfied with the world of sheds and sheep? Joey with his million questions?

She felt a stab of guilt that she had taken her brother's adventure for herself. She'd made the right decision —

Mr Sampson would have left Joey at Drinkwater like he'd wanted to leave her. But even getting that far would have meant a lot to Joey.

She took Kirsty's hand, holding the colt's lead rope in the other, as Sandy wordlessly took Sally's reins and led her behind the house.

Kirsty seemed to take in the young horse for the first time. 'Is that your new horse? Sandy said you rounded up a whole mob of brumbies. And you made a hundred pounds! Does the King of England have a hundred pounds?'

Flinty gently stroked Snow King's neck. The colt allowed it. He didn't even seem rattled by the small prattling girl, though he sniffed the scents around him, ears alert.

'I think King Edward has a bit more than that. I made ninety pounds.' Enough to pay the rates, she thought. To buy stores; for Joey and Kirsty to go to school again.

And Snow King will bring our Andy home too.

Chapter 15

29 November 1919

Dear Diary,

I put a saddle on Snow King today. Didn't fasten it, just let him feel the weight. He seemed curious, not frightened at all. I don't think anything frightens Snow King. He canters up when he sees me coming now. I don't think it's just for his apple. Maybe he does love me, like Sandy says.

No mist on the Rock today. I don't think ghosts come unless there's mist, otherwise everyone would see them. I wonder if there are other ghosts sometimes, not just me and Nicholas. I think there must be, because of the stories. But one ghost is enough for me.

I hope the mist is there tomorrow. I know I said I wouldn't be there for a few more days. I wish I hadn't. I wish I'd said it might be that long, but I'd try to be there earlier. I want to see him! It would be good to just know that Nicholas was there too, that I have a friend so close, even if he is a ghost.

The Rock was smooth and bare and mistless as Mr Mack's cart jolted up the track the next day, with Flinty leading Empress and Snow King.

She wanted to tell Nicholas about her ride so badly that she thought she might have to tie herself to the kitchen table to stop herself running back to the Rock, sitting there in case he came again. But of course she couldn't. There was the kitchen fire to light, the hens to feed and water, the swallows who were trying to build a nest over the front door to discourage.

Her brother and sister had needed reassuring too that she'd never leave them like that again. She'd had to coax Joey out of his sulks at being left out of the hunt by promising him the book on electrical engineering he'd read about in one of Mr Mack's old newspapers. There was money for a few luxuries like books now, new boots, material for clothes.

Of course Nicholas already knew that it had happened, that the girl from Snowy River had done her ride. But she wanted to tell him *everything*: how it had felt to soar down the hillside, she and Empress working as one; how Mr Clancy had both praised and told her off, and about Mrs Clancy too. Everything; but mostly to thank him, because without the words of a ghost she might never have gone at all.

She ran down to the Rock as soon as Joey and Kirsty were asleep. But the ledge was still resolutely mistless, in this first dry heat of approaching summer, even though she sat there while the stars wheeled overhead, until the Southern Cross 'turned over', just as it had when she'd sat here with Dad and Jeff and Andy to watch it.

At last she hauled herself back up the track to home, so tired she could almost have curled up on the tussocks. Of course Nicholas hadn't been there. She'd told him she wouldn't be back for ten days. She wondered if that was really why the mist wasn't there — not because of summer's dryness, but because he didn't expect her, wasn't there waiting for her.

The next days were too full to think too much of Nicholas, or even to spend more than ten minutes every hour admiring Snow King. There was bread to bake, kindling to chop, so many rabbits in the traps she had to spend an afternoon helping Joey skin them, and hang the skins to dry.

There was the letter to write to Andy, care of Drinkwater (they'd send the letter on), to tell him about Snow King waiting for him to train. There was so much 'now' there wasn't time to meet a ghost from the future.

There was the trip they all took to town with Mr and Mrs Mack in their cart, to get some of the ninety pounds Miss Matilda would have wired into the bank, staying overnight at a boarding house so Flinty could take out the money for the rates, buy supplies for the year ahead: sacks of flour, salt and sugar, tins of treacle, baking soda and cocoa, boxes of dried fruit, tea and soap, real soap, not home-made slush.

They ate ice cream at the café, three scoops with chocolate sauce each in a metal dish all frosted from the cold, and then another three scoops with strawberry sauce because it tasted so good.

They walked up and down the main street four times, just for the fun of seeing so many shops all together, and so many people. Kirsty commented on every woman's dress, and a car drove up the road, the horses skittering to one side, and Joey ran after it till it stopped outside the butcher's and even managed to convince the driver to show him and Kirsty how the engine worked.

There were Christmas presents to buy too, while Mr and Mrs Mack took Kirsty and Joey to eat sandwiches in the park — real *bought* presents, not home-made ones, which was good because she hadn't even had time to knit Andy a pair of socks. (She wondered briefly if the khaki ones knitted by her and Mum reminded him of the war too much, and promised herself she'd start knitting him some blue ones, even if not in time for Christmas.)

It was so good to have money for things they'd like for Christmas, not things they had to have. A jar of bullseyes (she'd have loved to buy chocolates in a silver box, but chocolate might melt on the way home), a box that played music when you opened it for Kirsty, a shotgun of his own for Joey, new boots for all of them — she wasn't having her brother and sister going barefoot to school, even if most of the other children did all through winter when the wombat droppings froze and grew white frost whiskers and the snow cloaked the mountain tops all around. A ready-made pink dress for Kirsty too, and white stockings; and a new apron with ruffles for Mrs Mack, to thank her for all her kindness, and a pipe for Mr Mack.

She would have liked to buy a present for Sandy too, to thank him for taking her on the hunt, for his help with the colt, for, well, just for being Sandy, but she was afraid that he'd think she was trying to put her socks on his feet, like the girls had giggled about when she'd been at school. When a young man wore socks you'd knitted him it meant you were engaged, or as good as.

That tradition had vanished with the war — you knitted socks then for every soldier you knew, and many you didn't, mates of Jeff's or Andy's who didn't have mothers or sisters or lovers to knit for them or make them cakes or write them letters. But a special gift for Sandy now might look like she was still making sheep's eyes at him.

In the end she decided to give the whole Mack family a giant Chinese-flowered porcelain jar of preserved ginger. Sandy loved ginger, and when the jar was empty Mrs Mack could use it as a vase.

She wished she could get Nicholas a Christmas present too. Would Nicholas spend Christmas in the mountains, or go back to his own home? She didn't even know what his home was like, she realised, only that, like Andy, it wasn't where he wanted to be now. But somehow she knew that any Christmas present to a ghost would stay here, in the past.

And then they were home: a home that smelled of cold ash in the kitchen stove, where swallows had built their nest (again!) over the front door, leaving bits of mud and grass they'd dropped all over the verandah — Dad had always laughed and said, 'Leave them to their nesting,' but it had been her and Mum who'd had to clean up the mess, and the bird droppings from the nestlings too.

She didn't bother with lighting the kitchen fire tonight. Mrs Mack had given them a big egg and bacon pie to eat for dinner, made by her daughter-in-law and almost as good as hers. At last Joey was in bed, Kirsty giving a slight snicker in her sleep. At last she could close the front door quietly behind her, run down the starlit path and up onto the Rock.

It was still mistless, still hot from the day's sun, its quartz crystals glowing slightly as if they saluted the stars. And there was still no Nicholas. The time wasn't up until the next day.

She sat with her arms around her knees, looking out at the valley, the hills and ridges dark against the spangled sky, the soft glint of the creek. Slowly her eyes adapted to the dark, and there were trees; and she grew still enough to hear the soft *whoosh* of a bat, no more than a foot away from her hair, the *boom* of a powerful owl below.

It didn't matter now if he came or not. It was just her, the valley and the stars. Then suddenly she felt the dampness of mist on her skin and heard the creak of wheels behind her. She turned.

He grinned, so obviously glad to see her that it soaked up some of the pain of Sandy's rejection. 'So, Flinty McAlpine, how did the muster go?'

She grinned back at him, feeling a gurgle of happiness spread through her. 'I made ninety pounds. And brought home the best colt I've ever seen.'

'Was there fire in the air, so that every gulp you breathed burned on the way down? Did Empress's sweat foam like the muddy froth of a flood?'

She stared at him. 'How do you know it was like that?'

'That's for you to find out.' The grin was self-satisfied now. He was enjoying this, she saw; he had been waiting for this meeting as eagerly as she had been. 'Maybe someone told me. Maybe I read it in a book. You'll know one day.'

'It wasn't really that great a ride,' she admitted. 'Not like "The Man from Snowy River".' Though the real man from Snowy River's ride hadn't been like the poem either, had it? 'Not enough to call me the girl from Snowy River.'

He was silent, as though considering what to say. 'That's not why they call you that,' he said at last.

She stared at him. 'But I thought that was what you meant ... Why else would they call me that?'

'Something happens that you don't know about yet. Something I shouldn't tell you. I can't go changing the past.'

You've already done that, she thought. If it hadn't been for him she'd never have gone brumby mustering, never claimed Snow King. 'But the past has already happened for you. So if you changed it, it's always been like that.'

'Now that makes sense, I don't think,' he said dryly. 'You know, I don't know all that much about you. Not the important things. The girl you are now, not the girl from Snowy River.'

'I was just thinking that I didn't know much about you.'

He shrugged. 'The main thing about me is this.' He gestured to his legless knees.

'No, it isn't,' she said softly.

He nodded at that. 'Maybe you're right. It was a few weeks ago. But not now. What about you, Flinty McAlpine? Are you happy? You didn't look happy when I first met you, but you do now.'

She considered that. 'Yes,' she said finally. 'I'm happy. I didn't even know till I thought about it now. After the boys enlisted we were just sort of waiting. Waiting for them to come back, for the war to end. Waiting for a telegram to say they'd been killed or injured; waiting for the lists in the newspaper. But since Jeff died, since Mum had her heart attack, since Dad got sick, well, that was just surviving. Getting through each day, doing as much as I could but knowing it was never really enough. But now ...'

'You won ninety pounds and got a horse.'

'It's not just that. It's ... it's the first thing I've ever done on my own. Not just carried on doing the things that have to be done. And it was fun,' she added honestly. 'Not having to put dinner on and make the bread, just being out there finding what was over the next ridge and the next, and the dew on my face when I woke up each morning. It was fun down in town, buying things. I even had ice cream. It's like snow but creamy and ...'

'I know what ice cream is.' He sounded amused. 'I think just about every house in Australia has ice cream in its freezer these days.'

'Every house!' It seemed impossible. She laughed. 'You've just told me about the future.'

'But not anything that affects you. You're not going to change your life because there's more ice cream in your future.'

'Well.' She tried to give the word as much importance as Mr Clancy did. 'It might if it was really good ice cream. I might change my life for really good ice cream.'

He laughed.

'What about you?' she asked. 'What has the last week been like for you?'

He remained silent for a moment. 'Better,' he said. 'I'm making friends up here. Didn't think I would,' he answered honestly. 'I just came up here, well, to escape, and this seemed the furthest I was likely to get. I thought no one up here would have time for a bloke in a wheelchair, much less a Vietnam veteran — that if a bloke couldn't ride he wouldn't be any use. But it hasn't been like that at all. You know, they even got me manning the telephone exchange three days ago, when there was a fire down the valley.'

'A bad one?' she asked anxiously.

'No. The wind changed. We got it under control by morning.' He shook his head. 'There you are. I'm saying "we" and all I did was man the exchange, relay messages from house to house.'

'You mean every house has a telephone too!'

'Most of them.'

'I've only ever seen pictures of telephones in the newspaper.' She tried to imagine a future where everyone had a telephone, even up here, and everyone had ice cream too. But Nicholas was still speaking.

'So, yes. It's been good. Getting good, at any rate. Still miss riding though. More than walking, in a way.'

'Why don't you try?' The words were out before she could stop them.

The laughter vanished. 'You know damn well why I can't.'

She'd never heard a man swear in front of a girl or woman before. 'You don't need feet to ride. Your knees work, don't they?' she added anxiously, suddenly afraid she may have underestimated his loss.

'Yes. They work.' He looked out at the valley now, not at her. She wondered if he saw the same valley she did. How would it change, in fifty years? 'I probably could ride, if it comes to that. Have to learn how to balance differently.'

He turned to her again. 'I think the real reason is that I couldn't get on a horse by myself. I'm sick of being handled like a baby. I've got some independence at last, in the chair. I'd have to be helped to ride.'

'Is that so very bad?'

'I don't know,' he said honestly. 'You've made me think, Miss Flinty McAlpine. You know, this is the first time your brother or sister hasn't called you away.'

'They're asleep.'

'And you should be too, by the look of you.'

And I've shocked him, she thought. He wanted to think about what she'd said. She hoped she hadn't hurt him. She hadn't meant to just as she hadn't meant to hurt Empress. Maybe she'd charged in here too fast and too hard too.

'You look done in. You go off to bed, Flinty McAlpine. Will you be here tomorrow?'

He looked so alone suddenly. Who could resist mist and starlight, she thought, and a ghost from the future? One who admired her, whose face lost its grimness when she arrived?

But Joey and Kirsty would wonder if she walked down to the Rock every day. She'd told them often enough not to go far by themselves. It was one of Dad's rules: if you go beyond the house paddocks there have to be two of you. That way if one of you were bitten by a snake or had a fall, the other could go for help. The only exception was if you went down the track to the valley, because someone could find you there. And anyway, there was no time for 'just a walk' these days, not with the rabbit traps to check, the firewood to gather, the winter cabbages and turnips and swedes to plant ...

But this was Nicholas, who smiled at her. Nicholas, who'd known she'd muster brumbies, but told her there was something else special to come, so special they'd call her 'the girl from Snowy River'. It was good to feel special to someone again.

'I'll come tomorrow night,' she said softly. 'It'll be late though, like tonight. Kirsty and Joey don't go to sleep till it gets dark.'

He grinned. The lonely look vanished. The man she'd met only nine days earlier wouldn't have grinned. 'Another news flash from the future. Eight o'clock isn't late at night these days. Not when you've got electric light.'

‘I’ve seen electric light,’ she told him proudly. ‘They have it down at Drinkwater Station. The generator is noisy though.’ She wrinkled her nose. ‘Electric light is too bright. It fills the whole room too, like it’s trying to take over the world.’

‘I suppose it has.’ He sounded amused, enjoying himself again.

She looked out at the valley. The half-moon had risen, sucking in the light from the nearby stars, leaving a pale grey ghost of itself around it. She glanced at Nicholas, suspecting that he saw the beauty there as well, didn’t just judge country by how many sheep it could run.

He was hers, just like Snow King. She’d be here the next night and the one after.

Chapter 16

23 December 1919

Dear Diary,

Nicholas told me about the horse he used to ride: Nightingale, 15.2 hands. He's agisted on the farm near where his family used to live. I nearly suggested that he bring him here, but I suppose having him close and not being able to ride would be worse than not seeing him. He said he missed his dogs too — a poodle and a Great Dane that Nicholas says is almost the same size as Empress, which I don't believe. But he can't have them here in case they chase the sheep, and anyway, they are his parents' dogs as well as his.

I told him about old Shep dying, and how we'll get another dog or even two when Andy gets back, and about, oh, all sorts of things, how Amy used to pinch me to make me give her the answers at school, and Mum growing up in the orphanage till she was sent as a servant out here, and even the box of chocolates that Sandy posted me from Sydney before they sailed. I've still got the box, and the wrappers, and even one of the chocolates — I didn't want to eat every one as they were my last link to Sandy. It's still in its gold wrapper. Probably bad by now.

I asked him straight out if he knew why Sandy came back so changed. He thought for a bit, then said, 'No,' quite honestly, not like he did know but wouldn't tell me.

I've met him every night for three weeks now. It's so good having someone to talk to properly, though Sandy and Johnno have been up, to bring us a forequarter of mutton and take back Joey's rabbit skins, and to tell us that Mr Mack will bring the cart up to take us down there for the Christmas service and for Christmas dinner.

The White boys called in too. They left some lamb chops which I know weren't theirs, because they don't have any sheep, just the cattle that straggle all over the place. But it was still kind of them. They helped stack up the woodpile as well.

No letter from Andy, not even a Christmas card, but he probably isn't anywhere you can post a letter, or even get mail.

Christmas beetles clattered on the roof. The black cockatoos arrived, as they did every Christmas, screeching and whirling giant wings against the sky. The sun shone straight and clear above Rock Farm, as though to say, 'Here I am, at the highest point of my year's journey.'

It was a good Christmas Day, better than the last: Andy still not home, even though they'd so hoped his ship would be back in time; Dad grieving, the absence of Mum and Jeff so deep that their empty places seemed more vivid than the chairs that were filled, all of them pretending a happiness that wasn't there.

Christmas 1917 had been even worse, Dad saying carefully Flinty's roasted rooster was 'the best he'd ever eaten', trying not to so much as mention Mum's name, all of them worried that another telegram might arrive, this time with Andy's name, wondering what the valley boys faced in France and Flanders.

The week before this Christmas Day Joey cut down a small she-oak from the gully for a Christmas tree. They decorated it with the cotton-wool snow and crepe-paper streamers kept in the box at the top of the linen cupboard, and made toffee to take down to the Macks' for Christmas dinner.

Mr Mack drove the cart up to fetch the three of them on Christmas morning — Empress wasn't up to carrying all of them on her back these days, though her leg was very much better.

The Macks loved their ginger. Mrs Mack exclaimed over the porcelain pot and Sandy said, 'Ginger. Good.' Flinty'd had a faint hope that Sandy might give her a present, one of her very own.

But instead, of course, there was just a present for each of them from all the Macks: a plaited stockwhip for Joey, coloured pencils in a wooden box for Kirsty and a handmade book for Flinty, all Mrs Mack's knowledge carefully written out in her laborious copperplate, learned long ago at school and rarely used. The lamington squares recipe Mrs Mack had found in a newspaper; instructions for jam drops, and lamb's fry and onions, and how to get candle-wax stains off a silk dress and make mock chicken from cold mutton.

It was a gift Mum might have given her, probably would have given her, to go in her glory box along with the embroidered tea towels and tray cloths that every girl slowly made and collected from the time she began to think of a home of her own.

Flinty hadn't added to her glory box since Mum's death. There was too much work keeping one house to think of another. She supposed, in some quiet corner of her mind, that she'd have to marry someone — everyone got married, except for a few maiden aunts, or drunks like Dusty Jim, though even he might have had a wife sometime, somewhere.

But sixty thousand Australian men had died in the four years of war, and more than twice that number would never quite recover from their wounds. How many young women would never marry now? She didn't want to think about it. Didn't want to think about marriage at all.

The dining-room table was so crowded that Mrs Mack had to put planking over it and cover it with two cloths, to fit them all around it. Two giant boiled puddings, and custard and brandy sauce, half a dozen cold roast roosters with hot gravy, because there was too much food today to fit in her oven and her daughter-in-law's; dishes of roast potatoes and pumpkin, parsnips and the last of the spring peas; boiled beetroot in butter and boiled carrots with mint; a massive trifle that had been cooling in the stone dairy since the day before, with sponge cake and bottled peaches from last season, and even more custard; and mince pies and shortbread. Later there was a singsong while Toby played his accordion, especially loud as though to hide the loss of Valma's voice, of Jeff's and Rick's and Andy's, and Mum's and Dad's. Sandy and Kirsty played knucklebones out on the verandah and Kirsty won three times — or Sandy let her.

Mr Mack drove them back in the cart, so drowsy from three helpings of pudding and the rum he'd been slipping into his teacup all afternoon that old Sally had to find the way up herself, which she did from long practice.

Joey and Kirsty went straight to bed — they'd been up since before dawn, discovering the oranges and new pencils Santa Claus had left in their stockings.

Flinty was tired too. Yes, it had been a good Christmas — not a wonderful one, not with Sandy still carefully not looking at her all through dinner — but a taste of happiness, at last, and a promise of more.

Although there were still things to do, even on Christmas night: checking Snow King and Empress in their paddock, adding wood to the firebox so there'd be coals for the next day's breakfast, mixing up a batch of bread to rise overnight. She'd told Nicholas she wouldn't be on the Rock tonight, that she didn't know what time they'd get back from the Macks'. She'd told him 'merry Christmas' the day before, wishing yet again you could give a ghost a present, hoping that his Christmas Day would be good with the people he was staying with (and still wouldn't name).

She wished she hadn't now. Kneading bread dough seemed an anticlimax after the celebration of the day.

It was dark by the time she'd finished mixing the bread. The moon rose out the window, fat as Mrs Mack's plum pudding, gold as the Christmas angel on her tree. And suddenly the house, which had seemed so full of Christmas happiness, was empty. The ghosts of those who weren't there, who would never be there again, seemed once again more real than the brother and sister sleeping in their beds.

She was tired, that was all, especially after so many late nights the last three weeks. She should go to bed herself. Instead she went out to the verandah and sat down on the big bush settler's chair Dad had made from snow-gum branches. Maybe if she shut her eyes she could pretend that he sat in the other chair, that Mum was just in the kitchen, that Jeff and Andy were playing knucklebones by the door, each shouting that the other was a dunce.

Instead she watched the moon float up the sky, its light shining on the mist about the Rock.

And she knew what you could give a ghost for Christmas.

'I brought you some toffee.'

He was there, even though she'd said she couldn't meet him, sitting in his chair in almost the same position as when she'd first seen him. He wheeled around as she approached. She loved the smile that lit his face; loved the fact that she could make him smile. Sandy hadn't smiled when she'd come into the Macks' this morning, just said, 'Merry Christmas.'

'I didn't think you'd be here,' she added.

'I'm here most of the time, these days. Got not much else to do. Unless there's another bushfire, I suppose.' There was no self-pity in his voice, just a statement of fact.

She looked at him, suddenly appalled at so empty a life when her month had been so full. 'Didn't your parents expect you to go home at Christmas?'

'No.' The word had walls around it.

'You just sit here? Even on Christmas Day?'

He smiled at that. 'It's not that bad. The people I'm staying with insisted I have Christmas dinner with them.'

'Who *are* you staying with?' Surely Dusty Jim's hut would have fallen down in fifty years — a high wind blew off the sheets of bark that made the roof even now, despite their being weighted down with big stones. 'It can't change the future to tell me just that! Do you live in our place — Andy's place, I mean?' It hurt a bit to think that sometime in the future she'd have to move from Rock Farm to her own home, leaving it to Andy and his family. But if Nicholas was staying with them it might explain how he knew so much about her.

He looked at her assessingly. 'No. Not Andy's place.'

'In a new house?'

Nicholas grinned, as though it was a game. 'Nope. A very old one. But there are more houses in the valley than in your time. I can see their lights from up here sometimes.'

'What do the people you're staying with think about your coming here so much?'

'They told me about you, remember. About the ghost of young Flinty McAlpine, here on the Rock. I have a good excuse to sit down here too. I'm writing a book and the words come better with all this around me. Mornings are best.' He grinned again. 'Even on Christmas Day. I don't try to write by moonlight, but it's still good to sit here. Besides, I hoped you might get down here tonight despite being so busy. And you have.'

'You're really writing a book?' She'd never met anyone who'd written a book before. Dad had told stories and they had books at the house, of course, two shelves full of books on horses as well as books like *Kidnapped* and *Rob Roy*, *Jane Eyre* and all of Jane Austen's books, and Rudyard Kipling, who Dad loved and who spoke to him of the Empire he'd been part of once. Even the Macks had the Bible and Shakespeare. People she knew might read books. But they didn't write them. 'What's your book about?'

'A war,' he said slowly. 'Not the war I was in. Not your war either,' he added. 'It's an imaginary war, set in the future. Science fiction.'

'So it's a science book?'

'No. A story. I s'pose it is a true story, in a way. I'd feel like I was dobbing on my mates, if I put about what happened to us back then in a book. But this way, well, maybe some parts of war don't ever change. Not fifty years ago in your Great War, or maybe a hundred years in the future. Don't know if it'll ever get into print,' he added. 'I've had some stories published, but not a book.'

She sat on the Rock next to him, her arms around her legs, fascinated. 'How do you get published?'

'Send it to a publishing company and cross my fingers. Why did you bring toffee?'

'It's Christmas.'

'I'm sorry, I should have brought you something too. Except I didn't know you'd be here tonight. And anyway, I think anything we give each other might vanish when we leave the Rock.'

'You can eat toffee here.'

'Good idea.' He smiled at her again. It seemed easier for him to smile today. She thought that whatever he'd been doing in the past month had been good for him. She handed him the toffee, watched him bite a bit, then make a face when it stuck his teeth together. He extracted it carefully and stared at it. 'It's good,' he said. 'Just, er ...'

'Sticky.'

He broke off a smaller bit and began to suck it. 'So how was your Christmas?'

'Good.'

'Except for ...? There's an "except" in your voice there, somewhere.'

'Except for Sandy,' she said slowly. She had told him about Sandy — a bit, at any rate: that she'd loved him, thought he'd loved her, that he'd been changed by the war. She tried to smile. 'Mrs Mack even had us sitting next to each other, but he changed places with Johnno.'

'Don't break your heart,' he said softly. 'You're a beautiful girl, Flinty.' He laughed at the shock on her face. 'Hasn't anyone told you that before?'

She shook her head. 'Only Mum. Mums don't count.'

'Well, you are.'

She felt her face grow hot.

'Surely there must be other young men around here who appreciate a lovely young woman?'

She thought of the White boys, Ron Mullins, even Toby Mack, and laughed. 'Not that I'd think of marrying.'

'Girls marry young in your time, don't they?'

It was a shock to remember how much separated them. 'Maybe. Mum was seventeen when she married Dad. Is that young in your time?'

He nodded. 'Girls are about twenty-one or twenty-two now, before they get engaged. Blokes are a bit older.'

'What about you?' she ventured. She had wanted to ask him before, but never had the courage. 'Is there — was there — anyone special for you?'

'Glenys.' For a moment she thought he was only going to say the name, and then he said, 'I gave her a friendship ring before I left. We talked about getting engaged when I came back. She decided she wanted a husband with legs intact.'

'I'm sorry.' The words seemed so little to offer.

'I'm not. Who wants a wife who doesn't have the guts to take a man as he is, wheelchair and all?' She saw his smile in the moonlight. 'You know, I've never realised that before. I tried to make excuses for her. But if it had been her who'd lost her legs, I'd have stuck with her. Still loved her. And you'd do the same, Miss Flinty McAlpine.'

'How do you know?'

'Because you look a legless man in the face, instead of staring at where his legs used to be.'

They were both silent, and then he said, 'Someone will come along for you.'

She tried to keep her voice light. 'I know. You told me I'd have children, the day we first met. I'm not the sort to have children without a ring on my finger.'

'Ah, that was a slip. Never mind. You were always bound to get married, a girl like you.'

She looked at him. Was he implying she *wouldn't* marry Sandy? Or just trying to cheer her up on Christmas night?

'Merry Christmas, Flinty McAlpine,' he said softly. 'May every Christmas to come be better than the last.'

'And yours too,' she said.

Chapter 17

January 1920

Dear Sis,

It is grand about the money and the horse. Well done, you. I'm glad the brats can go to school again. That colt will keep you out of mischief, eh?

I'm writing this from Brisbane. It's a funny place, hot enough to fry an egg on every roof and steamy as a shearing shed. The mosquitoes are the size of cricket balls, no joking. Anyhow, this is just to tell you that I met a good bloke who's looking for help to take some cattle out past the Darling Downs. They say it's grand country there, a stick will grow as soon as you put it in the ground. I'd like to see that. After that I might head up north a way too. It'd be a pity not to see more when I've come all this way, and now I know you and the brats are all right without me. I'll still wire half my wages back as soon as I'm cashed up and near a post office. Post offices might be a bit thin on the ground again for a while, so don't worry if you don't hear from me for a month or two.

Well done again on the brumby running. I'd have liked to have seen it.

Your loving brother,
Andy

She sat with the letter in her hand. Outside Joey and Kirsty dug potatoes, having a competition to see who could dig up the biggest. They both insisted on bare feet, so they didn't spoil their new boots before school started. Flinty hoped they didn't put the potato fork into their toes ...

She looked at the letter again. She wanted to feel angry. She'd waited for Andy to come home for nearly three months after Dad had died and within a month he'd been off again, leaving it all to her once more. This was his home! He owned it. The farm was his responsibility — and his brother and sisters were too.

But all she felt was — empty. She understood now that she never *would* understand. Nicholas had shown her that war was too big to understand unless you'd been there. War had sent Andy off with cattle now as surely as it had sent him to the trenches.

And, once again, all she could do was wait.

She wanted to cry too. But if she cried Joey and Kirsty would worry, think she couldn't cope. It was important for them to feel she could manage, that no matter what she'd always look after them.

But she could cry with the ghost, tonight.

She told Joey and Kirsty to put themselves into bed. She was going to sit on the Rock to watch the sunset, just like Dad and

Mum had done sometimes, dangling their legs over the edge as the sky turned the sifting mist red then pink then grey. 'Up here I own the sunset,' Dad used to say. 'Just me and your mum and no one else to share it.'

She had the letter in the pocket of Dad's cut-down trousers. She almost ran down the track, into the mist, then stopped.

He wasn't there.

Had something happened to him? She suddenly realised that if Nicholas ever stopped coming to the Rock she might never know why, or at least not for fifty years. Nicholas could find out what she had done, back in the past, but she could never know about the future, except by living it.

But she was panicking for nothing. He was expecting her later, when it was getting dark. Even if he sat here most of the day writing, he must go back for his tea, at least.

She sat on the Rock, her legs dangling from its bulk. The sun was behind the ridge now, the full glory of the sky above it seeming so close she could almost touch it. There was yellow too — was there yellow in every sunset, or had she just seen it now? The red faded to orange before it became pink, and there was a moment, almost too fast to see, when the cliffs turned red too, even the tree leaves flashed scarlet. Then, all at once, the sky had faded, like an old dress in the wash, and you wondered if it ever had been as bright, as wonderful ...

'I never get tired of it,' he said.

She turned as he rolled up out of the mist, his hands expert on the chair's wheels. 'Of the sunset?'

Nicholas nodded. He manoeuvred his chair closer. 'What's wrong?'

She handed him the letter. He read it, then looked down at her.

'What do you think?' she asked.

'Are you asking if he's a selfish so-and-so who leaves his sister in the lurch, or a man who's driven by his ghosts? Not ghosts like me,' he added. 'The ones in his memory. The ones you think you can leave behind if you run far enough.'

'Can you?'

'Yes. Being somewhere new you have to make new memories instead of always living with the old ones — it helps.'

'You didn't leave anyone did you, to come up here?'

'My parents. I ring them every Sunday night. I've hurt them, staying here.' He spoke as if he had just realised that fact.

'But they don't *need* you.'

'You're coping,' he said gently. 'Aren't you?'

'I ... I suppose so.'

'You're more than coping. Andy's right. Your brother and sister are happy and well cared for. You've got money in the bank and a grand colt in the paddock. So he thinks he can take another few months for himself, after what? Four years of war. Is it so very bad?'

'No,' she admitted.

'Responsibility,' he said. 'That's what he's landed you with. That's what you've been stuck with the last two and a half years. But you *have* managed, Flinty. Managed brilliantly. And if you really needed him, he'd be back again. That's what he's saying in this letter too.'

She was silent. She'd wanted him to be angry for her, be indignant that a brother could just ride off like that, even maybe to give her a story of something horrible that happened in war, like the newspaper stories of the Huns bayoneting babies, to show that Andy was wounded in his mind just as badly as Nicholas was wounded in his legs, except with Andy it didn't show.

Instead he'd told her that she'd read the letter wrongly. Andy was praising her, not abandoning them. And Nicholas was right. It did sort of say that if they'd needed him he'd have come back.

'I thought he'd want to train Snow King,' she whispered.

'Did you say so?'

'No. Just that he's here.'

'Then that's a compliment too,' he said gently. 'Snow King is your horse. Your brother thinks that you can break him in. Can you?'

'I don't know,' she said honestly. 'I've helped break in horses before. But none of them had Snow King's promise.'

'Anyone you can ask for advice?'

'Of course. Mr Mack, any of the Colours, though none of them are horsemen like Dad. I could probably write to Mr Clancy. They'd send the letter on from Drinkwater.'

'Clancy of The Overflow?' He gave another grin she didn't quite understand. 'Who better? There you are then.'

She put the letter back in her pocket. She'd thought she wanted to cry with him. Instead she felt touched by the sunset's gold. Sort of glowing. 'Thank you,' she said.

Chapter 18

2 February 1920

Dear Diary,

Nicholas brought me chocolate today! Real chocolate! Mum used to make chocolate fudge with cocoa, but it isn't the same.

It wasn't a box of chocolates, but a big fat block. I wondered if I could share it with Joey and Kirsty. Nicholas said, 'Try.'

I stepped off the Rock and out of the mist with the chocolate in my hand and suddenly it wasn't there. I think it felt stranger than even the first time I met Nicholas — the second time, I mean, when he said he was from 1969.

I also felt really stupid, because I'd lost a whole block of chocolate. I stepped back into the mist and there it was, just lying on the Rock.

'It dropped out of your hand,' said Nicholas. He looked shocked too.

I picked it up again, and we shared it. I felt guilty that the others couldn't have some, but even if I had been able to take it away I'd have had to explain to Kirsty and Joey how a block of chocolate suddenly appeared. I suppose I could've said I'd hidden it on top of the linen cupboard. That's where Mum used to hide our presents — where I hide them still. We all know we're not supposed to look closely at anything up there.

The chocolate was delicious, with dried fruit and nuts in it. I don't think you can buy blocks like that these days, but I've never been in a sweet shop so I don't know.

I felt disloyal to Sandy, somehow, accepting chocolate from another man. But he doesn't want to eat chocolate with me, and anyway, it wasn't a romantic box of chocolates, it was just a gift for a friend.

Nicholas told me that in his time women wear trousers even to church! But they are pretty trousers, in bright colours, like the shirts he wears. It's so funny to see a man in bright colours. Sandy wouldn't be seen dead in one of those psychedelic shirts. Nicholas is growing a beard too. I told him he looked like a swaggie, but he just laughed.

Ten eggs today. Fixed the netting so the goanna can't steal any more. The Bath apples are ripe. They're not good keepers, so I gave Joey a bag to drop in to the Macks on the way to school. He says Sandy is back from the sheep sales. I thought maybe he might look at farms to buy too, but Joey says Sandy didn't say anything about that. He asked Mrs Mack if they had any new stamps, because he's started collecting them again so that he can sell his collection one day, and she said they hadn't, so that means that Sandy isn't getting letters from anyone. So if he did meet someone they still aren't writing to each other.

'Good boy, King. That's a fine boy. Good boy now.' The colt looked at her assessingly, as though he knew exactly what she was trying to do, leading him round and round the paddock, the saddle on his back.

Dad would have ridden him by now, in the round horse yard, where Snow King would only have been able to circle endlessly and, if he was so inclined, to buck. But if a horse wanted to buck you off then you hadn't made friends with him, Dad had said. It was your own fault if you had a tumble.

Better to go slowly. There was no hurry. Snow King couldn't be hard trained for racing until he was a two-year-old. She reckoned he was only a year and a half. Nor did she have any idea how to enter a horse in a race, much less ride one to win. Only boys and men could be jockeys, though some races had special events for women — but not 'real' races, and not on potential champions like Snow King.

Flinty knew enough to realise it was going to be difficult even to register Snow King in the Stud Book. She'd have to hope that Miss Matilda would state that Repentance was his sire, and old Regret his great-grandmother, for him to have a chance to be considered. He'd have to show his form in picnic races too, before any racing trainer might take him on.

Horses that weren't Stud Book horses might win races, sometimes big races, but not often. Even if Snow King raced as brilliantly as she hoped, the stud fee would be low unless she could show he came from a line of champions and wasn't just one amazing horse.

She hoped Andy would be back before it was time to try to convince a trainer to give Snow King a chance, to give the young horse the best possible start in racing and a proper track to train on. It would be hard enough to get a trainer to take on an ex-brumby. It would probably be impossible to find one who'd take a girl seriously.

Meanwhile the school term had begun. Her days had another pattern now: waking before rooster crow to dress a sleepy Kirsty and a reluctant Joey, saddling Empress for their journey down the mountain to the Macks' so that Mr Mack could take them and the oldest two Mack grandchildren the next five miles down the valley to the one-room school.

These days she did the chores herself, with just the kookaburras for company, collecting the eggs and feeding the hens, weeding the vegetables, putting a stew on for dinner and, if she was lucky, a few hours like this with Snow King, before Empress ambled up, slightly faster than she'd gone down, eager for her hay and oats. Joey and Kirsty would be starving, sliding off Empress's back to run through the kitchen like a plague of grasshoppers, as Mum used to say, eating everything in their path.

She'd make scones today, she decided, two tins of them so Joey and Kirsty wouldn't eat the table legs. Or maybe pikelets. Mrs Mack had sent up a crock of butter two days earlier. She remembered Sandy saying how he'd thought of Mrs Mack's pikelets in France. Well, she could make good pikelets too, and there was the raspberry jam she'd made to go with them, the fruit from the thicket beyond the potato patch. She could just about murder a plate of pikelets herself now. Somehow she'd forgotten to have lunch.

'Come on, boy. Training's over.' She led Snow King into the pen at the end of the stables. The colt whinnied, lifting his head and rearing a little. Just to show me he's still King, she thought, doing what I want but only because he agrees to do it. She unbuckled the girth, pulled off the blanket and saddle, then opened the yard into the next paddock. The young horse made no move to go into it. Instead he stared at her, and pawed the ground.

She laughed. 'No, I didn't forget.' She bent and took the apple from the rock where she'd left it. The Bath apples were crisp when you first harvested them, but soft as snow after two days, not like the hard-fleshed apples of autumn. She held the fruit out on the palm of her hand, felt his warm breath as he took it, the whisper of his lips. He crunched it, grinning at its sweetness, then turned abruptly, swung his head down and cantered out into the paddock, out across the hill as though happy to pit his muscles against its steepness.

Oh yes, thought Flinty. You'll be a racer.

She glanced up towards the sun. Dad had shown her the old soldier's trick of telling the time, holding up her fist outstretched; if the sun had moved two fists, three hours had passed. Another hour perhaps till Empress plodded back up the hill.

Which meant she had time to meet Nicholas at the Rock and still make the pikelets. He was still there every day, writing in a spiral-bound notebook. Most weekdays she managed to get down to see him, during daylight now, guilty at the time 'wasted' away from chores, guiltier still when Mrs Mack patted her sympathetically and said how lonely it must be for her, all alone up there every day.

But she wasn't alone. She had her horse, and she had her ghost.

She ran inside to check her hair was neat and that there were no smudges on her face. Somehow, lately, it had become important to look nice for Nicholas. She could even put on a dress ...

She bit her lip, still watching her face in the mirror. Dresses were for going to church on Sundays or dances.

She looked out the window. Down past the mountains there were women who wore dresses every day of their lives, not men's trousers cut down to size and boots. They wore silk and lace, in the colours Kirsty loved, bright pinks and pastel blues, frills and lace and kid slippers.

Flinty wasn't sure what a kid slipper was, but she'd read about girls wearing them to balls. Kirsty probably knew already, even though she was only eight years old. Kirsty dreamed of going to a ball, of petticoats that rustled as you swept across the polished floor.

Flinty suspected that when Kirsty grew up she'd marry a man who'd take her away from the mountains, to a house with a skivvy to scrub the floor and sweep the stairs and fold the washing, where you didn't step out into slush up to your ankles every time the snow melted. Someone like Walter Green, who'd come back from the war and taken up an apprenticeship at the dockyards in Sydney.

But not her. She loved the mountains like Dad had loved them at first sight. He'd been going to buy a farm down on the flats and had just come up here because the doctor said it would be good for his health, after the fever in India.

Before the war it had never occurred to her that someone might know the mountains but choose to live somewhere else.

Mum's clock chimed two in the parlour. She gave her hair a final pat and ran out the door.

Nicholas was there, as he always was, sitting in his chair, his notebook in his lap. This time, though, something else lay next to the notebook. Roses.

She caught her breath at the sight of them. 'Hello.'

He smiled. 'Hello yourself.' He held the bunch of roses out to her. They were pink, with long straight stems that looked like they'd learned to stand to attention, not the white floppy roses or the little red ramblers that sprawled over the front fences in the valley, cuttings passed from woman to woman. She noticed a fragrance wafting up, put her nose down and sniffed.

'Oh,' she said. It was the first time anyone had ever given her flowers.

It was hard to interpret his look. 'I know they'll vanish when you leave the Rock. But I thought you might like them now.'

She lifted her head from the flowers. 'I've read about rose perfume in books. I thought maybe it was just made to smell like roses looked. I didn't realise that roses themselves could have a scent.'

'A lot of them do, I think. Not that I know much about roses. Picked them this morning,' he said. 'There's a bush by the front door. The old lady where I'm staying said you'd like them.'

'I love them.' She sniffed again, felt the softness of the petals on her cheeks. Heroines in books had lips like roses. She'd thought that meant red or white, but maybe it meant pink like these.

'Flinty ...'

Something in his voice made her look up at him. 'What's wrong?'

'I have to go away for a while.'

'What! Why?'

'I'm going to be fitted for new legs.'

'Wooden legs?' Peg legs, they were called in books. Sailors had peg legs, or an arm that ended in a hook where they'd lost a hand. She remembered he'd told her that false legs were different now.

'Not wooden ones these days. They'll be metal. They'll even bend at the ankle.'

'But that won't take long, will it?' she asked anxiously. 'Just a few days?'

'It isn't as simple as that. The legs have to be fitted specially. Then I have to learn to walk on them. It'll take many months, Flinty.'

Months! Empty months, scrubbing the kitchen floor, kneading bread, checking fences, Joey and Kirsty too tired to talk much when they got home from school, and anyway, they weren't like Nicholas. No one was like Nicholas. No one else understood.

'Why didn't you tell me before?' she whispered.

'I thought it wasn't going to happen for ages yet. But they had a cancellation. I got a letter this morning.'

'But you don't *have* to go now.'

'No,' he said steadily. 'I don't. But I want to walk again, Flinty. I need to. I didn't feel that a few months ago. But now I do. It's time for me to be part of the world again.'

'Yes. Of course.' She'd been thinking only of herself. Just like I did with Andy, she thought. And then: I'm selfish.

And what had she been dreaming of? That maybe one day she could push Nicholas's chair out of the mist and he could exist in her time? That she could take him up to the house and fix up hoists so he could lift himself, just like he said he'd done in his own time? That one day, somehow, he might be able to leave wheel tracks — or even footsteps — in the mud on the track?

Maybe it was best Nicholas was leaving for a while, she thought, before I live too much with ghosts and dreams.

He was still looking at her. Somehow he seemed far away already.

'Dad said that the mountains healed him.'

'Maybe they've healed me a bit then. Maybe you've healed me too, and the people here. I think, sometimes, when things are bad, you feel like you are the only person in the world. You shut out everything else because your pain is all that you can deal with. But then I met you. Suddenly I wasn't unique any more. Your brothers, the boys you knew ... they faced stuff like I did, or even worse. Some of them couldn't take it, but some did. And not just men,' he added quietly. 'Girls like you. Women like you. You kept going, Flinty McAlpine. And suddenly I wanted to keep going, get on with my life too.'

She tried to smile. 'You'll be walking next time I see you then. I ... I will see you again, won't I? You will come back?'

'Yes. I'll come back. I want to see you again. I love these mountains too.' He hesitated again, as though trying to find the words too hard to speak. She could see pain wrinkles around his eyes. Her breath caught in her throat. 'Flinty, I have to tell you something. I wish more than anything in my life I didn't have to tell you this. I can't even tell you everything, because if I do it mightn't happen, and it *did* happen.'

'I don't understand,' she whispered. It's all impossible anyway, she thought. Impossible to meet a ghost from another time. Even the war had been impossible. A whole generation of men couldn't just march away with bagpipes playing and children laughing, and a third of them never come home again. It was impossible that Dad could die, that she'd never see his grin again. Impossible that Mum had gone. Mum was always there — always.

Impossibles happened all the time.

'Flinty, dear Flinty. Something bad is going to happen to you. Very bad.'

'What sort of bad?' Her whisper was like the rasp of wind on the Rock. Surely the bad had already happened. How much more bad could there be? Mum, Dad and Jeff gone ...

'Joey and Kirsty,' she said in sudden terror. 'They're not going to be hurt too?' Her lips couldn't form the word 'dead'.

'No. Well, things will be hard for them for a while, but they aren't going to be hurt. They're going to grow up strong and happy.'

'Andy? Sandy? The Macks?'

'No. Your Andy is going to be all right,' he added gently. 'That will all work out too.'

'Then it doesn't matter. Nothing matters if they're all right.'

'This will matter. But I can't tell you more about it. If I did then you might do something to stop it happening.'

'You *want* me to go through something bad?'

'Of course I don't! That isn't even what I need to tell. What I have to tell you is this.' He took a breath, then took her hand in his. It was such a warm hand, for a ghost. 'Please, please remember this, Flinty. It's all I can give you. No matter how bad things seem — and they might seem impossible to face at times — it all works out in the end. You have to go through the bad bits to get to the good. But I promise, Flinty, it all works out.'

'Will you be here when the bad thing happens?' She hated how small her voice sounded.

'No. I wish I could be. You have no idea how much I wish that. But I can't be, because I *wasn't*. Do you see that? And even if I could be here, I couldn't help you.'

'Your just being here would help,' she whispered. 'Just being able to talk to you.'

'No,' he said gently. 'You'll understand why when it happens. I'm sorry. Flinty, you don't know how sorry I am. Truly. I can't say more.'

'I ... I sort of *do* understand.' She hesitated, looking down at the bunch of roses. 'I just ... don't want to. And you *should* go, I'd hate it if you didn't get your legs. It's just —' Like he'd told her a black cloud hovered behind the ridges, she thought, but wouldn't tell her what the storm would bring.

'I promise I couldn't help. Even my being here wouldn't help.'

She knew this time there was no point coaxing him, trying to get him to say more than he meant to. Didn't he realise that just knowing he was down here on the Rock — a friend, who smiled when he saw her, who thought she was beautiful — helped more than she could express?

But if she told him that he might stay. Might lose his chance to get new legs, or at least the life that they might lead him to. If only he would tell her more.

Men and their mysteries, she thought. Do all men have a world they can step into where women can't follow? All we can do is wait and see what happens next.

Nicholas sat, silent, staring out across the valley. A rainstorm was sweeping across the far ridges, a sunlit wall of white. She doubted the sun shower would reach up here though.

'I'm going to miss this so much,' he said at last. 'Have you noticed how every tree is different here? All twisted by the wind and snow, but if that was all, they should have been twisted in the same way. It's as though every tree has made up its own mind exactly how it wants to look. Flinty, may I tell you about how I lost my legs?'

Her mind felt buffeted: too much to take in. 'You already did.'

'No, I didn't. I told you what I told Mum and Dad and everyone else who wanted to know. I didn't tell the truth.'

'Why not?'

He faced the valley, not her. A wind slapped them suddenly, the snow wind that Dad said hid around the hill, then jumped out at you when you weren't looking; it pushed the sun shower further away from them. The wind tasted sharp, like tin, carrying the scents of far-off Kosciuszko. 'Because it hurts to remember. Because they love me and it would hurt them to know.'

'Then why are you telling me now? Are you trying to hurt me?'

'No. Flinty, I'd do anything I could to stop you being hurt. No, that's not true. I could tell you to go away — today, tomorrow. Take Joey and Kirsty and stay in town till winter.'

'The bad thing wouldn't happen if I did that?'

'I don't know,' he said honestly. 'Maybe something even worse would happen. What I'm trying to say is, there're bad things going to come, but good things too. Very, very good. If I stop you experiencing the bad you mightn't have the good too. Trust me, Flinty — the good is really good.'

'Tell me about how you lost your legs,' she said softly.

He nodded, his face expressionless, his hands flat on his knees as though to keep them still. 'I told you it was at Long Tan.'

She nodded, though the unfamiliar name had slipped her mind.

'It wasn't.'

'Then why did you say it was?'

He shrugged. 'Because we won that day, maybe. It was something to feel good about.'

'Then what did happen?' She spoke quietly, partly because his voice had grown so soft, partly because it felt like a loud noise would shatter whatever connection held them together.

'It was a couple of weeks later. A routine patrol ... We were walking through a village and suddenly something bounced out of a door. For a moment I thought it was a kid's ball. My mate Sam was walking next to me. He was quicker than me. He picked it up and threw it back, just as it exploded.' The wind muttered around the Rock as he added, 'He saved my life.'

'It was a bomb?'

'A hand grenade. A kind of bomb. I threw myself down and began to roll as soon as he reached for it. Saw someone in the doorway, managed to fire. Got him, saw him fall. Then I thought it had got cold. It's never cold in Vietnam. It was so cold it was hard to breathe. There was a pain in my chest — not in my legs; I told you the truth about that. They didn't hurt till much, much later, days after I woke up from what was probably the second, maybe the third operation.

'Anyway, I lay there, trying to get my breath. I tried to get up but nothing seemed to work, and then I thought about the person in the doorway, the Vietcong. I managed to push myself up onto my elbows again just as he looked back at me. I shot him again and this time I killed him, shot him right in the face ...'

He gripped the arms of the bathchair now. She put her hand on his, feeling its warmth, despite the fifty years between them, even though he was shivering, just as she supposed he had back then.

'So you stopped him killing anyone else.'

'He was ten years old. Maybe twelve. You said your brother was twelve.'

Joey's age! 'You shot a boy like Joey?' Shock bit like a dingo with a lamb. 'But he tried to kill you ...'

'I never knew. Maybe he was the one who threw the hand grenade. Maybe he was just there, inside the house. I never will know now.'

'And Sam? Your friend who saved you?'

'Sam was a spray of bones and guts all over me, all over the dust in the village. And that is how I lost my legs, Flinty McAlpine. Lost a lot more that day, and not just a mate. And until I came here I thought I'd never get it back.'

She didn't know what to say. Didn't know what to feel either. At last she said, 'Were children fighting the war in your time?'

'Yes.' He shrugged. 'We were in their country. If an enemy invaded your mountains, Flinty McAlpine, would you fight them? Would you let your brother fight?'

'Yes,' she said. Of course she and Joey would fight to keep these hills.

'Well, there you are then. Maybe he tried to kill me. Maybe he was one of the kids I was trying to protect. Like I said, I'll never know. Maybe ... maybe in some way I thought, the kid and Sam had lost their lives, so I lost my legs, sort of like a payment. Then I came here and I learned something. Flinty, promise me you'll do one thing. I don't know if it'll change the past or not, but I want you to do it.'

'All right.' The words were automatic. She was beyond thinking now. 'I'll do whatever you ask me to.'

'I want you to write to your brother and tell him that life goes on, that there's only one thing we can do for someone who's died — even thousands of someones — and that is to keep on going. Life should be good — life should be very, very good —

and the only duty we have to the dead is to make it good, for ourselves and other people. Will you do that for me? Please?'

'Yes.'

'Will you remember it yourself? If ... when ... the something bad happens, will you remember it too? Promise me the two things, Flinty.' He took her hand and held it in both of his.

She looked down at the roses, the precious first flowers that would vanish as soon as she took a step away from the Rock. 'I promise,' she said.

Chapter 19

3 March 1920

Dear Diary,

A letter came for Jeff today. I don't think he ever got a letter before. I didn't want to open it, but Joey and Kirsty stood there waiting, so I did. It seemed wrong to open something of Jeff's, even though he is dead.

At first I thought I just couldn't understand the handwriting, but then I realised it was scribble, not proper writing. I showed it to Joey and Kirsty. Joey finally worked out a couple of words that made sense. There was 'Jeff' and 'mate', and 'Morris' or maybe 'Boris', which was part of the signature. Joey said he thought he could make out my name — Felicity, not Flinty — near the start of the letter, but I couldn't see it.

I cried after Joey and Kirsty went to bed. I think the letter made me realise that Jeff really will never come home. Maybe none of us quite accepted it, except Mum. It would be different if we could have had a proper funeral, not just a memorial service, given him a grave down in the valley in the churchyard, with his stockwhip and hat on the coffin just like they did when Granddad Mack died.

It was so strange getting a letter so long after Jeff has died, even stranger getting one that didn't make sense. The address had been written by someone else, I think, not the person who wrote the letter, because it was clear as anything, but there was no return address, so I can't write back and explain about Jeff, or ask what the writer wanted.

The mist came right up around the house tonight. I wish I could have shown Nicholas the letter. I hope things are going well with his new legs. I hope that he is happy, and has made new friends. I heard the powerful owl call tonight, up past the horse paddocks, the first time since the cold snap last December. It seemed to cry, 'Lonely, lonely, lonely.'

Flinty stuffed a shoulder of lamb for dinner, with breadcrumbs and lemon and thyme, a recipe from Mrs Mack's book. The lamb was a present from old Mutti Green, handed to Joey in a hessian sack on his way back from school yesterday. There'd be cold lamb and chutney sandwiches for the young ones to take to school for the next few days.

We need a dog, she thought. A dog to eat the bones. A dog to keep me company, to bark if strangers come, to keep dingoes and native cats away from the chooks. Old Shep had died a few months after Dad, as though his heart had been broken like Mum's had been. Mr White had offered her one of their puppies but she hadn't wanted a dog then, another mouth to feed.

She thought maybe she should get one now.

She roasted potatoes, carrots, swedes and parsnips with the meat. No pumpkin — last year's were finished and this year's weren't ripe yet. Sometimes, this high up, the first frost killed the vines before the pumpkins sweetened, but the Whites had a paddock on a sunny slope that didn't get the frost till late. They shared their pumpkins with their neighbours in a frosty year ...

Kirsty chattered about Enid Brown's kitten, and Joey told her about the dead rat in the school water tank. 'It was just a skeleton really and Mr Ross says we may as well drink the water as we didn't get sick before. Flinty, why did all the skin and yuck dissolve and just leave the bone?'

'I don't know. You'd have to ask a doctor.' She tried to smile, to seem interested as they talked.

'Maybe I'll be a doctor,' said Joey. 'Or a vet. Doctors just sew up humans. A vet would be more interesting, because there'd be all sorts of animals. Do you think every animal is different inside? Or are some bits all the same, like sheep and rabbit have hearts and red wobbly bits?' He chewed his way through a hunk of swede. 'Flinty, if a lion had a sore paw, how could a vet treat it without being eaten?'

'I don't know.'

'Or a crocodile,' said Joey, warming to the idea. 'What if it had a sore tail?'

'Or a dragon with a tummy ache,' said Kirsty, carefully pushing her parsnips to the edge of the plate.

'Nah,' said Joey. 'No such thing as dragons.'

'Are too! St George fought a dragon! They said so in church! Would you fix up a dragon if a knight had fought it?'

Joey considered. 'I might,' he said.

'But then it would attack the knight again!'

The squabble brought Flinty back from far away. Was there any chance Joey could be a vet or a doctor? She had more than fifty pounds in the bank still, and Snow King might yet make their fortune. Was fifty pounds enough for him to go to boarding school for high school? Dad had hoped he would; and that he'd win a scholarship to university. Andy to get the farm, Jeff to be a soldier, Joey to go to university, the girls to marry …

'I want to fly an aeroplane like Mr Kingsford Smith,' said Kirsty.

'Girls can't fly aeroplanes!' objected Joey.

Kirsty poked out her tongue. 'Birds can fly so it can't be that hard.'

'Manners,' said Flinty automatically.

'Anyway, you don't make any money flying planes, not now the war's over,' said Joey.

'I'm going to wear a fox coat like Mrs White's and great big diamonds and a red hat, and people will pay to see me fly.'

'Where will you get diamonds?'

'I'll find them,' said Kirsty firmly. 'All sparkling in a stream bed. Flinty, do I have to eat my parsnips?'

'Yes, or there's no pudding.'

'What is for pudding?'

'Jam fritters.'

Kirsty stared at the parsnips in congealed gravy on her plate, weighing up the chore of eating them against missing out on jam fritters. Jam fritters won. She picked up her fork again.

At last dinner was over. Flinty washed up and put tomorrow's bread to rise. The others did their homework, Joey helping Kirsty with her spelling. Then Flinty sent him off to wash in the yard — the boys always washed outside in the warmer months — while Kirsty scrubbed herself by the fire in the kitchen and Flinty checked their school clothes for the morning. Joey had a rip in his trousers; he'd have worn them again tomorrow if she hadn't noticed.

She got them to bed, sat by lamplight with the needle and thread and made a hasty cobble darn. Mum would have told her to pick it out and do it again — a good darn should be invisible — but she was tired, deeply bone tired. A cobble darn was better than a hole. She'd pick it out tomorrow, or Saturday, maybe, and darn it properly so no one could see.

And at last, she was free to go to bed.

The days continued. Mr White promised her a puppy from the next litter. They'd be good pups, he said, a bit of dingo in them to make them tough, but not enough to make them wild.

She rode Snow King for the first time the week after Nicholas left, slipping into the saddle as he stood in the yard. The big horse shifted uneasily for a few seconds, accustoming himself to the weight, then seemed almost amused that she had taken so long. She urged him forwards, using the same hand signals she'd taught him to recognise when she had exercised him on the lunge rope in the paddock.

Snow King stepped up to the gate almost politely, paused while she bent to open it and then paced across the paddock like a gentleman. When she finally slipped off his back he stared at her, the liquid brown eyes seeming to say, 'We could challenge the wind, you and me. Why do we walk?'

She patted his neck and fed him his apple. 'One day we'll fly,' she whispered to him. For the first time since Nicholas had left, she did not feel lonely.

Chapter 20

11 March 1920

Dear Diary,

I took Snow King out on the road today. I let him canter, then move into a gallop, just past the Rock. His ears didn't even flicker as we edged through the mist. I don't think ghosts frighten Snow King. I don't think anything does.

The mist is still there, even though Nicholas isn't. I sit there sometimes, just in case he comes back, but I know he won't. He said he knows he doesn't, not for ages, which means that someone in the future must have told him. I've thought and thought about it, and the only person who could know I didn't see him for months would be me. Does he know me in the future?

Or maybe someone has read my diary. I keep it up in the linen cupboard, but maybe when I'm old I don't care if anyone reads what I wrote when I was seventeen.

I wish I'd asked Nicholas how many months he thought he'd be away. But maybe he didn't know how many. Maybe no one can tell how long it will take someone to learn to use new legs. But he said that we'll meet again. He said I'll have children. He said that something 'very, very' good would happen. I have to hold on to that, and not miss him too much, not be scared of 'something bad'. You get through bad things — I know, enough bad things have happened to me already. But I don't think getting through one bad time makes it any easier to deal with the next one. If anything it's worse, because there is less happiness to remember.

Sandy called by with a ham from old Mr Green. They've killed the weaner piglets to salt down, and make ham and bacon for winter. Ham and eggs again! There, that's a happy thing.

I'd made date scones. Sandy sat on the verandah and ate three, and had two cups of tea. That's a happy thing too, because we talked almost like the old days, before he kissed me, when we were just friends. We mostly talked about Snow King. He agreed there is no hurry to find a trainer. It can damage a young horse if you race him too soon. Snow King won't reach his full strength till he's about four.

I asked Sandy if he'd heard any more about his Soldier Settler block yet, but he just shrugged and said he'd chop some wood for me. That was the end of our talking. I don't even know if he's been offered a Soldier Settler block yet, or if he has to take the first one he's offered. He chopped the big stumps that Joey can't manage. They're tough and will burn overnight during winter, but I'd rather have talked to him more.

Mum used to say that no man could manage a farm alone without a good feed in his belly, and a wife to put it there. But Sandy isn't even going to the dances downriver, where he might meet girls. Joey says that Toby Mack and the Mullins boys and Amy all went down to the dance at Gibber's Creek —

they stayed at the Mullinses' cousin's place. But Sandy said he didn't want to go.

Amy is going to marry one of the Browns' cousins, the one whose sister married the Middletons' rouseabout and moved down to Sydney. I hope he knows what he's getting himself into. At least there's no worry about Andy marrying her now. Imagine having to live with her! Not that Andy would have married her, and anyway, he must have met girls a thousand times prettier than Amy White up north. She never even came up to say she was sorry after Mum and Dad died, but I bet she comes up now to show off her trousseau and engagement ring.

Amy is the only girl near my age in the valley, and now she'll be gone too. We never really got on — she and the White boys used to ping the rest of us with a pea shooter at school, and I don't think even Mr Ross got her to read a book in her life — but it feels funny that I'll be the only unmarried young woman in the valley, just the same.

The swallows are swooping high after flies. I suppose they'll be off for winter soon.

It was time to cut the grass hay to feed the horses through the winter, for the cold days when they would need more than the poor winter grass to give them energy and the colder days when snow covered the ground.

The hay cutter had lain unused in the barn since Viscount, the big draught horse, went to war: there were only the two horses to feed this winter, not the thirty to a hundred they'd been used to.

Flinty and Joey took turns with the scythe, swinging it back and forth through the red-stemmed grass, laden with seed heads, the clouds of finches flying up, chattering their annoyance, the mice scurrying. A weekend was long enough to cut two paddocks. It was harder work turning the grass, raking it back and forth over the next two weeks, hoping it wouldn't get rained on and spoiled. They could afford to buy hay, but that fifty pounds could be used for so many other things.

It didn't rain. Kirsty helped them rake the hay into mounds, and tie it in rough sheaves, then carry barrowload after barrowload down to the hayshed.

Time next to pick the pears and bottle them; to make crab-apple jelly; to harvest the late apples, wrapping each one in newspaper so it would last through the winter, and then the quinces and late pears, brown skinned and hard. And each week the washing, a full day stoking up the copper, stirring the clothes about, the rinsing, the hanging, the folding, the ironing; every day the milking, the hens, the meals to make. The jobs hadn't been so bad before, not with company. Now they were drudgery, each one no sooner finished than it was time to do it again.

The weekdays were lonely, except for the hours spent with Snow King, teaching him to trot, to respond to the pressure of knees, heels and hands, but never the whip. Flinty supposed that jockeys had to use the whip, but she hated the thought of anyone striking Snow King. He ran for the love of her, for the love of running. He'd win because he knew he was the king.

The weekends were better, with Joey and Kirsty at home during the day. Each weekend brought something they had achieved together, every success a sign that they could carry on, even without Andy or their parents; not just the shed full of hay but the big pile of firewood, the jars of crab-apple jelly as good as Mum's, the sacks of potatoes, enough to see them through to next Christmas when the first of the new potatoes would be ready, great plaited ropes of onions.

They spent two weekends harvesting the corn, storing the cobs in the big barrels to keep away the rats. The corn would be chook food through the winter, and extra energy for the horses too. Rock Farm had once grown oats for hay as well, but that was more than they could manage this year.

Flinty let Empress and Snow King into the corn paddock with its straggling stems for them to chew and trample down, and its soil ready for their manure. For the first time in longer than she could remember she felt a deep, sure happiness: the fulfilment of achievement, the joy in the mountain tops rearing up against the sky, the scents of gum trees and snow mixed with those of hot dirt and far-off chimney smoke. Dad had said you could smell the world up here, as the winds gathered the breezes together to roar across the mountains.

Sometimes Flinty could almost hear Nicholas's whisper just behind her: 'Something bad. Something bad.' But nothing bad happened, except for a bush rat that nested in the drawer that held Kirsty's woollens, so they had to spend a week washing them to get out the stink.

Kirsty's birthday. Flinty killed a rooster to roast, like Mum had done each birthday, and made her sister a new dress out of the material she'd brought back from town, using an old one of Mum's for a pattern, adding ruffles at the sleeves and hem. The newspapers Mr Mack passed on to them said women's skirts were belted about the hips instead of the waist, like the one she'd seen on Miss Matilda, and worn knee length now, but that didn't sound proper and, anyway, Kirsty wanted to dress like the other girls at school, not like a mannequin in the newspaper.

She watched them ride down the track to school the next day, Kirsty proud in what had been her Sunday dress — the new one was for best now — Joey behind her. Autumn had turned the birch trees yellow.

The mist swirled about the Rock again, but then it usually did, had done before she met Nicholas. It would still wisp down the gullies, she knew now, in fifty years' time, and maybe in another five hundred years too.

It was a grey day. Grey clouds. Grey air. The hawthorn berries down at the Macks' were deep red, which meant that it'd be a hard winter, but she reckoned there was rain coming before the snow.

She should go and feed the hens, collect the eggs. The brown snakes would get them if she didn't. Once a snake started raiding the henhouse it wouldn't stop. She'd have to wait with the spade then chop its head off, kill it like Nicholas had killed the little boy. That memory lingered, like the rat stink in Kirsty's woollens.

Maybe that's why the men don't tell us their stories, she thought dully. Because then we remember them and are haunted by them too.

She'd written to Andy, just like she'd promised. There hadn't been a reply. Perhaps Andy hadn't even got the letter yet. She'd addressed it to the station where he'd been working, but he might be droving for weeks or months before he got back there. Maybe the mail hadn't even got through. There'd been a flood up north. She didn't even know where Andy was exactly, so she couldn't look it up in Dad's old atlas.

And still nothing bad happened: it seemed impossible that anything *could* happen under the gentle autumn sky. Nicholas's words had implied it would be soon, before he would get back with his new legs. But nothing had. Nothing except being lonely, lonely like she'd never known you could be lonely, growing up with three brothers and a sister, like a mob of puppies underfoot, Mum said sometimes, riding up into the hills with Dad and Jeff, Sandy and Andy.

She should go and see Snow King. She could ride him around the paddock now, though she still used the yard to saddle him up and an apple to keep him sweet. He would never be a quiet horse — a kingfisher's swoop would make him shy. But he allowed her to saddle him, to sit on his back, to urge him forwards, faster or slower.

She needed a friend today, and Snow King was her only real companion now. She could talk to him about anything — about Sandy, about Nicholas, about her worry that Empress might stumble on the way down to school, or Andy have an accident way up north. It didn't matter that he didn't understand her words.

But she didn't feel like talking today. She fed Snow King his apple, stroking his mane. She was about to get his saddle and bridle, then hesitated. She didn't want the leather between them, the metal bit in Snow King's mouth. This once she wanted it to be just the two of them: the girl and horse. Only in the paddock, of course. It would be foolish to ride any further ...

He was a gentleman. A complete and utter darling. He almost winked at her, as if to say, 'This is just between you and me, eh? I know it's not the way it's done.'

He trotted around the paddock, with her leaning into his neck.

She couldn't resist. She nudged him, so he turned to the paddock gate. She bent down, unlatched it. Snow King waited till it had swung open, then walked out without her urging. Through the front gate, telling herself they'd head back in a moment, just a minute more. Out along the track and down the mountain. She kneed him to a canter.

He put his head down instead. He began to gallop, down the track, past the Rock. She gave him his head ... just her, the wind and the horse.

Impossible that she should control something so powerful. Impossible that he'd want to be controlled, that he'd accept her as his leader just as he'd accepted the stallion, his father. No, she thought, as the Rock vanished behind them in the turn of the track. This is friendship, not mastery. This is love.

She could hear Mr Clancy say, 'Well.' It was time to stop. It wasn't just the danger. Snow King was too young to be ridden hard, on a track of puddles and ruts. He hadn't had time to learn how to judge the ground with a rider on his back, nor did she have enough control riding bareback to guide him now.

Snow King would gallop until he tired, which might be hours. The wind was his brother just like it was hers, but she was the older friend, had to be the sensible one. She eased the pressure of her knees, just a little, and sat back to tell him she no longer wanted such speed. And then more, till he slowed to a canter, hardly out of breath.

You'll win the Melbourne Cup, you darling horse, she thought. And Kirsty will be there in a new pink dress, belted around her hips just like in the fashion pages of the newspaper, and Andy will put the Cup up on the mantelpiece. Wouldn't Dad have loved to win the Cup ...?

Someone moved in the distance. A man, on foot, plodding along the track. She sat back even further, to tell Snow King to settle to a walk, and peered at the figure shambling up the hill.

None of the neighbours would have walked up here — why walk when you could ride, or bring a cart? It was getting too cold for swaggies, now snow lurked in the clouds. Swaggies headed north with the swallows, where it was warm, not here among the rocks where a blizzard could trap you, freeze you till your body was found in next year's thaw.

The man on the track didn't belong here. The men of the valley were all angles, strong of arm and leg, from loping up mountains and sitting astride a horse. This man looked like his body was too heavy for his feet.

She rode towards him slowly, puzzled and wary. He was about Andy's age, she saw as she drew closer, dressed in what looked like an army uniform, but blue, not khaki. Men who have been wounded wear blue, don't they? she thought. Was this man still in the army? Or just wearing his uniform? Was that allowed?

The stranger peered up at her and she saw he had a scar running right down over his eye, puckered and purple. He blinked at her. His eyes looked clouded, and his face rippled with scar tissue.

'Hey, mister.' The man's voice was gruff, as though the inside of his throat was scarred too. 'This the road to Rock Farm?'

'Yes,' she said cautiously. Snow King stepped back nervously and tried to rear. She patted his neck to quieten him.

He tried to peer closer at the sound of her voice. 'You a girl? I don't see too good. It was the gas. See better when it's brighter ...'

'I'm sorry.' The words came automatically, but she meant them too. He looked alone and lost — a bit like she felt just now. 'Who were you looking for?' she asked more gently.

'Me mate. Jeff.'

Was this the person who had sent the letter? 'I'm sorry,' she said again, quietly. 'Jeff died in the war. Nearly three years ago now.'

The stranger looked at her blearily. 'I knew that. I was there. Saw him die, saw the holes in his guts. He was dead afore the gas hit us.'

Shock bit her. She could see it, see Jeff bleed. She could even smell the gun smoke and the blood. This is what Sandy wouldn't tell me, she thought. This is what Andy won't say. So I don't have to see Jeff's death every time I think of him. So I can think of him laughing, riding up the track, not bleeding in the smoke and noise.

The man still peered at her. He shook his head. 'It's Andy I want if Jeff ain't here. Can't be if he's dead, can he? Andy's me mate too.'

'You're a friend of Andy's?'

He took off his blue cap, the politeness so automatic even his fuddled brain didn't have to think about it. 'Sergeant Bertie Morris, at your service.' The words should have been military. They were slurred instead.

'Bertie Morris! But I wrote to you! Jeff,' she managed to say his name, 'Jeff wrote to us and said Sergeant Bertie Morris didn't have any family, and could I write to you! Mum and I made you a cake.'

'A fruitcake,' he said eagerly. He sounded more in control now. 'It were a real good fruitcake. And a pair of socks and a comforter.'

'Mr Morris!' Snow King began to edge away. She slid off, patting his neck, holding his rope halter. 'Don't mind Snow King. I'm still breaking him in. He's a beauty, isn't he?'

Mr Morris didn't even look at the horse. He stared at her, his neck poking forwards like a chook's. Trying to see me, poor man, she thought. 'You're Felicity. Felicity McAlpine.'

'Yes. But Andy's not here. He's up in Queensland droving. I don't know where he is, exactly.'

'Felicity McAlpine,' he said again, frowning as though it was too hard to think of more than one thing at a time, one important thing he mustn't forget ... 'You're the one I'm looking for. Not Jeff. Not Andy.'

Suddenly she was uneasy again. She stepped away slightly. Snow King whinnied and stamped his feet. 'Why are you still in uniform? Haven't you been demobbed yet?'

'Been in hospital,' he said. 'Don't like it. Said I could go home for the weekend.' He smiled and it looked like a baby's smile, innocent but sort of empty too. 'Told them I was going to my sweetheart's house.'

'Who's your sweetheart?'

'Why, you of course. Felicity McAlpine. You wrote to me, sent me a cake, the same day I got this.' He touched the scar over his eye. 'Gassed us too, but I didn't know till later. All of them coughing and screaming, but I missed that, on account of my head.' He grinned as though he had been clever, being blown unconscious while deadly gas seeped around him.

She couldn't handle this, not alone. He was worse than the swaggie who'd been here three years before, who'd had a friend called Blinky no one but he could see. Blinky had told him it was wrong to hurt people, the swaggie said, with strange intentness, and Mum had locked the door and made them hide under the bed till Dad came back and saw him off with the shotgun.

Sympathy warred with terror. She wished she had the shotgun now. Even empty, it might have scared this man away. She had to get him down to the Macks'. Mr Mack would know what to do. She grabbed Snow King's mane, intending to swing up on him again. Mr Morris snatched her hand. 'Don't go!'

'I'm not. I mean, I'm riding down to the Macks'. You can follow me down the track. Mrs Mack will give us some lunch. She'll give us apple pie.'

'Don't want apple pie.'

She tried to pull her hand away. He wrenched it back, so hard she let go of the lead rope. Snow King skittered a few paces off. She glanced at him desperately, then at the man. She tried to keep her voice calm. 'Mr Morris, please let me go.'

'Need someone to take care of me. That's what they said at the hospital. You'll take care of me, won't you?'

'Yes,' she said, edging away, wishing Snow King would stay still long enough for her to scramble back on him. 'Mrs Mack will too. You come down the valley with me to the Macks'.'

'Give us a kiss first,' he said. 'That's right, ain't it? You know I never been kissed. Went all that way to France and never a kiss. It ain't right. But Felicity McAlpine will kiss me.'

'No!' She backed away, his breath sour in her face, then tripped, falling heavily backwards. She landed on something sharp — a rock. It almost seemed to cut right into her body, the pain of it was so intense. The man was on her, his stink worse. His weight pressed her down into the rock so hard she screamed.

The pain blinded her. She blinked it away, trying to shove him off with her arms. Her legs must be trapped under his — she couldn't shift them at all.

She flung him back and realised she was stronger than him, her brain not as fuddled. ('Know what the greatest weapon in the world is?' whispered Dad. 'The human mind. An old sergeant told me that.')

She had to get away from him, find a weapon, a stick, a stone. She still couldn't move her legs even though he was off her, but she could roll. She rolled once, her back screaming pain, and then again, off the track then down the slope, faster and faster, rolling down while he scrambled after her, his hands groping in front of him now his feet had left the track. 'Felicity McAlpine? Where are you? Felicity McAlpine?'

Her back was fire. Her legs were cold. ('... it had got cold,' said Nicholas. 'It's never cold in Vietnam.' But Nicholas was fifty years away.)

'Felicity McAlpine!'

Her body tumbled against another rock, her face prickled by the grass. She forced herself up onto her elbows, saw a stick, managed to grab the end of it and haul it to her.

Where was Sergeant Morris? She held the stick, ready to poke it at his face, to shove, waiting for the thud of his footstep, the plaintive cry of his voice. Instead she heard hoofbeats and then a scream. The scream went on and on.

She couldn't move. She had to move. She pushed her head up. ('I managed to push myself up onto my elbows,' said Nicholas.) The man was lying on the ground. His head and chest were bloody. Snow King stood over him. The horse's hooves were red as well.

Chapter 21

10 April 1920

Dear Diary,

Even in these pages I won't write about what happened that day. Can't write about it. Maybe it would be easier if I could.

She tried to crawl. She couldn't. It was as though the rolling had taken all the movement that was in her. She managed at last to heave onto her back, which hurt so much the sky turned black, instead of grey.

The man in the scrub above her didn't move.

For a while Snow King stood over her. She felt his breath, knew if she turned her head she'd see red hooves.

She couldn't bear to.

She lay there. Time went on.

Snow King moved away. She heard his teeth tearing at the grass. The man — the soldier — Sergeant Morris lay quite still. She knew he'd never move again.

All she could do was lie there and try not to scream with the pain. And then she realised she should scream, as loud as she could. Maybe the White boys were up the mountainside after rabbits or trying to sneak off with any of the Greens' calves that hadn't been branded yet, or Mr Mullins could be out looking for a straggling sheep. She screamed and screamed and heard the echoes.

She screamed for Sandy, screamed for Andy.

No one came.

She thought instead. Thought about Nicholas, far in the future, getting his new legs. There're bad things going to come, he'd said. Well, this was bad.

Maybe ... maybe this was why he'd told her about the boy he'd killed, so she wouldn't cry, as she was crying now, for poor Sergeant Morris, off to war and never been kissed, his mind blown away in France, his body lying here as well as his poor silly dreams of a sweetheart, a girl who had written to him once, and sent him a cake, on the last day that he was whole.

War is all of us, she thought. All who fought, and all who cheered as they enlisted, as those young men marched away.

She hoped Sergeant Morris had eaten his fruitcake before it happened. She hoped he'd at least had that.

The sun was above her now, almost hidden in the clouds. Slowly, very slowly, it began to ride down the far side of the sky. Joey and Kirsty would be back soon. Her brother and sister shouldn't find her like this, but there was nothing she could do.

And then at last she heard the steady clop of Empress's hooves.

'Flinty!' She heard Joey dismount and then his shout: 'Kirsty, don't come any closer. I said don't get off! Go and get Mr Mack: ride fast as you can.'

'Tell them to bring a door,' she whispered. That's what they'd done when Billy Mullins broke his leg. Had she broken her legs? Was that why she couldn't move them?

'Tell him to bring a door!' yelled Joey. Suddenly he sounded just like Andy.

She let the blackness take her.

Chapter 22

I think of pain differently now. There is pain that hurts, pain that is agony, and there is pain that is so bad you can no longer feel it. Your body just says 'hold on'.

The blackness turned to white, and then to pain again. She woke to find her body flying up a hill. No, not flying, lying on a door, jolting so every movement hurt. Uphill — they were taking her home, not down to the Macks'. She was glad. She needed to be home, even if her legs were broken.

'Shh, girl, they've gone to get the doctor. Soon have you in your bed.' It was Mr Mack's voice.

'You'll be all right, Flinty.' That was Sandy's voice, from the end of the door by her feet. His voice sounded strange, rough, like he had an apple in his throat.

'Kirsty?'

'Don't you go worrying,' said Mr Mack. 'Kirsty's already up at the house. She'll have the fire all warm for you. Rock Farm's closer than our place, or we'd have taken you there.'

She tried to sit up, found it brought the blackness back. This time she managed not to scream.

'Snow King?'

'Joey led him and Empress back to the house.' There was a pause. 'That horse was standing by you. Guarding you,' said Mr Mack.

'The man ... he's Sergeant Morris. He knew Jeff, and Andy in the war ...'

'Toby said Jones the mailman gave a stranger a lift this morning. Says the bloke was acting all confused like. Poor fellow must have tripped,' said Mr Mack matter-of-factly.

'But —' She tried to speak through the pain.

'Hush, Flinty, hush,' said Sandy.

'He tripped,' said Mr Mack firmly. 'Fell down a cliff, I reckon. Easy to do up here. Managed to crawl back near the track afore he died. That's what we'll tell his folks. That's what it's best to say.'

His folks are dead, she thought. She couldn't say it. Instead she waited for the bouncing to stop, for the softness of her bed, for the moment when the pain would go.

Chapter 23

Why is it that you can bear pain, but someone's kindness makes you cry?

The pain didn't go.

She lay in her bed, still fully dressed, though Joey had gently pulled off her boots. She couldn't sit up to do it for herself or even move her legs. Kirsty sat with her, holding her hand. She had washed Flinty's face with a warm flannel and her hands too, and put a hot water bottle in her bed to warm it. Sandy sat by the bed, looking strangely helpless, as though he wanted to chop wood, build her a horse yard, do anything to help but just sit here.

'You'll be all right,' he said. He'd been saying it on and off for at least an hour. He made a move as though to take the hand Kirsty wasn't holding, but pulled back.

Flinty nodded weakly. She couldn't have been badly hurt! It was just a backward stumble onto a rock — poor sad Sergeant Morris hadn't had a chance to hurt her more.

A shadow darkened the door. She'd known Joey had been growing — she'd had to lengthen his trousers twice in the past year — but she hadn't realised how much. 'Kirsty, make us a cup of tea? Would you like a cup, Flinty?'

Flinty nodded. Actually she felt that she'd be sick if she swallowed anything, but Kirsty needed to do something, not just sit with her. It would be hours till Dr Sparrow got here, maybe not till tomorrow morning, as he didn't like riding at night — too drunk, Dad used to say. Drunk by lunchtime, dead drunk by dinner ...

Dead, like Sergeant Morris.

She waited till Kirsty had left the room. 'How's Snow King?' she whispered.

'He's fine. Safe in the paddock. I washed his hooves,' said Joey. Once again she thought how like Andy he was. 'They had mud all over them.'

Not mud. Blood, she thought, and Joey knew it too. So did Sandy and Mr Mack. But she didn't say it, knew Joey and Sandy and Mr Mack would never mention it again. Snow King was no killer. He had just protected what was his. He had killed but wasn't a killer, like Nicholas, like Andy too, and maybe even Sandy and Jeff, as well as poor Mr Morris ...

If she'd had a shotgun she might have shot him, and she'd have been a killer too. Or maybe she wouldn't have, and then he might have hurt her even worse than he had.

It was too hard. She shut her eyes again. Kirsty came in softly with the tea. Sandy held Flinty's head up so she could sip the hot, sweet brew. It was funny to feel Sandy's hands again after so many years, rough and strong and gentle. It was as though a little of his strength flowed into her. She felt better after the tea — not her legs, but her mind seemed to clear. Time passed, and pain stayed with it. Kirsty fed her a few spoonfuls of cut-up rabbit and potato stew, till the smell made her sick.

'Go and eat,' she told them.

'Kirsty will go,' said Sandy. 'I'll stay here until the doctor comes.'

Dusk had turned to dark. Kirsty drew the curtains and lit the lamp just as they heard hoofbeats outside. Surely it wasn't the doctor already.

She heard Joey's voice, then Mrs Mack's, asking him to see to her horse. But Mrs Mack never rode ...

Then she was there, taking off Mr Mack's oilskin coat, putting a carpetbag down on the floor, bending to kiss Flinty, all warm and with the scent of apple pie on her skin and in her hair.

'You don't ride,' said Flinty weakly.

Mrs Mack sat on the chair Kirsty had just left. 'I can ride if I have to. It's just easier with Sally and the cart these days. But Johnno has taken the cart to get the doctor. Don't you worry — the lamps will show the way and Dr Sparrow can sleep in the back till they get here.'

She turned to Kirsty. 'Could you unpack the saddlebags, dear? There are some supplies in there. My night things are in the carpetbag. I'll be staying,' she added to Flinty. 'Just for a few days.'

'But how will they manage without you?' She thought of Mr Mack and the boys coming into an empty house, an empty table. She doubted any of them had so much as toasted a slice of bread by the fire for themselves before.

'Annie will look out for them.' Annie was her daughter-in-law, who lived just across the creek. 'Sandy, you go and help Kirsty.' Then, as he protested, 'No, off with you. There are times when women need to be alone.'

Sandy left reluctantly, with a last unreadable gaze at Flinty. Mrs Mack waited till Kirsty was in the kitchen and Sandy had shut the door, then said quietly, 'Did that bloke hurt you, lovey?'

Flinty knew what she meant. 'He tried to. But I fell over getting away from him and rolled clear. And then —'

'And then the poor man died from the bad fall he'd had earlier. The rocks are slippery if you go off the track this time of year,' said Mrs Mack resolutely. 'That's what we'll tell anyone who asks, not that it's any business of anyone beyond the valley. No need to even say you met him.'

'But won't people think it's strange, the two of us being hurt the same day?'

'Strange things happen,' said Mrs Mack. 'The important thing now is getting you better.'

'It can't be really bad,' said Flinty.

'Of course not,' said Mrs Mack. 'You'll be up and about by tomorrow.'

Then why did you bring your carpetbag? thought Flinty. Why won't Sandy go home? But she said nothing, as Kirsty came in again, and Mrs Mack went to make up the bed in Mum and Dad's old room, and one for Sandy in with Joey.

It can't be that bad, she told herself again. Not from just a silly fall. It can't be that bad at all.

Chapter 24

I think my body knew before my mind did. Or maybe I just refused to listen to what I knew.

'It's a broken back,' said Dr Sparrow. His breath stank of rum; his clothes reeked of rum-soaked old sweat. His hands shook as he put them back in his trouser pockets after he'd examined her.

Flinty lay on her stomach, her shirt pulled up, her trousers slightly down, Sandy, Joey and Mrs Mack on either side of Dr Sparrow, Kirsty behind them. Mrs Mack had told her to stay in the kitchen, but she'd crept back. Flinty would have done the same.

'But it can't be! I only tripped. I landed on a rock.' The last sentence was hard to add.

'It snapped your back,' said Dr Sparrow, his words still slurred from his day's drinking, despite the long drive through the mountains. 'See this spot here?' She felt his fingers, surprisingly gentle despite the alcoholic tremor, trace a pattern on her back. 'Feel this lump? That's where the spine has broken.'

Flinty wriggled her hand around to feel it. He was right. It was like a chicken egg. Strangely it didn't hurt to touch it, although if she moved the wrong way the pain seared back like a branding iron.

'Are you sure that's what it is?' asked Mrs Mack quietly. 'Maybe you should look at her legs?'

Dr Sparrow stared at Mrs Mack blearily. 'Are you the doctor or am I, madam? What will looking at her legs tell me?' He blinked at Flinty. 'Do your legs hurt?'

'No, sir,' whispered Flinty. Her knee did hurt — she must have knocked it — but she wasn't going to bother the doctor with a bruised knee.

Dr Sparrow turned back to Mrs Mack. 'See? It's her back that's the problem.'

'How long till it gets better?' A broken leg takes months to heal, thought Flinty. Months, lying here in bed! She couldn't do it, not with so much that had to be done. But she'd have no choice —

'Never gets better,' said Dr Sparrow abruptly. Drunk or not, annoyed about having to come all the way up here, she could tell he didn't like saying this. 'Backs don't heal.'

'But ... but they have to. Other bones mend!'

'Not backs.' He snapped his bag shut, as though to say there was nothing in his bag that could help her. 'She's going to be like this for the rest of her life.'

'But she has to get better!' Kirsty made it sound like getting better was a dress you could make, a jumper you could knit.

'Shh,' said Joey. He picked Kirsty up, big as she was, and hugged her. Her legs almost dangled to the ground, but she rested her face on his shoulder, comforted. Joey knows, thought Flinty. Or he suspected. Maybe Mrs Mack had warned him what the doctor might say. Because Mrs Mack must have guessed how bad it was, or she wouldn't have come prepared to stay.

Sandy said nothing. She had to crane her neck to see him. His face looked as blank as the Rock, but she thought she could see tears. Sandy, crying! Crying for me, she thought. No, for all of us, for Joey and Kirsty too.

The doctor seemed impatient now. He knows we don't have any alcohol here, she realised. He'll have to get back to town to get more grog ... Her mind shied away from what he'd said, watching him sway out of the room, listening to Mrs Mack's low voice in the hall beyond.

'What should we do for her, doctor?'

'How do I know? I'm not a nurse. It's nursing she needs now, not doctoring. Feed her. Keep her clean.' The voice hesitated. 'There are homes for cripples down in Sydney. Places that will take her if she can't be cared for here ...'

Sydney! No, thought Flinty. Please, no ...

'We can look after her.' Joey's voice sounded far older than twelve.

'Flinty's not going anywhere.' Kirsty sounded older too, her tears gone.

'We'll manage,' said Mrs Mack, and suddenly Flinty knew that they would, that there'd never be any more talk of sending her to a cripples' home.

A cripple. That was her now.

Chapter 25

Sandy kissed my cheek when the doctor left. I think that made it all more real than anything the doctor said. A kiss on the cheek for a cripple, not on the lips for a girl you might love. How can any man love a cripple?

It had been the longest day of her life. She had started out whole and ended it here, helpless on her bed, not even able to sit up unless she called for someone to help her. And she couldn't stop the day by going to sleep. Her brain was as active as her body wasn't.

Surely Dr Sparrow was wrong! She tried to move her legs again, but she couldn't even twist her hips. Only her toes responded properly, though she could wriggle her feet a little. But what use were feet without the legs to make them walk, run?

Kirsty snuffled quietly in her bed across the room. A long snorting snore came from Mrs Mack down the hall.

Cripple, she thought. Cripple. Cripple. Cripple. I'm a cripple now.

What did life hold for a crippled girl? Nicholas had been crippled. Nicholas, who had told her that something bad was coming. This was bad ...

Life didn't end when you were crippled. But it stopped everything she loved. Nicholas could dream of riding again, of walking with new artificial legs. But there was no artificial back for her.

She'd never ride again, nor walk. Maybe they could rig up a chair for her, like his, so she could help in the kitchen, prop her up with pillows so she could sew.

She hated sewing. Hated cooking too. Housework was what you did because you were a girl, what you hurried through to get to the good bits outside.

Cripple. Cripple. No one would ever marry a crippled girl. When she'd dreamed of what her life would be it was always living in the mountains with a husband, children, horses. She'd have none of that now. That stupid, horrible glory box, sitting at the end of her bed. Kirsty could have it.

'Flinty? Are you all right?' A shadow that was Sandy appeared at the door.

'No, of course I'm not. I'm a cripple!' she wanted to yell and shriek. Instead she said, 'I'm all right. Just can't sleep yet.'

'Neither can I,' Sandy said softly, so Kirsty wouldn't wake. He sat on the chair beside her. For a moment she thought he was going to take her hand. But he didn't.

He sat silent for a while. She didn't try to talk either. What was there to say? But it felt good to have him beside her. The roof creaked as the night grew colder. A dingo howled, and another answered. At last Sandy said, 'We'll look after you, Flinty. Everyone in the valley will do what they can.'

'I know.'

Sandy hesitated, then bent down and kissed her on the cheek again. She watched him tiptoe out. Another kiss from Sandy, one that you'd give a child or an old aunt. Or a cripple, she thought.

The tears finally came, as though her body had been too shocked to let them out before. How would they ever manage up here now? Mrs Mack couldn't stay forever. She tried to cry silently, gulping down the sobs, so she didn't wake Kirsty. Kirsty had school tomorrow ...

But Kirsty couldn't go to school, not with her like this, nor Joey either. They'd have to stay to look after her, to do the chores that someone had to do, plant potatoes, fix the shingles, so they could eat and have a roof that didn't blow away in the first winter gale.

Maybe she should insist on going to a home for cripples, so Joey and Kirsty could be free — but they wouldn't let her. You couldn't just put yourself in a cripples' home. You had to go or stay where you were put.

Cripple. Not even able to sit up. Nicholas could sit, could move around. Nicholas was getting new legs, maybe a new life too. Lucky Nicholas.

Slowly the tears stopped. Sleep nibbled at her, sweet and dark, but she forced it away. There was something she had to remember. Something about Nicholas. About his chair, maybe ...

Then she remembered.

Something bad is going to happen, he'd said, or words a bit like that. But there'll be good coming, and it will be very, very good. That's what he said, isn't it? she thought. 'Very, very good' as though he had to say the 'very' twice so she'd know how good it was going to be.

Good. This was the bad. But there'd be good and she'd be happy. And that meant staying in the mountains, because she never could be happy down below.

They'd manage. Her ghost from the future had said so. He'd been right about the bad coming. Now she had to trust that the good would come as well.

The cuckoo gave its warbling three notes out in the maple tree. Dawn must be coming. At last she slept.

Chapter 26

20 March 1920

Dear Diary,

Kirsty propped me up on pillows and brought me my diary and the ink and pen. It's hard writing like this. I don't know what to say.

Every morning I wake up and then remember that I'm crippled. I think that is the hardest moment of every day — when I have to remember it again. Last night was hard too. I could see the sky turn that pale blue-gold that means the full moon is rising from behind the ridge. I wanted to be outside to watch it bob up from the dark, its light eating the stars. I have watched the full moon rise every month of my life, I think. One of my earliest memories is of sitting with Dad on the verandah waiting for that final jump from behind the black ridge into the sky, as though the moon was too excited to be held down any longer. But I can't watch it now unless someone pushes my bed around. I am enough bother already without that.

I think that without Nicholas's warning and his promise I'd have turned my face to the wall, and tried to pretend that none of this was real. But Nicholas said that something 'very, very good' is coming after the bad. I have to think of that. I have to.

Sandy has put a jar of everlastings by my bed. I touch them sometimes. They look like a glimpse of sunlight from the mountain. He comes and sits with me at night too, when the pain is bad and the others are asleep. It is funny how he knows just when it's at its worst. Last night he said that when he was wounded an Australian nurse told him to tell the part that hurt that everything was being done to help it. The nurse said that pain is the body's way of saying help and you had to reassure it. After that you should think of things to look forward to, never what you might have lost.

Maybe that was why Sandy said he thought of pikelets. No matter how bad his wound was — and he still won't speak of it — he knew that all he had to do was think of pikelets and get home.

I said I'd rather think of apple pie and we laughed. It was the first time I had laughed since it happened. Then we had to be quiet in case we woke Kirsty.

Sandy went back to bed. I managed to roll a bit — I've learned it hurts if I stay in one position for too long — and thought of apple pie, and Sandy and Kirsty and Joey and Andy and me all eating it. It's funny, but it did sort of make the pain a bit better and I could sleep.

Mrs White brought Amy in the sulky up here yesterday. They had made scones but they weren't as good as mine or Mrs Mack's. Amy wanted to talk about her glory box and the house her fiancé is building for them. Mrs White said they'd 'buried that poor soldier who fell down the rocks' last Tuesday.

Mrs Mack hadn't told me, though Mr Mack must have told her and Sandy when he came up here with the milk and papers and meat. Which means that even Mrs White doesn't know it had anything to do with me. I'm glad Amy doesn't. She'd tell everyone.

I just feel empty when I think of Sergeant Morris now. It's as though he was killed in the war, but it just didn't catch up with him till now. It's as though it had nothing to do with me or the valley or Snow King at all. I'd ask Joey to put flowers on his grave but someone might wonder. I'll keep him in my prayers.

It was strange how well they did manage. Flinty had forgotten that Mrs Mack had 'managed' for so many years before, when her Valma had the polio.

After only three days it was almost routine. Mrs Mack showed Kirsty how to wash her, rolling Flinty to one side and then the other in the bed; how to use a big soup bowl as a bedpan; how to prop her up and put a tray on pillows, so she could feed herself or write in her diary or read a newspaper; even how to make a bed with her still in it, putting on half a sheet and rolling her back and forth again.

Flinty couldn't move much herself — she could roll a little to each side, using her elbows and feet to move her unresponsive back, but every time she tried to sit by herself or roll right over her back screamed pain and refused to obey, though she remembered forcing her body to roll down the hill after her fall. (Even she called it a 'fall' now, pretending poor mad Mr Morris had never met her. Like Andy, like Nicholas running from the memory of war, she thought. And then: maybe they were right. It was easier to put those minutes with Mr Morris behind a door, somewhere in her mind, and never open it. Her life held all the pain she could bear right now.)

It hurt. Lying on her back hurt, and the longer she lay still the greater the pain grew. The only relief was being rolled on her side, till the pain began again, an hour or so later, and she bore it until she could no longer and had to call and ask to be rolled over again.

The nights were the worst. She'd sleep for an hour, perhaps, after Sandy had crept into her room and out again, but then the pain would wake her again, in her legs this time, from her hips to her knees, instead of her back. She didn't like to call for help. And so she lay there, she and the pain, counting the chimes of Mum's clock in the parlour, waiting for the cuckoo's call outside, and then the kookaburras, till someone could move her body, her stupid, horrible, pain-filled body, and make it bearable again.

On the third day Joey worked out that if they propped her on either side with pillows she could lie back one way, and then the other. It helped a lot.

Meanwhile Mrs Mack was 'cooking up a storm' as she said, in the kitchen, and teaching Kirsty at the same time, filling the food safe with long-lasting fruitcake and gingerbread and Anzac biscuits, making sure Kirsty knew how to feed the yeast each night and use half to make the next morning's bread, how to rub the eggs with clean dripping to keep them through the winter.

Outside Sandy and Joey filled the back verandah with split logs and piled the outside woodheap high, dug and bagged the first crop of potatoes, shovelled out the hen yard and spread the manure on the corn.

But at the end of a week Mrs Mack asked Joey to saddle her horse again. It was time to go back to her own home and duties, and for Sandy to go home too.

'But I'll be up on Saturday and I'll send one of the boys up every second day too. And if there's anything you need, you come on down,' she added to Joey. She bent down and kissed Flinty's cheek. 'There's always room for you all with us.'

Flinty shook her head, just as she had after Dad had died, after Andy went droving. There wasn't really room for them all at the Macks', even now the oldest boys had their own homes, and Valma and Rick were gone, though at least these days all the Macks left at home had a bed to themselves.

'We'll manage,' said Flinty. But it was good to be asked, to know that if managing was ever not possible — but they would manage, they *would* — the welcome was there.

'Well,' said Mrs Mack dubiously. 'Your Andy should be home soon.'

'I'm not going to tell him.'

Mrs Mack stared. 'Andy has a right to know!'

'No!' How could she tell Mrs Mack that Andy had been hurt by the war too? Somehow getting to know Nicholas had made her see that Andy needed time for his own wounds to heal.

Mrs Mack shook her head. 'You're stubborn as your father.'

'Yes,' said Flinty tiredly.

Chapter 27

5 May 1920

Dear Diary,

I thought there would be nothing to write about, stuck here. Maybe I notice little things more. A big tree fell over last night, up on the hill. No wind. I think it just decided it was time to fall, or it was long dead and a possum jumped on it. The possum must have got a fright.

I heard the first shoosha *as a native cat hissed out in the garden last night. They come down every autumn to try to get the hens. If we didn't pen the chooks up the native cats and dingoes would get them the first night.* Shoosha shoosha shoosha, *the cat said. I've only seen them a couple of times. Once it was a mother with two kittens. They don't look like real cats: more like tiny tigers but with spots.*

This morning I watched a daddy-long-legs eat a moth, one of the big fat ones with eyes on their wings. It took almost all day. I suppose a moth like that is a feast for a spider.

I have read every book in the bookcases this week. At least in a book I am away from my body for a while. But I want to do things, not just read about them. I want my life.

'You goin' all right?' asked Georgie Green.

She'd heard his horse plod up the track, Joey's voice yell a greeting, Kirsty's excited clanging as she put the kettle on then dashed into their bedroom to put on her red shoes and check her plaits were neat, the soft thud of Georgie's feet in socks coming down the corridor to her bedroom. (Mutti Green never let the men wear boots indoors, not on her spotless rag rugs.)

'I'm fine,' lied Flinty.

'Good-oh,' said Georgie awkwardly. He was fourteen and thin as a beanpole, with hair the colour of a winter fox. 'I was just passin', headin' up the mountain. Goin' rabbiting. Mutti wants some skins to make a blanket.'

As though there aren't as many rabbits down in the valley, thought Flinty. But the Greens would never make a visit look like charity. Georgie held up a hessian sack. 'Mutti sent you one of her cheeses and an apple cake.'

Flinty blinked away the tears. She cried at everything lately. 'Mutti's apple cake is the best in the world.'

Georgie grinned. He might not know how to talk in a girl's sickroom, but he knew his Mutti's apple cake. 'I know.'

Flinty remembered Mum talking about Mrs Grünberg's 'German apple cake' before the war. The cake had lost the German part of its name at the same time the Grünbergs became the Greens.

'Tea's ready!' Kirsty peered into the bedroom. 'You want a cup, Flinty?'

Flinty shook her head. She lay in her bedroom, trying to hear the voices in the kitchen.

'... and Hannah's had her baby,' said Georgie. 'A girl, but Vati says that's all right, plenty of time to have a boy later. And the Whites bought a new ram at the sale in Gibber's Creek. Well, they *say* they bought it but Vati has his doubts ...'

Life, she thought, and I am shut away from it.

Time passed. The sun climbed the sky each day, then fell down into the night. Nights of pain and days of ... managing, thought Flinty, but only just, only because all the work had been done for winter. Winter was the slow time, Dad said, the reward you got for working hard all summer and autumn, the time to make a new chair by the fire, or whittle a wooden spoon for Mum, a time to knit and make new trousers, all the picking and bottling and jamming done till the next summer.

Joey exercised Snow King for her, keeping to the paddock, riding the horse round and round, which bored them both. He took Empress on longer rides, to check his rabbit traps.

She had lost track of days and had to ask Sandy what day it was when he called by with a forequarter of mutton and a bag of flour he refused to let them pay for and a crock of butter well salted to last for weeks. She drew up a calendar after that: twentieth of April, twenty-first ...

The first snow fell at night, a thin scatter like flour on the kitchen floor, gone as soon as the sun was a handspan above the ridges. She saw it from her bedroom window, the only glimpse of the mountains she had now, and shut her mind to the possibility it might be all she would see for months or years, perhaps forever.

She needed a bathchair like Nicholas's. Joey was strong enough to help her into it and out again. But a chair like that cost money — as much as ten pounds perhaps, or even twenty, maybe even more.

She thought she might have fallen into a grey hole of pain and despair those first two months, if it hadn't been for neighbours. Sandy came twice a week, at least. Mrs Mack visited every Saturday, as she'd promised, always bringing some treat, coconut cream pie or damson pie or apple and blackberry. She brought books too, borrowed from every family in the valley. 'Your dad was such a reader,' she said, as though reading was something peculiar, like a white kangaroo. 'I thought you might have a taste for it too.'

Somehow every few days someone else 'just happened to be passing by', as though there was any real reason to come so far up the mountain. Even old Dusty Jim — 'just out for a Sunday ride' — stopped to help Joey bring in more firewood from the yard pile. Pat and Snowy White stayed to nail down a bit of flapping roof, and left a chunk of home-corned beef.

She watched the patch of blue turn white, then grey. Rain oozed rather than fell. She knitted — socks, because that was the most complicated pattern she could think of — her fingers, at least, busy. She wriggled her toes, her feet. Sometimes in the afternoons she could move her knees too, but every morning they were just lumps again.

More feet down the corridor, in boots this time. Joey.

'How you going, Flint?'

'Fine,' she lied again. 'How are the horses?' She tried to keep the yearning from her voice.

'Snug in their stalls. Reckon Empress showed Snow King what a stall is for. Don't worry,' he added, 'there's hay in the rack for them.'

She nodded. They'd need extra food in the cold, but the hay would do for now. No need for corn when neither was being worked or ridden much. Suddenly the paddocks seemed further away than Sydney or Calcutta or London.

'How are the onion seedlings? Have the peas come up?'

'It's all fine.' He spoke wearily. 'I know what to do.'

'Joey,' she said impulsively. 'Please move my bed into the kitchen.'

'The kitchen!' It was as though she'd asked him to move the chooks into the parlour or Empress into Mum and Dad's bedroom.

'Please. It's ...' She hesitated. She couldn't say she was lonely: that would seem like a reproach. Joey and Kirsty had so much to do, with no extra time to spend with her. Nor could she say she wanted a better idea of what was happening on the farm. 'I can do things more easily in the kitchen. We would only need the one lamp too.' She dreaded the dark of the long winter nights, lying here unable to read or sew to save the cost of lamp oil or candles.

Joey looked at the bed, considering. 'We could move the kitchen dresser into the dining room,' he said. They never used the dining room now.

'Please.'

'Kirsty's bed is lighter. Takes up less room.'

'I'll swap beds with her then.'

He nodded. 'It's a grand idea, Flint.'

And it was. For the first time since her accident dinner almost seemed normal, Joey and Kirsty sitting at the table and her with her tray on the bed. She'd peeled the potatoes for dinner and chopped the carrots for the stew.

I can help shuck the corn when it's ripe, she thought. Plait onions, pod the beans for seed. Now they didn't need a fire in her bedroom, didn't need to light an extra lamp. She could supervise Kirsty's attempts at cooking too. Above all she had company; she was part of it all again.

For now, it had to be enough.

Dad always said the third snow was the one that stuck. They woke to find the world white, the snow hanging heavy on the gum trees, carpeting the ground in long white drifts that grew thinner as they passed the Rock. Snow never lingered in the valley, but it could lodge up here for weeks, until the wind warmed and brought rain to send the snow gushing into the gully, the creek swelling to a river, speeding silver between the she-oaks down below.

She saw a glimpse of the newly white world through the window, then through the kitchen door, as Kirsty slipped out to get more firewood. Already the novelty of being in the kitchen had worn off. Day by day she saw Joey's face grow more set, weighed down by the burdens of the farm and household.

How long had it been since Kirsty had laughed? Kirsty should be playing with friends down at school. Joey should be planning his life, not living with the burden of a useless sister. All his dreams needed school to make them real. But how could he get there with a crippled sister to care for?

Even if they moved down to the Macks', she knew Joey would feel he owed them his work in return for all their help, and the Macks would accept it. None of their boys had ever gone to high school, much less taken an apprenticeship or gone to university. It would never occur to the Macks that a young man might feel confined in the valley, instead of free.

She picked up her sewing. She'd already darned the edge of nearly every sheet and tea towel in the house; pulled apart an old jumper of Dad's, worn through at the elbows and tatty at the hem, and used the best of the wool in new socks for Joey. She had read every book twenty times, even the Shakespeare.

It should be Joey and Kirsty who were reading, not her!

Kirsty slipped back into the kitchen, opening the door as little as possible to keep out the cold. Flinty wanted to yell at her to leave it wide open, so she could smell the wind, not the stale kitchen air, so she could see the sunlight and the hills. But any complaint would just make Kirsty's face bleaker.

The sky began to weep again by mid-afternoon. Joey put his wet boots by the fire to dry. He sat silently, his hands on his legs, his still-thin frame exhausted.

'Is there water in the trough for the horses?'

'Yes, Flinty.'

'Did you give them some corn? They'll need extra in this cold wind.'

'It's all done.' His voice seemed to echo with what he didn't say: *All that I can do.*

She wanted to ask more: not from any real fear that he had left things undone, just to remind herself of the time when she'd been able to do it. But any more questions would sound like nagging.

'If you can pass me the flour and the dripping and a bucket of apples from the larder I'll make a crumble,' she said.

Joey smiled at that. She saw the effort that went into it, knew how hard it was to give a smile back. It wasn't just the sky that was grey now. The light and warmth seemed to have been sucked from their lives just like it had from the winter world around.

The apple crumble brightened up a meal that consisted of a tough haunch of kangaroo — not even a day's boiling could soften it — with boiled potatoes and cabbage. They ate as the shadows lengthened, partly to save lamp oil and partly because there was nothing else to do, and the wind played hide-and-seek around the shutters.

Six months earlier they might have played knucklebones or checkers after dinner, but the last eight weeks had left her brother and sister too tired for after-dinner games.

Suddenly Joey halted, his fork halfway to his mouth. 'You hear that?'

'No,' said Flinty. All she could hear was the wind.

Kirsty's eyes were wide. 'It's not that man again? The man who hurt Flinty ...?'

Flinty clenched her fists. Kirsty wasn't supposed to know about Sergeant Morris, but she supposed people whispered about what you weren't supposed to talk about. She wondered what her little sister had overheard. She forced herself to speak calmly. 'Sergeant Morris died falling down the rocks. He can't hurt anybody now.'

'Maybe it's his ghost —'

'There are no ghosts —' She stopped. No ghosts, except on the Rock, in the mist. Instead she said, 'Ghosts can't hurt us. Anyway, all the ghosts here would be kind ones.'

'How do you know?'

'Shh,' said Joey, and now Flinty could hear it too: Snow King's whinny of challenge to another horse, the *clomp* of hooves. Well, ghosts didn't ride horses, unless there were ghost horses too, and none of the neighbours would have come up the mountain as late as this.

It must be a stranger, though few swaggies rode horses ... They'd have to offer a stranger hospitality on a night like this. But in the barn, she thought, with two quilts, never mind if he steals them in the morning. They weren't having a stranger sleeping in the house.

'The shotgun,' she whispered. 'Joey, put it under my blanket.'

Joey nodded, eyes wide. He fetched it quietly. She felt the shotgun's reassuring coldness as he slid it down beside her. She'd stay on watch with her hand on the trigger all night if she had to.

They waited for the knock on the front door. Instead she heard footsteps on the side verandah. The stranger was coming around the back. Everyone would know on a night like this the family would be in the kitchen, at the back of the house, and anyway, whoever it was out there would have seen the cracks of light under the shutter.

The footsteps sounded like a man's. Kirsty shrank back on Flinty's bed. Flinty put one arm around her, the other hand on the hidden shotgun. 'Who is it?' she yelled.

The back door opened with a flurry of snowflakes and wind. 'Well, that's a fine welcome,' said Andy. 'Any dinner left for me?'

Chapter 28

15 May 1920

Dear Diary,

Until tonight, when I realised just how much we'd missed Andy, it had never really bothered me that we didn't have aunts or uncles like other people. Even the Whites have cousins, though they're mostly in prison.

Mum was an orphan — she didn't even know where her people came from. Dad's parents were dead too. His father had been in the Indian Army as well — I think that was one of the reasons he let Jeff join up early, because he'd always hoped Jeff would follow his family tradition. I don't know how our McAlpine grandparents died. I think from something he said once it may have been in some battle or raid on the North-West Frontier, but Dad never told me, though he may have told Andy. He did have cousins in England, but I think they lost touch when he became an officer and went out to India again.

So it was just us. But everyone in the valley was family, really, even the ones who didn't like each other, like me and

Amy, and Snowy White and Barry Brown. They even had a punch-up after church one day, till the Reverend Postlewhistle put off his surplice and punched both of them on the chin. They hadn't known he'd learned boxing!

The next week one of the Browns' haystacks caught alight, and Snowy saw it first and burned his hands lashing at the fire with green wattle branches so it didn't spread to the rest of the haystacks in the paddock. Although that didn't stop them having a punch-up three Sundays later, but down at the creek that time so the Reverend didn't see them.

'I came as soon as I heard.' Joey and Kirsty were bathed, in bed, their excitement turned to exhaustion, as though the responsibility of caring for their sister had been a boulder they could only now set down, after two months.

Andy sat by her bed in the kitchen, tall and sandy haired, more freckles than ever. He'd grown a moustache too: a big red one that turned up at the ends as though he waxed them. He looked tired, but the bruises under his eyes, the ones that looked as though the war had left him bleeding inside, had gone.

'I'm sorry,' she said. It was the seventh time she'd said it since he got back.

'Not your fault, Sis.' He'd been saying *that* over and over. It was good to have him call her 'Sis' again. He'd brought his new name for her back from the war. He took her hand. It was a sudden shock how much his hand looked like Dad's, the rider's calluses Andy had lost in France back again. 'It's my fault. I should've been here for you.'

'Wouldn't have made any difference. I'd still have slipped.' She carefully didn't mention Sergeant Morris.

'Or maybe you wouldn't have.'

He's heard exactly what happened, she thought. Had Sandy written to him, or Mrs Mack? It had to be one or the other, because Mr Mack couldn't do much more than sign his name, though he could read the newspaper.

Suddenly she had to know. 'What was Sergeant Morris like when you knew him in France?'

Andy was silent for a moment, tweaking one end of his moustache: a new mannerism. Wondering how much to tell me, she thought. Wondering if he should tell me anything.

'I need to know.'

'He was a good bloke. Did his share without complaining. Saw him give his bully beef to a stray dog once. He'd grown up in an orphanage, said he knew what it was like to be a stray. Jeff knew him better than me. I only met him that one time we were on leave together.'

Andy gave an almost grin. 'I spent my leave with a couple of mademoiselles. Right goers, they were. Caught up with Jeff and the others at this café where they knew the word for "beer". Jeff and Sandy and Bertie told me all about the churches they'd visited, and this palace. Churches.' He shook his head.

It hadn't occurred to her that Sandy would also know Sergeant Morris. But of course Sandy and Jeff had served together, after their march from the Snowy to Goulburn.

'Were you there when Sergeant Morris was wounded?'

'No. Heard about it though.' She knew from his tone he wasn't going to say more than that.

'Did you ever see him afterwards? When he got better, I mean.' Or as better as he ever got, she thought.

'No. His wounds were what they called a blighty one. Got him sent to Blighty, to England, and then shipped back home. Except there wasn't any home for him, I suppose. No family to take him in. Just the repatriation hospital. I should've looked him up when I came through Sydney. Didn't even think of it. He was one of so many I met once or twice. They were in the same trench as you, or you met them in a café on leave, and then they were gone. That's no excuse, I know. I suppose I just wanted to forget the war and all that was in it. Flinty ... he was a good bloke when I knew him. Not the sort to hurt a girl.'

'He was ... confused. Not all there.'

'Having part of your skull shot away does that to a bloke,' he said, then added, 'Sorry. Shouldn't have said that.'

'No, I'm glad you did. I'm glad he was a good bloke. Glad that I wrote to him.' It wasn't entirely true. Part of her wanted him to be a villain, so she could rage against him. But even when she'd tried to run from him there'd been a desperate pity with her terror too. 'I'm sorry that he died that way, but I think by then he was a different man from the one you knew.' Or maybe he wasn't, she thought. Maybe the good bloke had still been inside that poor fumbling shamble of a man, just hadn't known what to say or how to say it, how to court a girl he'd once had a letter from, the only girl he sort of knew. Or perhaps inside the good bloke in the trenches had been the one she'd glimpsed, inside the one who'd force a kiss.

Andy had never known Bertie Morris in normal times. She had a feeling Sandy wouldn't want to look at churches these days, just as Andy didn't cavort with mademoiselles any more. If he'd wanted that sort of life he'd have stayed in Sydney, not gone to Queensland droving.

Andy wouldn't speak of Bertie Morris again, she knew, just as he'd probably never tell her more about the day Jeff died, or what he saw in his nightmares. Well, she had her secrets now too. It was impossible to tell Andy about Nicholas, or the promise of something 'very, very good' that kept her going. He'd think that she was mad.

'What's that smile for, Sis? Glad I'm home?'

'Yes.'

'Never should have gone away.'

'We needed the money.'

Andy gave her a look she couldn't interpret. 'Well, I've got my wages now. Miss Matilda wired me extra too, when she heard I was coming home. She said her manager told her that they'd never have got Repentance back without you. They're good people down at Drinkwater.'

'They're good people up here too. They've looked after us.'

'Like I should have done. I could have got a job here, Sis. I *have* got a job, rouseabout three days a week down at Mullinses'. Won't take me more than an hour or so to ride there and back each day. Might spend the night there sometimes. But I'll mostly be here.' He looked at her steadily. 'There was another reason I had to get away.'

'Because I kept questioning you?'

He looked surprised. 'Why would you think that? You always have asked questions, goose. No, it was just ...' He shrugged. 'For four years I kept dreaming of home. The mountains. Mum and Dad and you lot. But when I got back —'

'It wasn't home,' she said flatly. 'Mum and Dad were dead. And Jeff.'

'It was home all right. But it was too ... sudden. That's not the word for it. I'd had those months in camp and on the boat before I got back here. But I needed, well, *space*, I think, before it was all real. Does that sound barmy?'

She squeezed his hand. 'No.'

'It was beautiful, Sis. Not like it is up here, ridge after ridge. Plains that go on to the sky, trees with no grass under them at all, just red sand as far as you can see. A flood came down while we were out there — just a little one, but one morning a dry gully was under ten feet of water. No rain. It just came up from nowhere, not even any sound.'

'How can water come from nowhere?'

He laughed. It was good to hear him laugh. 'Not really from nowhere. It rained up north and the water flowed south, week after week, month after month, till it got to us. But my word was it good. We even had a wash.'

'Bet you stank.'

'I did at that. You should see Brisbane too — the river's even bigger than the Snowy. You should just taste their bananas and pineapples. I'll buy you all a pineapple one day, and the ladies of Brisbane ...' He grinned, and touched his moustache again. 'Well, you don't want to hear about that. I'm glad I did it, Sis. But I won't go away again. Truly. I'm not just saying that.'

There was too much that could be said between them both. Too much pain. Too much loss. He hadn't asked about her back, her legs. She was so sick of telling the same lie, over and over: 'It hardly hurts at all'; and the same truth: 'I can't sit up unless I'm propped up. I can't move my legs either.' She understood a little more now of why Andy and all the others wouldn't talk of what they'd seen, what they'd been through.

Instead he said, 'That's a grand horse out there, Sis. He came up to the fence to give us the once-over when I rode up.'

She grinned. 'His name's Snow King. And he's mine,

remember. But you can train him. Split the money when he wins his first race.'

'Sell him after that?'

'Only if we have to. Mr Mack says we should lease him to a trainer next year. I'd like to breed from him too when he's older.'

'We'll get some grand foals from that one. Have to find a few good mares first though. Can't see Empress as mother to a racehorse.' He stretched and yawned. 'It's good to be back, Sis.'

It was so good she didn't even try to find the words. Instead she said, 'Joey and Kirsty can go back to school again now. They've missed too much already.'

'Sis ...' He hesitated.

'What?'

'Joey can go to school. But not Kirsty. Someone has to stay here with you.'

'I'm fine by myself.'

'No, you're not. And even if you were ...' He looked away. 'I can't do it all, Sis. Not work at Mullinses' and keep the garden going and the housework too.'

And care for her. Wash her, make her bed, bring her food. Flinty was silent. Andy was right. It was almost dark by the time Joey and Kirsty got back from school in winter. By then the fire would be out, the stove cold, the hens eaten by the dingoes.

Girls married. Boys had to make their way in the world. If only one of them could get an education it had to be Joey. Girls were so often kept at home to care for frail grandparents, or even when there were too many brothers and sisters for their mother to manage. Schooling was still a luxury for girls. It isn't fair, she thought. But then, nothing was. The world didn't work on fair. In a fair world only those who made a war would suffer from it.

'Joey wants to be a vet,' she said.

He looked at her steadily. 'Sis, there's no way we can manage that. He'd have to spend years studying. It'd cost hundreds of pounds.' He shrugged. 'It would be different if we had relatives he could stay with in a town. But we don't.'

'Dad wanted Joey to go to university if he could.'

'Dad's plans are no use now, Flinty. He had his pension, and the income from the horses. He thought his old army mates would get Jeff a commission and that he and I could build up the farm again when I came home. But I'll never be the trainer Dad was. And now ...' He shrugged again.

Now you have a crippled sister to support, she thought, and empty paddocks.

He yawned, the new moustache almost reaching to his eyes. 'I'm beat, Sis. It's been a long day. It'll be good to sleep in a bed again.'

'When do you have to go down to Mullinses'?'

'Day after tomorrow. Any stores we need?'

'Only a billy of milk, if they've got some. We've got enough food to feed an army. Everyone has been so kind.'

'We've good neighbours.' He stood up. 'Better get some shut-eye. Is there anything you need ...?'

He meant did she need the chamberpot put under her, but Kirsty had done that before she went to bed.

'I'll sleep too. Good night, Andy. I'm so glad you're home.'

'Me too,' he said.

For the first time in months she slept deeply, despite the pain, waking only when the kookaburras carolled from the branches outside.

Chapter 29

3 June 1920

Dear Diary,

I dreamed I could run last night. Not walk, just run across the mountains, faster than I ever have before. I kept trying to get back to the dream even after my body began to wake up.

The others were still asleep. I can't do much, of course, till someone helps me, so I just lay there, thinking. Nicholas had told me how he had a bar rigged up so he could haul himself in and out of his chair from and to his bed. But he could move his hips. It hurts so much when I try.

I wonder if Nicholas is able to walk on his new legs yet? I suppose you need to learn to balance, like on a bicycle. I've never ridden a bicycle, but I saw them down in Gibber's Creek. Even women ride them. I'll never ride a bicycle now. Sob sob. Get a hold of yourself, Flinty McAlpine. You never even wanted to ride a bicycle anyhow.

The chooks have stopped laying. I've told Kirsty to give

them more corn and a hot bran mash each morning. I should have told her before.

Sandy came up yesterday afternoon. He and Andy played checkers, and Sandy won three times. He's going to bring up their draught horse so Andy can plough the corn and potato fields, and oats too, and later cut the hay. Andy wants to use some of my fifty pounds to buy a draught horse of our own. I'd rather buy a good mare, for breeding. But there's no need to do either this year, not with the Macks so kind and Snow King too young.

'*It's a long, long way to Tipperary*,' sang Kirsty as she scrubbed the kitchen floor.

Flinty watched from her bed, her fingers clicking her knitting needles, trying to remember the pattern. These were to be gloves for Mrs Mack, to thank her, just a little.

It was as though a small sun shone over Rock Farm, now Andy was home. Even the weather changed: the sky was blue, the days warm and each night cloudy like a blanket holding in the day's warmth.

Kirsty seemed happy. Among Andy's presents for his family were green gumboots for her ('Green,' said Kirsty blissfully. 'Green!'). She wore them even indoors now, with three pairs of socks because Andy had bought them big for her to grow into.

Somehow most days Mrs Mullins or Mrs Mack or one of the Colours women made 'a little bit extra' — a billy of soup or stew for dinner, or syrup dumplings or a plate of pumpkin fritters for Andy to bring home, acknowledging without saying anything that a nine-year-old girl wouldn't have the cooking skills to feed a family easily, even with her older sister's direction.

Meanwhile Empress carried Joey down to the Macks' to go to school and back, while Snow King paced his paddock alone, except for the days that Andy rode him up and down to the Mullinses', leaving Lord George to crop the grass instead. Next summer, said Andy, he'd take the young horse down to the valley flats, give him his head and start racing him against the valley horses. There were no locals with Snow King's potential, but he needed to learn to want to win, as well as be guided by a jockey in a race.

'And then we'll see,' Andy had said, which meant taking him to a race in Gibber's Creek perhaps, or even Goulburn, where a proper trainer might agree to take him on.

Kirsty carried the bucket of dirty water outside and threw it on the rhubarb patch. Flinty breathed in the sharp winter air. 'Leave the door open,' she said as Kirsty came back in, eggs in her apron now. 'The floor will dry faster. There's no wind today. How many eggs?' The hot bran mash had worked.

'Five.'

Not bad for mid-winter, thought Flinty. 'What's it like outside?' She tried not to make her voice wistful.

'Not a cloud anywhere, except for the mist on the Rock.'

For a moment she longed for Nicholas. He would understand what it was like to be crippled. At least she was still whole. But it might be months before Nicholas was back, and even then she couldn't reach him, not down on the Rock.

Was he still writing his book, wherever he was now?

'Will I make scones for lunch?' Kirsty was proud of her scones. The first ones had been small and black as sheep pellets, but she had the knack now.

Flinty nodded. 'Kirsty — do you miss school?'

Kirsty carefully looked at the mixing bowl, not her sister. 'No.'

'Really?'

Kirsty shrugged. 'Well, Enid and Meg.' Enid Brown was just her age, Meg Green a year older. Rocky Valley school still had far more boys than girls. 'Andy said he'll invite them to come up here for a few days in the school holidays.'

'Good,' said Flinty absently. But a few days with her friends wouldn't make up for months of learning. 'Kirsty, how about I give you lessons?'

Kirsty looked so horrified that Flinty laughed. 'Spelling and things?' Kirsty made it sound like her sister was offering her green slugs.

'Spelling's useful,' said Flinty.

'I *despise* spelling,' said Kirsty. 'I *despise* the little Red Maths Book too. And I *despise* my copybook.'

Mr Ross might be able to get Kirsty to do her spelling and sums when she didn't want to, backed up by the school inspector and the truant officer. But Flinty doubted that she'd be able to.

What did a girl need to learn at school? How to read and write and do her sums, and what the world was like beyond the valley? I can teach her reading and writing and sums, thought Flinty, as well as Mr Ross can. But only if Kirsty wants to learn.

She looked at her sister, carefully shaping her scones, humming 'It's a Long Way to Tipperary' again under her breath. 'How about you write something now?'

Kirsty wrinkled her nose. 'It's lunchtime.'

'After lunch?'

'Don't want to.'

'Please. For me.'

Kirsty poked her lip out stubbornly. 'I've got to ...' She stopped while she tried to think of an urgent job.

Flinty grinned. Joey brought up the water from the well every morning before he left for school and Andy made sure the horses were fed. There wasn't anything urgent left this afternoon. 'You've got to learn to write, Kirsty.'

'I *can* write.'

'Write better then. More words. Neat ones that people can read.'

'Tomorrow.' Kirsty bent to put the tin of scones in the oven.

And tomorrow she'd decide to clean out the henhouse — wearing Joey's shirt and trousers so she wouldn't get hers mucky. Then Joey would yell at the pong when he got home. Flinty reckoned in Kirsty's mind even shovelling chook poo was better than her copybook. But once you left school there were so many other things to write — letters and diaries. A world to read in books. 'With a shelf of books I can have a universe in my lap,' Dad used to say, 'and still sit here on my mountains.' She had a sudden image of Nicholas's hands, with his strange pen, writing in the notebook on his lap. She wished he'd read some of it out to her, but he'd always refused, saying his novel was still coming together in his mind. Suddenly she had an idea.

'How about I tell you a story,' she said, 'and you write it down?'

Kirsty looked cautiously interested. 'A story? Like the bedtime ones you used to tell us before Mum died?'

Flinty stared at her sister. She'd forgotten about the stories she used to tell. They'd vanished at Mum's death, she realised.

Maybe her brain had tried to shrink into the smallest corner it could. But Kirsty didn't seem to notice the impact of her words.

'Tell me a story then,' the little girl ordered, sitting on the edge of the bed and rubbing a smudge off her gumboots.

Flinty came back to the present. 'This is a story for writing down.'

Kirsty looked at her stubbornly. '*You* write it down. You write in your diary all the time.'

'You need to write it so you get the writing practice. I'll talk and you write.'

Kirsty looked at her consideringly. Kirsty knew all about negotiating a bribe. 'Maybe,' she said at last. 'But only if it's a *really* good story. A *really*, *really* good one.' She got up to take out the scones and get the plum jam from the larder.

A really, really good story, thought Flinty, as they ate their scones, as she washed up in the bowl of water on the bedside table while Kirsty dried and put away, then peeled the potatoes and chopped up cabbage and swedes for dinner. Where was she going to find a really, *really* good story?

Kirsty and Joey — and even Jeff, though he'd never have admitted it — had liked the stories she used to tell, but that was because they were bedtime stories, an excuse not to go to sleep till they were done. Where was her brain going to find *new* stories anyway?

It was all right for Nicholas. He'd done exciting things. The only exciting thing she had ever done was run the mob of brumbies.

She could make up a story about that ride, but Kirsty had already heard the best bits.

A ghost story? Like the one she'd told once about the ghost who turned out to be a goat eating a sheet from the washing line?

No, not when real apparitions haunted the Rock below the house. If there *were* ghosts other than Nicholas she didn't want Kirsty even thinking about them. Books were about fascinating things, orphans, like Jane Eyre, who was sent off to an orphanage and met a romantic rich man with a mad wife, or about heroes like Rob Roy. The only heroes she knew were in books. Or just possibly her brother, and Sandy and Toby and maybe even Snowy White, but if they'd been heroic they wouldn't tell her.

Maybe she could make up a story about a king or a prince; but the only one she could remember from school was King Henry the Eighth with his six wives, or was it eight? Anyway, she couldn't tell Kirsty a story about a king chopping off his wives' heads. And Napoleon, but she hadn't been paying attention when Mr Ross had taught them about him ...

There were the stories in the books she'd read, but she instinctively rejected those. They'd been told already; and anyhow, none of them interested Kirsty enough to read them. Shoes, she thought. Kirsty would love a story about shoes ... magic shoes that tapped along the mountain road. That would fascinate Kirsty ... and might give her nightmares too.

Which left only one thing she knew about. Horses. A magic flying horse? But where would it fly to? Gibber's Creek?

And then she had it. She'd tell a story about Snow King. No, not Snow King. Lamentation! The great racehorse who had escaped from men's fences, and led his brumbies up in the high country. But she would call him Mountain King.

In her story no man from Snowy River would catch him — and no girl either. Mountain King would stay free.

Yet he was still the horse who had won every race on every track, who had known what it was like to lead the field, hearing the pants of lesser horses far behind, the cheers of the crowd as once more he galloped past the winning post.

Great horses don't forget.

She caught her breath. It was suddenly so clear that she could see it. The country race track, out of town below the hillside where the brumbies had camped the night before, the men spreading the blankets on the grass, the women with their picnic baskets, the girls in hats with ribbons, the boys brushed up and at their best.

Mountain King had led the mob away from the noise. But the sounds and smells had lured him back, leaving his mob with the lead mare. Now he stood among the trees, above the race track.

The horses lined up at the starting gate. The crowd gathered at the rail. And on the hillside the great stallion watched. He heard the starter's pistol ...

The horses surged along the track. Suddenly the great brown stallion leaped the fence, behind them at first, then slowly gaining, hooves thundering and tearing up the grass, riderless, knowing he had to win. And then the cheers, as the stallion passed the winning post.

Hands tried to catch him. But Mountain King reared, so they all stood back in fear. He bent his head and charged, out of the crowd, over the fence again, and up into the mountains with his mares.

Until the next race. The brown stallion would become a legend, the wild horse who could not be beaten. Time after time the men would try to catch him. But every time he'd beat them, and run free.

It was so real she felt tears of excitement on her cheeks, a longing to know what happened next. She'd call it *The Dance of the Mountain King.*

'Kirsty?'

Kirsty looked back from stirring the rabbit stew. 'What? I'm not letting it burn, Flinty. I'm stirring it right to the bottom, like you said.'

'What do you think about a story called *The Dance of the Mountain King*?'

Kirsty considered. Flinty could see the interest in her eyes. 'I don't know,' she said warily. 'What's it about? What mountain is he king of? Why does he want to dance?'

'I'm not going to tell you anything till you've got paper and pencil. You have to write the story down.'

'What if it's boring?'

'It won't be.'

'But if it's boring I can stop?' bargained Kirsty.

Flinty nodded, trying to think. It was a good story, but if Kirsty didn't like the first sentence she'd refuse to write.

She reached under her pillow and pulled out the exercise book that held her diary. Blank paper was precious, and empty books even more so. But there were no slates up here in the mountains. This was all she had. She tried to think of the most non-boring sentence to start the story with.

And then suddenly the words came, as though the mountains had whispered them, as if a ghost was dictating from down in the mist.

'Turn the book upside down and start from the back, where the pages are still blank,' she said, and now she longed to have the words secured on paper before they could float away. 'Do it in pencil first, so you can rub it out if you make a mistake. Then go over the words in ink when you've got them right.'

If this worked she was going to have to tear out her diary pages before Kirsty read them. But she could do that tonight.

For a moment she thought Kirsty was going to say no. But she was bored too — bored enough even to write a story down. She took the book, turned to a blank page, then picked up the pencil. '*The*,' she said, writing laboriously. 'How do you spell "dance", Flinty?'

'D–a–n–c–e,' said Flinty, hoping she had it right and it shouldn't have an 's' in it somewhere too. She'd hated spelling as much as Kirsty had, at school. She'd have to be careful not to use words she couldn't spell. Andy's spelling was even worse than hers.

'He was the king of the mountain,' she began softly. 'Brown as the sunlight on the autumn creek, glossy as an apple.' Flinty could almost hear her father's voice. He'd talked like that sometimes too. 'Once Mountain King had won the greatest horse races in the land. But no man can own a king. No paddock fence can hold him.

'Now Mountain King looked down at the horses and riders gathering at the starting gate. He reared up, his front hooves pawing at the air, and whinnied a challenge.

'He would join this race. And he would win. He had to win. He was the king! The strongest and tallest horse who had ever galloped across the ridges.

'He reared again, in scorn. No man alive could catch Mountain King.'

Kirsty looked up, her mouth open, the pencil in her hand. 'Does he win?' she whispered. 'Please, Flinty. Do they catch him again? Tell me what happens next. Then I promise I'll write it down.'

Chapter 30

15 July 1920

Dear Diary,

Three eggs today. Sandy brought up a whole pile of women's magazines that a friend sent from Sydney. Sandy didn't say who the friend was, but it must be a girl or they wouldn't be women's magazines.

So there is someone, just as I thought. He must be writing to her without letting his family know. Maybe he's asked Jones the postman not to tell anyone — I never thought of that. Dad said that in the early days the mail was put in a hollow tree, down where the creek joins the Snowy, and it waited there till someone rode out to pick it up. Maybe Sandy has asked Jones to use the hollow again, so everyone doesn't gossip about his business.

Or maybe Mrs Mack just takes any letters to Sandy out of the box and gives them to him privately. I've been living in story land too much with Kirsty. I'll be imagining Sandy is going to gallop away with a Ruritanian princess on his saddle next.

Sandy sat with me for ages, telling me and Kirsty all the valley news. Joey and Andy are too tired to tell us things when they get home, or maybe they don't realise how much we want to know, up here away from everyone. Snowy White was had up as drunk and disorderly at the dance at Gibber's Creek last Friday, but he asked the policeman's sister to go to the next one with him when she brought him his breakfast, and she said yes! Annie Mack is expecting again, and Mutti Green had a 'turn' after church, but is all right again now. Mrs Mack loves her new gloves.

It was good to get the magazines though. I wouldn't read them to Kirsty — I made her read them aloud to me. The dresses are higher than the women's knees in some of them and every skirt is above the ankle! The women even have short hair!

At least Kirsty really likes the story now. She even coaxes me to tell her more after dinner, and writes it down without any complaining. Or not much. Joey likes it too, and even Andy grinned last night when Mountain King outraced the bushranger then led his horse to freedom in the hills. Andy has let his beard grow, so you can't see the moustache any more. His moustache looked funny at first with those red waxed points, but I miss it now.

Boiled mutton and dumplings with onion sauce for dinner, and apple pie. The stored apples are starting to wrinkle and go off. Apple cake tomorrow, then I'll make apple dumplings. Joey can take cold dumplings down for lunch.

I am trying to be glad that Sandy really might have a girlfriend. Even if he still liked me that way, even if we had been engaged, I'd have had to break off the engagement now. I do want Sandy to be happy. If anyone deserves happiness it is Sandy Mack.

The story grew. It filled the rest of the diary and half of the new exercise book she'd asked Sandy to bring her. A trap was set for Mountain King at the next race meeting — a trap to catch the greatest racehorse in the land. Kirsty spent an hour each day writing the words. Flinty wrote some of the story down too, partly because otherwise it went too slowly to keep Kirsty interested, but also because when she wrote she was no longer lying in a narrow bed in the kitchen, but galloping back up the mountains to freedom with the king.

Mountain King could run while she was trapped in bed, could gaze across the ridges while all she could see was the small patches through the kitchen door and window.

Mountain King chose his own destiny, not like a crippled girl, slicing swedes for lunch.

But she could call herself happy, some of the time at least, the times when the pain didn't snake down her legs, so that whichever way she lay it hurt, the hours when she could forget what might have been, and enjoy the small joys around her.

Kirsty sang her times tables now as she plaited long strings of onions with Flinty, or worked out that if Andy gave her a penny a day, she could have new red shoes by Christmas, if she gave the cobbler her old shoes as part of the payment.

Kirsty even read the newspaper because she was interested now, not because Flinty coaxed her to do it. It was more than a month old by the time Mr Mack had read it and passed it round the valley. But it still spoke to them of the world 'down there': short skirts and a campaign to make women's wages in the public service four-fifths of men's for the same job, instead of less than half; Australian Bert Hinkler flying non-stop from London to Turin, trying to be the first to fly the almost impossible distance from London to Australia.

'Imagine a plane flying over us,' said Kirsty dreamily.

'He'd never get it over the mountains,' said Flinty.

'Yes, he would,' said Joey. 'Mr Hinkler flew over ten thousand feet high above the Italian Alps.' He spoke as though Mr Hinkler was his own friend — which he may have been in Joey's dreams. 'Our mountains are not much more than a quarter of that.'

Flinty imagined balancing like an eagle on the updraughts ... but maybe a plane was noisy, like the motorcar they'd seen when they went down to town, its engine hiccuping and jolting along. She looked out the door at the slim patch of blue sky, the slip of winter-brown hillside. There'd been no more big snowfalls, just flakes that drifted in the breeze and two days of wind and sleet so sharp that Joey's cheeks looked red and bruised from the journey back from school. He stayed at home till the wind died down, while Andy slept over at the Mullinses'.

I want to fly, thought Flinty. I want to gallop on a horse again. I want to run as fast as the wind so the rain and snow can't catch me.

I want to walk.

Flinty woke early on her birthday. The coals glowed from the fireplace. Outside she could hear the mutter of the wind as it slid around the house. Mum had said Flinty had been born in a snowstorm, the drifts so thick there'd been no chance to get old Grandma Mack up to help, or the doctor if anything had gone wrong.

But it hadn't. 'You didn't even cry,' said Mum. 'Just looked around as though you were happy to be here. So we called you Felicity. It means happiness. You've always been a happy child. We're the happiest family in the mountains.'

Until the war, thought Flinty. The war ate ten million men and took chunks of our family too. Mum might be alive if it hadn't been for the shock of Jeff's death. Dad wouldn't have died of the influenza, spread by the troops coming home.

She heard the scrape of the chest of drawers in Joey's room. He must be up then. Andy had spent the last few nights down at the Mullinses' farm. The days were too short now for him to come home every night.

Would Joey or Kirsty remember it was her birthday? She hadn't wanted to remind anyone. She was probably the only one who kept a note of the date on the calendar anyway.

I should have told them, she thought. When they realised they'd forgotten all about it they'd be embarrassed not to have made her a present or a cake. Best to pretend she had forgotten it too.

'Morning,' muttered Joey. He wore his going-to-school clothes, not quite as patched and darned as the ones he wore on the farm. He bent and shoved some kindling onto the fire. It flared as he added some to the wood stove too.

He had forgotten. Flinty swallowed her disappointment. Joey looked at the clock on the mantelpiece. 'I'm late.' He sawed off a hunk of damper, spread it with dripping and treacle. 'This'll have to do me. See you tonight, Flinty.' He picked up the bag with his lunch in it.

'Have a good day,' she said, as Kirsty came bleary eyed along the corridor to help her wash and dress.

It was hair-washing day, Kirsty decided, putting on every saucepan they owned as well as the kettle so they could both have hot water. Afterwards she built up the fire to help their hair dry, spread across their shoulders like rain running down the hill.

'And let's put on your Sunday dress,' said Kirsty.

'Why?'

'Because we look pretty with clean hair,' Kirsty replied, with perfect logic.

Flinty nodded. It was easier to agree. At least her Sunday dress would make it feel a bit like a birthday, even if they hadn't had breakfast yet.

Kirsty fussed, sitting on spread-out old newspapers, polishing her red shoes. Flinty's tummy growled. She didn't have much appetite these days, but it must be nearly ten o'clock. The hens hadn't even been fed. 'Kirsty,' she began.

'I've got boot polish on my sleeve.'

'Give it a scrub with sand soap before next wash day.'

'It's on my *sleeve*, Flinty!' Kirsty sounded as though Flinty expected her to dress in cobwebs and ashes. She hauled the sand soap out from under the bench and scrubbed the sleeve anxiously. 'It's out!' she exclaimed at last. She sat back on the newspapers. 'I'll wear my sleeve protectors next time.'

'Good,' said Flinty. She really was hungry now. 'Look, leave those and put the porridge on. Or we might even have pancakes. How many eggs have we got?'

'Done,' said Kirsty, ignoring Flinty's question. She held up her shoes. 'Look at the shine on them!'

'Yes, but —' Flinty stopped at the sound of hoofbeats outside, the familiar sound of Empress's whinny and Snow King's high trumpet call in reply. Joey must have forgotten something. Or maybe Empress had picked up a stone. She thought with guilt about the hind leg that Empress sometimes still favoured.

She waited for the sound of Joey's boots on the verandah. But there was silence. 'That was Joey,' she said to Kirsty.

'Was it?' Kirsty looked innocent. Too innocent. 'I'll go and see,' she said.

She vanished out the door.

Flinty waited. Wheels, she thought. I can hear wheels too. And creaking, like the Macks' cart. And then more hoofbeats, and the mutter of voices.

What was happening? For a moment she felt fear: fear of swaggies, old soldiers, all the terrors that might happen to those she loved while she was helpless here. Then at last — or two minutes later — she heard the tap of Kirsty's shoes.

The back door opened.

'Happy birthday!' yelled Kirsty. She held a bright red balloon. Joey grinned behind her, and Andy and Mr and Mrs Mack, and even Amy White and her mother, and Sandy holding another bunch of everlastings (Where could he have found them in mid-winter? He must have searched for days!), and Ron Mullins and his mum, and Barry Brown with his little sister Enid, and Meg and Hannah and Mutti Green, someone from every Colour of the Valley, the women all carrying plates of food.

'Oh,' said Flinty, and burst into tears.

There was a giant sponge birthday cake with cream, and five sorts of pie, and jam tarts with eight types of jam, and rock cakes and custard slices, and mutton and chutney sandwiches, and the chocolate coconut-covered little cakes called lamingtons that Flinty had never had time to make before her accident.

None of it was proper for breakfast, but it was morning-tea time for everyone else. They ate and talked and drank a dozen pots of tea. They sang 'Happy Birthday' as Flinty blew out the candle on the cake and Mrs Mack and Mutti Green put on kettle after kettle of water.

Suddenly there was a creaking sound along the verandah. Flinty looked enquiringly at Andy. He grinned. 'Happy birthday, Sis,' he said quietly, as Mr Mack wheeled in her present.

'It's from all of us,' said Mr Mack.

It was a bathchair. Not like Nicholas's all-metal one. This was mostly wood and wicker, with bigger wheels, more cumbersome. It looked like Nicholas's chair's grandmother, like you'd need to push it hard to get it along a track.

It looked like freedom.

'We asked Dr Sparrow,' said Mrs Mack. 'He said it couldn't hurt you to sit in the chair for a while each day.'

Which probably meant he said that nothing could injure my back any more than it is already damaged, thought Flinty, staring at the chair.

'It was Sandy's idea,' said Andy, and Sandy blushed and moved from one foot to another.

'Got a nurse friend in Sydney who knows about bathchairs, that's all,' he muttered.

'Come on, lass,' said Mr Mack. She lifted her arms as he bent to pick her up; he placed her in the chair.

It hurt as he moved her, but it wasn't bad when she was

sitting down. It did feel unsteady, till Mrs Mack propped pillows around her to sort of jam her in. She sat there in her Sunday dress while they all stared anxiously until she smiled, thrilled despite the pain of moving.

'Where do you want to go?' asked Andy.

She wanted to go up the tallest mountain, up above the tree line, find the snow line and run back down. Instead she said, 'Out onto the verandah.'

Andy pushed her down the corridor, with everybody following, out the front door, onto the verandah. The valley stretched away on one side, brown now except for the always-green she-oak trees along the creek and the silver gleam of the Snowy River at the junction of the hills. On the other side the mountains were topped with a blaze of white, dressed for winter, whiter by far than the clouds above.

She took a deep breath. She could smell mothballs, from Mrs White's fur coat, wood smoke and old boots and horse droppings. She could smell the mountains too.

She wriggled her feet under her Sunday dress, lifted them as far as they would go, let them fall down. Even that small movement was exciting. She looked up to find Sandy looking at her strangely.

'That's all that will work,' she said apologetically.

'Now, not too much on the first day,' said Mrs Mack. 'You don't want to tire her out.'

'I'm not tired,' said Flinty.

It wasn't true. The pain, the shock, the happiness, the hope had all exhausted her, though they'd given her energy too.

She glanced down the track at the Rock. Mist hovered above it, trickling down the gully. Soon, she told it. I can come to you soon.

Chapter 31

1 August 1920

Dear Diary,

I am in love with my chair. Who would have thought it a year ago? Four wheels instead of two legs. But I watched the moon rise from the front verandah last night. Isn't that wonderful?

It took her a week to be able to roll the chair by herself, pushing the wheels with her hands. She could make her way around the kitchen, even out to the woodpile on the back verandah to bring in firewood. As long as the wood was stacked high enough for her to reach, she would put it on her lap to bring in and place in the fire compartment of the wood stove.

She could wheel herself out to the front verandah, watch the mist trickle down the gullies or enjoy the days when it spread like a white plate below Rock Farm, hiding the valley below. When someone visited now she could make her way to the window to see who was riding up, instead of having to lie helplessly, waiting for whoever came in the door.

Slowly the awareness of what she couldn't do began to seep into the joy.

The chair was cumbersome. She needed to go back and forth six times to manoeuvre around the kitchen table. It had no brakes, so even if she could somehow get down the stairs she couldn't push herself down the track herself — or up it either. This chair was for use on smooth level ground only and was easy to tip over, unlike Nicholas's lighter and more compact chair. On any slope it could run out of control, unless strong hands pushed her and controlled it. The chair was a prison, still, as well as a friend.

But on the second weekend Andy carried the chair down off the verandah onto the grass, then lifted her into it. If he thought it was strange that she wanted to be taken down to the Rock he didn't say so. It had the best view of the valley after all.

The mist was almost too thin to be visible, but she still felt its chill as Andy pushed her into it. It wasn't like the breath of winter, with its tinny scent of rock and snow. The Rock had a scent all its own.

'Sure you want to stay here, Sis?'

'Please. I've been in the house so long. I'm happy here by myself. Really.'

He didn't argue. He'd needed time to himself too. He never did say much these days, though at least his nightmares seemed to have gone. She watched him stride up the hill, then past the house and into Snow King's paddock, to shovel the droppings out of the stables and barrow it down to the vegetable garden for the spring's cabbages. Then she turned to watch the valley.

A new green rectangle of paddock at the Browns' — they must have put in a field of oats. Smoke rose from the chimneys of the Greens and Mullinses, hidden among the green, a faint haze from behind the hill that would be smoke from the Macks' stove. Across the valley the mountains wore their winter patchwork of green and white and slashes of black shadow, where the low-angled winter sun wouldn't kiss the rocky gullies until spring.

Something moved behind her. She turned. A wallaby gazed at her, as though it couldn't believe a human could sit so still, then blinked and hopped off into the hop bush. A currawong began its liquid descant, echoing across the valley.

She snuggled further into the rabbit-skin rug that Kirsty had tucked around her. She could hear the wind moan up on the mountains, as though complaining about the high hills that made it creep and roll instead of flying straight ahead. Here on the Rock the air was still, the fog thickening, like a stew after you'd added flour and water. The mist grew deeper, and deeper still. The valley slowly vanished. The world was white and still and cold.

And Nicholas didn't come. She had known he wouldn't come after the first few minutes. If he had been on the mountain he'd have been here all day.

She had known he'd be away for many months. It felt like years had passed, but it had only been six months. She had hoped nevertheless that he might be here today. If it was impossible that a ghost from 1970 would appear then maybe another impossible could happen too.

But Nicholas had known what was going to happen to her too. Probably he thought she wouldn't be able to get down to the Rock, or at least not so soon. Besides, visitors didn't come to the mountains in winter. They came after the spring thaw, to fish, to climb the hills.

Of course Nicholas wasn't here today. She realised she had simply hoped he might be so that he could reassure her that there *was* a future for her. Good things, he'd said.

The chair was good. But it wasn't really, *really* good, as Kirsty would say. The chair just made what had happened a little less bad. Andy's return was good too, and Sandy visiting again, talking to her, to Andy and the others, almost as though the war had never been. But none of it made up for all she'd lost.

Her future — and any good bits — were still lost then. No, not lost, just still to come. She had to believe that, just as she had to carry on.

When she heard footsteps behind her now she knew it was Andy. She smiled at him, her kind big brother with the long red beard he never bothered to trim these days. She let him push her up the hill, to the kitchen where Kirsty had pancakes ready with plum jam.

Chapter 32

2 August 1920

Dear Diary,

Andy wants a motorbike! I just sat there with my mouth open when he told us while Joey cried, 'Wacko!'

'Why do you want a motor anything?' I asked.

He looked at me like I was crazy. At last he said, 'To ride to work and back. What if Empress or Lord George go lame after Snow King goes down to a trainer?'

'But a motorbike,' I said. 'You can buy ten horses for the price of a motorbike.'

'A second-hand motorbike,' he muttered. 'Fellow down in Gibber's Creek has one for sale. It's got a sidecar too.'

I said, 'You want to use my money —' but Andy didn't let me finish. He just slapped his napkin down and said, 'Well, I'm earning the money we're actually living on, miss, and I'll buy a motorbike if I want one. What else is there for a bloke in this place? Not even a woman under forty.' Which isn't true, but is in a way because they're either married or at school.

Then he stamped out and slammed the door, and Kirsty burst into tears and ran to her room, and Joey just looked at me reproachfully and said, 'A motorbike, Flinty,' as though I'd said they weren't allowed to go to Heaven or eat bread any more.

Andy came in about an hour later, and apologised, and I said a motorbike sounded fun.

I never realised Andy was so bored up here, just working down at the Mullinses' — I bet he gets the worst jobs too — and looking after us. But of course he couldn't tell me, because I'm the reason he has to be here, and has to work at the Mullinses' too, because if I were able to help we could muster brumbies again, try to get the farm working like it used to. Andy is as trapped as I am.

I wonder if he's let his beard grow because there is no one he wants to look good for. I thought the moustache looked funny at first, but now I wish he would shave and twirl it up again.

I'm going to suggest he go down to the dances at Gibber's Creek sometimes. At least he'd find dancing partners there, and enjoy himself, and he won't get locked up like Snowy White. But I won't say it yet. It would look like I'm fussing.

I'm writing this on the back of some sales brochures Dad kept in a drawer. Kirsty's story has filled all my old diary book and nearly filled the new one too. I'll ask Andy to get me another two exercise books when he goes to Gibber's Creek, and a slate and slate pencils for Kirsty too.

Trimmed the lamp wicks this afternoon, which is why I'm making smudges on the paper. Somehow you can never get really clean after trimming the wicks, not unless you have a proper bath, which I can't do. I'd be much too embarrassed to have Andy pick me up out of a bath and he is the only one strong enough to do it. I would love to soak in front of the fire in the tin tub like I used to do while the others were at school. I am so sick of wash cloths!

There were icicles dangling down from the roof this morning. They went drip, drip, drip, then suddenly they dropped like daggers, one after the other. I suppose the ice that held them to the roof melted. Joey said the water trough was frozen this morning again, so he had to lug up buckets from the well.

Kirsty and I had toasted cheese for lunch the way old Mutti Green showed us, with lumps of cheese and bread threaded on a green stick held over the fire. You have to hold it just right or the cheese melts into the fire or the bread burns before the cheese is soft. It is fun and very good if you do it properly. Made suet pudding for dinner, and apple dumplings. I thought we'd have enough for tomorrow's lunch but Joey ate them all. He eats like Andy and Jeff used to do, and Mum said they had hollow legs. He will be as tall as Andy soon.

She dreamed of Nicholas that night, Nicholas bending to kiss her in the mist. His lips were cold, colder than the Rock. She woke to find that she had pushed the quilts off in her sleep.

She hauled herself over to the edge of the bed, reached down and pulled the quilts up again. She was glad she hadn't had to wake Kirsty to do it. The extra exercise in her chair had made her able to move in new ways. Her arms were regaining the strength they'd lost from months in bed. She could twist her waist more easily too.

She snuggled under the quilts and waited for sleep to pull her back to her dreams. To Nicholas saying 'I love you', because only Nicholas could understand how even if you lost your legs you were the same person. No, that wasn't right. You were different, deeper, because you knew pain and understood what it could do. Nicholas had brought her roses, which must mean that he liked her ...

She suddenly thought of the faded bunch of everlastings in Sandy's awkward fist. Sandy must have searched half the mountain to find ones still with all their petals in mid-winter. Roses would have lost their petals by now, vanished almost as fast as Nicholas's had when she stepped off the Rock and into sunlight. Sandy's everlastings still sat in the bud vase on the mantelpiece.

She wondered about the nurse Sandy knew in Sydney, the one who had helped buy her chair. Had she sent the magazines?

She could admit, now that all hope was lost, that even when Sandy had painfully ignored her in the past year she had still hoped that somehow they'd be together, that maybe he needed to get over the war before he thought of marriage, like Andy had needed to go off with cattle.

But even if Sandy did think of her that way, she couldn't marry anybody now. A farmer needed a wife who could work, not one who required a carer even to use a chamberpot.

She was glad, though, that Sandy was still a friend. A good friend. So many good friends, all down the valley ...

Sleep came, as softly as the mist.

The clouds had swung down over Rock Farm the next morning. You couldn't even see to the Rock.

'The fog will clear once I get past the Rock,' said Joey confidently. 'It always does.'

Flinty shook her head. 'There's a storm coming. I can smell it.'

'You're as bad as a brumby,' said Joey. 'Sniffing at the wind.'

'Yes. Well ...' said Flinty. 'Promise to stay at the Macks' tonight if it's raining?'

Rain down in the valley could mean sleet or snow up at Rock Farm. Thick snow could even be a white-out — you couldn't even see your feet, much less the track. Dad had made sure that none of them ever went out of doors in a white-out, except to check the horses and, even then, not alone, and with a rope tied to the verandah post so they could feel their way back.

'It's different now I've got the chair,' she added. 'Kirsty and I are fine here for a night or two by ourselves. I can even get between the bed and the chair now you've put up the rail for me. But I don't want you heading up the track into a blizzard.'

'All right, I promise.' Joey grabbed his jam sandwiches — half for lunch and half to eat on the way down. 'Did you know that mist keeps the heat in, like a blanket? It was in one of Mr Ross's books.'

She shook her head. 'No. What books?' The only books she'd ever seen at school were the tatty textbooks.

'He's got lots of books in his cottage,' said Joey. 'He says he only lets the best students read them though, otherwise they'd get as battered as the school ones. He's going to start giving me Greek and Latin lessons,' he added, a bit too casually. 'He says if I go on to do my Leaving or go to university I'll need Greek and Latin.'

'That's wonderful,' said Flinty hollowly. She'd been Mr Ross's best student when she was at school — she'd even learned to read just by following the words as Mum read to them. But Mr Ross had never let her read his books. She supposed he didn't want to waste his time on a girl. And now Joey was studying Greek and Latin, still with no chance to go on to high school, much less university.

She wondered if Joey knew and was just pretending so he didn't have to let go of his dream. Or maybe he's hoping for a miracle, she thought. If impossibly bad things could happen maybe impossibly good ones could too. 'I'm really proud, Joey.'

He grinned at her cockily. Mum's grin, under Dad's fair hair. The door slammed behind him as he clattered down the stairs.

She looked at the bread rising in the bowl by the fire, then wheeled her chair into the larder and got out the flour and a couple of eggs. She'd make date and walnut buns instead of bread today. It was good to be able to cook properly again. Even better to be able to dress herself, wash her hair and the rest of herself — mostly — from a bowl, work at the kitchen table. Good to let her sister sleep in sometimes now too.

Kirsty emerged, still yawning.

'Water's hot,' said Flinty, nodding at the big kettle and stew pot on the stove.

'I smell buns.'

'Not till you've washed. There's enough water for a proper bath today.' A few weeks earlier Kirsty would have been the one to take charge. Maybe the best thing of all is letting my sister be a little girl again, thought Flinty. Next week Kirsty is going to school again, she decided, no matter what Andy and Joey say, at least for part of each week.

She suspected that Kirsty was learning more up here at Rock Farm than she'd ever learned at school. But even a couple of days a week with her friends would be good for her. And if

Kirsty ever wants to learn Latin Mr Ross can jolly well teach her, she thought. Or Joey can. She guessed Kirsty was more likely to want to learn how to hunt for diamonds, or make a ball dress, than sit down with Latin grammar.

She lifted the tray of buns from the oven, then rolled down the corridor and let herself out the front door onto the verandah while Kirsty bathed.

The cloud was rising from the mountains as though the sun sucked it up, little streams and eddies heading towards the sky. A few snowflakes fluttered from the deep blue sky, what Mum had called a sun shower, the flakes gusting from the clouds that still lurked behind the mountains.

Flinty breathed deeply. Yes, there would be a storm, tonight or maybe tomorrow, and a big one. The world seemed to be waiting, the ants scurrying down into their nest by the steps, the white goshawk skimming purposefully above the grass as though it knew it needed a good feed before a couple of days of huddling in the snow up here or sheltering from the rain down in the valley.

The mist had almost gone now, except around the Rock. Even as she watched, a figure emerged, so suddenly her heart lurched.

But it wasn't a man in a bathchair — or a man with new legs either. It was a horse, Sandy's piebald, Bessie, with Sandy and a strange woman in jodhpurs on her back. This must be his nurse from Sydney.

She dragged her sinking heart back into place. It was good of Sandy to bring the visitor up here, another woman to talk to. Of course Sandy would want to introduce his girl to his best mate's sister. And just possibly, she thought, her cheeks flushing, make it clear to a girl he had once kissed that she was a friend, and just a friend, no matter how often he might visit.

Sandy lifted his hand in greeting. Flinty inspected the woman as they rode closer. She didn't look like the delicate roses she'd seen on the recruiting posters. This woman was at least five years older than Sandy, her face sallow rather than pink and white. Her clothes were the sort that any sensible woman would wear to ride up a mountain in winter: no hint of lace or frills.

Flinty rolled closer to the steps. 'Hello!' she called.

The woman dismounted without waiting for Sandy to help her down, then strode up the stairs as Sandy took Bessie around the back to the stables, away from the buffet of the wind. The woman pulled off leather gloves and held out a swollen hand knotted with red scars. 'Gwendolyn Burrows,' she said.

Flinty took it hesitantly. She had never shaken hands with a woman before. Only men shook hands. 'Flinty McAlpine.' She couldn't ask them in before Kirsty had finished her bath, but Kirsty appeared almost immediately, resplendent in her too-tight red shoes. She'd even had time to put ribbons on her plaits.

Kirsty looked at the new arrival curiously, inspecting everything from her boots to her short haircut as Sandy came back and climbed up the stairs to join them.

'Miss Burrows,' said Flinty. 'This is my sister, Kirsty. Kirsty, this is Miss Burrows.'

'Sister Burrows actually. I'm a nurse.' Sister Burrows looked ruefully at her hands. 'Well, I will be when my hands settle down again in summer. The cold weather's always hard on them.'

Sandy looked strangely awkward. 'Sister Burrows is visiting for a while.'

'In winter?' asked Kirsty. Flinty could see she was trying not to stare at the scarred hands.

'Sandy invited me.' Sister Burrows shrugged. 'I was bored out of my skull in my Sydney flat.'

Flinty looked from one to the other. Was Sister Burrows really Sandy's girlfriend? She wasn't very pretty, but she seemed ... Strong, thought Flinty. Capable. The sort of woman a man might like to travel through life with.

'Come into the kitchen. It's warmest there. I'm afraid there's no fire in the parlour. I'll put the kettle on. The date buns are just out of the oven.'

'Fresh date buns. Heaven,' said Sister Burrows.

They followed Flinty's chair into the kitchen. Sandy, Kirsty and Sister Burrows sat at the kitchen table while Flinty served the tea and buns and Kirsty asked about the train journey from Sydney. Sister Burrows held her teacup awkwardly, using both hands, as though afraid she might drop it if she used only one.

The small talk dried up. Flinty could feel Kirsty wanting to ask if Sister Burrows was Sandy's girlfriend, but Mum had drilled into them you didn't ask personal questions. You waited for people to tell you. And somehow Sandy and Sister Burrows didn't act as if they were walking out. Sandy called her Sister Burrows too, not Gwendolyn or even Gwen.

Something relaxed inside her. She chose a bun herself and took a bite. She looked up to find Sister Burrows watching her.

'I met Sandy in France,' she said abruptly.

Flinty glanced over at Sandy. He said nothing, looking into his teacup. It must have been when Sandy was wounded, she thought. 'You were a nurse there?'

Sister Burrows nodded, just as Sandy said, 'She was my doctor.'

'Well, I was a nurse,' said Sister Burrows. 'But our surgeon had been blown up by a stray mortar — Dr Nigels, a good man, such a tragedy. The army in its wisdom didn't get round to sending up another doctor for three months. That was when Sandy's lot were there. Well, the casualties kept coming in. We coped as best we could.'

'First time I met her she'd just sawed off a bloke's arm.'

'Nonsense. It was hanging by a shred when he was brought in. I just tidied it up. If you can sew a hem you can sew up an arm.'

Flinty held her breath. Beside her Kirsty's mouth hung open around some half-chewed bun. 'Was that when you were wounded?' Kirsty asked.

Sandy shrugged. 'It was my mate who was hurt that time. I brought him in.'

'Carried him two miles under fire and won the Military Cross,' said Sister Burrows firmly.

Flinty gazed at him. 'You ... you never said.'

Sandy still stared at his cup of tea.

'Can I see the medal?' asked Kirsty. 'I've never seen a medal.'

'Hasn't Andy shown you any of his?'

'What medals? Has he got more than one then?' demanded Kirsty, while Flinty said slowly, 'No.'

'Well.' Sandy shrugged again. 'There's not much to medals, really. We were just there.'

Sister Burrows met Flinty's eyes. 'We were all just there,' she said quietly. 'We did our best, and if it wasn't good enough ...' her mouth twisted in an almost smile '... if we were lucky we learned to forgive ourselves.'

Flinty shivered. The fire could warm the cold air of the mountains, but not the memory of war.

'I didn't get to know Sandy till later, when he was wounded himself,' added Sister Burrows.

'She sewed me up,' said Sandy simply. 'I reckon I'd have died if she hadn't been there. Then later she was in charge of the convalescent hospital in Brighton.'

'They sent me back to England when my hands got too bad to work. The Brighton Hospital was mostly administrative, so it didn't matter if I dropped the bandages.' She made it sound like a joke, not a test of endurance and pain.

Flinty tried to take it all in. Did Mrs Mack even know how badly Sandy had been hurt? She wanted to ask what his injuries had been, when there was no scar on face or hands, just that strange hunching that seemed worse sometimes. But if he'd wanted her to know — wanted any one of them to know — he would have said.

'Thing is,' continued Sandy doggedly. 'Sister Burrows is as good as any doctor.'

'No, I'm not,' said Sister Burrows. She looked at Flinty again. 'But I might be better than a drunken old sot who's forgotten most of what he learned half a century ago. You see, I've seen men with their backs broken. I remember,' she glanced down at Kirsty's wide-eyed gaze, 'well, no need to tell you the whys and wherefores.'

'Thing is,' repeated Sandy. 'A man with a broken back can't move his feet.' He flushed as he looked at Flinty. 'Not like you can.'

So that was why he'd been looking at her feet on her birthday. Flinty flushed too. She'd hoped maybe he'd been looking at her because she looked pretty, with clean hair and in her Sunday dress. But he was just interested in her feet moving.

'I can move my knees sometimes too, in the afternoon when I've been in my chair. But I can't stand up. My back really is broken,' she added. 'Dr Sparrow showed me the lump where the break is.'

'Is the lump still there?'

She nodded. 'Not as big as it was — not as swollen, I suppose.'

'Have you tried to stand up?' asked Sister Burrows gently.

'Of course I have! Every day!' Flinty stopped, shocked by the anguish in her voice. 'Yes, I've tried,' she said more quietly. 'But if I put any weight on my feet the pain is so bad, well, it isn't even really pain. The world goes black and I have to lie down.' She turned to Sandy. 'It's really ... kind ... of you to bring Sister Burrows here. But it's no use.'

Sister Burrows put her teacup carefully on the table. 'May I have a look at your back?'

Flinty nodded, trying to beat down small flames of hope. A doctor knew more than a nurse, didn't he? But on the other hand this woman had probably seen more severe injuries in a few years in France than Dr Sparrow had in his whole life — and she was sober.

Flinty turned the bathchair, flushing again as Sandy watched her manoeuvre it back and forth away from the table without speaking, glad he didn't spring up and try to push her. At last she had it pointed in the right direction. Sister Burrows followed her into her bedroom and closed the door.

'Do you need help getting onto the bed?'

'I got my brother to put bars up so I can pull myself in.' And a ghost told me how to do it, she thought. But she couldn't tell this calm-eyed woman that.

She rolled parallel to the bed, grabbed the bar at the bedhead with one hand and hauled herself, sliding, onto the mattress. She lay face down, panting for a moment till the pain eased, then began to roll over.

'No, stay like that,' said Sister Burrows. 'Do you mind if I pull up your dress?'

'No,' said Flinty.

It was chilly in the bedroom. Sister Burrows's fingers were cold as they touched her swollen back gently. 'Can you feel that?'

'Yes,' said Flinty.

'I'm going to use a hatpin now. I'll try not to hurt you. Can you feel that?'

'No.'

'How about this?'

'No,' said Flinty. 'Ow! Yes, I can feel it now.'

'Sorry,' said Sister Burrows. She put the pin back into her hat. 'Now when I run my hands down your legs ... what can you feel?'

'I can feel your hands. They're cold,' she added.

'Sorry. Can you feel when I touch your feet?'

'Yes.'

'Any pins and needles in your toes?'

'No. They just feel like feet.'

'I see.'

Flinty felt Sister Burrows pull the dress back about her legs. 'Come on, I'll help you back into the chair.'

'I can do it!'

'So I see,' said Sister Burrows calmly. 'But you're doing your back no good by jerking it that way as you try to get up. If you won't let me lift you I'll call Sandy —'

'No!' She let herself be lifted. She was surprised at the strength in the nurse's arms, one under her legs, the other in a practised movement around her shoulders. When she was in her chair again, Sister Burrows sat on her bed and looked at her.

'I'm not a doctor,' she said at last. 'If we were in Sydney or even Goulburn, I'd advise you to see a specialist. But I suspect that the jolting journey down to the city would do you more harm than good.'

'Dr Sparrow said that nothing can be done about a broken back.'

'He was correct. But there are ... different ways ... a back can be broken. If the spinal cord is severed ... you know what the spinal cord is?'

Flinty nodded. She'd cut up enough mutton and rabbits to know what a spine was. 'It's inside the bones that run down your back. They're all connected.'

'That's right. Well, if your spine had been broken completely you wouldn't have any feeling or movement below the injury. That's obviously not the case.'

Flinty glanced at her with dawning hope. Sister Burrows held up a warning hand. 'You have, however, done major damage. There's an area on the right side where you can't feel anything, and it extends part of the way over onto your left side too.'

'What ... what does that mean?'

'I think — and I have to emphasise this is only my opinion, and I am scarcely an expert in these matters — but I believe you have broken one, or maybe two, of the tiny "spurs" on the edges of your backbone. These bits of bone are causing inflammation and swelling in the soft bits around them, and that is pressing on the nerves. Am I right in thinking that you are able to move more now than when it first happened?'

'Yes.' Flinty gripped the arms of the chair. 'You mean ... you mean I might keep getting better?'

'That depends. You may have improved as much as you're ever going to. Or perhaps you'll slowly find you can move more easily, even stand up and walk.'

Sister Burrows reached over and gripped Flinty's hand. 'My girl, I'd dearly love to be able to promise you that you'll walk again. But I can't. I can't even promise you that you'll be able to stand by yourself. But I can promise that there's hope.'

'Hope,' whispered Flinty.

Sister Burrows nodded. 'There'll always be damage. Any jarring or bruising will make it swell again. You'll probably never be able to ride again — it would jolt your back too much. That's why I want you to accept help to get in and out of your chair, try not to pull or jar your back as you attempt to move, whether you're lying in bed or reaching for things from your chair or pushing yourself around. Be gentle and let yourself heal.'

'You mean I have to lie in bed?' I've only just got out of bed's prison, thought Flinty. Please don't send me back there with a promise of 'perhaps'.

'Certainly not. Lying flat on your back is the worst thing you can do. When you lie on your back your weight will press down on the injury ...' She hesitated. 'I'd say, do whatever causes least pain and, if it hurts, stop. The body is very good at knowing what's good for it. Try hot bran poultices wrapped in a towel or pillowcase against the base of your back. Do you know how to make one?'

'Dad showed me for the horses.'

Sister Burrows grinned. 'They work for people too. Use them like a hot cushion for your back, as often as you can. Don't let the spine get chilled or jarred. Heat will bring the swelling down and anything that brings down the swelling will make it easier for you to move and for the injury to possibly heal more too.

'But mostly keep on moving gently.' Sister Burrows shook her head. 'You won't find many doctors who'll agree with me on this. Male doctors are happiest with patients all lined up neatly in bed to be inspected. But we nurses found that injured men got better fastest if they kept moving. Nurses are the ones who see what works and what doesn't. So the best advice I can give you is to move as much as you can without pain. And hope,' she added. 'I've seen hope create miracles, and giving up kill a man who might have lived.'

'What do I tell everyone?' She felt adrift. She had finally accepted she was crippled. Now, it seemed, the sky was neither clear nor cloudy, but obscured by fog that might or might not lift.

'The truth,' said Sister Burrows gently. 'Tell them your back is badly hurt. It may improve, or it may not. But if you are careful — and give it time and don't aggravate it — then we will see.'

Chapter 33

4 September 1982

Dear Diary,

I thought Sister Burrows was the first woman I'd ever met who actually did things. It took years for me to realise that Mrs Clancy, Mrs Mack and Mum were just as capable in their own ways. They're just not ways that men pay much attention to — unless their socks aren't darned or dinner isn't on the table at six o'clock. The life I've lived in the past sixty years has been built on the achievements of those strong women of my youth.

Kirsty had put the kettle on the stove. The sound of an axe came from outside — Sandy must be splitting more wood for the stove, and Kirsty was stacking it. Flinty suspected he was using the activity as a way to prevent more questions about his own injuries too.

She suddenly realised that Sandy had known what Sister Burrows's diagnosis would be, was so confident that he didn't need to ask now. He had probably even reassured Kirsty.

Just how long had Sandy been in hospital or a convalescent home, she wondered, as she poured fresh water into the teapot, to be so familiar with back injuries like mine?

'Could we have our tea on the front verandah?' asked Sister Burrows. 'I seem to have spent my life in rooms or tents that smell of antiseptic. It's a treat to be in the open air for a while.'

Flinty nodded. She didn't trust herself to speak yet. Sister Burrows carried their cups out the front door and Kirsty came to fetch Sandy's tea. Flinty leaned back in her bathchair as Sister Burrows sat in the settler's chair, gazing down the valley. 'Beautiful,' she said at last. 'You're blessed.'

'I know,' said Flinty.

Sister Burrows shot her a glance. 'More than you realise, perhaps. An injury like yours might have meant a nursing home. A row of beds of hopeless people and hopeless lives, nothing to look forward to but a visitor bringing buns at the weekend, friends slowly forgetting you as the years go by.' She sipped her tea. 'I don't think your friends up here forget anyone.'

'No,' said Flinty. 'Are ... are you and Sandy good friends? It's just,' she added, as Sister Burrows looked at her enquiringly, 'it's a lot to ask someone to come all the way up here to look at me.'

'We've been close friends, but not like that. I was engaged to his older brother.'

'Rick?'

Sister Burrows nodded. 'We met when Rick was on convalescent leave in England after his first wound, and so was I — my hands again. We had nine days.' She smiled at the memory. 'He took me to a teashop and ended up holding the teacup for me to drink and cutting my teacake into pieces for me. We walked and we walked, every day — pebble beaches, not sandy ones like here. The wind in our faces, trying not to listen to the rumble of guns across the Channel, talking about cicadas and wattle trees and how you can't ever explain to a French farmer why you can't harness a kangaroo.

'Then he went back to France, and a week later I did too. By some stroke of magic our casualty post was the nearest one to where he was stationed. We managed to meet every week or so, and the ambulance girls carried letters. We would have married, but then I'd have had to resign and come back to Australia. At least that way we saw each other, even got a note to each other most days.

'We had it all planned — we'd get married the day the war ended. We'd buy a farm near enough to a town. I'd trained as a midwife before the war, and I'd go back to that. We even chose the colour of the kitchen curtains, the children's names: Gladys and Pamela, George and Arthur. I know it sounds silly, but it really mattered at the time. Then Rick was gassed.' She gazed out at the twisted trees. 'He was blind after that, you know.'

'No,' said Flinty. 'I didn't know. Not about the engagement, not about him being blind before he died. Did his parents know how badly he was hurt?'

'No. Not the first time, nor the second. He didn't want them to know.' Sister Burrows shook her head. 'Most families just got that same form telegram, and then the postcard: *I have been wounded, but I am in hospital now and recovering well.* The same words over and over, saying so little, hiding so much.'

'We had a right to know,' said Flinty.

'Perhaps. But the men had a right to privacy too. It helped them, sometimes, to know that their families weren't too worried. Time enough,' said Sister Burrows lightly, 'to work out what would happen to a man blinded by the gas, or coughing blood, when he was able to be shipped back home. I used to write letters for them then — all of us nurses did — trying to prepare the families so they weren't too shocked when their men were led or carried off the ship.'

Sister Burrows looked out at the valley again. A fox trotted past, its red coat tipped with winter white. It seemed startled by the unexpected humans and darted up into the scrub.

'When Rick learned he wouldn't see again he tried to break off our engagement. I said it didn't matter, though of course it did. But I'd rather have had him blind than not at all. And then he went and died anyway — many of the gas cases just got worse, no matter what we did. We had six weeks and four days together, all in all. I don't know if that's enough for a lifetime, but it's all I'll get.'

'Do his parents know you were engaged?'

'They do now.' Sister Burrows blew her nose suddenly. She was crying, Flinty realised.

'Sorry. Excuse me. I never cry ... Rick was about to write of our engagement when he was gassed. It all happened so quickly. Things do in war. And then ...' She shrugged. 'I'm glad Sandy insisted I come here, and not just to see you. It's been wonderful to talk to Rick's parents about him in the last couple of days. It's like he lives in the marriage that might have been now. There'll always be family who knew him, who I can remember him with. Mrs Mack wants me to have her engagement ring.' She smiled and blew her nose again. 'But she can't get it off her finger, even with butter and tugging.'

Flinty thought of Mrs Mack's thick fingers, the swollen knuckles.

'She says she's going to have a jeweller cut it off, next summer when they go down to town. Then he'll repair it for me. I ... I should say no. But it will mean a lot to me.'

To Mrs Mack too, thought Flinty. 'You won't marry anyone else?'

'I don't think I can,' said Sister Burrows quietly. 'When I see a man's body now all I think of is pain and death. And when I look at my hands I see that too.' She held them up. 'Our hands were always wet, always working with infected wounds, so any cut or graze became infected too. The war is still with me every time I try to hold a cup of tea.'

'Maybe your hands will get better. Maybe you'll meet someone.'

'Maybe your back will heal. We live in a world of perhapses.'

'I didn't know there were women in the war. I mean, I knew about nurses, but I thought you were all far away from the fighting.'

'Oh no. Sometimes the shelling was a mile away, like a bad thunderstorm. Other times the battlefront would move. We'd have to move too, and be quick about it. Sometimes we weren't quick enough.'

She looked steadily at Flinty. 'The men would go to the front for weeks, months sometimes, then have a break. We didn't get any break at all, except when our hands were too swollen to work. Day and night sometimes. At one stage there were three of us sharing a single bed, but it didn't matter, as we each only got two or three hours' sleep before we had to be up again. Lived on cocoa and bread and dripping. The volunteers didn't even get any wages.

'Year in, year out ... Never think, Miss McAlpine, that women can't put up with as much as men. It's women who bear the children and women who lose them too. And maybe that's another reason why I'll never marry now. I couldn't bear that a son of mine might go through what I have seen. Not George. Not Arthur.'

'But there won't be another war. The Great War was "the war to end all wars".' Suddenly Flinty remembered Nicholas saying 'World War I' as though there had been a World War II — and maybe even III and IV. She wished she could tell Sister Burrows about Nicholas. Perhaps, if she had been whole, she might have. But an injured girl, shut away from real life, could so easily have imagined such a companion, a handsome young man who came from the fog.

Sister Burrows was already shaking her head. 'Do you think war ends so easily? To me it seems no more than a ceasefire while the generals work out ways to recruit more men, so they can be at it once more. But maybe I'm wrong. I hope I'm wrong. Miss McAlpine, will you forgive a personal remark?'

'Of course.'

'You've had significant courage to manage as well as you have over the last years. Do you have enough courage to say yes if Sandy Mack asks you to marry him?'

'But he won't! He's never even kissed me properly since he got back!'

'Sandy Mack used a chunk of his savings to come to Sydney to talk to me about your case, and buy my train ticket and pay for a night at the Gibber's Creek Boarding House so I could come here and take a look at you. He asked me not to tell you. I haven't broken my word, because I just nodded, and let him draw the conclusions he wanted to. That young man cares for you very deeply.'

'He was my brother's best friend.'

'That sounds like a good recommendation for a husband.'

'You don't understand. He just feels responsible for me.'

'Somehow,' said Sister Burrows, 'I doubt that's all there is. By the way, if you are wondering, I don't see any reason why you shouldn't have children, even if you are forever confined to your bathchair. If you wish to, that is.'

Flinty thought of Nicholas, so far away. Of Sandy, chopping wood at the back door.

'Sandy needs a proper wife. One who can help him run the farm.' Scrub floors. Round up the sheep, she thought. Chase brumbies across the hills.

'There are many kinds of marriage,' said Sister Burrows. 'If Rick had lived, even if he had remained blind, I think we'd have had a good life. I enjoy my work — it would have been no hardship for me to be the breadwinner, extraordinary as that sounds. Well, as I said, we live in a world of perhapses.'

She glanced up at the clouds creeping over the mountain, swollen as plums and almost as purple. 'And now I had better tell Sandy we need to go, or perhaps I will miss my train.'

Chapter 34

3 August 1920

Dear Diary,

I think I met an angel today, one in jodhpurs and with swollen hands. I can't really believe it yet. I might walk. And Sandy … there are even more 'perhapses' with Sandy. I wish now I had asked Sister Burrows how he was wounded, how bad it was. I knew Sandy as well as my brothers for thirteen years, or even better. Then there were three years when I didn't know what was happening to him at all, and those might be the most important ones of his whole life. Or maybe those are to come. Happy ones. I hope so.

Oh dear, I'm hoping now. Hoping about so many things. Hoping hurts, but, oh, it's good.

It snowed that afternoon and all through the night, deep steady falls that leached all sound from the world, except the creaking of the roof. Flinty was glad Andy and Joey were down in the valley. The snow would probably be rain down there, and even the sight of Rock Farm would be cut off by its cloak of snow and cloud.

It was impossible to sleep. There was too much to think about: the possibility that one day she might walk, a gift from Sandy, quiet Sandy with his freckles and blushes, who had never spoken a word of love and maybe never would, just like his Military Cross would probably stay hidden under his clean socks.

Was Sandy waiting to see whether her back got better? But then why had he been so cold before her accident? He'd kissed her once. Why not again? Sandy ... Sandy was a perhaps ... a wonderful perhaps, but still just that.

There was more to think about. Somehow today the world had stretched and expanded. For eighteen years Flinty had assumed that women existed as a help to men, feeding them, cleaning for them, so that men could do the small or great deeds of the world.

But Sister Burrows had done great deeds in her own right. Even the war had been made up of women too. Not just the women and babies bayoneted by the Huns, their homes destroyed, but women who had done things.

Mrs Clancy rode with her man, even if she had to be disguised as a drover's boy to do it. And there was Miss Matilda down at Drinkwater, running the biggest property in the district, and all the wives and daughters during the war who had also run farms with their men gone. Maybe the world is full of women who do things, she thought, but they're women men don't see, don't write about.

I did something once, she thought. I rounded up a mob of brumbies. She glanced at Kirsty, snuffling across the room. Even if she hadn't longed to get up from her bathchair for her own sake, she owed it to her sister. If she could stand then Andy would have no excuse not to send Kirsty back to school.

And what of Flinty herself? What would she really want, if she had the choice? To be a nurse, like Sister Burrows? Women could be teachers too, at least until they married, and telegraphists. But all she really wanted was to live here on the mountain, just as Mum had.

No, she acknowledged. Not like Mum. She wanted to train Snow King, to ride out after brumbies again and this time do it right, to be the farmer, not the farmer's wife.

And neither might be possible. Even if she could walk, she might never be able to do the sustained work in the saddle needed to train horses or face the rigours of a hill ride after brumbies. And Sandy, gentle Sandy, was the fourth son of a small farmer. Even when he had his own land, it could never be Rock Farm. Rock Farm belonged to Andy. One day Andy would live here with his wife. He would always give his sisters a home, but when they married they would be expected to live in houses of their own.

Yet Sister Burrows hadn't waited for a husband or brother to support her. She had even spoken as if a woman was capable of earning enough to keep a family.

Dawn glowed from the chink in the shutters. Flinty pulled herself as quietly — and gently — as she could into her chair. Kirsty muttered as the wheels passed her bed.

Flinty peered out the back door. The world was white, the snow-gum branches heavy with their load of snow. Something moved, up on the hill, white on white. Snow King, prancing in the snow.

She smiled, grabbed a lapful of wood before her hands and nose froze, shut the door against the chill and put wood on the fire, then slipped her old pillowcase of bran into the oven, to warm up for a poultice.

She slipped it in against her back as she sipped a cup of tea. The warmth helped almost immediately, dulling the ever-present pain. Experimentally she slid forwards, put her feet on the floor, and tried to push herself upright.

Nothing happened. Of course nothing happened, thought Flinty. Sister Burrows had promised hope, not miracles.

And yet something nibbled in a dark shell of her brain. Something she knew, something that mattered. Something she could possibly do ...

She grabbed a blanket from the cupboard, tucked it about herself and rolled herself out the front door. The sky shone sharp and blue against the white. Even the Rock was cloudless this morning. And it was as though the clarity of the day cleared her mind too, so she could see the thought that had been bubbling up inside her brain all night.

Nicholas was writing a book. Now she had written a book as well, admittedly a little blobbed and blotted in one and a half exercise books. But that shouldn't matter, should it? Books were printed, so it didn't matter how messy they were at first.

Could you really make a living writing books? Nicholas must think so. He'd have an army pension too, of course, but she was pretty sure he expected his book to make money.

She wheeled herself inside and reached up for a copy of *The Man from Snowy River and Other Verses* by Banjo Paterson.

Mum had given it to Dad the last Christmas before the war. She had rubbed out the price on the title page, but you could still see the pencil mark — three and sixpence.

If a man could write a book, maybe a girl could too. After all, Miss Brontë had written *Jane Eyre.* Miss Austen had written lots of books.

If a book sold say, a hundred copies, that was a hundred times three and sixpence. But it would cost money to print them, maybe a shilling a copy. Two shillings a copy would mean a book might earn two hundred shillings, or nine pounds two shillings and tuppence.

It wasn't enough to buy a farm. But if she wrote two books a year and Andy bred horses, like Dad, it might be enough to help support them without Dad's pension, so that Andy didn't have to work down at the Mullinses', could afford to support a wife, might even — possibly — let Joey at least go to high school.

It was a start.

She looked at *The Man from Snowy River* again. The publisher's address was on the next page: Angus and Robertson in Castlereagh Street, Sydney.

She carefully tore a blank sheet of paper from the back of the exercise book, added water to the ink gunge in the bottom of the pot, took up the pen and began to write as neatly as she could. There was no use wishing for blotting paper, because they didn't have any. The best she could do was not smear any splodges that dripped from the pen.

Rock Farm
The Track
Rocky Valley via Gibber's Creek
4 August 1920

Dear Mr Angus and Mr Robertson,

I hope you are both well.

My name is Felicity McAlpine and I have written the book in this parcel. I am sorry the words are not clear at times. My little sister did most of the writing. She was not very good at forming her words when she started, but as you will see her writing gets much better soon. I am sorry about the blots too. We do not have any blotting paper left. The smudge on the cover of the second exercise book is not blood. It is strawberry jam which was spilled on the kitchen table.

I hope you like the book. If you like it I can write more. Could you tell me how much it will cost to publish the book? I have forty-nine pounds five shillings and threepence in my savings account.

Yours sincerely,
Felicity McAlpine (Miss)

Flinty looked at the letter. It seemed to lack something. Or maybe there was too much.

But it was a good story. If Kirsty liked it, it must be good, or even *very* good. She wondered if she should tell Mr Angus and Mr Robertson that. But she'd either have to write the letter again, or put a PS, and a PS wasn't good manners when you wrote letters, except to friends.

Anyway, she thought, it was the book that counted. Even if they just read the first sentence they might want to hear more, as Kirsty had.

She wrapped the exercise books and letter in brown paper, and tied the parcel carefully with string. She'd ask Andy to give it to Mr Mack to post when he went to the next sheep sale.

Her bran poultice was cold. Her feet were chilly too. Kirsty would need three pairs of socks and Mum's old gumboots to feed the hens (Kirsty never soiled her own gumboots with chook poo) and check that Snow King's water trough hadn't frozen over, and to give him a few forkfuls of hay.

The brown-paper parcel stared at her from the sideboard.

Chapter 35

14 September 1920

Dear Diary,

Kirsty says Harriet is sitting on ten eggs. She is sitting well, so I hope they all hatch. She was a good mother last year. Only three eggs from the others, so I boiled one each for Kirsty and Joey for breakfast; I kept the third for pikelets for afternoon tea.

Sandy comes up here every Sunday now, just as if we were courting, except he spends more time with Joey and Andy, helping with the ploughing, than with me. He hasn't brought me flowers again. But at least we talk these days, just like we did before he went to war, about the lambs and dingoes and how the ploughing has gone, and how Mutti Green's goat ate Vati Green's best trousers and then a petticoat drying overnight on the verandah, and then Hannah saw something white move and thought it was a ghost, and screamed in terror instead of rescuing the petticoat, just like the story I told about the goat eating the sheet. Maybe that shows that stories can come true, or maybe it just shows that goats like to eat washing.

My own ghost hasn't been back. Andy takes me down to the Rock once a week. I tell him the few hours there are my 'day out'. But there is no Nicholas.

Maybe I really did imagine I had met him, after I was hurt. I know I met him long before that, but maybe I only dreamed a ghost from the future told me my life would get better, like I dreamed I ran across the mountains.

Or perhaps Nicholas has decided not to come back to the valley or he is still getting used to his new legs. Perhaps I will never know what happens to him till I'm an old lady, in fifty years' time. I'll have grey hair then, or maybe white, like Snow King.

Snow King is so beautiful. I keep wanting to ask Andy to put me on his back. But that would be the worst thing for my spine, all the jolting, especially as I couldn't grip but would have to balance. It wouldn't really be riding at all. I think I'd almost rather never to ride again, than ride like that.

Almost.

Spring arrived with new red shoots on the snow gums, and lime-green ones on the oaks and maples that Mum had planted, and diamond-crusted spider webs between the tussocks.

The oak and maple shoots died in the next frost, a hard one that left more icicle daggers dangling from the roof. Snow gums knew how to live with the mountain, Dad had said. The newcomers had to struggle.

But the oaks and maples were big enough to survive now. They put out more shoots when the frost was gone. Even the next snowstorm didn't hurt them, flakes as big as a baby's hand whistling and swirling across the valley, melting as they touched the ground.

Every morning Flinty tried to stand, and every evening before she went to bed. But, although she could move her legs easily from the knee down now and even lift her feet from the floor a little bit one by one, her back ignored the order to support her.

Nothing more had been said about the motorbike. Flinty hoped Andy had seen they couldn't afford it, that any money needed to go towards horses, or be kept for an emergency. His wages barely covered expenses. How could they even pay for a motorbike's fuel?

They were lambing down in the valley now. Andy spent most nights down at the Mullinses' farm, helping to check the paddocks by lantern light. Sheep, it seemed, liked to lamb in darkness. Sometimes one needed help to get her lamb out, especially when there were twins. Others got 'cast' — the ewe lay on her side and the heavy wet wool stopped her from getting to her feet. A cast sheep could die by morning.

Dingoes prowled the mountain too, looking for lambs or ewes too weak to resist. But they knew the smell of men, even if they didn't understand the guns they carried.

'The dingoes bred up in the war,' said Andy wearily one evening, as he stretched his feet in their thick socks before the kitchen fire after Kirsty and Joey had gone to bed. 'Like the bunnies. Not enough men to keep the numbers down. Half the fences in the valley need replacing, and it'll be worse when the thaw comes and the floodgates are washed away.'

The floodgates were the fences strung across the creek that would swell to a foam-rimmed river, tossing boulders as though they were knucklebones, in the spring floods.

'The floodgates go every year,' said Flinty, peering down at the hem of Kirsty's new skirt, made from an old dress with the top half turned into a frill at the hem. Kirsty was all legs like a colt these days. 'We got them back up all right during the war.' Even Mrs Mack had put on an old pair of trousers to help in those days, she remembered.

'It's not just the floodgates, Sis. The land's been starved of men for too long. The Browns' hayshed is leaning so far it'll go in the next big wind. All the best horses have gone. Most that are left are either too old or too young.'

Andy was silent for a moment, staring at the fire. Flinty wondered if he was remembering when there were horses in every Rock Farm paddock. Andy had enlisted before the stock was sold and led away. She'd cried for three nights after the horses left, almost as much as she'd cried for her brothers. At least Andy and Jeff had enlisted willingly, knowing something of what they were going to. The horses had trusted the men who led them into horror.

But of course no man had known what the last war would bring. The Boer Wars, the battles on the North-West Frontier — none of them had been like the mud and endless inching back and forth of trench warfare. She tried not to think of the Rock Farm horses, so far from their mountains, amid the noise and death.

Where were their horses now? Prince Albert and Blossom Queen and the horse Dad called the Duke of Wellington because of his big nose? Were they with the Indian Army? Pulling a plough in Belgium? Or dead, perhaps, killed by shell fire or even their own riders, determined the beasts would not be shipped off to servitude in India or the Middle East.

'Flinty,' said Andy suddenly. There was a new note in his voice. Hope, she thought. How long had it been since Andy spoke like that?

She leaned forwards. 'What?'

'I've been offered a job at Drinkwater.'

'But ... but you have a job.'

'A real job.' His face was lit as though a fire shone on it. 'I'd be deputy manager. Manager even one day. I got used to command in France, Flinty. I'm good at it. Mr Sampson is getting on, and his sons have places of their own. Miss Matilda's husband is no farmer. A good bloke, but he's more interested in machines than stock.'

She thought of the neat Drinkwater paddocks, the station that stretched to the hills. Andy manage all that? But he could, of course. Would love the challenge of it. Terror nibbled her heart. She forced her voice to sound confident. 'We manage all right here.'

'No, we don't. Well, maybe, yes, we do. But that's not the point.' He took a deep breath. 'There's a good house goes with the job, as big as this place. You should see the Drinkwater cottages, Flinty. No bark huts there. It's like a small town.'

'I know,' she said dully. 'I've seen it.'

'Then you know how good it is. There're so many opportunities, Flinty. Joey can go to high school at Gibber's Creek. He can get an apprenticeship down there too, if he wants one, might even manage university if he can get a scholarship. It would be easier for Kirsty to go to school as well — one of the cars takes the kids every day.' He grinned. 'I'll get to drive one if I'm deputy manager. Might even get a car of my own.'

She looked at him in horror. 'You want us *all* to go down there!'

'It's the only thing to do, Flinty. Maybe if I'd saved my pay during the war I'd have enough to stock the place again, but even then —'

'When Snow King starts winning races we'll make more money,' she said desperately.

'I can train him as well down there as here. Better, probably. It'll be easier to prove he's out of Lamentation too if he's from Drinkwater. Sis, it's not just that this is the best thing for us. I don't want to spend my life perched up here with the eagles. I want a real life. Men working under me. Dances every Friday night. They're even getting an ice-skating rink in Gibber's Creek this year.'

She stared at him, as though he had ripped off the familiar Andy face, leaving a stranger in their kitchen. Ice skating, when they had icicle daggers on every tree each winter here? 'Then *you* go! I'm not going anywhere!'

His look was half sympathy, half the shut-off expression she knew so well, which meant he wasn't going to argue. 'You don't have a choice. I'm Kirsty and Joey's guardian in the eyes of the law. And yours too, till you're twenty-one. Besides, the farm belongs to me.' He took another deep breath. 'I'm going to sell it, Flinty.'

'No!'

'No point letting it stay empty for the dingoes. I could do with the money too. Get set up properly down there.'

No, he was still her brother. And in an anguished crumb of her heart she knew he might even be right, that this was best for him, for Joey and Kirsty, that Andy had never chosen this life as Dad had. Drinkwater would give him a new life — even perhaps a wife.

She sat, her hands on the arms of her bathchair, her heart as cold as the Rock. Sell Rock Farm? She couldn't live anywhere else. Rock Farm and the mountains were who she was.

A Flinty McAlpine might live down on the Drinkwater flats, but she wouldn't be *her*. She'd be a shell: talking, even smiling, but never really there. The real Flinty would be flying with the white goshawk, twisting with the trees. Every time she saw the black swans flying in their arrow overhead she would be with them. I'd be a ghost, she thought, away from my real place like Nicholas was away from his own time.

How could she live in a land where she wouldn't understand whether the clouds were hinting at thunder or a flurry of snow, where the birds no longer talked to her in a language that she knew?

'Maybe no one will buy it.' If Rock Farm was too barren for Andy to make a living, why would another farmer want it?

'It's a good house. Worth more than the land, really. Sometimes city people want a place in the mountains where they can come when it's too hot in summer, like the visitors who come for the fishing. If someone buys the house Mullins will want to add our paddocks to theirs. If I got some money for the house I could let Mullins pay it off, a bit each year.'

But not Sandy, she thought. Sandy loved the mountains, but he would know as well as any farmer that you could break your heart on acres like Rock Farm's. He needed fertile fields for the money he'd saved, somewhere he could feed a growing family, not paddocks covered with snow for months of the year. Rock Farm would cost him far more than a Soldier Settler block.

This was The End, she thought, like they put at the bottom of the final page of books. Impossible to think of herself living down below. But it was all too possible to imagine The End.

'When do you want to go?' she asked dully.

'Miss Matilda says there's no hurry. After Christmas, maybe. That's when most of the fishermen come up here. I spoke to the land agent at the last sales. He said houses sell best when they look lived in. But if the house hasn't sold by the new year, we'll have to move anyway. Maybe one of the Mack families will rent it till it's sold.'

One more Christmas, she thought, that mingling of hot air up from the plains and the mountains still breathing the last of the ice. One more thaw with its drip and trickle and roar. One more spring of mountain daisies and billy buttons and tiny pink slippers, and then the hot Drinkwater plains down below.

No Rock, she thought. Never to see Nicholas again either, or not for fifty years. Not to see the swallows arrive each spring. No native cats hissing under the windows. No echoes of Jeff cantering down from the top paddock, or Mum's laughter or Dad's boots on the verandah. No Sandy.

I want my ghosts, she thought. I want my life.

'I'm sorry, Flinty. I wish it could be different.'

She looked at him. Her kind big brother. But all at once she realised that the brother she'd known never *had* come back from the war. This man needed a new challenge, needed a place where memories wouldn't bite him, needed to forge a life of his own.

He was still her brother. She loved him; she knew he would always do his best for her — had tried his best to find a way she might stay here. But the old Andy had disappeared, just as the Flinty she was now would on the plains.

Chapter 36

24 September 1920

Dear Diary,

No one has come to see the farm but Andy says he doesn't expect anyone till summer. Joey is looking forward to moving, especially the motorcars. He is already planning to learn to drive. Kirsty is excited about shops and dances, but she came in red eyed from the chooks yesterday, and I've even seen Joey look wistfully at the mountains, as though he doesn't want to say goodbye.

It's only a day's drive to Drinkwater, so they can come back and see their friends. I suppose I could come back in a motorcar. I'm not sure I could bear to, even to see Nicholas, and anyway, I couldn't meet him if other people were in the car, looking on. Couldn't even bear to see the mountains, knowing I'd have to let myself be driven away again.

Used the last of the bottled tomatoes. The potatoes in the sacks in the shed have begun to sprout — will leave the rest for seeding. Andy is still going to put in the corn and potatoes and other vegetables. Even if we don't get to harvest them, Andy says it will make the farm look more prosperous.

Sandy says he will caretake the place if it still hasn't sold after we move. I asked him if he would consider buying it, but it's just what I thought. He can't afford to. Somehow it wouldn't seem quite as bad to know that Sandy bought Rock Farm, even if we're not here. But that won't happen either.

Made dumplings for the lamb stew. No more stored quinces or apples. Jam roly-poly for pudding, a big one made in the big stew pot so that the others could take some for their lunches.

Still no sign of Nicholas. If he doesn't come back till after Christmas I may never see him again. Maybe I can scratch a note on the Rock. But what would it say? Gone to Drinkwater. Goodbye. Flinty. I want to say much more than that, but those are things you can't scratch on a rock.

The hardenbergia bloomed first, mauve blooms twisting through the thorn bush. The native sarsaparilla turned the hillsides into purple flame next, then the orange and yellow of the bitter-pea and then the billy buttons. Wonga vine hung its cream and purple cups from the kurrajong trees, and then the clematis shone like a white arrow up the mountain.

Later the everlastings would flower and the yam daisies and the bushes Mum called red shaggies. The red-capped robins and the swallows would come back, and the black cockatoos to tear the old bark from the trees. But would she still be here to see them?

The echidna that lived in the front garden emerged, nosing around the walls for ants. The plovers nested up by the chookhouse — trust plovers to nest where humans went every day, shrieking and bobbing at Kirsty every time she collected the eggs.

The creek burbled and babbled, loud enough to hear from the house but not a roar. The 'melt' was gradual this year, thin seeps from snowdrifts and icicles each warm day, but no sudden heat to send the melted snow and ice roaring in one great torrential swoop down the creek.

Instead two warmer than usual days sent a small flood gushing and grinding loose rocks, big enough by the time it reached the valley to push down the floodgates with its accumulated logs and debris. There were none of the great washes Flinty had seen when she was small, after the drought years before her birth, the great past floods when all the lower paddocks were brown water and white froth, and the smell of melted wombat and roo droppings had seeped into every crevice of the house for weeks.

Joey saw the first snake of spring — a big red-bellied black sunning himself on the Rock, as though borrowing the Rock's stored heat to give it strength to hunt the bush rats or the tiny mountain mice that scurried between the tussocks — but never inside the house, not with Dad's stone walls and well-fitting doors.

Flinty longed to be out in it. This might be the last mountain spring she'd ever see. But all she could do was wheel herself onto the verandah, trying to store each memory, stretching each second to make it last. Perhaps the mountain spring would come to her in dreams, down on the Drinkwater flats. At least she'd have the memory, when the miracle of the experience itself was lost to her.

Spring brought more visitors: Sandy, of course, almost the old companionable Sandy, telling her about the two giant eagles that had built their nest in the old red-gum tree, how Toby had wanted to shoot the pair of them but he'd persuaded him not to. The eagles didn't take chooks, and the only lambs they carried off were the dying ones. Better the eagles took them, said Sandy, than the smell of dead sheep attract the dingoes.

Now the track was clear of snow he drove Mrs Mack up in the cart again each Sunday afternoon too, bringing a couple of her pies and even more gossip. Sometimes Mutti Green came along, with an apple cake or her delicate almond biscuits covered in icing sugar, which dissolved almost before you had a chance to bite them.

Dusty Jim emerged from his winter hibernation with his usual smell of old dog and dunny — all Dusty Jim needed to see the winter out was a case of rum and a sack of flour for damper. Flinty suspected he didn't remove his clothes from one year to another, simply putting on another coat or two in winter. Dusty Jim built up the woodpile again in return for a pot of stew and dumplings and a giant gingerbread.

But there was still no ghost upon the Rock. Andy pushed her bathchair down there every Saturday morning. It was almost a ritual now. But her only companions were lizards, golden skinks darting after mozzies and the first of the season's flies.

Had she dreamed him? So much had happened since. Maybe her memory was playing tricks, confused by pain and tiredness in those first weeks when agony refused the retreat of sleep.

Easy, perhaps, to dream of a soldier, lost in time like Jeff was lost forever, crippled as she was crippled.

Maybe in those nights when she seemed never to properly sleep, she had created his promise that good things would come. The story she'd made up for Kirsty, that even now might be sitting on a publisher's desk, had seemed so real when she created it. Had her imagination made Nicholas real too?

Visitors came at weekends, the Sunday afternoons that even cocky farmers allowed themselves off, to sit in their socks digesting their lunch, or mooching over to their neighbours to inspect a new bull or plough or litter of pups. But it was midweek when her most unexpected visitors arrived.

It was one of Kirsty's days at school — Andy now allowed her to join Joey three days a week, as long as she did her chores before they set out and spent the other days catching up on the scrubbing and clothes washing and whatever else Flinty couldn't manage from her chair.

Flinty heard the horses canter up the track, not the slow plod of the Macks' carthorse or the well-known gait of Sandy's Bessie. Snow King whinnied a challenge as she wheeled herself down the corridor and out onto the front verandah. The front door was open, to let the spring breezes warm the house and rid it of the scent of winter soot. The shotgun always stood behind the front door now — since the tragedy with Sergeant Morris she had lost her confidence with strangers.

But these were not strangers, she realised, as the couple dismounted, unsaddling their horses but leaving them unhobbled as they left their saddles and blankets on the front fence for the horse sweat to dry.

It was the Clancys: Mr Clancy with his white beard, freshly trimmed, and Mrs Clancy, still wearing her dingy drover's boy's shirt and much-washed trousers held up with baling twine. The big hat hid her long hair.

'Just passing,' said Mr Clancy, standing just outside the front gate.

Why don't they come in? thought Flinty. Oh. Stockmen might accept Mrs Clancy out droving, but even those who had eaten her roast ducks around a campfire wouldn't ask a native — man, boy or woman — into their homes, to sit with their wives and family.

'Come in!' She was glad she and Kirsty had been spring-cleaning, that the parlour was freshly swept and polished, the ornaments dusted, the carpets beaten and left to freshen in the sun. Mrs Mack and Mutti Green might sit in the kitchen, she thought, but the Clancys would sit in the parlour.

She owed them that, and more.

'Like to see how the colt's goin',' said Mr Clancy, as he followed her inside. 'The wife here wanted to come up the mountain too. Says all those white flowers dripping off the trees were planted by her people.'

'You mean the clematis?'

'Like a road, I reckon. The wife says that the young girls used to follow the white way to get their stringy bark for baskets. So, the colt's goin' good?' He had yet to comment on the bathchair. Mrs Clancy hadn't spoken at all.

'My brother Andy has come home. He's training him. He's shaping up well.' She didn't mention that any further training would be down on the flats, not here. She gestured at the velvet sofa and Mum's chintz armchairs, a bit faded now. 'Please sit down. I'll just get the tea.'

She was glad neither offered to help her. She needed to do whatever she could by herself. The kettle would be on the boil, and she'd put scones into the oven as soon as she'd heard the hoofbeats, just as Mum had always done.

She arranged the best cups on a tray with an embroidered teacloth, the crab-apple jelly in a bowl, not the jar. There was no butter, but she didn't think the Clancys would mind, or maybe even notice. She balanced the tray on the arms of her chair, wheeling carefully so she didn't knock it, then allowed Mr Clancy to put it on the tea table in front of the sofa and armchairs.

They ate and drank silently. Mr Clancy as always had no small talk. He seemed focused on his tea and scones, less comfortable in the soft armchair than when leaning against a tree. Mrs Clancy looked around curiously, gazing at Mum's clock, the statue of the sphinx Andy had brought back from Egypt, the postcards both boys had sent and the ones from Sandy too, still displayed on the mantelpiece, at the bookshelves, the footstool and the Persian rug.

At last Mr Clancy swallowed the last of the scones. He stood up and brushed off the crumbs as though the freshly beaten carpet was a patch of grass. 'How about I see how the colt is goin'?' he said. 'While you and the wife have a catch-up? Heard about your trouble when we called in at Drinkwater,' he added. Flinty wondered exactly what they'd heard — whether the story had included Sergeant Morris, or just the fact she'd fallen. 'Thought maybe the wife could help.'

'I don't understand.' She looked from one to the other. Was Mr Clancy suggesting his wife help them with the housework? They couldn't afford to pay for help, or even to feed another couple for long, even if they lived on rabbit and roo. 'I'm managing well now, thank you.'

'The wife knows some native medicines,' said Mr Clancy. 'They do all right, some of them.'

Flinty shook her head. 'A nursing sister from Sydney has already been up here. She says there isn't any medicine that will make a difference.'

'Yes. Well. Heard about that too. But I went to a doctor who said that about me rheumatism, must have been twenty year ago now,' said Mr Clancy. 'The wife's emu oil fixed it a treat. How many men my age do you know still droving?' He grinned at the question good manners wouldn't let her ask, showing the gaps in his teeth. 'I'm eighty-three.'

She'd taken him for twenty years younger. The grin grew wider. 'You listen to the wife, all right? Now I'll go see this horse.'

Flinty sat awkwardly as the sound of his boots headed out the back.

'This is women's business,' said Mrs Clancy. 'Don't need men around for this. He's a good man but. A real good man. Now, you hurt your back? Not your legs?'

Flinty nodded.

'Yes. Well,' said Mrs Clancy, sounding so like her husband that Flinty almost smiled. But of course Mrs Clancy would have learned most of her English from him. The old woman reached into her trouser pocket, then brought out what looked like a ball of dead grass. Flinty wheeled closer and saw it was a small woven basket, hinged at the top. Mrs Clancy opened it. Inside were lumps of dried tree fungus.

Mrs Clancy rose without speaking and went out into the corridor, turning towards the kitchen. Flinty wheeled herself after her in time to see the woman open the stove and hold the fungus to the flame. When it smouldered she placed it in the basket again. Mrs Clancy handed it to Flinty. 'Smell,' she ordered.

Flinty lifted the basket to her nose reluctantly. The fungus smoked rather than burned. It smelled strangely sweet, almost of Nicholas's roses, or even oranges. She breathed in again. Somehow her breath seemed to go deeper this time, then deeper again.

How could smoke help a back?

But there was something in Mrs Clancy's gaze that stopped protest. Instead she breathed, again and again. Each breath seemed deeper still. Slowly her body *lightened*. She smiled, not knowing why she smiled, and Mrs Clancy smiled back.

Suddenly the native woman stepped forwards and put her arms under Flinty's armpits.

'No,' said Flinty fuzzily, as Mrs Clancy began to lift. Did the old woman think that the smoke was magic, had made her light enough to stand?

Mrs Clancy ignored her. Her arms were as surprisingly strong as Sister Burrows's had been. Flinty put a hand out to cling to the kitchen table in case she fell.

Mrs Clancy stepped back, leaving Flinty alone at the table. Yet somehow she wasn't falling. Somehow her legs were standing, and she was on them, unsteady but upright.

'Back can't lift you up,' said her visitor. 'But once you're up you stay all right.'

She was standing! Not quite straight, it was true — her back was bent like a roo's — but on her own two feet, even if she had to keep hold of the table to steady herself. My back isn't strong enough to get me to my feet, thought Flinty, but there is nothing wrong with my legs.

It all made sense. Despite the confusion brought by the

fungus smoke — or maybe because of it — the bits all came together.

She tried a step. Her legs didn't move. Mrs Clancy made a lifting motion.

Flinty let go of the table. She bent slightly, all her back would allow, and used her hands to lift her right leg and move it forwards a tiny step. Somehow she drove her body after it, pushing with her shoulders to make her left leg follow the first.

She pushed again and took another step, this time without having to lift her leg, grabbing the table again both for steadiness and to help push.

It wasn't quite walking. But it *was* standing, and she was moving, moving without wheels, without anyone lifting her.

She wanted to cry. But tears wouldn't come. Maybe her mind was too full for tears or the smoke had dried them up. Maybe, she thought vaguely, the fungus had smoked away her despair, planted by Dr Sparrow when he had told her she'd never walk again. The smoke had let her trust a native woman's hands, instead of the mumblings of a drunk white doctor.

'Well,' said Mr Clancy from the doorway. He grinned. 'When Pete Sampson told us what that nurse from Sydney said to your Sandy, the wife said she reckoned she knew what you needed.'

'You got the jar?' demanded Mrs Clancy.

Mr Clancy had evidently been to his saddlebags. He held out an old tin that had probably once contained tobacco. 'Rub this green stuff on your back before you go to bed,' he ordered. 'Stinks a bit, but you get used to it. Brings the swelling down a treat.'

Sister Burrows had said that it was the swelling on her back pressing on the nerves that stopped her moving. Suddenly she was willing to believe that the ointment would help, just as the smoke had done.

'Bring you more later,' said Mrs Clancy. 'Not the season for the leaves now. When the wattle seeds turn dark, that's when you pick the —' She added a native word, spoken too fast for Flinty to hear it properly. She looked at Flinty thoughtfully. 'Might tell you more women's business then. If you want.'

Mr Clancy nodded. 'Got to get another emu too, to boil it down for fat. That's what the wife uses for her ointments: emu fat. I'm running low meself.' He grinned, showing every one of his remaining tobacco-stained teeth. 'Glad you're standing, girl. Who knows? One day you might even get on a horse again.'

And just then, with the solid floor beneath her slippers, the chair two blessed steps behind her, Flinty believed him.

Chapter 37

1 October 1920

Dear Diary,

I waited till after dinner to stand up again. I didn't dare take a step, in case I fell in front of them all. Kirsty cried and hugged me so hard I nearly did fall over and Andy kept saying, 'By Jove,' over and over and Joey said, 'Wait till I tell them at school,' and then wanted to look at my back to see if the lump moves when I stand up (I wouldn't let him). He wants to be a doctor now, though I bet it'll be a vet again by next week.

I thought my back would hurt more tonight, but it's funny, it hurts less than it has since I fell. Maybe Sister Burrows is right: the more I move it the better it will be. And now I can really move. It is so good to look down at things again, instead of always up.

I'm tired but I'm too excited to sleep. Nicholas said that bad things would happen, but they would pass. Maybe that means that I will be able to walk properly again. But he said that very, very good things will happen too.

Maybe now I can walk — or might be able to walk and won't need nursing — Sandy will … it's funny, I can't even write it down, perhaps because I want it just to happen, not imagine it by writing it. Maybe Sandy could get a Soldier Settler grant on another mountain near Batlow, not as high as this, of course, with better soil. But even if he did, I'd still miss the Rock. Dad said once that when he stood on the Rock he could feel his feet connected deep to the centre of the earth, and ever since I've felt the same.

Somehow the Rock isn't just Nicholas, but Sandy — Sandy as he used to be and Sandy as he is now — and Mum and Dad and the brumbies, and everything that made up my life.

Things change, of course — so much has happened in the past few years, in the last year too. I can accept things changing, but I don't think I can bear losing the Rock.

Although that's silly. You bear what you have to bear. And if you can't, maybe you die, like Mum. But I don't want to die, not for a long, long time. Not even if I have to leave the Rock.

It was a day of heavy clouds, fat bellied and green tinged. First they covered the mountain top, then the paddocks and, finally, the house. At last the rain began, not so much falling as sweeping from all around.

Flinty was glad she'd sent Kirsty and Joey off to school with a change of clothes. They could both stay at the Macks' tonight, while Andy stayed at the Mullinses'. She'd be alone here for the first time in her life.

It felt strange, but good too. She could never be truly alone up on the mountain. Not just because of Snow King in his paddock and the hens, but the wallabies pulling at the shrubs to eat the new shoots, the sugar gliders munching at spring blossom, even the tiny bats that flew across the house at night. One had got into Mum's wardrobe once. Mum had screamed, but Dad had lifted it carefully and put it on the stand by the water barrel ...

Only a few weeks earlier it had seemed that she would never be alone for more than a couple of hours again, that someone would always need to lift things for her, even help her use a chamberpot.

Now she could walk slowly around the kitchen and down the corridor, holding on to the walls for support. It was still a long way from walking outside, much less climbing a hill or riding a horse, but one day that would come too.

She still couldn't stand up by herself, unless she pulled herself up by her hands on the kitchen table, or lay down on the bed, holding her legs out straight, then rolled off at an angle so that her feet touched the floor while her arms pulled at the bar to heave herself upright. It was clumsy, and took too long and was so awkward she wouldn't let even Kirsty watch her. But at least it got her upright. Every day of movement made her back feel better. When the pain screamed at night she could even walk around till it eased. She was careful not to lift anything heavier than a teapot or saucepan of potatoes, and tried to move smoothly so her back didn't jar. And each day she was sure that it grew better.

The house creaked around her. Any ghosts on the mountains are kind ones, she thought. I need this time. Time to drink it all in, to store my memories, instead of bustling about getting meals and making sure Joey has dry socks.

She'd promised Andy not to get out of her chair and try to walk when she was alone unless she really had to. He was scared she might fall. But it was too tempting to resist and, after all, what could happen to her with the chairs and tables for support? She stood carefully, and walked around the table — really walked, she thought, able to lift her knees now too.

No need to make a proper dinner just for herself. There were cold potatoes — Sandy had brought some new ones up from the Macks', where they'd been in the soil over winter — and dripping in the food safe, and half a cabbage in the scullery. She fried it all into a big pan of bubble and squeak, ate a third of it and left the rest to reheat for tea and breakfast.

She stayed in her chair darning that afternoon. The half-hour on her feet had exhausted her. As the shadows lengthened she brought in firewood so she didn't have to go out in the dark. She wheeled herself onto the front verandah in the late afternoon to look down the track, just in case the others decided to come home. The rain had washed away the fog: it eased slowly as the darkness grew. Stars swept across the sky in their own strange tides, until clouds smeared them into black again.

No one was coming. She wheeled back in, chilled, ate her bubble and squeak, and warmed a bran poultice to take to bed, with the luxury of the lamp beside her so she could read as long as she liked, an old book of Dad's called *Mr Midshipman Easy*. She'd read it so often she could almost recite it now, but that didn't change the joy of the words, or the feeling that she too was there, facing the grey waves and flapping sails.

Would she ever see the sea? She was happy enough to see it only in books, especially if seeing it meant getting shipwrecked. Besides, it would take days to get to the seaside. She'd rather have the pinky-purple haze of indigofera, or the white fuzz of thorn bush, or the shine of new bark that left the snow gums streaked with grey and green and red. You only get that once a year, Dad said. Three score and seven years for a man, so you only get that many springs too, and Christmases and birthdays.

Dad hadn't even managed three score ... No, she wouldn't want to miss even one of the seasons of the mountain, just to see the sea. But maybe it would be different when she had to live down on the Drinkwater plains.

She blew out the lamp and slept deeply, waking at rooster crow, the kookaburras chuckling afterwards. There was a new note to their call this morning. An almost ... shocked sound. Apart from that the world was strangely silent.

She slid into her chair and wheeled over to the window to open the shutters. The world glowed so bright she almost had to shut her eyes.

Snow! Pure white, too recent to even be flecked by wombat and bird prints or the longer marks of the roos. It was deeper than she'd ever seen it: two feet high about the house perhaps, piled up even on the edge of the verandah. But up on the mountain ...

It was as though giants had played in the night, making new cliffs and mountains. But these cliffs were snow — massive tall drifts right across the mountain above the paddocks, the edges crumbling as she looked.

The clouds hung below the Rock, across the valley. This was her miracle then, unseen by the valley below, her world of ice and trees and beauty.

What miracle of cloud and wind had made this frozen landscape? She dimly remembered Dad saying that spring snow was always the deepest.

There'd been spring snow the first year he'd been on the mountain, so soft and deep he'd sunk to his knees, when the house was just what was now the kitchen and scullery. Spring snow sucks in the sunlight, then beams it out tenfold, he'd said. She looked up at the harsh blue of the sky and smiled. It really did look darker because of the snow, just like Dad had said, as though most of its light was below.

Well, today's snow wouldn't last. Even now, as the sun rose above the ridge, the first icicles were dropping from the roof. She could almost see the soft top of the snow turn to a brittle crust of ice and the snow below it melt. She turned to stoke up the fire. By midday the snow would have melted into a flood ...

She stopped, her hands still on the chair's wheels. She had never seen snow as deep as this. When this snow melted it would bring a flood, perhaps the biggest the valley had ever known.

No one down in the valley would be able to see the snow, not through the layer of fog. The fury of water would appear with no more warning than a few seconds of roaring and thunder. It would surge across the creek flats, where the sheep grazed on the new grass that had sprung up after the last floods, where the men and horses ploughed to put in the spring crops.

This flood might grasp higher than any flood before — even, maybe, to the schoolhouse nestled by the road. It would come in a torrent, gaining speed as it crashed down the mountain till it was captured by the Snowy far below.

Nothing could withstand the strength of a thaw flood down from the heights, she thought. How many sheep and cows or pigs would die today trapped in the paddocks as the flood wave washed them against the fences? How many farmers might be ruined? The Macks, the Mullinses, the Colours of the Valley, all the kind, dear neighbours ...

She had to warn them. She couldn't warn them! She had an hour, perhaps, while the snow melted and the flood gathered, another hour while it hurled itself down the mountain ...

It took an hour to ride to the Mullinses', another half-hour to ride to each farm in the valley. Less, if you galloped. But there was no one here to gallop down to the valley, only a crippled girl in a chair. No horse to ride, except Snow King in his paddock.

If only a yell could reach the houses below. If only someone might call by, Sandy or Mrs Mack. But no one would be coming up through the mud today, not till Joey and Kirsty late this afternoon, and Andy tonight.

By then it would be too late. Far, far too late.

There is only me and Snow King, she thought. You'll probably never be able to ride again, Sister Burrows had said. Riding could damage her back more than it had been before. And galloping Snow King might strain his legs, split a bone or strain a tendon, be damaged so that he'd never be a racer, maybe never even canter across the hills. Both horse and girl crippled, if they galloped down the mountain now.

A blob of snow slid off the roof and landed with a *plifff* outside. The thaw was coming even as she hesitated.

She couldn't do it. It was impossible, even without the risk to herself and Snow King. She couldn't even walk as far as the paddock, much less get on a horse.

Impossible. But she had to try.

Chapter 38

19 November 1920

Dear Diary,

I think last week I felt a tiny breath of what the valley men must have felt facing the enemy. You do what you have to do, because if you don't it's worse.

No time for warmer clothes. Even boots would be a struggle, taking minutes she couldn't spare. She wheeled herself out to the back porch, planted her slippered feet on the ground, then stood by the back steps.

Stairs. It had been eight months since she had walked down steps. Nor was there solid ground to walk on after that, just slush more than ankle deep. She could manage to lift her knees as she walked around the kitchen. How could she struggle through snow?

She grabbed the railing, and twisted one leg down, twisted again, and the second leg followed it.

Another step. Another. Her slippers were already drenched, but the woollen socks would help keep her feet from freezing. Even wet wool keeps the heat in, Mum whispered, years away but still a comfort in her mind.

Help me, she said softly to her parents, to the Rock and to the mountains. Please help me now.

At last — ten seconds or ten years later — she stood at the bottom of the stairs, grasping the rail. The paddock gate was maybe fifty yards away.

Fifty yards uphill, with nothing to hold on to, through melting snow in lumps and bumps across the ground. Fifty yards might as well be fifty miles.

She had to let go of the railing now. She had to walk properly, to climb. She lifted a leg ...

Her back wasn't strong enough to lift her foot above the snow, and there was no way she could force it up through the slush. Desperate, she bent and lifted her knee with her hands, moved it forwards, let it fall down.

Squish! Her foot landed in the snow, met solid ground below. Somehow she was still upright, even without the rail to cling to.

She lifted her other leg. Up and down. *Squish!* Up and down ... again ... again ... again ...

She must look like Frankenstein's poor monster, like the picture in the book, the wretched creature lurching about on legs that weren't really his. Her legs didn't feel like they belonged to her either. But somehow she made them move.

One step. Another step lifting her knee with her hands each time. She had to go faster, but if she went too fast she'd fall. If she fell perhaps she'd never get up again, would lie in the snow freezing. If the thaw came Joey and Kirsty wouldn't come home to find her for perhaps days. Too late for her. Too late for the valley.

Another step. Another.

There was no pain. Almost no pain, just a blankness where pain would be if she let herself think of it. Pain could come later, when she had time to deal with pain. Small cascades of chilly water trickled off the stable roof. The sun, that great beaming bully, was climbing higher.

Another step, another. Sweat trickled down her back. Pain sweat, not from heat. Almost to the paddock gate now.

Stupid! She should have brought some bread, an apple — something to tempt Snow King to come to her. Would he even remember her? He had only known her for a few months and hadn't seen her all winter and spring.

He knew her. She heard his whinny, heard the hooves, half muffled, half crunching through the crust of snow. He cantered up to her, tossing his head, then pig-rooted, part showing off, part rejoicing as she had been in the sheer abundance of light and snow.

No saddle. She couldn't carry it, much less put it on. At least he wore a headstall, though of course no bit and reins. There was a piece of rope hanging on the gate latch. She could attach that to his headstall so at least she had a lead rope — not much with which to control a spirited horse like Snow King, but better than nothing. She would be able to use it against his neck to indicate to him when she needed him to change direction and pull on it to slow him down. But without a saddle, how could she get on?

Once she would have grabbed a handful of mane, sprung up and, dropping her left shoulder, swung her right leg over easily before settling herself on his warm, broad back. But her legs couldn't spring now, not without a whole spine to tell them how to move. Instead she opened the wooden gate and hauled herself up onto it with her arms, strong from months of wheeling. She managed to get her feet up onto the second rung, to balance there. 'Here, boy! Here!'

Snow King tossed his head as if it was a game. She bit her lip. '*Please*, boy! Come on, Snow King.'

He stopped prancing and skittering. For a moment the brown eyes looked at her. She realised suddenly that *he understood her*. Not what was important perhaps, or why, but that this *was* important, the most important thing she'd ever done or asked him to do. Slowly, miraculously, he settled. He walked towards her, and then stood next to the gate, as quiet as Empress.

She pushed herself from the gate towards him. She landed lying across his back, half on, half off. He snorted in surprise, trotting a few steps so she thought she would slither off. But then he steadied again.

Her arms couldn't lift her legs and cling to Snow King too. Her legs had to move themselves. Move! she told them. Lift! The right foot shifted just a little. She made another effort, sweat trickling down inside her shirt despite the cold, and suddenly her leg obeyed, twisting onto one side across his back while the other stayed where it was, her body lifting so at last she was where she had longed to be all those months indoors. Astride Snow King's back among the blaze of white and mountains.

Balance was second nature. But to gallop over rough country you had to grip with your knees and thighs — not to mention use them to signal to the horse you rode. Instead her legs just hung there.

Impossible to gallop down the track. Even more impossible to take the short cut, to guide Snow King over wombat holes and through thorn bushes, balancing on a horse's back, no saddle to keep her steady. No stirrups, though even if she had them they'd be no use.

But it had been impossible to get from the house to here. The impossible had to keep on happening.

Her back screamed. She ignored it.

She tapped Snow King's neck lightly with one hand and clicked her tongue, hoping he'd understand hand gestures instead of the nudge of her heels.

He did. He began to walk, through the gate, down to the track. She bent low, over his neck. Even before she urged him with her voice he understood.

He surged like the stream in torrent, like the Snowy down its bed. He galloped as smoothly as water, neck arched before her with his head almost statue still as he scanned the track in front of his flying hooves. It was as though they had suddenly become part of the mountain, like the wind itself made way for them, parting to let the horse and rider through.

Past the Rock, with its breath of chill. Snow King didn't even falter, as other horses did, although his ears pricked up a little. Around the corner, then another ...

She had to turn him off the track here to take the short cut. She pulled on the lead rope and shifted her weight in the direction she wanted him to go.

Perhaps he sensed the old tracks where Empress had been. But at any rate he leaped over the first of the bushes, his hooves sure even in the slush.

The fog was below them, like a massive wall shutting out the world. Snow King plunged into it, as though trusting his rider to take him where it was safe. All at once the world was another kind of white: the snow invisible under his hooves, the air clammy and cold.

And then they were out into clear bright air. She glanced back at the smooth white barrier. You'd never guess the deadly burden of snow above.

A branch lashed her, almost unseating her. She cried out, bent down again as low as she could go onto Snow King's neck. He had never been ridden in rough country, as far as she knew, only in the paddock and on the track. But perhaps he understood, because he kept clear of overhanging branches now. Even when he soared above the wombat holes his stride stayed so smooth it was as though they flew together, horse and girl.

It was terrifying. It was beyond any dream of wonderful. She was scared, exultant, wishing she was safe back in her chair, wishing this would never end, frightened that she would be forever crippled, elated that she'd had this last ride, at least. She was the eagle flying; a small child wanting to cry for help. She was horse and rider, one instead of two. She was the land, the breath of mountains, the beat of kangaroos. And then she was a girl again, with a desperate job to do.

The creek glinted to her left, snaking its way through the rocks, quartz winking at the sun. It was already twice as big as usual. But anyone seeing how it had risen would just think there'd been rain up top and this was the worst it would be. The true flood would come quickly, a wall of water as high as the half-grown she-oaks, powerful enough to lift boulders and uproot trees.

Snow King leaped again. Flinty tried not to think what the impacts would be doing to his still-growing leg bones.

Bad enough to gallop him at all, so young, so long, without taking him on rough ground like this. Another leap, landing awkwardly this time. She grabbed his mane even harder, trying to keep her body moving with the rhythm of his.

If she fell now the hooves might crush her. If she fell now …

No. She would not fall. She couldn't.

Snow King soared again. But this jump took him across the final hop bush onto the track again. It was muddy, rutted, but clear of wombat holes. At least here the young horse could see where he was going, as long as he kept clear of puddles; the muddy water was deceptively deep.

Round one bend … and another … and there was old Dusty Jim's shack. Please, she prayed, don't let him be asleep with his rum bottle. If she had to get down to find him she might never get up again. Old Dusty only had a dozen sheep he kept for meat and the few quid he got for the fleeces, but they too would be on the creek flats now.

There he was, on the verandah. He *was* asleep, and there was an empty rum bottle on the floor under his chair. But he woke when she pulled at Snow King's lead rope and shouted, 'Flash flood coming! Snow melt on the mountain!'

'What? When?' He stared at her blearily from age-clouded eyes.

'Get your sheep in! Now!' she yelled.

Was he too drunk to understand? But he took off at a shambling jog towards the creek flats, shouting for his dogs. Rum or not, he knew what flash flood meant.

Snow King's sides heaved, and he gasped for air. But he surged forwards down the track again, as soon as she shook the lead rope and clicked her tongue. He was born to race, thought Flinty, trying to erase her promise never to ride another horse this hard from her memory. The king horse, just like in her book, proud of his strength, determined to outrun even a flood.

And she might cripple him, she who knew all too well what it was to be a cripple.

'I'm sorry,' she whispered as they pounded on. 'I'm so sorry.'

He couldn't hear. He couldn't understand. And suddenly she realised that this was a horse who was born for more than simply racing. His great-grandmother may have been Regret, the greatest racehorse of them all. But his ancestors had been bred to be partners with humans too. Snow King had been born to run with her today, to break his heart, his legs, just like the poor horse who'd belonged to the real man from Snowy River. He'd do what his rider wanted even if he died in the attempt. She had created the king of horses in her book. Was she destroying a king horse too?

The Mullinses' next. She'd hoped to see Andy — if he was already mounted he could take over the run. But instead there was old Vati Green, steering the plough behind his big Clydesdale. He and his sons must have come up to help with the ploughing, not knowing this field would be under water in an hour. She pulled Snow King back to a jog and waved frantically. 'Mr Green!'

'Felicity, mein Gott —'

'Flash flood coming!' She pointed to the creek, then up to the ceiling of cloud. 'Blizzard up there last night — and now the snow is melting! It'll be the biggest flood ever. Get the animals out of the lower paddocks, and people too. You understand?'

'I understand!' He slapped the Clydesdale on the rump to turn the plough, taking them uphill. 'Heinrich!' he yelled. Flinty heard the answer: 'Ja, Papa?'

She jerked the lead rope to head down the track again. The swerve jolted her back so badly she felt not pain, just sweat, springing from every pore, prickling her scalp, a wave of blackness that tried to take her into unconsciousness. She had to wrap her mind around Snow King, the smell of him, the rhythm of his hooves. Slowly her vision cleared again, though the world still spun. Snow King was wet with sweat too, his back and neck slippery.

The Macks' next. She pulled the colt's head towards the gate. He responded at once, hopping across the cattle ramp, cantering up the road towards the house.

What time was it? Mid-morning, she supposed. There was no one working in the paddocks nearby. She pulled at the rope as Mrs Mack hurried out of the front door.

'Flinty love! What on earth —'

'Flash flood coming. Snow melting! Got to warn them, move the stock —'

'The boys are down on the river flats —'

'I've got to find them. Got to warn them.'

'You'll do no such thing. You bide there.' She reached up to the bell outside the front door. The jangle filled the valley. *Clang, clang, clang* ... Snow King skittered sideways, Flinty clinging on grimly. She heard a far-off answering whistle from beyond the trees.

'They've heard,' said Mrs Mack, wiping her hands on her old sacking apron. 'Someone will be down in half a jiffy.'

'I can't wait! I've got to warn the others —' She stopped as a horse broke through the trees, its rider urging it forwards, and then another. Toby, she thought, and Sandy.

'Ma! What is it?' yelled Toby. 'You ain't been bitten by a snake?'

'Pa's just coming,' panted Sandy. He reined his horse as he saw Flinty. 'What the flaming hell —'

'Language,' said Mrs Mack. 'Flood's coming. Snowstorm melting up above.'

'A big one,' gasped Flinty. 'It'll cover the lower paddocks. It's going to come fast too.'

Sandy slid from his horse and ran to Flinty. 'Come on,' he said. 'I'll help you down.'

'No! I have to warn the others ...' All the Colours of the Valley, she thought. She had to warn them as well.

'I can do that,' said Toby, then as she opened her mouth again, 'I'll warn the school too, make sure everyone is up safe.' She realised with desperate relief he was right. She had done all she need to.

Toby dug his heels into his mare. She sprang to a gallop, fresher than Snow King, whose sides were still heaving and running with sweat.

'What's all the fuss, Ma?' Mr Mack drew his horse to a standstill too. 'Thought the house must be on fire, all that clanging.'

'Flash flood's coming. Big one, and fast. Snow melt,' said Sandy shortly. 'Flinty, slide off this way. I'll catch you. Dad will see to Snow King.'

'Cold poultices, for his legs,' panted Flinty. If they could stop them swelling it might limit the damage. Oh, you poor horse. You darling horse, she thought. What have I done to you? Taken a king from the brumbies and then destroyed him ...

'Dad knows what to do,' said Sandy. 'Don't worry, love. We'll do our best for him.'

Suddenly Mr Mack was barking orders. 'Bernie, you come with me; Sam, you take the dogs down to the lower paddock ...'

Hands covered hers on the sweaty rope now, unwrapped her fist from the hank of Snow King's mane. Sandy's hands. 'Come on, Flinty darling,' he said quietly. 'You can let go now.'

'I … I can't get off.' Her back seemed frozen. Perhaps it would be frozen forever, the broken bones jolted so much that maybe even more were broken now. Darling, she thought. He called me darling. Now, when I may never move again.

'It's all right, love,' said Sandy. He tugged at her gently and she slid into his arms. Warm, safe arms that carried her up the stairs and into the sitting room, and placed her softly down onto the sofa, as though she was as light as a feather pillow.

'Hot bran poultice for her back,' he said to Mrs Mack, who had followed them in. 'And blankets too.'

Mrs Mack vanished. Flinty tried to focus through the pain and growing fear.

'Don't worry,' Sandy said. 'Leave it to Toby and Dad. Toby will have told Mr Ross already. They'll bring everyone's sheep up. And as long as the paddock gates are open, any they can't round up will hear the water and run.'

She nodded, trying not to cry. Mrs Mack was back, tucking the poultice behind her. It helped, but only a little.

'I can't feel my legs,' she whispered. 'Not even my toes. Even when it was worst I could still feel my toes.'

'You'll feel them again,' said Sandy. His eyes looked like he would tear mountains down if that could help.

'Tea,' said Mrs Mack, in the tone of someone who knew that anything was better with hot tea. She disappeared towards the kitchen again.

It *was* better with tea, well sweetened. She sipped and the nausea slowly eased. The shock of the pain ebbed, even if the pain did not.

Her legs were still numb, but faintly, very faintly, she felt pins and needles in her toes. Outside she could hear barking and the annoyed baaing of sheep. A smell of pikelets cooking and hot butter came from the kitchen — another of Mrs Mack's remedies for the woes of the world.

'I used to dream of Mum's pikelets,' said Sandy. He sat on the rag rug on the floor next to the sofa. Somehow he was still holding her hand, the one that didn't hold the teacup.

'You told me. That's about all you ever have told me about the war,' said Flinty.

He shrugged. 'Not much to tell, except what I put in postcards. No,' as she began to protest, 'it's the truth.'

'But the danger ... people being blown up and the rats ...'

'Most days were pretty much the same,' said Sandy. 'Seen one trench rat you've seen them all.' He gazed at her. Time seemed to stretch, years in a few seconds.

At last she said, 'Snow King ... do you think he'll be all right?'

He didn't try to reassure her, to tell her not to worry. Sandy would never do that. 'We won't know for a few days.'

'I'll sit up with him tonight, keep changing the poultices ...'

'You'll be resting that back of yours, in this house,' said Sandy.

'But it's my fault! If Snow King ends up a useless cripple it'll be because of me. I ... I can't bear it, Sandy.'

'Yes, you can,' he said softly. 'You'll bear it because you have to, Flinty McAlpine. You did what you had to. Remember that.' He looked at her steadily. 'I had a horse killed under me once. I had to watch him die. Black Thunder, you remember him? It was my fault he died, my fault that he was in the war at all. But I was doing what I had to, Flinty. Just like you.'

It helped, a bit.

'Flinty.' He was clearly hunting for words now. 'It was my fault Jeff died too. It was twice my fault.'

'What? I don't understand.'

'I dared him to join the march with me that day. Dared him to say he was eighteen. I'm sorry, Flinty. I've been trying to bring myself to tell you since I got back.'

Sister Burrows was wrong, he wasn't keen on her. It was just guilt ... She wanted to cry: cry with pain, with shock, the relief that she'd been in time to warn the downstream families, weep for Snow King, for Jeff and for herself. But tears seemed locked away in a cold dark place she couldn't find.

'You said it was twice your fault?'

He nodded, his gaze still caught on hers. 'He saved my life, Flinty. At Bullecourt. They ordered us out of the trenches — a full moon, they could mow us down like shooting skittles, but we had to go. I was halfway through the barbed wire of no-man's-land, between our trenches and the Huns', when a shell burst in front of me. Don't know what happened for a while. But when I woke I was trapped there, in the wire. Cold, I've never known such cold; I was too weak to move.

'Our blokes had fallen back then. The only ones around me were dead. I knew when dawn came the Huns would have me. I was like a rat caught in a trap. One shot and I'd be dead.

'But Jeff came after me. I swore at him, told him to go back. But you know Jeff. He cut the wire, bit by bit. It took forever, but he kept on going. He pulled me out, dragged me through that mud. He was lifting me when the next shot came, the one that had been meant for me.'

He stopped, as though his own small flood had died down. She said softly, 'That's when he died?'

'Yes. It wasn't quick, Flinty. I lied. We all lied, time after time, about things like that. He screamed for hours, growing weaker all the time. And I just lay there helpless, listening to my best mate die.'

The teacup was on the table. Somehow her arms had gone around his shoulders; his head was pressed into her. 'Sandy ... Sandy, it's all right. What ... what happened to you then?'

'I lay there,' he whispered. 'Don't tell Mum, will you? Don't want her to know. I lay there for three days. I think that's what saved me, Flinty. That's what Sister Burrows said.'

'I don't understand.'

'I had shrapnel cuts from my chest right down to my legs. That mud — it was half blood. I should have died of gangrene. But then the maggots found me —'

'Sandy, no ...'

'The maggots saved me. They ate the dead flesh. After Sister Burrows sewed me up she said the wounds were clean, and that I'd live, if I wanted to. She said that it was up to me.

'I didn't just dream of pikelets,' said Sandy. 'I dreamed of you. That's what I wanted to come back to. It's always been you, even at school. When things were at their worst I dreamed of you and me up on the mountain. I'd think: I only have to get through this and I'll be there.'

The cold dark place melted, leaving a glow instead. 'I thought you'd changed your mind. You didn't even kiss me when you got back. You'd seen so much. So many girls —'

'No one but you,' said Sandy.

'Why didn't you tell me?' It couldn't just have been guilt about Jeff's death, she thought.

Sandy glanced at the door, but there was no sign of Mrs Mack, just frypan noises from the kitchen. 'I didn't think I could marry anyone. Not and make them live with this.'

He moved away from her and began to unbutton his shirt.

Flinty gasped. The scars were purple, ridged and heavy lipped, like giant worms wriggling across his skin.

'It's like this all down my body. All the way, Flinty, down to my knees.'

She saw what he meant. It wasn't just the ugliness he was trying to show her now.

'You mean you ... you think you can't have children?'

'I think I can. Perhaps it'll be all right. But you can't ask a girl to marry you with a "perhaps", Flinty. Not a girl like you.'

Your children, Nicholas had said. What had he said about her children?

It didn't matter. When she had children they'd be with Sandy, because she wasn't marrying anyone else ever, no matter what.

'Perhaps is good enough,' she said. She took his hand again. 'But I reckon we can do better than perhaps.'

'That's what Sister Burrows told me. She said I should stop dilly-dallying and ask you.'

Flinty could just imagine the way she'd said it too.

'When I took her back to Gibber's Creek to catch the train I bought this.'

He felt in his pocket and pulled out a box. It was small and square, covered in fine brown leather. He opened it. The ring inside was a thin gold band, with a small row of blue stones, clear as the mountain sky. A betrothal ring, thought Flinty. The stones glowed against the deep blue velvet, even in the dimness of the room. 'I've been carrying it in my pocket ever since.

Didn't want to let the boys see it, or Mum.' He swallowed. 'All right if I put it on you?'

'Why?' she said stupidly, then realised it was probably the most unromantic proposal and the silliest answer in the history of marriage.

'So that every bloke who sees it on you knows you're mine.'

'Sandy ... dear Sandy ... are you sure you want a wife who can't walk?'

'You'll walk again. And even if you don't, we'll manage. But like you said, I reckon we'll do better than perhaps.' He gazed at her steadily. 'You saved every farm in the valley today. You're a heroine, Flinty McAlpine. I reckon you can do anything you set your mind to.'

It wasn't a great speech, not like in books, but she was crying anyway. 'All right,' she said. She wanted to say, 'With you beside me we can do anything,' but she couldn't quite say romantic words either. On paper, perhaps, where romantic things belonged. But not out loud.

She held out her hand. He slipped on the ring.

'Too big. I knew I should have got a size smaller.'

'I've been wondering for two years when you were going to get around to that, Sandy lad.' Mrs Mack stood in the doorway, holding a plate of pikelets. 'And don't think you hid that jeweller's box from me, because you didn't. Wrap a bit of rag around your finger, lovey,' she added to Flinty. 'That way you can wear it till he can get a jeweller to make it fit.'

A rumble began to shake the valley, vibrating even through the sofa. The flood had hit the creek flats. Flinty heard the first crash of a fallen log bashing its way through the trees, the grind of boulders carried by the mountain tide.

'Will Toby have got to everyone in time?'

'Plenty of time,' said Sandy, still gazing at her, both her hands in his. 'All the time in the world.'

'I'll go and make some dumplings for the stew,' said Mrs Mack. 'They'll be hungry when they come in. You can kiss her when I'm in the kitchen,' she added.

'All right,' said Sandy. He grinned at Flinty, and moved towards her.

His lips were warm. The taste of him, the strength of him, filled the world. He was the most real thing she had ever felt. She wanted to stay next to him for her whole life; she knew in all the ways that counted that she would.

Chapter 39

25 November 1920

Dear Diary,

All things in their season, Mum used to say. I wish I could tell her about this. I hope she knew that there would be so much good as well as pain. The land has its seasons, and so do people. We've had the season of war. Now, finally, it is as though we are getting our season of peace. It is blossom time at last, and the season of fruit to come.

Sandy drove her back to Rock Farm in the cart a week later, lying propped between pillows, with Mrs Mack and Kirsty in case she needed anything. Snow King stayed in his stall at the Macks'. One hock was badly swollen, though Andy told her it would mend.

'Do you think it will?' she'd asked Sandy.

He'd just smiled and said, 'Hope so.' Sandy's smile seemed always ready now, a gift to her each time she saw it. I make him happy, she thought. And then: I always did.

It had been a week of pain, worse even than when she'd first been hurt, not even able to feel her toes apart from the pins and needles. But at last there was a little movement, and then some more. She'd need the bathchair for weeks, or even months. But once again she had hope.

And Sandy. He glanced back and grinned at her, then nodded towards a young wallaby peering at them from the hop bush, as though hoping this strange many-headed cart-beast would keep to the track. She smiled to show she'd seen.

It was good hope too: a strong rope that tethered her to the future. Nicholas had told her bad things would happen, and they had. He'd promised good things too. Sandy was one good thing, but there would be more. Perhaps walking again was one of them, and Sandy finding a farm to buy on a mountain for them both.

They neared the Rock now. Bessie flickered her ears and hesitated, just for a second, till Sandy flicked the reins. She plodded on.

No mist on the Rock today. But there would be tomorrow, maybe, or the day after. And somehow she knew, with a certainty as strong as the mountains, that next time Nicholas would be there.

The cart rounded the bend for home. Andy was standing on the verandah, waiting for them. Joey waved his hat and ran down to the gate towards them.

She hoped the boys hadn't made too much of a mess while she'd been gone.

Dirty saucepans and dishes were piled in the washing-up bucket. The porridge pan was so crusted she knew they'd used it over and over without cleaning it, so the porridge had cooked on. The kitchen table needed scrubbing and scrubbing again. She managed that from her bathchair, while Kirsty cleaned the floor and lit the copper to boil water for the washing. It took a whole day to get the house straight again: a cake in the food safe, a stew on the stove.

The sun shone as if it had never met a snow cloud the morning she asked Andy to wheel her down to the Rock, so she could watch the valley and feel the sun.

'You're as bad as Dad,' he said, as he settled her into her chair after he'd lifted her down the stairs. 'Remember how he'd be sitting there when Mum drove the cart back with us from church?'

'He said he did all the praying he needed on the mountain, not within four walls.'

Andy began to push her out the gate. 'He told me once that after sitting there he knew things were going to be all right. Didn't say what things, mind you. But he looked happy.'

Suddenly Flinty remembered the day Dad had died. 'Won't tell you to care for the place,' he whispered, as he lay there in the bed. 'I know you do.' And then the final whisper: 'Give my love to the mountains.'

Had an older Flinty been a ghost for Dad, like Nicholas was hers? Maybe Dad had even built his house here because he'd met her on the Rock or perhaps he'd even met his granddaughter, if there was a granddaughter among the children Nicholas had sort of told her she would have.

And maybe she'd never know. We live in a world of perhapses, said Sister Burrows. She'd been lucky to have some certainties to guide her too.

'You'll be all right here, Sis?'

Flinty nodded.

She listened to Andy's footsteps, striding up the hill. Almost at once she heard new steps; hesitant and uneven, and the thud of sticks too.

She wheeled her chair around as Nicholas had turned in his bathchair a year back.

He didn't seem surprised. He's known I'd be crippled all along, she thought. That was why he gave me roses. Not for love, but as you'd take flowers to someone who was sick.

Then he smiled, and she thought, Maybe a little bit of both. For there were many kinds of love — more, perhaps, than there were roses.

He looked younger than when she'd seen him last, even leaning on his sticks. Or maybe I've grown much older, she thought, and he has lost the look of pain.

He looked happy too, a deep happiness that wasn't just from seeing her.

'Good morning, Miss Flinty McAlpine.' He stopped, using two metal sticks to keep his balance.

'How are your new legs?'

'Magnificent. I'd bend down and lift my jeans up to show you, but I'm still not that steady yet.' He looked at her steadily. 'I will be though. It's going well. My whole life is going well, Flinty McAlpine.'

'Maybe you should just call me Flinty.'

He grinned. 'I'll call you Flinty at dinner tonight, shall I?'

She looked at his blue eyes. All at once so much became clear.

An old woman had invited an injured soldier to stay at their house in the mountains. A schoolfriend of her grandson. She bet that the older Flinty had been the one to invite him.

The sixty-seven-year-old Flinty had sent the soldier down onto the Rock, to gaze over the valley, to meet herself, fifty years before.

Would she have had the courage to muster the brumbies, to write the book for Kirsty, to make that desperate bold dash down the mountainside, even to wait out the agony on her back, if it hadn't been for this man?

She didn't know. She had a feeling that she wouldn't know in 1969 or 1970 either.

It didn't matter. Those things had happened. He was here, and so was she.

He reached for her hand. 'Happy, Flinty?'

'Yes. Are you?'

He nodded. 'I've met a girl.'

'One who looks at your face, not your legs?'

'She's seen my legs now too.'

'Are you going to marry her?'

'If she says yes.'

Flinty nodded. She didn't ask if this woman in the future was her granddaughter. She didn't ask about her children either, whether they were well and safe and happy in this land that was the future. There was time enough to come to know all that.

With life came loss. The war and the years since had taught her that. There'd be sadness in her life to come, as well as happiness. Even the most blessed lives had both. She'd live them as they came.

He still held her hand. Such warm fingers for a ghost. He examined her ring. 'So Sandy has proposed. I didn't like to ask you ... the older you ... exactly when that happened. You'll be a bit formidable, you know. But kind.'

'And happy?'

'Yes,' he said. 'Not happily-ever-after happy, perhaps. But you have had the most fulfilled life of anyone I know.'

'Then ...' She hesitated, not knowing how much he'd tell her, or even how much she wanted to know.

'You'll be walking again by Christmas,' he said. 'You'll walk down the aisle too. There's something else as well. I'm supposed to show you this.'

He reached into his pocket and pulled out a newspaper cutting, held in a strange soft transparent cover. The newspaper cutting was yellowed and brittle at the edges.

She read the headline: *The Girl from Snowy River Saves the Valley.*

'A journalist came up for the fishing two days ago in your time. One of the White boys told him about your ride. His article will be in *The Sydney Morning Herald* tomorrow — the same day an editor at Angus and Robertson picks up a couple of grubby exercise books. He'll be about to throw them in the bin when he'll recognise your name. So he'll begin to read, and when he's read the first sentence he'll keep on reading.'

'They ... they'll publish my story?' she whispered.

'And many more. I reckon even in my time you're still a long way from ending your writing career.'

'And what about Rock Farm? Can books make enough money for us to live here?'

He shook his head, grinning. 'I'm obeying instructions. You'll find out, Flinty McAlpine.'

She grinned back, still dazed, still supremely happy. Because he had already answered her, even if he didn't realise it; had told her that the older Flinty still lived here, that he would see her tonight, at dinner. Maybe she and Sandy bought Rock Farm next year. Maybe they had to wait five years to do it.

Her life would be here, where she belonged. But there was one question she had to ask.

'What about Snow King? Please! Have I crippled him too?'

The grin faded a little. 'I think you know the answer to that already, even if you haven't admitted it to yourself.'

He was right. 'He won't ever race now,' she said softly. 'Yes. I knew it.' She put her chin up. 'But he'll have sons and daughters. They'll be champions, and their children will be too.'

All at once she knew something else as well. 'We're not going to meet again, are we? Not like this, as we are today.'

He shook his head. 'You told me we don't — the older you told me, I mean. Today is goodbye, you said.'

She wondered if she'd meet other ghosts, perhaps, here on the Rock. She also wondered what the older Flinty might have decided not to tell him.

Suddenly she had an image of Mum and Dad, sitting on this Rock as they had done so often at sunset, smiling at glimpses of their children and grandchildren, their daughter faintly heard through the mist. But those thoughts she'd keep for later.

Just now, there was only him.

'Be happy,' she said.

'I will. You've been a good friend, Flinty, both then and now.' He hesitated, then smiled. 'Not sure I'd have made it without you.'

'You would have.'

'Well, maybe. And so would you.'

They smiled at each other.

'Nicky?'

The young woman sounded a bit like Kirsty. But this wasn't a voice from 1920. This voice was calling him.

He looked back, out of the mist, towards the house. 'I have to go.'

'Does she know about me?'

'You'll find out,' he said. 'See you in fifty years, Flinty my dear.' He bent forwards and kissed her on the forehead. This kiss was cold, not warm. For the first time she saw him dissolve into mist in front of her, knew that she was vanishing for him too.

She listened, hoping to hear his voice again, or the voice that might be her granddaughter's, and was the girl he loved. But there was only birdsong, and the distant beat of horse hooves.

Sandy, cantering up the mountain. Smiling, she rolled the chair out of the mist onto the track to meet him, to tell him about ghosts, and love, and what a ghost had said would happen tomorrow when an editor down in Sydney picked up a tattered exercise book.

Above her the snow-streaked mountain gleamed its too-hard white light.

Epilogue

21 DECEMBER 1926

The cicadas gave their first morning buzz from the gum trees beyond the garden. The sky was clear blue above the sunrise red above the ridges. It would be hot today.

Flinty shut the front door, then tucked the cotton bunny-rug Mrs Mack had crocheted around Nicola. She gazed at the shiny green car as she carried the baby down the steps. 'Are you sure that thing will get us back up the mountain?'

'Of course,' said Andy easily. 'It got me up here yesterday.' The ends of his moustache had been newly waxed. They shone, just like the car.

'Yes, but it's got to carry us all back after Christmas.' And all the Gibber's Creek dresses that Kirsty 'just had to have', she thought, and the new suitcases that Joey would need for university next year. Her first book had paid off the debt for Rock Farm. Her most recent one was paying for all they wanted. Not a fortune, but enough.

'Motorcars are stronger than you think,' said Andy. He winked at her.

Flinty grinned as Andy absently took out his hanky to polish a fingerprint off the gleaming door. The car even had a vase with rosebuds on the dashboard.

But it wasn't a horse. You can't love a car, she thought, glancing up at the paddock behind the house where a grey foal tried to dance with a butterfly.

She looked back at Andy. Well, maybe you could love a car, a bit. But a car would never push its heart and lungs to breaking point because it loved you back.

Sandy opened the car door for her. 'Come on, love. The chooks will have gone back to bed before we even set out.'

Flinty slipped into the front passenger's seat with Nicola. Sandy checked the luggage strapped on the car once more, then crammed himself into the back with Kirsty and Joey.

'You've got the books for Drinkwater?' Flinty asked Kirsty.

'Under my feet with the nappies,' said Kirsty.

'And I've got the Thermos and ginger cake and sandwiches,' said Joey.

Sandy smiled at her. 'Stop fussing, love. We've got everything.'

She grinned back. They had.

Andy turned the crank. The motor caught. He climbed into the driver's seat and did complicated things with levers. The car gave a sort of burp, then began to rumble, surprisingly smoothly, down the track.

Fog covered the Rock like a tablecloth this morning, but the car didn't hesitate as it chugged past. Cars didn't see ghosts either. Not like a horse.

She turned her head as they passed the Rock, just as the rising sunlight slid down into the shadow of the valley.

And she saw him. A horse, black as the mountain cliffs, rearing against the sun-red sky, and on his back a rider in blue trousers and a sky-blue shirt.

He looked older. Of course he looked older. His face was at peace. What remained of his legs were thrust into strange high stirrups. The horse lowered its forelegs as its rider took off his hat and saluted the rising sun. Just for a second she saw joy, the exultation of a rider at one with his horse and bush and sky.

The mist shimmered and they were gone.

Had he seen her too?

It didn't matter. He knew her past ... and her future, what her life would be. He'd said that she'd be happy.

Now she knew that he was happy too.

She looked back at Sandy, saw his questioning look, nodded and gave him a reassuring smile. The green car bumped its way down the mountain, through the twisting valley and along the dusty track above the glinting river, down towards the plains.

Author's Notes

This is a book about war. Officially World War I ended on 11 November 1918, but that was only when the battles ceased. The war itself would be a shadow changing the lives of many generations. The years immediately after were as strange and disturbing as those of the war itself, to the men and the families and especially to small communities, where so many had been lost, or returned with wounds and nightmares that few would speak of.

In those days it was felt best to 'just get on with life' and not dwell on the past. It is only now, as the diaries and letters from World War I are published by the participants' descendants, that we can hear the voices of those who were there.

The Girl from Snowy River is fiction. Many of the incidents referred to in it, such as the Snowy River enlistment march, are based on real events, but no character in this book is based on a real person. You may find echoes, though, not just from the bush poets and old songs, but from my life and others'. This is the place to say, perhaps, that I have never met a ghost from the future, nor known an ex-serviceman crippled after the Vietnam War.

Who was the man from Snowy River?

Banjo Paterson may have written his poem as homage to the Snowy River riders generally, or it may be based on the feats of a single person. Contenders include stockman Jack Riley (1841–1914), who lived at Tom Grogan, participated in brumby running and is buried in the Corryong cemetery, or young Charlie McKeahnie, who made the ride described by Mr Clancy in this book. Bush poet Barcroft Boake wrote a poem about the ride, 'On the Range', in which the brumby dies running into a rocky outcrop, and it's believed that Paterson was told that version of the story. McKeahnie was killed in a riding accident in 1895 and is buried in the Old Adaminaby cemetery, on the shores of Lake Eucumbene. Paterson himself claimed that 'the man' was a composite of many bold mountain riders.

The poems referred to in this book

These include, of course, Banjo Paterson's iconic 'The Man from Snowy River', as well as 'Clancy of The Overflow' and Henry Lawson's 'Andy's Gone with Cattle', but you will find references to a dozen or so less well-known poems from that era. I will leave to the reader the pleasures of reading the bush poems that this book is based on. Three of them appear over the following pages, but you might also look at the song 'The Snowy River Men' and the poems 'Black Swans', 'Do You Think That I Do Not Know' and many others. (I am deliberately not giving even the songwriter's and poets' names, so as not to deprive you of the joy you will find in many more works if you choose to hunt for them.)

'The Man from Snowy River' by AB 'Banjo' Paterson (1864–1941)

There was movement at the station, for the word had passed around
That the colt from old Regret had got away,
And had joined the wild bush horses — he was worth a thousand pound,
So all the cracks had gathered to the fray.
All the tried and noted riders from the stations near and far
Had mustered at the homestead overnight,
For the bushmen love hard riding where the wild bush horses are,
And the stockhorse snuffs the battle with delight.

There was Harrison, who made his pile when Pardon won the cup,
The old man with his hair as white as snow;
But few could ride beside him when his blood was fairly up —
He would go wherever horse and man could go.
And Clancy of The Overflow came down to lend a hand,
No better horseman ever held the reins;
For never horse could throw him while the saddle girths would stand,
He learnt to ride while droving on the plains.

And one was there, a stripling on a small and weedy beast,
He was something like a racehorse undersized,
With a touch of Timor pony — three parts thoroughbred at least —
And such as are by mountain horsemen prized.
He was hard and tough and wiry — just the sort that won't say die —
There was courage in his quick impatient tread;

And he bore the badge of gameness in his bright and fiery eye,
And the proud and lofty carriage of his head.

But still so slight and weedy, one would doubt his power to stay,
And the old man said, 'That horse will never do
For a long and tiring gallop — lad, you'd better stop away,
Those hills are far too rough for such as you.'
So he waited sad and wistful — only Clancy stood his friend —
'I think we ought to let him come,' he said;
'I warrant he'll be with us when he's wanted at the end,
For both his horse and he are mountain bred.

'He hails from Snowy River, up by Kosciusko's side,
Where the hills are twice as steep and twice as rough,
Where a horse's hoofs strike firelight from the flint stones every
stride,
The man that holds his own is good enough.
And the Snowy River riders on the mountains make their home,
Where the river runs those giant hills between;
I have seen full many horsemen since I first commenced to roam,
But nowhere yet such horsemen have I seen.'

So he went — they found the horses by the big mimosa clump —
They raced away towards the mountain's brow,
And the old man gave his orders, 'Boys, go at them from the jump,
No use to try for fancy riding now.
And, Clancy, you must wheel them, try and wheel them to the
right.
Ride boldly, lad, and never fear the spills,
For never yet was rider that could keep the mob in sight,
If once they gain the shelter of those hills.'

So Clancy rode to wheel them — he was racing on the wing
Where the best and boldest riders take their place,
And he raced his stockhorse past them, and he made the ranges ring
With the stockwhip, as he met them face to face.
Then they halted for a moment, while he swung the dreaded lash,
But they saw their well-loved mountain full in view,
And they charged beneath the stockwhip with a sharp and sudden dash,
And off into the mountain scrub they flew.

Then fast the horsemen followed, where the gorges deep and black
Resounded to the thunder of their tread,
And the stockwhips woke the echoes, and they fiercely answered back
From cliffs and crags that beetled overhead.
And upward, ever upward, the wild horses held their way,
Where mountain ash and kurrajong grew wide;
And the old man muttered fiercely, 'We may bid the mob good day,
No man can hold them down the other side.'

When they reached the mountain's summit, even Clancy took a pull,
It well might make the boldest hold their breath,
The wild hop scrub grew thickly, and the hidden ground was full
Of wombat holes, and any slip was death.
But the man from Snowy River let the pony have his head,
And he swung his stockwhip round and gave a cheer,
And he raced him down the mountain like a torrent down its bed,
While the others stood and watched in very fear.

He sent the flint stones flying, but the pony kept his feet,
He cleared the fallen timber in his stride,

And the man from Snowy River never shifted in his seat —
It was grand to see that mountain horseman ride.
Through the stringybarks and saplings, on the rough and broken ground,
Down the hillside at a racing pace he went;
And he never drew the bridle till he landed safe and sound,
At the bottom of that terrible descent.

He was right among the horses as they climbed the further hill,
And the watchers on the mountain standing mute,
Saw him ply the stockwhip fiercely, he was right among them still,
As he raced across the clearing in pursuit.
Then they lost him for a moment, where two mountain gullies met
In the ranges, but a final glimpse reveals
On a dim and distant hillside the wild horses racing yet,
With the man from Snowy River at their heels.

And he ran them single-handed till their sides were white with foam.
He followed like a bloodhound on their track,
Till they halted cowed and beaten, then he turned their heads for home,
And alone and unassisted brought them back.
But his hardy mountain pony he could scarcely raise a trot,
He was blood from hip to shoulder from the spur;
But his pluck was still undaunted, and his courage fiery hot,
For never yet was mountain horse a cur.

And down by Kosciusko, where the pine-clad ridges raise
Their torn and rugged battlements on high,
Where the air is clear as crystal, and the white stars fairly blaze
At midnight in the cold and frosty sky,

And where around The Overflow the reed beds sweep and sway
To the breezes, and the rolling plains are wide,
The man from Snowy River is a household word today,
And the stockmen tell the story of his ride.

First published in *The Bulletin*, 26 April 1890

'Clancy of The Overflow' by AB 'Banjo' Paterson

I had written him a letter which I had, for want of better
Knowledge, sent to where I met him down the Lachlan years ago;
He was shearing when I knew him, so I sent the letter to him,
Just on spec, addressed as follows, 'Clancy, of The Overflow'.

And an answer came directed in a writing unexpected
(And I think the same was written with a thumb-nail dipped in tar);
'Twas his shearing mate who wrote it, and verbatim I will quote it:
'Clancy's gone to Queensland droving, and we don't know where he are.'

In my wild erratic fancy, visions come to me of Clancy
Gone a-droving 'down the Cooper', where the Western drovers go;
As the stock are slowly stringing, Clancy rides behind them singing,
For the drover's life has pleasures that the townsfolk never know.

And the bush has friends to meet him, and their kindly voices greet him
In the murmur of the breezes, and the river on its bars,
And he sees the vision splendid, of the sunlit plain extended,
And at night the wondrous glory of the everlasting stars.

I am sitting in my dingy little office, where a stingy
Ray of sunlight struggles feebly down between the houses tall,
And the foetid air and gritty of the dusty, dirty city,
Through the open window floating, spreads its foulness over all.

And in place of lowing cattle, I can hear the fiendish rattle
Of the tramways and the buses making hurry down the street;
And the language uninviting of the gutter children fighting
Comes fitfully and faintly, through the ceaseless tramp of feet.

And the hurrying people daunt me, and their pallid faces haunt me
As they shoulder one another in their rush and nervous haste,
With their eager eyes and greedy, and their stunted forms and weedy,
For townsfolk have no time to grow, they have no time to waste.

And I somehow rather fancy that I'd like to change with Clancy,
Like to take a turn at droving, where the seasons come and go,
While he faced the round eternal, of the cash-book and the journal
But I doubt he'd suit the office, Clancy, of The Overflow.

First published in *The Bulletin*, 21 December 1889

'On the Range' by Barcroft Boake (1866–92)

On Nungar the mists of the morning hung low,
The beetle-browed hills brooded silent and black,
Not yet warmed to life by the sun's loving glow,
As through the tall tussocks rode young Charlie Mac.
What cared he for mists at the dawning of day,
What cared he that over the valley stern 'Jack',
The monarch of frost, held his pitiless sway? —
A bold mountaineer, born and bred, was young Mac.

A galloping son of a galloping sire —
Stiffest fence, roughest ground, never took him aback;
With his father's cool judgement, his dash and his fire,
The pick of Monaro, rode young Charlie Mac.
And the pick of the stable the mare he bestrode —
Arab-grey, built to stay, lithe of limb, deep of chest,
She seemed to be happy to bear such a load
As she tossed the soft forelock that curled on her crest.

They crossed Nungar Creek, where its span is but short
At its head, where together spring two mountain rills,
When a mob of wild horses sprang up with a snort —
'By thunder!' quoth Mac, 'there's the Lord of the Hills.'

Decoyed from her paddock, a Murray-bred mare
Had fled to the hills with a warrigal band.
A pretty bay foal had been born to her there,
Whose veins held the very best blood in the land —
'The Lord of the Hills', as the bold mountain men,
Whose courage and skill he was wont to defy,
Had named him; they yarded him once, but since then
He'd held to the saying 'Once bitten twice shy'.

The scrubber, thus suddenly roused from his lair,
Struck straight for the timber with fear in his heart;
As Charlie rose up in his stirrups, the mare
Sprang forward, no need to tell Empress to start.
She laid to the chase just as soon as she felt
Her rider's skilled touch, light, yet firm, on the rein.
Stride for stride, lengthened wide, for the green timber belt,
The fastest half-mile ever done on the plain.

They reached the low sallee before he could wheel
The warrigal mob; up they dashed with a stir
Of low branches and undergrowth — Charlie could feel
His mare catch her breath on the side of the spur
That steeply slopes up till it meets the bald cone.
'Twas here on the range that the trouble began,
For a slip on the sidling, a loose rolling stone,
And the chase would be done; but the bay in the van
And the little grey mare were a surefooted pair.
He looked once around as she crept to his heel
And the swish that he gave his long tail in the air
Seemed to say, 'Here's a foeman well worthy my steel.'

They raced to within half a mile of the bluff
That drops to the river, the squadron strung out.
'I wonder,' quoth Mac, 'has the bay had enough?'
But he was not left very much longer in doubt,
For the Lord of the Hills struck a spur for the flat
And followed it, leaving his mob, mares and all,
While Empress (brave heart, she could climb like a cat)
Down the stony descent raced with never a fall.

Once down on the level 'twas galloping-ground,
For a while Charlie thought he might yard the big bay
At his uncle's out-station, but no! He wheeled round
And down the sharp dip to the Gulf made his way.

Betwixt those twin portals, that, towering high
And backwardly sloping in watchfulness, lift
Their smooth grassy summits towards the far sky,
The course of the clear Murrumbidgee runs swift;

No time then to seek where the crossing might be,
It was in at the one side and out where you could,
But fear never dwelt in the hearts of those three
Who emerged from the shade of the low muzzle-wood.

Once more did the Lord of the Hills strike a line
Up the side of the range, and once more he looked back,
So close were they now he could see the sun shine
In the bold grey eyes flashing of young Charlie Mac.

He saw little Empress, stretched out like a hound
On the trail of its quarry, the pick of the pack,
With ne'er-tiring stride, and his heart gave a bound
As he saw the lithe stockwhip of young Charlie Mac
Showing snaky and black on the neck of the mare
In three hanging coils with a turn round the wrist.
And he heartily wished himself back in his lair
'Mid the tall tussocks beaded with chill morning mist.

Then he fancied the straight mountain-ashes, the gums
And the wattles all mocked him and whispered, 'You lack
The speed to avert cruel capture, that comes
To the warrigal fancied by young Charlie Mac,
For he'll yard you, and rope you, and then you'll be stuck
In the crush, while his saddle is girthed to your back.
Then out in the open, and there you may buck
Till you break your bold heart, but you'll never throw Mac!'

The Lord of the Hills at the thought felt the sweat
Break over the smooth summer gloss of his hide.
He spurted his utmost to leave her, but yet

The Empress crept up to him, stride upon stride.
No need to say Charlie was riding her now,
Yet still for all that he had something in hand,
With here a sharp stoop to avoid a low bough,
Or a quick rise and fall as a tree-trunk they spanned.

In his terror the brumby struck down the rough falls
T'wards Yiack, with fierce disregard for his neck —
'Tis useless, he finds, for the mare overhauls
Him slowly, no timber could keep her in check.

There's a narrow-beat pathway that winds to and fro
Down the deeps of the gully, half hid from the day,
There's a turn in the track, where the hop-bushes grow
And hide the grey granite that crosses the way
While sharp swerves the path round the boulder's
broad base —
And now the last scene in the drama is played:
As the Lord of the Hills, with the mare in full chase,
Swept towards it, but, ere his long stride could be stayed,
With a gathered momentum that gave not a chance
Of escape, and a shuddering, sickening shock,
He struck on the granite that barred his advance
And sobbed out his life at the foot of the rock.

Then Charlie pulled off with a twitch on the rein,
And an answering spring from his surefooted mount,
One might say, unscathed, though a crimsoning stain
Marked the graze of the granite, but that would ne'er count
With Charlie, who speedily sprang to the earth
To ease the mare's burden, his deft-fingered hand

Unslackened her surcingle, loosened tight girth,
And cleansed with a tussock the spur's ruddy brand.

There he lay by the rock — drooping head, glazing eye,
Strong limbs stiffed for ever; no more would he fear
The tread of a horseman. No more would he fly
Through the hills with his harem in rapid career,
The pick of the Mountain Mob, bays, greys, or roans.
He proved by his death that the pace 'tis that kills,
And a sun-shrunken hide o'er a few whitened bones
Marks the last resting-place of the Lord of the Hills.

First published in *The Bulletin*, 30 May 1891

'The Snowy River'

When Banjo Paterson wrote 'The Man from Snowy River' the Eucumbene River too was known as the Snowy River, and the Snowy River region was even larger than the one we refer to as the 'Snowies' today. The Snowy was — and still is — a long river, traversing many different kinds of country. Rocky Creek and Rocky Valley are not based on any particular area, but do include the bushland — and rocks like the Rock — that I'm familiar with.

The Snowy's floods have been tamed by the Snowy Mountains Scheme and the Eucumbene Dam, which also removes much of the flow. It is no longer the river that Flinty would have known. Farms and farming methods in the area also changed greatly in the 1930s and during the '50s and '60s, with small settler farms like those in the valley giving way to larger ones.

Drinkwater

Those readers familiar with *A Waltz for Matilda* will recognise references to Drinkwater Station, Miss Matilda, Tommy (Thomas) Thompson, Mr Sampson and Pete Sampson.

As is evident in *The Girl from Snowy River*, Matilda, although married, is still known as Miss Matilda in 1919. Tommy has set up an engineering business at Gibber's Creek, and Matilda has made good her promise to give her Indigenous relatives part of the Drinkwater estate.

At the end of *A Waltz for Matilda* she had sold much of her stock. When this story begins she has stocked Drinkwater with cattle during the latter years of the war, when supplies of canned 'bully beef' were needed to feed the armies overseas, but is now selling the remnants up in Queensland.

The Men from Snowy River March

World War I was fought with little regard on either side for the loss of thousands or even tens of thousands of troops in each engagement. Although enlistment numbers were high in Australia in 1914, by the end of 1915 the reality of the war as revealed in letters from servicemen abroad, and a shortage of labour at home, meant that enlistment numbers were dwindling rapidly and needed to be boosted. The 'snowball' recruitment marches began in 1915. A small group of men would begin a march from a country town or village, enlisting men as they went, 'snowballing' until eventually a large number arrived at a city army camp.

The first march from Gilgandra in October 1915 was known as the Cooee March — twenty-six men left Gilgandra and by the time they arrived in Sydney a month later there were two hundred and sixty-three recruits.

The Men from Snowy River March started with fourteen men at Delegate, near the New South Wales–Victoria border, on 6 January 1916. They marched through Craigie, Mila, Bombala, Bibbenluke, Holts Flat, Nimmitabel, Summer Hill, Rocks Flat (which is not the Rocky Valley in this book), Cooma, Bunyan, Umeralla, Billylingera, Bredbo, Colinton, Michelago, Williamsdale, Queanbeyan, Bungendore, Deep Creek, Tarago, Inveralochy and Tiranna to Goulburn. They marched three hundred and fifty kilometres in twenty-three days, with other men coming from places like Bega and Williams Creek to join them, reaching Goulburn on 29 January 1916 with one hundred and forty-four volunteers, which, despite all the excitement, was considered disappointing by army recruiters.

At each stop they were met by local dignitaries, music, feasts and children running alongside them. At times — or possibly for the whole march — they were accompanied by a bagpipe player and a drummer, as well as the handmade wool banner made by the women of Delegate, proclaiming that they were *The Men from Snowy River.* The banner, scarcely faded, is now held by the Australian War Memorial in Canberra.

All of the men who enlisted on the Snowy River march were in battle on the Western Front. Of those one hundred and forty-four men, thirty-nine were killed in action and seventy-five were badly wounded. None, probably, survived unscathed, whether in mind or body. Perhaps every community lost men, knew sons or neighbours killed or wounded, and had to cope in the years the men were away, as well as face challenging changes when the men returned. It was not always the 'happily ever after' expected when they rejoiced at the November 1918 Armistice.

None of the characters in this book are based on any of the real men who were part of the Snowy River march, although their stories are based on letters and diaries from that time.

You will find the names of the real men on the memorials in the towns and villages where they lived, and their sacrifice is still remembered each Anzac Day.

Catching brumbies

I have based the brumby hunt in this book on accounts from a hundred years ago. (Modern brumby hunting uses different methods from those of the round-ups back then.) Many of the horses were taken to be boiled down for tallow and for their hides. The young ones were broken in and sold as riding horses — most weren't valuable, though some were excellent, strong and hardy. As in Paterson's poem, the brumby stallion in this book was a well-bred horse who had escaped and 'joined the wild bush horses'. His foals were likely to be excellent horses, unlike those of brumby stallions; brumby stallions had won their position by fighting with other stallions, not because of their speed or endurance, and other qualities prized by humans.

Flinty's back injury

I have given Flinty a more severe case of my own back injury — the spurs on two of my lower vertebra are broken. About a decade ago, at its worst, there were times when I couldn't move my legs or back, as the swelling pressed on the nerves. Thanks to good medical care and MRI scans, I knew that my back wasn't broken and that my spine was still sound. While spines can't regenerate, exercise, a good diet that lowers inflammation and physiotherapy mean that I rarely have much of a problem any more or, if I do, a few exercises relieve it. Just occasionally, though, especially if there is a cold snap at night, I can wake unable to move my legs till I roll off the bed, stand up like a zombie and slowly move forwards until movement eases. A hot shower usually fixes things from there.

If it hadn't been for X-rays and scans, however, I would have worried, like Flinty, that my back *was* broken, and if I hadn't had good medical assistance I might not have kept moving to strengthen the muscles around the injury. If Flinty had had a better doctor — or modern medical knowledge — they would have known that she needed to move gently to regain her mobility and that lying still, with pressure on her back, would make the problem worse and slow her eventual recovery.

Women in Australia to 1920

Women were among Australia's earliest settlers, farmers and explorers. Australia's first professional shearers were women from what is now Germany, brought to teach men the craft. You will find few mentions of them though.

Women's voices from our history mostly survive in their letters and diaries. Men's accounts were more likely to be published at the time. The Matilda Saga is written to try to change that perception. The famous poems work just as well if you change male to female: '*"You'll never catch me alive!" said she*' or '*I doubt she'd suit the office, Nancy, of The Overflow*'.

Lawson and Paterson and the other 'bush poets' immortalised the Clancys. It is time the 'Nancys' were acknowledged, the strong women who shaped our nation, who didn't fit into the sentimental clichés of strong silent men and 'the little woman' who waited at home.

A womanly woman was supposed to tend the home and her family, not go droving, run a farm or work for wages after she was married, except in extreme necessity. Many jobs forbidden to women were even more out of bounds for married women; others were unattainable simply because no man would hire a female, nor would men work with one. Women might be nurses or teachers or telegraphists and telephonists, but usually they were forced by regulations to give up even these jobs as soon as they married.

The home-maker was the ideal. Many women, mostly from poverty, did work outside their own home after marriage, but usually in 'home-like' occupations — as servants, cooks and laundrywomen — although many factory workers were women too, employed at a small fraction of the men's wage. One of the reasons for the strong feeling against working wives was that they undercut the wages of men.

By 1920 Australian (white) women had fought for and won the vote (see *A Waltz for Matilda*) and the right to go to university and be awarded degrees, although the careers of most would be as 'assistants' in academia, medicine, laboratories, publishing and journalism and other professions where the men got the credit for much that their 'assistants' achieved.

World War I was a time of enormous change in the way many women thought about their lives. They were forced to become farm managers, replace men in professions, and cope with families alone while waiting with dread for the casualty list or telegrams to say a loved one had been lost. For the women volunteers and the official nurses, telegraphists, drivers and VADs, the war was their proving ground. Many died from infection, wounds, disease and exhaustion, but others emerged indomitable.

Yet even before the war, women had run farms, 'gone with cattle', dug for gold, trained and broken in horses — all activities that were not seen as womanly and so were best ignored. Even in World War I, while the role of official nurses and VADs is acknowledged, the extraordinary role women played in feeding, transporting and providing unofficial medical aid is ignored (see also *A Rose for the Anzac Boys*).

The drovers' boys

One of the unspoken traditions of the bush was 'the drover's boy', an Aboriginal wife who could not be acknowledged, but who would be a partner for life on the road and at home.

Some of the native plants in this book

She-oak — *Allocasuarina spp*, probably *glauca*
Christmas bush, thorn bush — *Bursaria spinosa*
Gorse, bitter-pea — *Daviesia ulicifolia*
Cascade everlasting — *Ozothamnus secundiflorus*
Native sarsaparilla — *Hardenbergia violacea*
Austral Indigo — *Indigofera australis*
Native heath, heather — *Kunzea spp*
Snow gum — *Eucalyptus pauciflora*, *E. dalrympleana*, *E. rubida*, *E. viminalis* and *E. stellulata*

Snow grass, tussock — *Poa spp*
Narrow-leaved peppermint — *E. radiata*
Alpine ash — *E. delegatensis*
Red shaggies, royal grevillea — *Grevillea victoriae*
Hop bush — *Dodonaea spp*
Native cherry — *Exocarpos cupressiformis*
Yam daisy, murnong — *Microseris lanceolata*

I have deliberately not given any clue about the fungus Mrs Clancy uses in this book. Fungi can be and often are fatal if not correctly used and identified. The source of the green ointment and the wattle species she recommends are also left deliberately vague. The bush is a living larder and chemist shop, but it takes many years to learn what can be safely used, and how to do it, and as long to learn how to diagnose medical conditions. Please don't attempt to learn either except from well-qualified and experienced practitioners or widely recognised places of study.

Timeline of books

The Girl from Snowy River is part of The Matilda Saga:

A Waltz for Matilda (1894–1915)
A Rose for the Anzac Boys (1915–20)
The Girl from Snowy River (1919–26)

The trilogy above will be followed by another three sequels, covering the era 1932–72. The final book in the series will be set in 1969–72, when the wounded Vietnam veteran of *The Girl from Snowy River* wheels himself down to the Rock and meets the girl from the past, and when Flinty Mack, Matilda and 'Nancy of The Overflow' dance to the most ancient music of their land. Although my book *Somewhere Around the Corner* is set in the Depression and *Pennies for Hitler* covers the years 1939–42, these tell unrelated stories.

Acknowledgements

A book like this is made up of gifts from many people, over many years, sharing their skills and knowledge of the land. Once again the 'two Kates', Kate Burnitt and Kate O'Donnell, guided and cosseted book and author to make it the best book possible. To Lisa Berryman and Liz Kemp too, I owe more than I can express. They assess the manuscript, rip it apart and show me where it should be mended. Mostly, they demand that I write the difficult parts, the ones where I'd rather say, 'And the rest is a row of dots ...' Without their determination, unfailing honesty and friendship, this, like so many of my books, would be a shadow of what it might be. Many, many thanks as well to Jane Waterhouse who took the words of the book and created the perfect image to go with it.

Angela Marshall, with this book as with so many others, not only turned pages of badly spelled and scarcely punctuated mess into an acceptable form, but added her encyclopaedic knowledge of horsemanship and history, as we exchanged emails about her lambs and my wombats, our respective vegetable gardens and offspring.

And of course my debt to the poets and songwriters long gone. I fell in love with 'Clancy of The Overflow' when I was seven years old, and the vision of the bush created by Banjo Paterson and Henry Lawson. It may not quite be the 'bush' I found (they did tend to leave out the women, except in severely restricted roles as mother, wife and sweetheart), but I lived with their words till I was old enough to find the bush myself. My love always to my husband Bryan, who helped take men to the moon rather than droving cattle up to Queensland, but who shares Clancy's love, kindness and knowledge of the land.

Perhaps I owe most gratitude to the valley and the mountains where I live. They and their inhabitants, human and otherwise, are the heart of the book, and of my life.

Other titles by Jackie French

Historical

Somewhere Around the Corner • Dancing with Ben Hall
Soldier on the Hill • Daughter of the Regiment
Hitler's Daughter • Lady Dance • The White Ship
How the Finnegans Saved the Ship • Valley of Gold
Tom Appleby, Convict Boy • They Came on Viking Ships
Macbeth and Son • Pharaoh • A Rose for the Anzac Boys
Oracle • The Night They Stormed Eureka
A Waltz for Matilda • Nanberry: Black Brother White
Pennies for Hitler

Fiction

Rain Stones • Walking the Boundaries • The Secret Beach
Summerland • Beyond the Boundaries
A Wombat Named Bosco • The Book of Unicorns
The Warrior — The Story of a Wombat • Tajore Arkle
Missing You, Love Sara • Dark Wind Blowing
Ride the Wild Wind: The Golden Pony and Other Stories

Non-Fiction

Seasons of Content • A Year in the Valley
How the Aliens from Alpha Centauri
Invaded My Maths Class and Turned Me into a Writer
How to Guzzle Your Garden • The Book of Challenges
Stamp, Stomp, Whomp
The Fascinating History of Your Lunch
Big Burps, Bare Bums and Other Bad-Mannered Blunders
To the Moon and Back • Rocket Your Child into Reading
The Secret World of Wombats
How High Can a Kangaroo Hop?

The Animal Stars Series

1. *The Goat Who Sailed the World*
2. *The Dog Who Loved a Queen*
3. *The Camel Who Crossed Australia*
4. *The Donkey Who Carried the Wounded*
5. *The Horse Who Bit a Bushranger*
6. *Dingo: The Dog Who Conquered a Continent*

Outlands Trilogy
In the Blood • Blood Moon • Flesh and Blood

School for Heroes Series
Lessons for a Werewolf Warrior
Dance of the Deadly Dinosaurs

Wacky Families Series
1. My Dog the Dinosaur • 2. My Mum the Pirate
3. My Dad the Dragon • 4. My Uncle Gus the Garden Gnome
5. My Uncle Wal the Werewolf • 6. My Gran the Gorilla
7. My Auntie Chook the Vampire Chicken
8. My Pa the Polar Bear

Phredde Series
1. A Phaery Named Phredde
2. Phredde and a Frog Named Bruce
3. Phredde and the Zombie Librarian
4. Phredde and the Temple of Gloom
5. Phredde and the Leopard-Skin Librarian
6. Phredde and the Purple Pyramid
7. Phredde and the Vampire Footy Team
8. Phredde and the Ghostly Underpants

Picture Books
Diary of a Wombat (with Bruce Whatley)
Pete the Sheep (with Bruce Whatley)
Josephine Wants to Dance (with Bruce Whatley)
The Shaggy Gully Times (with Bruce Whatley)
Emily and the Big Bad Bunyip (with Bruce Whatley)
Baby Wombat's Week (with Bruce Whatley)
Queen Victoria's Underpants (with Bruce Whatley)
The Tomorrow Book (with Sue deGennaro)
Christmas Wombat (with Bruce Whatley)
A Day to Remember (with Mark Wilson)
Dinosaurs Love Cheese (with Nina Rycroft)

Jackie French is a full-time writer and wombat negotiator. She writes fiction and non-fiction for all ages, and has columns in the print media. Jackie is regarded as one of Australia's most popular children's authors and has won numerous awards. She writes across all genres — from picture books and history to science fiction.

www.jackiefrench.com